MATCHED

PIPPA GRANT WRITING AS

JAMIE FARRELL

To Regina -

Jamie Farrell

aka

Pippa Grant

Cover photos Copyright © Regina Wamba

Cover Design by Lori Jackson Designs

Editing by

Penny's Copy Sense

ISBN: 978-1-940517-62-9

ONE

LINDSEY CASTELLANO'S love-hate relationship with love was trumped only by her hate-hate relationship with microphones. Yet here she was, at her sister's second wedding reception, as the maid of honor again, staring down a microphone again, to toast the newlywed couple again, before an enormous crowd in her hometown of Bliss, Illinois, the Most Married-est Town on Earth.

And, once again, Lindsey wished Natalie had picked Mom to stand beside her instead.

At Nat's first wedding, Lindsey had wanted to relinquish the attendant duty for several reasons. Because she hated microphones. Because she hated crowds almost as much as she hated microphones. Because Nat had picked the wrong groom.

This time, though, Lindsey wished she could've passed the honor to Mom simply because she wished Mom were still here.

"Good evening," Lindsey said into the evil microphone. Her voice bounced off the white textured walls. The audience —a mix of family and wedding crashers—eyed her from the dance floor as though they could see her smiley face panties. Despite the blustery late December weather outside, Lindsey needed a fan and a cold drink. "I was told this would be a small thing. Friendlies only."

A few people snickered. A few grimaced. Natalie, resplendent in her wedding attire of jeans and the *Second Chance Misfits* T-shirt that she and CJ had asked all their invited guests to wear, offered her a sympathetic smile and a thumbs-up. Behind her, CJ grinned like the evil redheaded SOB that he was. But he made Nat and her four-year-old son, Noah, happy. He also gave Lindsey free drinks at his bar and was always good for a laugh, so she actually liked him a lot.

Lindsey sucked in a breath that the microphone caught and amplified so loud, the Mars rovers probably heard it. Her champagne flute wobbled in her sweaty hand, and her pulse hammered hard enough to crack a diamond. Words. She had to say a few more words, then she could return to obscurity.

"So I'll make this short." She had to, because her tongue was getting thick and dry, and there was no telling what she'd say if she didn't. She'd had ten years of practice as a divorce lawyer. She should be able to handle a few words. But microphones did her in every time. "To my favorite sister in the whole world, and the man who had better not ever have reason to see me in a professional capacity. Congratulations, and many happy returns."

Dad lifted his glass. "To Nat and CJ!" Clapping and shouts of "Cheers!" spread through the ballroom, from the deejay to all eleven of CJ's sisters—Lindsey's new competition for Most Favored Aunt status—to the whole of Bliss's bridal brigade, Knot Fest committee members, and Bridal Retailers Association honchos who had crashed the wedding.

Lindsey passed the microphone to the deejay and chugged her champagne, letting the sting of bubbly in her throat wash away her discomfort, then escaped the spotlight.

Nat grabbed her in a hug. CJ joined in. The goober knew Lindsey hated enclosed spaces, but he had thirty years' worth of experience in tormenting sisters.

"Isn't that the same thing you said at my first wedding?" Nat said.

"Yes, but this time I'm optimistic you won't need me." Lindsey's voice was almost steady. "Mom would've liked CJ."

Nat squeezed harder. "You're still coming to karaoke afterward? Family only this time. Cross my heart."

As if Lindsey could tell Nat *no* for anything today. "Absolutely. But no singing for me."

"That's a given," Nat agreed with a laugh.

Lindsey gave CJ a well-placed elbow to the ribs, and he backed off with an amused chuckle. Nat let go as well. Lindsey bent and planted a smacker on Noah's cheek, and while the deejay announced the first dance, she eased away.

She needed air.

Her dad squeezed her shoulder on her way past. "Beautiful, hon. Your mom would've loved every word."

Lindsey's eyes misted.

Melancholy wasn't her favorite mood, but it was something she'd gotten used to since Mom passed away.

Lindsey held up her glass and reached deep for her normal poise. "I'm going for a refill. You need anything?"

He declined. Lindsey headed for the bar. Other guests offered what she took as pained smiles and nods. Or, possibly, the townsfolk of Bliss were not at all disturbed by her presence, and Lindsey's discomfort, loneliness, and awkwardness here had only been amplified by the liquid courage she'd needed to make the toast.

She returned the smiles and nods with as much dignity as she could manage. She *did* regularly have semi-friendly conversations with many of the people here, and she'd dated at least three of the single sons on The Aisle, Bliss's equivalent of Main Street, over the years since law school. But she still needed space.

And another glass of wine.

She stuck to the perimeter of the room and inched toward the bar while Nat and CJ danced with Noah between them. The deejay, the flowers, the big ballroom in the exclusive country club, the buffet, and the centerpieces were not things Nat had planned for her wedding reception, but the townsfolk of Bliss had decided to give them to her anyway. It wasn't every town that could pull off a surprise reception, but Bliss was unique. The local economy revolved around the wedding industry. Lindsey's family had been in the bridal gown business for four generations now, with their boutique nestled in amongst jewelers, florists, tux shops, the party supply store, other bridal boutiques, and every other bridal shop imaginable on The Aisle. As of last summer, Nat was a local hero. CJ was popular in his own right, and so the folks who ran The Aisle had crashed the wedding and brought gifts as only they could.

Including an open bar.

Lindsey thanked the bartender for a glass of Honeymoon Paradise wine from the local winery, then turned to watch the newlyweds while she tried to slow her still-pounding heart.

"Hey, you okay?" said an elegant Christmas tree beside her.

Lindsey peered closer at the tree.

Kimmie Elias peeked out between the branches. Her normally unruly dishwater hair was tucked in a braid, and her pale skin glowed in the twinkle of the white fairy lights.

Lindsey nodded. *Normal*, she reminded herself. Calm, cool, collected. She slid behind the tree with Kimmie. "I haven't seen you alone all day. Having fun?"

Kimmie winced. "Not exactly."

"Your mother's idea?"

"Yes. Again."

Kimmie had talked, dined, and drank with nearly every single guy at the reception tonight. Not because she wanted to, if Lindsey knew Kimmie.

"Were any of them—you know," Kimmie said. "Even close to not a bad match?"

Lindsey sipped the cool wine. She *hated* that question. It didn't come often—thank *God* she'd wised up during college and quit talking about her *gift*—but her family and friends and a decent number of the guests here tonight knew she'd been calling bad relationship matches with eerie accuracy since puberty. Since she'd come home as a divorce lawyer, though, she was rarely asked for her opinion on relationships.

Which was fine with Lindsey.

"Jake wasn't so bad," she said to Kimmie.

Kimmie squeaked, then buried her face in her hands. "Oh, *pumplegunker*. He's my *cousin*."

Breathing was getting easier, and Lindsey's racing heart

was almost back under the speed limit. "You could move down South," she said. "You'd fit right in. *And* you'd get away from your mother."

"Mom's gonna slice my fruitcake if she hears about this."

Lindsey gave Kimmie a sympathetic nudge. "I'm teasing. He was actually the worst of all of them."

Kimmie blew out a breath. "Did I tell you my fortune cookie said unexpected friends would play a pivotal role in my love life? I almost came down with the floosles today, but I didn't want to miss Nat's wedding."

"The floosles?"

"A fake case of the flu and measles." Kimmie peeked around the tree at the dance floor. "Mom would pretty much roast my chestnuts if I weaseled out of a singles night though."

"It's Christmas time. Surely she wouldn't roast your chestnuts during the holidays."

"Yes, she would. And her master plan—you know what? Never mind. Are you thirsty? The winery sent eight cases. It goes great with the cupcakes."

Lindsey lifted her glass.

"Oh, right."

"You want some?" Lindsey asked.

Kimmie's lips tightened into an unusual grim line. "Not really. I—you know I like CJ, and I'm happy for Nat, but I always thought we'd be the three Bliss-keteers. You know. You, Nat, and me. Single and happy and weird together. Or close enough."

Lindsey and her melancholy totally got it. "You'll find your match one day," Lindsey said. "I'd bet all your cupcakes he won't be in Bliss, and your mother won't like him, but he'll make *you* happy. And that's all that matters."

"I don't think so," Kimmie said, "but you will."

Lindsey didn't bother masking a laugh. Years of being saddled with her unfortunate talent had taught her a few things. One was what to look for in short-term hookups to maximize benefits and minimize the pain of the breakups.

The more important thing she'd discovered was that she didn't have a match.

Most days, she was okay with that. But every once in a while, something would happen, like when Mom died, or Nat had Noah, or Nat got married, or Lindsey had to talk into a microphone—*especially* Lindsey talking into a microphone—that would remind her of the one she'd gotten too attached to.

The one she'd loved and left. The one who hadn't been meant to be hers, no matter what her young heart had wanted. "Some of us are better off single," she said to Kimmie.

"Hey, y'all," a feminine voice said over the sound system.

Lindsey peeked around the tree and a cluster of crashers for a better view. One of CJ's sisters had captured the microphone. And—Lindsey winced—she had a guitar.

"Which one's that?" she murmured to Kimmie. Lindsey was trying to learn Nat's new family—she *was*—but CJ had eleven sisters. *Eleven*, scattered all over Illinois. Two had moved to Bliss since CJ decided to settle here, but the sister with the guitar wasn't one of them. And every last one of CJ's sisters was thrilled to finally have a nephew in addition to their plethora of nieces.

Noah had gotten the best Christmas present ever. Lindsey was happy for the little guy, but Kimmie was right. They weren't the three Bliss-keteers anymore. Nat—and Noah—had a new family.

Kimmie peered around the tree too. "That's Saffron. I made her wedding cake last year. She's the one who used to be in Billy Brenton's band."

"Billy…? Oh, right." Some country music blah blah guy. Noah mentioned him from time to time, but Noah was also easily distracted, which saved Lindsey from ever having to listen to country songs.

"CJ, Natalie," Saffron continued, "since everyone else has a surprise for you tonight, we wanted to contribute one as well." Saffron's husband, also with a guitar, nodded beside her. Lindsey almost smiled. Like Nat and CJ, Saffron and her husband didn't spin Lindsey's internal match-o-meter into stormy weather territory. It was a refreshing break. "Although, this is more for Noah," Saffron said. "Congrats, you two crazy kids. Natalie and Noah, welcome to the family."

Saffron adjusted her mic. She swept a gaze over the crowd, grinned big, then nodded to Dylan. They did some counting thing until both of them were bopping their heads to a silent beat, and then they started plucking and strumming their guitars.

Twang came out.

Lindsey had a clear view of Nat, who laughed. CJ did his pretend wince thing, as though he dreaded hearing his sister sing, but affection shone through. And Noah—sweet, innocent, dark-haired little Noah, the best nephew in the whole world—jumped and clapped. "Yeah!" he shouted over the music.

Saffron and Dylan smiled bigger, then the two of them launched into some lyrics.

Something about second chances and being ready for love and getting over the past.

For country music, it wasn't bad. Very appropriate too, given that this was a second marriage for both Nat and CJ. The twang gave Lindsey another hit of melancholy—there went that old memory again—but at least there wasn't anything about getting drunk or breaking up or dogs running away.

"I love this song," Kimmie said over the music. "It's so—*Oh!*"

She was looking past Lindsey. She straightened, put her hands to her cheeks. Lindsey turned, but Kimmie grabbed her. "*Don't look*. Omigod, don't look. Ooooh, *pumplegunker*. He's—"

Whatever else she was about to say was suddenly absorbed into the sounds of a third guitar.

A third guitar that sent a shivery tingle from Lindsey's toes to her tailbone and up to her touched-up roots. And then a third voice joined in. Softer, deeper, not amplified, but nearby.

Lindsey's shivery tingle went spastic.

And despite Kimmie's grip on her arm, Lindsey turned and sought the voice.

She knew that voice. Deep and strong and steady, with a drawl that made the smiley faces on her panties sigh in pure feminine satisfaction.

Her heart—an organ Lindsey tended to consider petrified by professional necessity—thumped along to the music, climbing higher and higher and bigger and bigger until it threatened to choke her.

He strolled through the tables on the other side of the bar, guitar on a strap over his shoulder, rugged stubble on his chin and jawline, short, sandy curls poking beneath his brown ball cap. His fingers coaxed magic from the strings, and his voice swirled into the room like a warm breeze. The hypnotic sound filtered into her empty parts, her lonely parts, her melancholy parts, amplifying the cracks in her soul. Ancient memories and regrets and guilt split the fractures bigger, wider, deeper.

Her heart beat out a thousand country songs of its own in the span of three seconds.

It was *him*.

Singing, strumming, making a path through the crowd. Beneath the *Second Chance Misfits* T-shirt sleeves, his arms were more toned than she remembered, the spread of his shoulders wider, his jeans the right kind of perfect to show off his delectable backside.

But it wasn't his body that had done it for her.

It was his voice. His smile. His eyes.

Him.

Kimmie was saying something, but Lindsey couldn't understand the words. The wedding guests squealed. Some reached out and touched him. As if they recognized him. As if they knew him. As if he was famous.

Her Will.

Everyone in this room knew her Will.

Except he wasn't *her* Will. He never had been.

She'd simply wished, a long, long time ago, that he could've been.

He reached the front of the room, climbed two steps to the small stage and joined Saffron and Dylan, who were both sporting smug grins while they all sang. Will stopped at the third microphone onstage, then his voice came through the speakers too. Lindsey blinked. She straightened against the wall, shrunk farther behind the tree and inhaled deeply. The room was too small. Too small, too crowded, too hot.

I'm going to be president.

It had been almost fifteen years ago, but she could still hear herself.

I'm going to be president, and the world isn't ready for a first Bubba.

She needed to find a way to breathe. To shut off the memories.

And the memories were coming fast and furious.

Will by a fireplace in the ski lodge in Colorado over spring break, watching her with those honey-brown windows to his soul, plucking his guitar.

His adorable country boy smile flashing at her during a snowball fight.

His open, raw, unguarded affection when they'd made love the first time.

Her first time.

Lindsey blinked. Her lungs shuddered for air. She glanced desperately around the ballroom, looking for something— someone—else to focus on before the melancholy beat her. And she found him.

Noah was dancing like a dinosaur with three left feet and crooning along to every word.

With the wrong words, if she knew Noah, but he was giving it everything he had.

Will scanned the crowd, smiling and nodding to the people of Bliss. Making instant friends with the village that had raised Lindsey.

The song came to a drifting halt. Cheers erupted in the room—clapping, hollering, whistling, all of it combining into a celebratory cacophony that was beyond what Lindsey could bear. The noise made her ears ache until the pain spread to her temples, down her neck, to her throbbing, pounding heart.

She didn't know if she should laugh or cry.

Will stepped away from his microphone, reached around both his and Saffron's guitars for a hug, then did a man-shake with Dylan.

Saffron returned to her mic, a grin lighting her pixie face beneath her carrot red hair. "Hope y'all don't mind. We invited one more wedding crasher."

Most of the guests laughed.

"Billy can crash my party anytime," Nat called, and the laughter started all over again.

Will treated Nat to a wink and a heart-stopping country-boy grin.

"I can't believe Billy Brenton is here," Kimmie whisper-shrieked.

The pressure built behind Lindsey's nose.

Her Will had grown up to be the famous Billy Brenton. And now, he was here. In Bliss. At Nat's wedding.

He'd done it.

He'd reached his dream.

She wanted to walk onto that stage and hug him and laugh.

But she didn't have the right. *She'd* left *him*. Cruelly. Publicly. Humiliatingly.

And how long had he been a success? Two years? Three? Longer? She didn't know. She didn't follow country music.

She didn't even follow wedding music trends anymore.

She hadn't, not since that spring break.

But he'd done it. He'd made it. And he probably wouldn't care that she was happy for him.

He probably wouldn't remember her at all.

She hoped.

Kimmie gripped Lindsey's hand. "I just want to watch. Don't let my mom find me, okay? She'd—well. You know."

Lindsey winced. Kimmie's mother was formidable enough when she put her mind to regular tasks. Having the opportunity to offer Kimmie to *Billy Brenton*? She'd be unbearable. And although Lindsey hadn't been a good match for Will—for *Billy*—all those years ago, she'd wanted him anyway.

He was the only one she'd ever truly wanted. The one she could've loved. And so a not-all-that-small, selfish part of her didn't want to know if Will—if Billy Brenton—would be a not-bad match for Kimmie.

For *anybody*.

She looked at the stage again.

And gulped.

He wasn't—he wasn't a bad match for Saffron. The two of them together put Lindsey's match-o-meter in sunny beach-day mode. But Saffron was already married to a guy who wasn't a bad match for her.

Was Will—was *Billy*—a better match?

The room shrunk again.

"What do you think, Billy?" Saffron said into the mic. "You got another song in you tonight?"

Noah bounced. "Yeah!" he shouted.

Saffron grinned at him, an indulgent I'm-going-to-spoil-my-new-nephew-rotten grin. Will leaned into Saffron and said something. She nodded, and he went to his own microphone, chuckling. "Noah, bud, you got some moves," Will said in that easy, warm, husky voice of his. "What's your favorite tune?"

Noah shrieked something Lindsey couldn't understand, but everyone around him cheered too. Still smiling, every bit as at ease onstage as if he'd been born there, Will looked at Saffron and her husband. "Y'all up for it?"

They nodded. There went the heads bopping again, but this time, Will started playing first.

First, and alone, his fingers picked individual sounds out of the guitar in such a way to inspire a nostalgic melancholy.

As if seeing him wasn't enough inspiration.

He was mesmerizing. Larger than life. Owning the stage, owning the room.

Just a man, she reminded herself.

Saffron joined in plucking her own guitar. Her husband did too.

And then Will sang.

Ain't never been the kind who liked the cold, but there I was on that slope, praying for a quick way down.

Lindsey's breath caught. Her shivers got the shivers.

They'd met on a ski slope.

*Learned right quick to be careful what I wish, 'cuz soon I was tumbling
into the snow, with my face all about to hit the ground.*

He looked about the room, smiling, playing, living it up, as comfortable in the limelight as Lindsey was suffocated by it. The crowd loved him. Half of them sang along, and they stopped while he held a note on his guitar.

But then a snow angel caught me.

Lindsey's hold on her wineglass slipped. She pressed into the wall and hoped it didn't give way.

Or maybe she hoped it did.

*She had an easy sassy smile that hit me like a baseball, big brown eyes
that could make an ol' boy drown, and I said, "Baby, that ain't no way
to break a man's fall."*

The pressure spread behind Lindsey's eyes. They burned and stung like they hadn't since Mom died.

That ain't no way to break a man's fall.

It was exactly what he'd said fifteen years ago when he'd crashed into her on the bunny hill.

He remembered her.

He'd written a *song* about her.

And the whole town of Bliss was singing along.

He was strumming the guitar hard and fast now. Noah was spinning. Nat and CJ were dancing and singing too.

*And now she's showing me her pretty smiles, funny smiles, sexy smiles,
her sassy smiles,
She wears her biggest smiles, her brightest smiles, her secret smiles, her
underneath-it smiles,
And she's wearing them just for me.
My snow angel shows her smiles just to me.*

A horrified sputter slipped through Lindsey's lips. Will launched into the second verse, natural as could be. Noah was dancing with three of his new aunts. CJ was twirling Natalie. Dad was nodding his head. Kimmie was singing along.

While Lindsey's first love—her *only* love, despite her knowing better—stood onstage and sang a song about her.

No, not a song about her.

A song about her underwear.

TWO

WILL Truitt hadn't hung out in a karaoke bar like a regular Joe in what felt like a decade.

Lot of fun, this little country joint. It was made to look like a barn, and Will wouldn't have minded doing some two-steppin'. He was mighty glad he'd accepted the invitation to come on over after the reception. Hadn't had fun like this in a while. Given how hard he worked, he'd earned a night out.

Saffron's family took up most of the room, some dancing, some taking their turns singing, some chatting. The place wasn't normally crowded on Sunday nights, Saffron told him, so he wasn't worried about not arranging security. Though after her grandmama had goosed him, Will had taken care to have his backside firmly on a seat or against the bar when he wasn't on the stage with Vera, his trusty six-string who was strapped behind him.

There was a time when the karaoke gods wouldn't let him take his own guitar onstage.

Billy Brenton wasn't a bad thing to be.

"Hey, Billy." One of the younger sisters appeared beside him at the wooden bar. She was a redhead with the same gonna-cause-trouble tilt in her grin that Saffron had when she was in his band. "My sister Pepper over there can sing 'Goin' Creekin'" better than you can," the girl said.

"Gonna have to point her out," he said. "Can't keep all y'all straight, so I call half of you Pepper."

"What do you call the other half?"

"Salt." Named after spices, the whole dang family. Couldn't talk to Saffron without getting hungry when she started jabbering about her sisters.

"Let me know how that turns out for you," Little Red said.

They were a fun bunch. His family wasn't so big. Colorful in a good ol' down-home Southern way, but not big.

Little Red looked over at the stage and clapped her hands together. "Ooh! Look! It's—"

A chorus of *boo*s interrupted her, started by the groom himself.

Will took a swig of beer and eyed the stage. He made out a blonde reversing direction on the stairs to the stage, but that was it.

Cheers erupted. Little Red cocked a hip. "*Seriously?*"

On his other side, Saffron laughed. "The pool," she said to Will. "Cinna here put her money on CJ getting booed out of karaoke quickest. But he at least made it onto the stage."

CJ stood in the middle of the dance floor, high-fiving his new missus. Little Red pranced off to join them, and the sister she'd called Pepper angled closer.

Which he appreciated greatly when he realized their grandmama was eyeing him again.

"Ain't everybody in the family got your musical talents?" Will said to Saffron.

"That wasn't my family. That was Natalie's sister."

The beer in Will's stomach tilted funny, like it found a few extra bubbles it didn't know what to do with.

"You should meet her," Saffron said, the impishness coming out in her own grin.

She was the smallest of her siblings, stature-wise, with a few freckles that didn't go away even this far into winter, but there wasn't a man on Will's crew who hadn't learned the hard way not to underestimate the size of her personality or the depth of her knowledge of practical jokes. "She set Nat and CJ up," Saffron said.

"And a few others too, I've heard," Pepper said.

"How long's it been since you had a girlfriend?" Saffron said. "Isn't that bad for your reputation, going too long without dating anyone?"

"I'd tell you to ignore her," Pepper said over the first few notes of "Friends in Low Places" coming from the speakers tucked between straw bales in the rafters, "but I suspect you're already pretty good at that."

"Hey, you should date Pepper," Saffron said.

Will eyed Pepper. It *had* been a while since he dated anybody.

He hadn't had much urge since his old pup, Bandit, died. His management team had mentioned before Christmas that people were speculating on his love life too. They suggested he go out and get seen with a girl to keep people remembering he was here and he was hot.

But Will had the luxury of telling them to shove it. He'd played the get-seen-with-the-actresses-to-get-some-attention game in his twenties. Now, his songs sold because they were good and people loved *him*, not who he dated.

But that luxury would be short-lived if he couldn't find his music again.

"One date, Billy," Saffron said. "You both need it."

Pepper's face went the same shade as Saffron's hair. She gave her sister a headshake.

"What?" Saffron said to her. "It's a brilliant plan. You'll have fun, and he'll break your streak for you."

Will tugged at Vera's strap. Time to leave this conversation.

"Please ignore her," Pepper said to him. "You've done plenty for our family already."

"But this is for *him*," Saffron said. "He'd be doing himself a favor too if he took you out."

"No, he wouldn't," Pepper said, some singsong *shut up* coming through her lips.

Saffron snickered. "Billy, you want to get married?"

"Ladies," he said, "that right there's my cue to go see a man about my next song."

"Chicken," Saffron teased.

"Yes, ma'am."

"You could do worse. No, wait. You *have* done worse. *Much* worse."

Too much truth in that to argue the point. He'd given up the idea of finding love somewhere between being nineteen and making it big. Now, he didn't know who wanted him for him, and who wanted him for Billy. He liked the ladies well enough, but he didn't date the settling-down type. Especially with his family history.

Saffron snapped a finger. "Oh, hey—here. We'll do a test. I'll drop it if you're a bad match. If not, you have to take Pepper out for dinner. Because she's had a rough time with boyfriends lately, and it would make her day. And you're already here."

His gut tilted more sideways at the way she said *bad match*, and a tingle of a memory made his shoulder twitch. "Leaving in the morning," Will said. "Have to get to New York for New Year's Eve."

Saffron poked him. "Then you can take her to breakfast. And have fun with a *nice* girl, Billy. See what it feels like."

He shook his head and took another swig, but she turned and lifted her hand. "Hey, Lindsey! Over here!"

Will had spent the better part of the past decade onstage, and the better part of the five years before that doing everything he could to get himself on that stage. Performing was almost second nature.

All that practice performing was the only reason he didn't spit out his beer.

Because he suddenly understood what all that gut tilting was about. What his body knew that he was ignoring.

Saffron was saying something again, something about spotting people who shouldn't be in relationships, a sixth sense, telling the relationship weather, but he didn't need Saffron to explain.

He knew who *she* was and what she did.

He knew before that blonde head turned their way.

He knew before her slender shoulders twisted to follow her head.

He knew before she stepped through the crowd and came into full view.

Ten years of touring the States, and he'd just found the only girl who had ever broken his heart.

Will took in the white wool coat she was buttoning over her breasts, the downward cast to her light lashes, the way her blonde hair fell forward and brushed her high cheeks in straight, silky strands. His leg muscles quivered, his heart went on a bender, and his breathing wasn't slow enough to be normal.

He'd spent almost half his life wondering if this day would ever come.

"You're leaving?" Saffron said to her.

She nodded while she finished her buttons. "My work here is done."

"Oh, not yet." Saffron latched onto her arm. "Have you two met yet? Billy, this is Nat's sister, Lindsey. Lindsey, you've heard of Billy, right?"

Her hair was blonder than it had been, her face thinner, her brows more arched. Legs still long and slender, lips still a natural pink, ears still dainty. She carried herself with the nose-tilt he would've expected of the president. And if she remembered him, if she knew who he was, there wasn't an ounce of recognition when she turned those brown heart-crushers on him.

Not a flicker of an eyelash, a tremble in her mouth, a flare of memory anywhere.

She offered a smooth hand with perfectly polished pink nails. "Billy. Nice to meet you."

Billy. She wanted him to be *Billy.*

They might've only had a week together, but that week had changed his life.

Changed *him.*

It hit him right in the ego that she didn't know—or was pretending she didn't know—who he was.

By all rights, he was the one who shouldn't have remembered her.

He set down his beer and took her hand, barely keeping

his own steady, and had the reward of feeling a tremor in her grip.

"Miss Lindsey," he drawled.

Her left eyelid fluttered. Will's heart flung itself against his ribs, banging for a way out. "You look familiar," he said. "We ever met?"

That kicked the dust up in her composure. Her hand twitched and her lips tilted into the likeness of a smile, but her eyes didn't follow. No surprise, if she'd heard him sing "Snow Angel Smiles."

"Does that line actually work for you?" she said.

"Darlin', I don't need lines." He tugged Vera's strap, felt her steady, reassuring weight. "You ever been to Charlotte?"

"No."

"Orange Beach?"

Her eyes narrowed. "No."

"Wait, wait. I got it. Seattle. We met after the Seattle show, right?"

She pulled her hand from his grip. "I've never been farther west than Colorado."

"Huh." He slouched and stroked his whiskers. He had to hand it to her. Any other girl would've jumped in his lap, talked about the good times, pretended they'd parted on good terms so she could get close to the superstar.

Not Lindsey.

He also gave her points for saying *Colorado* out loud without flinching.

"You sure?" he said.

"To be honest, I don't care for country music." She added another of those smiles that kept to her lips, a smile that was probably meant to look like an apology. Like a *nothing personal*.

Right.

He gripped Vera's strap.

It was personal.

"Got a notion I might could change your mind," he said.

She visibly swallowed. They'd had this conversation before. Near about word-for-word, if his dusty ol' memory recalled.

"So far, you haven't," she said.

Saffron howled. Will started. He'd forgotten she was there. "You're wasting your time, Billy," she said. "Looks like Lindsey's the only woman on the planet who's never heard of you."

Will forced a smile—a good one, too, a Billy Brenton classic—because it's what was expected of *Billy*. "Aw, now, that can't be true." He waited a beat, let Lindsey's eyelid flutter some more—she had, after all, heard of him long before Billy Brenton came to be—then added, "Planet's big. I'm just a kid from Georgia. Lots of people ain't heard of me."

Saffron leaned closer to Lindsey. "I'm trying to convince Billy to take Pepper out."

Probably he shouldn't have jumped when he got Saffron's text suggesting he come crash her brother's wedding. Sounded like fun, getting out of Pickleberry Springs, away from moping over his writer's block. Plus, Maroon 5 crashed weddings. Ed Sheeran crashed weddings. Billy Brenton could do it too. That was as good for publicity as picking a token girlfriend.

But it was hell on his heart.

"He has notoriously terrible taste in women," Saffron said.

"I do," Will agreed.

Lord have mercy, that one hit its mark. Lindsey's eyes flared and her lips flattened, but all her poise came back quick. "We all have our difficulties."

"Wouldn't they be cute together?" Saffron said.

Will leaned against the bar to give her a better view of him and Pepper.

Not because he wanted to be an ass—well, not *all* because he wanted to be an ass. It *had* been fifteen years, but then, she was the one pretending she didn't know him.

Lindsey's gaze flicked between him and Pepper, then him and Saffron. Her brows pinched together, then smoothed out.

And his heart went to doing that bouncing to get out thing faster and harder while the hairs on his arms stood at attention.

She'd been right all those years ago about Mari Belle. Shocked the hell out of Will when his sister divorced her husband, but Lindsey had called it.

He should've been grateful she'd called herself a bad match for Will in the end too, but she'd done it in such spectacular fashion, he still couldn't fully offer his thanks. Even now.

Some scars went deeper than flesh wounds.

Will swallowed. "Saffron says you match people up."

"Does she?" Lindsey gave Saffron one of those looks that usually came before a good ol' cat fight. "How lovely that she likes to talk about people."

Will's lips still couldn't remember how to smile natural. "You the resident matchmaker here in Bliss?"

Her mouth settled into a grim line. "No. In fact, I prefer the term *unwanted relationship correctionist*. And only when unavoidable."

"She's a divorce lawyer," Saffron said.

Lindsey nodded. "I eat babies for breakfast."

Will choked on his own spit. "That right?" he managed.

"They taste the best."

Her straight-faced delivery was almost believable.

"How's a pretty girl like you end up with a job like that?" he asked.

If she was going for serene and unaffected, she almost hit it. But her lips tightened, her brows slanted down, and she pulled herself taller.

"Local lore is that she makes matches in her spare time," Saffron said, as though she couldn't see the storm brewing.

"Prevents bad matches usually," Pepper said. "But the point is, she's never wrong."

Of course she wasn't. *That*, he remembered too. *We're bad for each other. I know these things. Deep down in my gut. I know. And I'm never wrong.*

"Did you hear about the couple who—" Pepper started.

"I appreciate the warm welcome into the extended family," Lindsey interjected, her knuckles going white while she yanked her coat belt, "but you can feel free to leave me out of the gossip."

"Absolutely," Saffron said. "As soon as you tell us if Pepper's a good match for Billy."

Lindsey flicked another glance at Will. "Pepper is a lovely

person. You could certainly do worse here in Bliss, if you honestly need my opinion, which I suspect you do not."

He absolutely could do worse. Had a notion he was looking at *worse* right now.

But he wanted to get inside her head and translate all that stuff she wasn't saying for what she was.

To ask her—everything.

Mari Belle said he was a hopeless romantic for wasting time thinking on a girl he met when he was still a kid, but he hadn't felt like a kid that week. He'd felt like his mind and his soul and his emotions had finally grown into his man-size body. Wanting answers about why she left him like she did— now, fifteen years later when his career was on top of the world, when he had a top-notch team and a handful of good friends surrounding him to boot—was a good sign he needed to haul his rear end home before he did something more stupid than that time he reminded Mari Belle that Lindsey had predicted her divorce.

Saffron straightened beside him. A draft of cold air slunk through the bar. Pepper straightened too and looked at the door. Lindsey turned that way as well.

Two dozen people were streaming in, and they weren't in the matching wedding shirts, nor did they seem to want to sing.

Nope. They looked to be looking for someone.

Namely, him.

Will liked meeting fans well enough, but this wasn't the place. Not controlled enough, and if there were two dozen now, there would be a hundred in five minutes.

He checked Vera's strap and felt behind him for his coat.

Saffron signaled the bartender.

"Does this place have a back door?" she said to Pepper and Lindsey.

"Yes, but it'll set off the alarms," Lindsey said. "The best way out is through the kitchen."

The hordes had spotted Will and were moving through the crowd.

Got Fired from Pickin' Chicken Parts.' Here. I'll play it for you."

She looked to be fighting a smile herself, but even with only the moon to light the night, he could tell that smile still wasn't spreading to any of the rest of her face.

Might've been his imagination, but he thought there was some sad lingering in there. Maybe some regret.

Proof she had a soul. Wasn't something he would've given her credit for.

"You should go," she said quietly. And this time when she turned, he swore she murmured something that sounded like, "I'm proud of you, Will."

Even if he wanted to chalk it up to his imagination, he couldn't stop the flood of pure, simple affection those five little words brought about.

With the flood came something else.

She kept walking away. She didn't know it, and Will didn't like it, but she left a part of herself behind.

He knew, because for the first time in near about two years, he wanted to write a song.

THREE

BEING home at Aunt Jessie's house always put Will in touch with old memories. Usually of her homemade turnip soup, playing cards with Sacha, and Hank Williams and Willie Nelson on the record player. Despite his offers to buy Aunt Jessie a nicer, newer house, she'd clung to this old place as *home*. Will's old room was nearly unchanged from when he'd moved out at nineteen—his Greg Maddux poster on one wall, Faith Hill and Shania Twain on the opposite, the old dresser still missing a knob and the springs on his twin bed still squeaky.

Most of the days he was lucky enough to spend here, he appreciated the cozy comfort. It was the home that a kid who'd lost his mother at six craved, and the where-I-come-from that the Billy Brenton part of him needed to stay grounded.

But today, with the Georgia winter bearing down on the dreary, nippy side, all he could remember were his last months here as a kid, before he moved to Nashville.

They hadn't been good months. About as ugly as a wet warthog and messed up as a bumblebee in a snowstorm.

He shook his head. Too much work to do for him to waste time wallowing in the past.

Coming home seemed a smart thing after he left New York

yesterday, but now he was itching to get to Nashville. Away from haunting memories and closer to —

Something.

He knew what he didn't want, but he couldn't rightly say what it was he did want.

He pulled on his boots, then pocketed his phone, wallet, and keys. There was another new tune bobbing around in his brain. He needed to write it down, smooth it out, polish it.

Not think about how long it'd been since the music talked to him.

How the new tune had snuck in while Will was standing in a cold, dark, icy parking lot in Bliss, Illinois.

"You leaving, honey?" Aunt Jessie said when Will stepped into the cozy living room. She was hunched over a card table in the center of the room messing with yarn, buttons, a map, and a brown jar of something. Whatever it was, Will didn't want to know.

Could be anything, since Sacha was there too. Sacha lived next door and was Aunt Jessie's psychic. She was also practically Will's third mother—she'd been there for all of them since Aunt Jessie took in Will and Mari Belle. Sacha wasn't blood, but she was family.

"Yeah. Hitting the road soon as Mikey gets here," Will said. He and Mikey had been best friends since second grade, growing up and writing music together. Now Mikey played drums in Will's band, and he was as good at picking up ladies' phone numbers as he was at banging buckets.

Aunt Jessie threaded another button onto a length of pink yarn. Her warm blue eyes lit in a twinkle beneath her trademark dye-and-perm job. "Mikey's momma ask for grandbabies again for Christmas?"

"Nah, this year she threatened to trade me in for them instead," Mikey himself said from the front door with an unrepentant grin. He let himself in and kissed both Aunt Jessie and Sacha in turn. "And how are my favorite ladies today?"

"Don't you be bringing that charm in here." Aunt Jessie waggled her string of buttons at him. "I'm a happily married lady."

"Don't see ol' Donnie here today though," Mikey said. Donnie had come into the family about two years ago as Aunt Jessie's fourth husband. Will could take him or leave him, but Aunt Jessie liked him, he treated her right, and even Mari Belle couldn't find much wrong with him, other than the part where Donnie was a man.

Aunt Jessie giggled. "He's in Macon. Got a lead on a winery he might invest in. But he'll be home tonight, so don't you go trying anything."

"And I've got your number," Sacha said to Mikey. She was tall and dark to Aunt Jessie's plump and light, Morticia Addams to Betty White. Sacha drew a finger along the map, tracing the creek that ran through town. "You can save your flirting for young ladies who fall for your malarkey."

Will copied Mikey, treating both of the ladies to a peck on the cheek. "Thanks for a good Christmas. Don't know what y'all are planning with those buttons and that map, but call if you need bail money."

"We're fixin' to find the treasure," Aunt Jessie said. "We've been looking all the wrong places."

Ah. The legendary Pickleberry Springs treasure. Will should've guessed.

"I had a vision," Sacha added. "And that's all we're telling the likes of—"

She suddenly stopped and stared at Will with a singular concentration that gave him a familiar creepy sensation along the back of his knees and neck.

"William." Her coal-black brows slanted together over her long face, but it was the tone more than his full name that got Will's attention.

He knew that tone.

The dramatic, voice-dropped-an-octave, I-had-a-premonition tone.

Always gave him a shiver. She was right as much as she was wrong, but she'd called a few big moments in his life.

You need to go to Colorado with your sister. There's something there you have to do.

Follow your dream. Follow it to the top. You have the gift, young William.

You'll see her again. Your story isn't over.

Will's shiver turned into a shudder.

Aunt Jessie turned to watch with parted lips. Mikey leaned back and tucked his hands in his pockets with his normal healthy dose of skepticism.

Sacha's dark gaze swept over him, lingering on his chest.

Right where Vera's strap was.

There went the shivers tickling Will's neck again. He latched onto the strap, half from habit, half from protectiveness.

"You need her gift," Sacha said in the freaky premonition voice. There weren't any candles lit like when she was over here doing a reading, but Will smelled the sickly sweet scent anyway.

His grip tightened on Vera's strap. "Been using her gift since you gave her to me." Two days after Will and Mari Belle moved in with Aunt Jessie, Sacha arrived with a doll for Mari Belle and Vera for Will.

Took him a few years before he was big enough to play her *right*, and another couple after that before he named her, but he never forgot where Vera came from.

"Not Vera." Sacha took his hand in both of hers, his calloused from playing, hers smooth and cool. *"Her.* You've seen her."

"Her?" Mikey said.

"Her?" Aunt Jessie whispered.

There was one *her.* There had always been only one *her.*

Will's jaw tightened. "Don't know what you're talking about."

Sacha pinned him with a dark stare.

It wasn't a *you're lying* stare, necessarily, though she'd always been able to see through him as well as Aunt Jessie could. Better, some days.

More like another of her *I'm having a vision* stares.

He had a flash of memory—several, matter of fact. Most of them fifteen or so years old, but another more recent.

All surrounding a blonde lady he couldn't shake out of his mind.

You'll see her again some day, Sacha had said fifteen years ago. *You'll see her when you need her.*

The shivers he got when she was right went deeper than his skin. They were somewhere inside, somewhere he couldn't reach.

"You need to go to her," Sacha said. "Now. For you. For Mikey. For the music."

Mikey cleared his throat. No secret what he thought of Sacha's visions.

"You need to go to her for all of us," Sacha whispered. She blinked once, twice, and then stood. As she always did after a vision, she turned and floated out of the house, flowery fabric swishing softly about her as though she hadn't dropped a psychic bomb on his life.

Will tried to shrug off the heebie-jeebies giving him goose bumps. He could say all he wanted that he didn't believe. She'd been wrong about his debut album going gold and that his house would burn down with something important in it — seven years and two electricians later, all was still standing in the Nashville burbs — but when she was right, she was on the money.

More than whether she was right or wrong, though, she shared her *visions* because she cared.

She always had.

She'd steered Aunt Jessie through three divorces and then introduced her to Donnie. Sacha had predicted that the dishwasher would get possessed by the devil, and a week later, the darn thing sprang to life with the door open and rained all over the kitchen. She convinced Jessie to take a spur-of-the-moment vacation to see Will in Nashville two days before a tornado wiped out the Pickleberry Springs Library where Aunt Jessie was supposed to be working.

"She in Nashville?" Mikey asked.

He was asking about Lindsey, and everyone in the room knew it. Will shook his head before he could stop himself.

Aunt Jessie stood and wrapped him in a hug. The top of her head barely reached his shoulders, but she squeezed tight as she did when he was little, like that's all it would take to banish evil and danger from the world.

"Be careful, my sweet boy," she whispered.

"We're going to Nashville, Aunt Jessie," he said. "Nowhere else."

She pulled back and frowned at him, but it was a wobbly, shiny-eyed frown. "You need to go where you need to go. Listen to Sacha. Trust her."

"All due respect," Mikey said, "but Will's got too many people depending on him for us to be anywhere but Nashville right now."

Mikey was half right. Will had a big crew, and they depended on Billy Brenton for their bread and butter. For their families' bread and butter. Will was supposed to be in Nashville, writing songs and getting in the studio, so he could keep his crew employed and have a reason to tour again next year.

But Billy Brenton needed to find his music again. And last Will checked, the music hadn't been talking to him in Nashville. Not for writing his own songs, not for finding anyone else's that worked for him.

The music hadn't talked to him anywhere except Bliss.

His palm was sweaty over Vera's strap, but her weight was comforting. She'd be there no matter what he did. She was always there.

"Sacha has never steered me wrong in my love life, and she's never steered you wrong in your career," Aunt Jessie said. "You go find that girl." She turned to Mikey. "And you. Watch out for my boy. You watch him good."

Mikey's steel gaze was flat and hard. "Always do, Miss Jessie. Won't let him do anything knuckleheaded. Promise."

Anything knuckleheaded like go anywhere but Nashville.

God willing, Mikey would deliver on that promise.

JANUARY WAS busy season for Lindsey at work. New year, new clients with new resolutions to get out of misguided marriages. If Lindsey had her way, there would be more clients coming in for prenups and adoption proceedings instead.

Of course, if Lindsey had her way, she wouldn't be able to see when couples shouldn't be together. But since she'd first started calling breakups in junior high, she hadn't been able to shake it. So she lived with it, and she corrected what she couldn't prevent, and she thanked her lucky stars she had a job demanding enough that she could bury herself in it.

But her job wasn't enough to keep the memories from nipping at her heels this week. She rubbed at her temples.

It had been ten days since Nat's wedding. Ten long, cold, overcast winter days spent at her carved mahogany desk in her dark walnut–paneled office, with the coffee-colored leather client chairs staring at her when there weren't unhappy divorcées-to-be sitting in them. Several of her fellow attorneys at the firm had asked about Nat's wedding—and Billy Brenton, of course—but otherwise, life went on as normal.

Except for the memories.

And the unusual guest who popped in late Wednesday afternoon.

"My dear Lindsey," an annoyingly authoritative female voice intoned from her doorway.

Lindsey's shoulders bunched in on themselves, but she forced herself to relax, sit straight, and greet Marilyn Elias with her best baby-eating divorce lawyer glare. "Marilyn. You weren't on my calendar."

Behind Marilyn, Lindsey's assistant made the universal *I'm sorry, she steamrolled me* gesture.

Marilyn stepped into the room and closed the door on Lindsey's assistant with a definitive *click*. "By the power vested in me as—"

"Cut to the chase unless you want me to start charging to listen to you," Lindsey interrupted. Marilyn was Kimmie's formidable mother. She was also president of Bliss's Bridal Retailers Association, chairperson of the town's annual Knot Festival, a direct descendant of Bliss's founders, the unofficial

Bliss Propriety Police, owner of Bliss's most prestigious bakery, and a general pain in the ass. Most of Bliss feared and revered her. Nat called her the Queen General, or QG for short.

Marilyn was also Dad's unofficial quasi-girlfriend, which was the only reason Lindsey hadn't started counting minutes already.

Marilyn cleared her throat and eyed the brown leather chair across from Lindsey.

"It's clean." Lindsey waved a hand at the other chair. "But that one has the divorce cooties."

Marilyn's eye twitched over the forced smile plastered across her lips. "I had no idea you worked above ground."

"Closer to the man upstairs," Lindsey said. "By the power vested in God as God, he grants second chances through me. And speaking of second chances, Nat's wedding cupcakes were delicious. Now, are you here to lose a debate about my profession, or is there some other reason you've come to the dark side today?"

"My dear Lindsey," Marilyn said again.

Lindsey lifted a brow. This *was*, after all, the same woman who had quietly spread word almost ten years ago that any real estate agent willing to show Lindsey homes in Bliss would never sell another house in the entire county, which was why Lindsey both worked *and* lived in Willow Glen, the trendy city thirty minutes from Nat and Noah and Dad. Not many people had the guts to cross Marilyn.

But Marilyn couldn't take anything from Lindsey.

Not anymore.

Marilyn draped her coat over the *clean* chair and lowered herself onto the edge of the seat. "My friendship with your father has made me consider reevaluating some of my life truths," she said.

Lindsey waited. She'd seen love—and hate—do remarkable things to people, but Marilyn lived and breathed leading the Most Married-est Town on Earth. Divorce attorneys didn't belong in Marilyn's life picture. Period.

"While it would've been preferable for your sister's first

husband to perish of natural or heroic causes rather than to have departed her life through divorce," Marilyn said, "it's obvious that Natalie's second marriage to our dear CJ is a blessing for all involved, and that Bliss is better for the opportunity they had to become one. And that"—Marilyn's eye twitched again—"would not have been possible without the intervention of professionals such as yourself."

Tonight would be a two-glasses-of-wine night. "That's very open-minded of you," Lindsey said.

"And as you seem to have a good deal of practice with… breakups… it occurred to me that we have a unique opportunity to capitalize on your… talents, and to benefit Bliss at the same time."

Marilyn was still peering down her nose with her crystal blue laser-flingers, and other than a brief show of pink that had quickly receded from her cheeks, her Queen General poker face was firmly in place.

Good thing Lindsey had plenty of practice reading between the lines.

Bliss had been without a professional matchmaker since their last one retired seven years ago, and Marilyn thought her friendship with Dad could open the lines of communication for Lindsey to come home and do what she was supposedly born to do.

Lindsey's refusal to live up to Marilyn's idea of her destiny was the other reason Marilyn had put a bounty on the head of anyone willing to show Lindsey real estate in Bliss all those years ago.

Marilyn's way or the highway, and Marilyn's way was having Lindsey trained and ready to be the next woo-woo psychic matchmaker in Bliss.

Lindsey preferred the highway. "I'm quite happy with the profession I have now, thank you."

"Of course, my dear," Marilyn said. "I would never suggest you abandon your… profession."

Lindsey cleared her throat.

"But Bliss would be so grateful if one of our own returned home to judge the Battle of the Boyfriends next month."

Lindsey's lips parted.

Then snapped shut.

The Battle of the Boyfriends had started as a wedding band competition in the seventies. The winning band was typically booked for the biggest and best weddings in Bliss. But over the years, the battle had evolved as competitors used their time onstage to dedicate love songs to their girlfriends or crushes. Now every year, a dozen or more men got onstage to sing for their women, and every year, there were hookups, proposals, heartbreaks, and earplugs. It wasn't as big as the Husband Games—a series of Olympic-style domestic challenges for new and old husbands alike that capped off the week of Knot Festival every June, and which Nat now organized for Bliss in Mom's place. But the Battle of the Boyfriends was legendary in its own right.

A music-blind divorce attorney as a judge for Bliss's annual competition didn't fit. Even if Marilyn was trying to make nice with Lindsey for the sake of her special friendship with Dad.

"What do you really want?" Lindsey asked.

"My dear Lindsey—"

"Don't 'my dear' me."

"I'm simply offering an olive branch."

"I've never much liked olives."

Marilyn smiled brighter. And though Lindsey had nothing this woman could take away, her stomach dipped. Nothing good came of Marilyn smiling like that. "A grape vine, then," Marilyn said.

Lindsey studied her. Her short, dyed-and-highlighted-to-perfection brown hair was immaculate as always, her white business suit cut entirely too similarly to Lindsey's light gray business suit, the determined set to her square jaw hiding the beginnings of a natural sag beneath her chin. Her lipstick was bloodred and perfect, her shoulders square as though she'd been raised by Southern debutante mamas. All in all, she exuded *I will not take no for an answer*.

Marilyn wanted more than to offer peace.

She wanted Lindsey back in Bliss, acting as matchmaker.

No—that wasn't exactly what Marilyn wanted. At least, it

couldn't be the only thing Marilyn wanted. A gasp of surprise slipped from Lindsey's lips before she could stop it.

Marilyn arched her brows—mildly, so as not to cause wrinkles most likely—and her smile didn't waver. But then again, if Marilyn knew what Lindsey suspected, she wouldn't show it.

Lindsey stood. "It was kind of you to think of me, Marilyn, but Bliss has far better options for everything you need. I'll consider the olive branch extended though."

"Think it over for a few days," Marilyn said. "Take a week, if you must. It would be lovely to have a daughter of Bliss return home as a judge for the Battle of the Boyfriends."

"My answer is final. And I have work to do."

Marilyn's lips pursed, but she stood as well. "Regardless, the position will still be open should you change your mind. Talk it over with your father. I'm sure he'll have a level-headed opinion on the matter."

She tucked her wool coat over her arm, gave Lindsey another gracious smile that made her look as friendly as a hungry tiger, and then strolled to the door.

"Oh, and Marilyn," Lindsey said.

"Yes?"

"I won't help you marry Kimmie off either."

Marilyn's shoulders visibly twitched. "That's quite presumptuous," she sniffed.

But long after she left, Lindsey had no doubt Kimmie was the real reason Marilyn had stopped in today. And if Lindsey was right, Marilyn would return with more carrots until Lindsey agreed to help find Kimmie a man. It was a little-known secret that Marilyn had sold half of her bakery to a distant relative to fund Knot Fest a few years ago, after a flood had nearly wiped Bliss off the map. And it was even less well-known that Marilyn's relative had passed away, leaving her half of the bakery to a Chicago playboy who had spent the last year taunting the Queen General. Marilyn wanted Kimmie married off to someone who could both help Kimmie manage the bakery she would inherit one day, and also manage—or get rid of—their silent partner.

Lindsey smiled to herself. Marilyn, the bakery, the matchmaking scheme—this was normal for the antics in and around Bliss. And the closer Lindsey got to life returning to normal, the further she got from remembering the blip in her life that was Will.

FOUR

WILL WANTED to believe he should've stayed in Nashville, but by Wednesday, it was clear Nashville didn't have what he needed.

By Friday night, Will conceded defeat. He'd irritated half of the songwriters in Nashville and a good portion of his label's management by not liking any of the songs he heard from anybody else. He'd also lost all the tunes whispering in his ear after his trip to Bliss. Even Vera couldn't find the music again for him.

He was swinging his bags into his truck when Mikey arrived at Will's Nashville mansion.

"Ain't enough to aim for the Country Music Hall of Fame? Have to aim for the Dumbass Hall of Fame too?" Mikey tossed his own bags in the truck and climbed into the cab. "Know better than to talk you out of it. So let's go be stupid together."

Now, two nights later, they were settled in a furnished rental house in a quiet neighborhood in Bliss that Will's assistant had arranged for them.

But the house didn't have food yet—or tunes—so that night, Will and Mikey climbed out of Will's truck in the frigid, half-empty parking lot at Suckers, an aptly named watering hole not far from the house. A giant neon sign that wouldn't have been out of place in Vegas lit the night. "Can't help thinking being here is a bad, bad idea, buckaroo," Mikey said.

"It's this or a couple years off touring."

"Had a good run."

"Yeah, might as well close out my career with *Hitched*."

Mikey's shoulders twitched.

Next to Mari Belle, Mikey had been the loudest in protesting Will's last album. *If you're going back to that dark place, you're going alone this time*, Mari Belle had said. *I thought you burned those songs.*

You should've *burned those songs*, Mikey had chimed in.

Probably they were right. For Will's peace of mind, though not for the Billy Brenton empire.

Two years ago, Will had gotten drunk at his label's Christmas party. He'd started talking about all those old songs he'd written about Lindsey. Apparently he'd sang what he could remember of a few of them.

There was a reason Will didn't drink much.

The brass had called him two days later, wanting to hear more. And since Will never got rid of a song, he still had 'em tucked away. He'd thought he could handle it, that enough time had passed, that the songs probably sucked worse than ten straight nights of sharing a bus with nine other guys on a straight chili diet.

He'd been wrong. About everything.

Pure, raw Billy, the label brass had called the songs.

They had no idea.

He hadn't either.

He'd polished the songs with some of the best and brightest songwriters in Nashville. The album came out a year ago. Went platinum within a month of release. He'd had five other albums go platinum in his career, but never that fast.

And Will had felt completely unsettled—and unable to write a song he liked—ever since.

He grabbed the door to Suckers. "Can't write on an empty stomach," he said.

Mikey grunted. "Security in place?"

"Yep."

"Ready to turn up the Billy factor?"

"Let's do this." Will flipped his cap around and swung open the door. The joint wasn't too crowded. A good number of the tables and booths were occupied, though half the stools around the semicircle steel bar were empty. Nary a head turned at first. But then a gasp of surprise came from one of the tables. Will stood taller and slapped on his show smile, prepared to channel Billy's slower drawl. Squeaks and whispers went through the room while he and Mikey swaggered in. Two more couples looked their way. So did a group at the far end of the bar.

Will started to nod to them, but mid-nod, he nearly tripped over his own cowboy boots.

The middle woman—*Lindsey*.

Her blonde hair was tied at the base of her slender neck, showing off small diamond studs in her delicate ears. A soft ivory sweater molded to her shoulders and breasts. Her lips were tipped up in a grin at a dark-haired woman and big redheaded guy beside her—the newly minted Mr. and Mrs. CJ Blue. But Lindsey's smile slid off her face when her brown cowboy-killers landed on him. Her brow took on a slight pinch, and then everything about her went still and blank. But the pinch was enough to send his brain reeling back about fifteen years.

They'd made unlikely friends when he plowed into her on the ski slope, and after that, he'd waited for her every breakfast, then every lunch and every dinner, fascinated by the girl who could chatter on about any subject Will's slow brain could think of, whose friends kept ditching her, who had a plan to be president of the whole country one day so she could change the world. She was a funny combination of confident and vulnerable, all rolled into the prettiest package a kid from the Georgia sticks had ever seen.

Halfway through the week, he'd overslept. She'd been gone when he went running down for breakfast, and he couldn't find her on the slopes. Dummy that he was, he hadn't gotten her number—not that either of them had cell phones back then—and he'd been sure she'd slipped away, lost to him forever. He'd been all kinds of smittened by then, and he'd had half a mind to go drown his sorrows, when he turned a corner of the lodge and took a snowball to the face.

You stood me up, Lindsey had said.

She hadn't said a word about all of her friends lying to her about where they were having dinner, about when they were meeting, about which slopes they'd be skiing, but she'd hit Will with a snowball because he missed breakfast.

Because he hurt her.

He'd known she had secrets—knew there was a story for why she let her friends treat her as bad as they were—but her eyes had pinched, her voice had wobbled, and right there he'd sworn he'd spend the rest of his life protecting her.

Friends don't stand friends up, she'd said.

And then she'd lobbed another snowball at him.

Are we friends? he'd asked.

I could use a friend, she'd said.

The rest was hazy—how they got to tumbling in the snow, her beneath him, their coats between them, those big brown eyes asking him questions his nineteen-year-old mind couldn't understand. He'd kissed her. *Friends kiss all the time, right?* she'd said.

And because he'd been a red-blooded nineteen-year-old kid outside of Pickleberry Springs for near about the first time in his life—with a sexy, sophisticated sorority girl willing to kiss him—he hadn't taken the clue that she wasn't falling for him like he was for her.

And he'd fallen hard. Fast.

Forever, by the feel of it.

But it hadn't been forever, and now, fifteen years later, he was watching her in a bar, his fingers twitching for Vera, because Will was suddenly hearing a melody.

Just as well Vera was back at the house. Wasn't *good* music he was hearing. More like an out-of-tune marching band made of people playing the wrong instruments.

The ring of a bell exploded in the bar and pulled Will fully back to the neon purple track lighting and the silver and red décor inside Suckers. "Phones and cameras away," CJ Blue said to the room at large. Much like he'd been dressed at his wedding, he was in a T-shirt and jeans. Even on the wrong side of the bar to be in charge, he had everyone's attention. "What happens at Suckers stays at Suckers, or Jeremy will toss you out on your ass. Got it?"

A bigger, darker, tattooed dude on the other side of the bar nodded, and everyone—including Lindsey's crowd—made their phones disappear.

"Don't even think of being stealthy," a familiar, shorter, sassier redhead behind the bar called. Another of the sisters from the wedding, Will realized. The baby of the family. "I got every one of your numbers."

"Aw, shit," Mikey said. "Is *everyone* in here related to Saffron?"

"You mean through blood or through marriage?" a dark-haired girl with Lindsey's crowd called in answer. Pepper. She was the one whose name really was Pepper. She was also the one smart enough to be eyeing Mikey like she knew to keep her phone number to herself. "Only four or five of us, but Cinna's the one you have to worry about." She pointed to Little Red behind the bar.

"Time to go, Billy-boy," Mikey said.

Pepper laughed. "You *are* Mikey. I thought I recognized you. But the chicken part clinched it."

Any other time or place, Will would've had a good laugh at Mikey's expense. Instead, he had to work just to find a smile. "Always does," Will said.

Mikey grunted.

Pepper patted the seat beside her. "Make yourselves comfortable. Food's good, beer's good, and Saffron's not here to make any outrageous suggestions."

"I'm happy to fill in for her," Cinna said behind the bar.

"Not if you want to keep your job," CJ replied.

"You're such a spoilsport, Princess." She flipped two glasses onto the bar. "Get you boys something to drink?"

"Beer and grub." Will swallowed the butterflies climbing in his throat. He was Billy Brenton. Blonde divorce lawyers in bars didn't make him sweat, dammit. "What's good?"

"The redheads." Cinna winked and pushed her shoulders back, lifting her chest.

"Feeling more in the mood for brunettes tonight," Mikey said. He winked at a table of brown-haired twenty-somethings, and all three of them giggled.

"You really *are* like this in real life." Pepper seemed equally horrified and impressed.

"Maybe you should date *him*, Pepper," Cinna said.

Pepper flipped her off.

Cinna laughed. "Two brown ales, coming up."

"Corner booth's open too if you want it," CJ said to them. "Company's good at the bar though."

Will could've picked the corner booth. Will *should've* picked the corner booth.

But he was here looking for inspiration.

And she was sitting right there, though all she was inspiring was a headache.

"So long as you don't have any more relatives coming tonight." Will slid onto the stool next to Pepper.

"None who are as annoying as Cinna," CJ said.

"I'll drink to that." Pepper lifted a glass toward her brother, then turned to Will. "So, what brings the great Billy Brenton into Suckers tonight?"

The woman sitting three seats down. Not that he'd tell her that. "Needed a place to get away and write some songs for a few weeks. Where better than here?"

Mikey coughed. He'd taken the stool next to Will, and Will didn't have to look to know that his buddy was scoping out the single ladies.

All the single ladies.

But unlike most nights when Mikey was trolling for numbers, there was an extra level of awareness to him tonight.

"Don't worry, we won't tell people you're here," Pepper said.

The girl on her other side went pale. Might've whimpered, matter of fact.

Cinna slid two beers across the bar, then followed them

with a napkin for Mikey. "From the twins by the door," she said with an eye roll.

Mikey raised his beer and treated the identical brunettes across the room to his I'm-a-country-rock-drummer-god smile.

"Ain't so sure that not-telling-people thing will work for long," Will said to Pepper.

"Right. The Mikey handicap. Oh! He was the one who—"

"Most likely," Will said.

"Near about definitely," Mikey agreed.

No telling which of Mikey's exploits Saffron had told her relatives, but odds were, it was accurate.

The blonde on Pepper's other side peeked around and looked closer.

"Saffron told us about you and the girl in Dallas who—?" Pepper wiggled her eyebrows.

"And Kansas City," Mikey said.

"Boston and Minneapolis too," Will said on a sigh. Mikey didn't kiss and tell, but the girls he picked did.

Some days, Will wished he could've been like Mikey. Living it up, having fun, embracing the moment.

But Will had never been the kind who could keep his heart out of it.

"And the three—" Pepper started.

"You know it, sweet pea," Mikey said.

"Ain't never proved that one," Will said.

"What?" Natalie leaned across Lindsey. "The three what?"

"Mikey's a total dog," Pepper whispered loudly.

At least four women giggled, and none of them were sitting at the bar.

"Had a dog or two what would take exception to that," Will said.

Everyone laughed, and Will smiled.

It was what they expected, and here, he had to be Billy Brenton.

"Oh! Introductions. Sorry. Billy, you remember CJ and Nat," Pepper said.

"Sure do," Will drawled. "Good to see you again, Mrs. Blue."

"Oh, Billy, the pleasure's all mine," Natalie said.

"You remember Nat's sister, Lindsey?" Pepper continued. "And this is Kimmie Elias."

Kimmie inhaled a loud breath. "I had a dream you were the love child of Bugs Bunny and the abominable snowman, but in my dream that was a good thing, and you lived in a mushroom that had secret passages into outer space," she said.

And here he thought he'd already heard it all. He was working up one of his *No need to be nervous, I'm just a guy* smiles when Lindsey shifted on Kimmie's other side, her gaze passing him by with a barely noticeable warning look.

"The chocolate outer space, or the one with cupcake moons?" Lindsey asked.

Kimmie settled in her chair, the creases in her forehead fading. "This one had stars that were actually frogs. Weird, right? I like the cupcake moons better."

"Ditto," Pepper said. She smiled at Will and Mikey. "Kimmie made the cupcakes at the wedding last weekend."

"I like cupcakes," Mikey said with a brow-wiggle.

"I can make your face out of fondant and put it on a cupcake," Kimmie replied.

Mikey's jaw slipped. He pulled his cap off and scratched his bald scalp.

And for the first time in ten days, Will found an honest smile. "I'll take two dozen," he said to Kimmie. "Gonna mail 'em to Mikey's momma, show her he finally made something of himself. She'll get 'em bronzed and put 'em in her china cabinet."

"You take us to the best places, Billy," Mikey said.

"It's a gift."

Cinna cruised past and put two more napkins on the bar for Mikey. Par for the course when Will was out with Mikey. Apparently Billy Brenton's drummer was more approachable than Billy himself. Plus, anybody who had ever seen a BillyVision video knew Mikey loved the ladies.

"This'll get old fast," Cinna grumbled.

"He tips good," Will told her. He glanced at Pepper's group. "Y'all meet here every Sunday?"

"We have Knot Fest committee meetings most Sunday nights," Pepper said. "We come here to recover."

"Not Fest?" Mikey said. "I like Yes Fest better myself." He winked at another girl at the bar, then gave a slow smile to another sitting with her boyfriend at one of the tables.

"You wanna tone down the dog factor?" Will said.

"We all have our talents, Billy-boy. Gotta use what God gave me."

Cinna slapped one more napkin on the bar. "You need an intervention," she said. She snapped her fingers at Lindsey. "How about you do your good-match/bad-match woo-woo and put us all out of our misery before I spend the rest of the night living out a bad version of *The Playboy's Secretary's Secret*."

"I liked that book," Natalie said.

"One of Mae Daniels's best," Pepper agreed.

"I'm kinda liking Ava Bee novels more these days," Kimmie said.

"Woo-woo?" Mikey said flatly.

"Ignore her," CJ said. "She has a permanent case of being-a-pain-in-the-ass-itis."

Will took a long drink of his beer. Wasn't anything he could add to the conversation, so he was staying far, far out of it.

"Hey, I watch BillyVision too," Cinna said. "And it's quite obvious Mikey wouldn't be such a manwhore if he found the right woman. And the first step is weeding out the wrong ones. Mikey, dude, you have terrible taste in women."

"I have excellent taste in women," Mikey said. "Every last one of them."

Will should've kept his mouth shut, but this was too easy. "Mikey, you make me look like I got good sense when it comes to the ladies."

"Wouldn't go that far," Mikey said dryly. "But you're right about something else. I tip good. So, Little Red. Tell me more about the good-match/bad-match woo-woo. Not something I've tried before."

That was Mikey's wink-wink voice, but it had an edge Will recognized all too well.

"She's talking about me," Lindsey said. She wasn't the frosty lawyer lady about it, but she wasn't let's-be-best-buds either. "Call it woo-woo if you like, but you can't be a divorce lawyer for a decade without learning a few things about body language and relationships. And I'm terribly sorry to disappoint you, but this woo-woo isn't up for being *tried* tonight."

"Not even in a professional capacity?" Will said. "Mikey *could* use the help."

It was like poking a wounded bear, if the bear happened to have a good poker face. Will could *feel* the tremors of a storm brewing behind that calm demeanor.

Or maybe that storm was all his and he needed to take his hind end out of this bar *now*.

Mikey was right. Coming here was a bad idea.

Will had a sudden flash of his momma, both fuzzy and clear as day. She was sitting at a scarred oak table in the dim light spilling out from under the sink, cicadas buzzing outside the open window, the stench of something sharp and hard biting his nose while she tilted a thick, dark bottle to her lips and slid an unfocused look at the little boy he'd been. *Some of us ain't meant to carry a pretty tune, son. And some of 'em out there will kill our music, and there's nothing we can do about it.*

"If your dear friend Mikey needs a divorce before pursuing the girl of his dreams," Lindsey said, "my firm is accepting paying clients at the moment. Otherwise, I hear MisterGoodEnough.com is a wonderful online dating service."

Kimmie made one of those squeaky noises again. Lindsey's sister choked on a laugh. Her brother-in-law, though, inched closer, watching more intently than he should've.

"Don't need online dating," Mikey said. "*Or* a divorce lawyer."

Will scratched his chin and looked at Lindsey again. "You sure knowing bad matches comes from all those years of splitting couples up? Thought that was you Saffron was talking about, doing all that matchmaking. Doing it right good too, I heard. Unless the pretty bride over there has another sister?"

"I find one's reputation can become irrationally inflated based on the company one keeps," she said.

"Fancy words, ma'am. You ever thought of running for president?"

Yep.

Definitely poking a bear.

Will never did claim to be the smartest guy in the room. Apparently he wasn't much for self-preservation either, because there was a fire growing in those flashing eyes of hers. She was tamping it down good, but not good enough to hide the tight lines at the corners of her mouth and the way her nostrils flared.

And danged if that didn't put all that noise between his ears back in tune.

He'd be writing something good tonight. A power ballad. About a breakup. Being better off. Moving on. Something between Carrie Underwood's "Before He Cheats" and Jerrod Niemann's "Lover, Lover."

"Don't look like the matchmaker's up for the job, Billy," Mikey said.

Natalie leaned across Lindsey. "Billy, did I hear you're here for a while? I should warn you, when the BRA president hears, she'll want to host a welcome reception."

Mikey choked on his beer. "The BRA?"

"Can't spell brains without it," Lindsey muttered. "Excuse me." She slid off her stool and left her coat behind.

"Bathroom break. Me too," Kimmie said, and she, too, scurried away.

"The Bridal Retailers Association," Natalie said. She moved into the seat Kimmie had abandoned and gestured to Pepper, who had been quieter than Saffron ever could've been. "It's one of the many organizations we're in that keep Bliss's reputation what it is. Are you guys hungry? The cheese fries here are amazing."

With Lindsey gone, Will had an easier time slapping on his Billy face. "Sounds right good, ma'am."

Heading out, grabbing a drive-through burger, and getting home to Vera sounded better.

"Hey, um, Billy?"

Will twisted to the new voice, coming from a middle-aged woman with a perm that reminded him of Aunt Jessie.

"I know you hear this all the time," she said, "and I don't want to bother you, but I'm your biggest fan *ever*, and I was wondering—"

"You want a picture?" Will said.

"Oh, yes, please. I promise I won't put it online. Well, not until tomorrow." She giggled like a teenager, and Will smiled at her.

"Mikey. Quit making eyes at that girl and get over here and take a picture for this nice lady."

"Aw, now, Billy, I think you got it wrong." Mikey winked at the lady. "Think this sweet young thing wants her picture taken with *me*."

And just like that, Mikey had her all charmed too. Then folks gathered round for pictures and autographs, and instead of returning to Vera, Will settled into the easy rhythm of being Billy.

Wasn't how he'd planned his dinner to go, but being Billy beat being Will Truitt tonight.

IN HIGH SCHOOL, Lindsey thought her gift was cool. She liked knowing what other people didn't, being right about who would break up and who would make it to the end of the school year. In college, she'd learned to hate it. Because in college, her friends had serious intentions of dating for the long haul, and until Lindsey learned—the hard way—to keep her mouth shut, her *gift* had lost her more friends than it gained.

As an adult, she liked to pretend it didn't exist, but it was always there, in the back of her mind, in a subtle pressure in her sinuses, a twitch in a random finger or an ache in her knees or elbows, telling her the relationship weather around her as surely as an old farmer could predict rain coming in three days.

She'd learned to keep her mouth shut, but she'd learned something else too.

Most people had at least one not-bad match. Sometimes two. But Lindsey?

Lindsey had never looked at a man and felt anything other than bad match vibes for herself.

Will wasn't the only man she'd ever been attracted to, but he was the only one she let herself fall for. With the rest, she'd kept her heart out of it, called it quits early, didn't get vested. She dated to scratch an occasional itch, and she was always brutally honest about what she could and couldn't offer her dates.

She didn't kid herself. She'd never have children of her own. She'd go home to an empty house every night of her life. She chose to be satisfied that she had Nat and Noah and Dad. When her time came, she'd look back on her life and know that she'd helped flawed people with good intentions correct their marital mistakes. That a good number of them had gotten the same second chance Nat had. That they'd gotten it right the second time, or that they were at least happier and healthier alone than they'd been while in an unfortunate marriage.

Most days, that was enough.

But tonight, with Will—with *Billy*—walking into Suckers, into her hometown, into her world, nothing felt right. Her internal match-o-meter had gone haywire. Early morning thunderstorms morphing into ice storms, with sunshine and rainbows bouncing around in there too.

He wasn't supposed to be here. He *shouldn't* have been here.

And the questions and suppositions she had about why he was here weren't things she could afford to contemplate.

If she were one to run away, she'd be ducking out through the kitchen now instead of standing in the Suckers bathroom, sucking in the chilly air and trying to steady her pulse and her breathing.

He was just one more ex-boyfriend, she told herself. If he chose to be here, she could choose to maintain a distant, platonic relationship with him, as she did with every other man she'd ever dated. Why he was here was nothing for her to stress over. She could go out there and be her normal self—guarded, claustrophobic, and unapologetic—and ignore the fact that she and Billy *freaking* Brenton had a history.

Liar, the throbbing in her chest said.

A chunk of rocky casing had fallen off Lindsey's petrified heart, and that little organ was coming back to life with painful thumps.

He was just another man. He shouldn't have affected her.

The bathroom door swung open, and Kimmie darted in. "My mom's gonna frost her cookies when she hears this." She gripped Lindsey's arm. "I will pay you a million gazillion s'mores cupcakes if you start a rumor that I'm a bad match for Billy."

Lindsey's match-o-meter had declared Billy a cool summer breeze with Pepper, a warm spring day with Kimmie, and a bright sunrise over the beach with Mikey. Lindsey didn't have any not-bad matches, but that was *all* Will had.

Lindsey's gift could go toss itself off a cliff.

"I'm sure someone like Billy Brenton has people who can handle your mother," Lindsey said.

Kimmie dropped her forehead against the gray stone wall. The purple lighting in the bathroom put a blue hue on her curly dishwater blonde hair. "My last fortune cookie said my love life would one day soon be fodder for public judgment."

Normal. Kimmie talking fortune cookies was normal. Lindsey loved normal. "Are you getting your cookies at Wok'n'Roll? Mine always say *Fortune smile on he who smile at life.*"

"But you're not a freak. The cookies know. They pick me."

Lindsey was a freak in her own right. She leaned a hip against the stainless steel sink. She hated crowds, but hanging with Kimmie had a strangely calming effect, and Lindsey's pulse was almost steady again. "You're out in public now, and we're discussing your love life. Fortune cookie solved."

"Good. Thanks. I mean, he's hot and all, but I am *so* not the celebrity girlfriend type. We'd go to an awards show and someone would ask me what I was wearing and I'd say *giraffe bubble skin* or something else out of one of my dreams."

Lindsey found a smile for her friend. "Tell your mother that if she gets any ideas."

Kimmie suddenly squeaked. "Oh, *pumplegunker*. Do you think Mikey's rich too? My mother's not above suggesting second best if he has the cash. We were a bad match too, right? He's cute enough, but in a scary way. Like a motorcycle gang, dominant billionaire romance, groupie-loving way. Not like Billy is, like that trusty gentleman country boy way."

"Trust me, no one in this bar is a good match for Mikey," Lindsey said.

She couldn't honestly say the same about *Billy*.

"Nat's right, you know," Kimmie said. "Mom will have a welcome reception planned within the next two hours. And she'll have my wedding china and silver and crystal picked out by Thursday. If she doesn't already."

"Your mom won't marry you off to Billy Brenton," Lindsey said. "She can't afford to. You'd go move to wherever it is he lives and she'd lose you at the bakery."

"Unless she makes him move here. She could do that, you know. I think she bakes voodoo cakes, I really do. Maybe I *shouldn't* put Mikey's face on a cupcake."

"Speaking of cupcakes, how did the fruitcake cupcakes go over?"

Kimmie launched into a story about fruitcake cupcake samples, and the two of them returned to the bar. If they hadn't, Nat would've come looking, and Lindsey didn't feel like offering explanations.

When they emerged, *Billy* and Mikey had spread out and were signing autographs and taking selfies with the other patrons. CJ had circled the bar and was chatting with Jeremy, his co-owner here at Suckers, while both of them kept an eye on the celebrities. Nat and Pepper were chatting, probably about Knot Fest stuff or the bridal boutique. Pepper had moved to Bliss and bought into the shop as co-owner last summer, and she ran the floor operations while Nat was branching out into designing an original line of wedding gowns.

Lindsey couldn't have been prouder of Nat for all she'd

accomplished. She'd floundered for a while before finding where she truly fit in Bliss.

"You leaving?" Nat asked.

"Have to get my evil overlord sleep so I can eat some babies tomorrow," Lindsey said.

Nat snorted. "Right." She reached out and gave Lindsey a hug. "You free Saturday? I'm almost ready for your next fitting."

"Sure. So long as I can borrow Noah afterward." The downside of Nat's launching her own line of bridal gowns was that she'd talked Lindsey into being one of her models for the first photo shoot for her marketing materials. Kimmie was getting a dress too, along with Pepper and some of Nat's other new sisters-in-law.

"Dad claimed Noah already, but I'm sure he'll share." Nat angled her head toward Billy. "Crazy, isn't it?" she whispered.

"How long do you think we can keep my mom from finding out?" Kimmie whispered back.

"Not long enough." Nat grinned, a spark of the devil flashing in her dark brown eyes. "Although, I can't deny wanting to see what Marilyn thinks of Mikey."

Lindsey shot a glance at Mikey. He wasn't as classically handsome as Will was—too tall, too lanky, too bald under his Billy Brenton ball cap—but he oozed womanizer charm, and he was working it tonight. He had a lady on each arm and was wiggling his eyebrows suggestively at a third. Lindsey's match-o-meter pegged a tornado, a hurricane, and a sandstorm. None of them were good matches.

No surprise there.

Without her history with Will—with *Billy*—Lindsey would've found Mikey ideal for an itch-scratcher. But he was here with Will, and she didn't have any itches that needed scratching right now.

None that sex would solve.

And she got the distinct impression Mikey didn't much care for her anyway.

The door opened behind them, and Dahlia Mallard strolled in. She ran The Milked Duck, Bliss's charming ice cream shop around the corner from Nat's bridal boutique. She marched past Mikey without a second glance.

Lindsey smelled roses.

She straightened and looked closer, but Dahlia was past Mikey, waving at CJ and Jeremy with a paper in her hand. While CJ stood, Dahlia glanced around. Her baby blues went wide behind her glasses, and her lips parted.

The ice cream lady had spotted Billy Brenton.

Lindsey turned to Nat. "Saturday at nine, then?" Mikey's love life wasn't Lindsey's business. And she didn't know Dahlia well, but Dahlia always fussed over Noah when Lindsey took him into The Milked Duck for ice cream and had never been anything but sweet and kind.

She could *definitely* do better than a womanizing drummer.

"Nine works," Nat said. "How about you, Kimmie? You free, or are you on wedding cake duty?"

"I'll be done by nine-thirty or so," Kimmie said. "We have two weddings next Sunday, though, so I have to be back by two."

Lindsey's gaze drifted across the bar. CJ had met Dahlia halfway, and they were talking over the paper. Dahlia's cheeks matched the red streak in her brunette hair, and she kept shooting glances at Billy. Kimmie and Nat were still talking, something about cupcakes and an ice cream tasting at The Milked Duck. Dahlia gave CJ a quick hug, then turned and paused.

She was watching Will—*Billy*. Or possibly Mikey. Her shoulders squared, her mouth took on a determined line, and she marched toward Will. But halfway across the bar, Dahlia bumped into Mikey.

Lindsey smelled roses again, and this time, she felt warm sunshine beaming from clear blue skies too.

She blinked once, twice, vaguely aware of Nat, Kimmie, and Pepper giggling beside her. She smiled, because it seemed like the right thing to do.

Mikey helped Dahlia steady herself, still grinning his wicked ladies-love-me smile, still flashing it at the other three women around him too, oblivious to the fact that he was touching a woman who was a not-bad match for him.

Lindsey shook her head. This wasn't her business. She didn't play matchmaker. She spotted bad matches, not good ones.

Time to go home. She turned to say her goodbyes—

And Will was watching her.

He'd moved while she was watching Mikey, and now he was behind Nat. His golden brown eyes were trained on her.

There wasn't a smile, but there wasn't animosity either. Nor was there curiosity. Or wariness. Or trust.

Simply steady, concentrated focus. As if he could see through her, deep down to the darkest, most secret parts of her.

As if he knew what she'd seen.

"Hey, Billy, these three ladies ain't had their pictures taken yet," Mikey said behind Lindsey.

Right behind her. Too close.

"Suppose we better fix that," Will drawled.

He broke eye contact with Lindsey, shifted his attention to Mikey, then tucked his hands in his pockets and strolled past her without another look.

"Okay, Saturday at nine," Nat said. She touched Lindsey's arm. "I'll start with you first, so you can—hey. You okay?"

Lindsey blinked again. She pulled a big breath in through her nose, then gave Nat a sardonic smile. "As okay as I ever am when I'm thinking of wedding dresses," she said.

Nat laughed, and Lindsey reached for her coat. "Make lots of brides happy this week. I'll see you Saturday."

Because that was normal.

But Lindsey's life?

Her life was suddenly anything but.

FIVE

MIKEY DIDN'T SAY a word about Lindsey on the ride to the rental house.

He could've. Probably should've, matter of fact. After that spring break trip where Will fell for Lindsey, Mikey had been there, watching Will disappear from his life to make something of himself for a girl who would never care. Then the two of them had gone to Nashville together. Three years later, Mikey got an offer to join another band, an opportunity to go touring with Tim McGraw's opening act, and he had taken it. Opened for all the big names eventually—Toby Keith, Kenny Chesney, Brooks & Dunn. Will had been happy for him, and put that much more effort into making Billy Brenton a success too, which came not long after. He was happier, though, a few years ago when Mikey came back to play with him. They'd always written songs together, even before Will believed they could go big, so having Mikey with him should've been good.

Normal.

Except now, there was a girl between them.

A girl who, unless Will's imagination was running away with him, had pegged Mikey with a girl tonight.

Not something Will would be mentioning to his buddy.

Ever.

But he'd felt it. He'd felt those shivers he got when Sacha made predictions, but he'd felt them in different places.

Wrong places, deep in his gut, in his chest.

Would be nice if he could be as ignorant as Mikey about it.

When they got back to the house, Mikey left Will and Vera in peace for a while, and Will's favorite guitar helped him work out a few melodies.

And there were melodies.

New melodies, new lyrics, new beats. Good or not, he couldn't say. He was too close to it.

But it was more than he'd done anytime since he started work on *Hitched*.

"Mari Belle hear about you chasing your snow angel yet?" Mikey said from the doorway to the kitchen a while later. Will caught sight of thick, heavy snowflakes lit up by the porch light outside the front window. A space heater glowed in one corner, and a fire popped and crackled in the fireplace, both effectively cutting the chill out of the drafty house.

Good sign, working so hard he hadn't noticed Mikey in the room. Hadn't been into the music like that in ages.

Will picked at Vera's strings. "Ain't chasing anybody. Using a change in scenery to find the music. That's it."

Mikey flung himself onto the other end of the couch with a snort. "You want to lie to yourself, fine. But don't lie to me. We both know why you're here."

And they both knew Mikey was only here because he couldn't stop Will from coming. "Not my first choice of where to be either." The skin on Will's left shoulder twitched. He bent his neck. Concentrated. That melody was drifting away. Had to catch it.

His fingers worked over Vera's steel strings while his other hand slid down the well-worn wood of her neck.

"But you're staying. Even after tonight, you're staying."

The disgust in Mikey's voice wasn't unexpected, but the worry part made Will taste the bitter flavor of guilt. "Starting to sound like an old grandmama."

"Wish you had a grandmama to kick your sorry ass. Pack your bags. I'm calling Mari Belle, and we're —"

Will cut him off with a riff on Vera. Raw, new, and *good*. He went for a few measures, then a few more measures, switched the chords, let his fingers fly, listening to Vera.

He played.

And he played.

And he played.

Until he finally clapped a hand over Vera's strings, plunging the room into silence, save for the crackling fire and the hum of the house's ancient and inadequate furnace.

Mikey muttered something his momma would've taken as grounds for washing his mouth out with lemon dish soap.

"I'm staying," Will said.

"Then you need to stay away from her."

"Got this covered."

"No. You don't. You're here because Sacha sent you here for *her*."

"She sent me here to find the music. That's all."

"You planning on telling the brass that you're here because it's what your psychic told you to do? And Jessie agreeing with her—all y'all are touched in the head," Mikey said. "Except maybe Mari Belle. That girl lives in the good ol' United States of Reality."

"Don't go bringing Mari Belle into this." Will strummed a G chord. If Vera could smile, she'd be grinning at him. Giving him a high five for finding his listening ears again. "She doesn't need to know."

"You're a grade-A dumbass sometimes."

Will scribbled a lyric and a chord in his notepad. "Y'all are fussing over nothing," he said.

"The way you were looking at her wasn't *nothing*." He pointed at Vera. "And that sound isn't *nothing*. You're playing with fire, Will."

Will grunted. He'd already written all the songs he ever wanted to about Lindsey. Inspiration striking was coincidence. Nothing more than the influence of a town devoted to love.

If Lindsey was influencing Will's music, it was because of all that talk of matchmaking. Probably Lindsey hadn't thought Mikey was a match with the girl in the glasses anyway. Probably she was wondering how much money she could make working his divorces if Mikey got in a mind to start marrying all the girls he flirted with.

Will shut the world out, plucked at Vera's familiar strings, looked for the right chord. He'd had another melody. It was there a minute ago, something sweet. Sweet and rich. Something bigger than what he could pull out of his fingers tonight.

That was the whole problem he'd had since *Hitched* came out. The music was beyond reach, way back there, locked in his mind. But this time, it felt bigger than he was. Like he wasn't enough of a songwriter, enough of an artist, enough of a man to do it right.

Like he'd written all his best songs before he was of drinking age.

"Any music you find here won't be songs worth recording," Mikey said.

"You didn't like 'Goin' Creekin'" either, and look how that turned out," Will said. That song had launched his career ten years ago.

"You're a real shithead sometimes."

"Yeah, but the fans love me. You gonna help, or you gonna sit there and whine?"

Mikey rubbed a hand over his scalp. "Could take a year or two off," he grumbled. "You work too hard."

"Sweet of you to worry, Grandmama, but who's paying the crew and band if I take a year or two off? Like my crew. Like my band. And I'm fixin' to find my songs again. You in, or you out?"

Mikey grunted and grabbed a notebook. "Let's do this. So we can go home."

Sounded good to Will.

WORD SPREAD FAST that Billy Brenton had settled in Bliss for a month. Even in Willow Glen, it was all people were talking about.

Monday, Lindsey ignored it. Or tried to. Should've been

easy with all the insanity at her office. One client's soon-to-be ex had gone off the rails and refused to return the kids after his weekend with them. Another client had dropped by with incriminating photographs that would invoke the infidelity clause in her prenup. Lindsey didn't stumble home until almost nine.

Tuesday, she had to wear her growly baby-eater face at two final hearings, and then returned to her office to find her paralegal and her assistant bent over a computer, watching episodes of BillyVision.

She snapped at them to get back to work, then slammed her office door.

And she admitted defeat.

She wore smiley face panties as a personal reminder that life was what you made it. That she could choose to make a positive difference with her attitude and her demeanor despite the ugly parts of her job. But this week, they weren't working, and it didn't take a psychic anti-matchmaker to know why.

She needed to talk to someone. Preferably Mom. But since Mom wasn't an option, Lindsey texted Nat to see if she was free tonight.

Nat had plans — she'd gotten a babysitter so she could hang out at Suckers while CJ worked — but she told Lindsey to come on over and join her. An hour after Lindsey left the office Tuesday, she pushed through the door of the funky bar. Twitter was reporting that Billy Brenton was due to crash Melodies Karaoke Bar any moment now, so Lindsey settled into her normal seat at the steel semicircle bar in the center of the room and breathed in the peace while she waited for Nat.

She didn't have to order. As soon as she claimed a red leather bar stool, CJ appeared with a glass of white zin. "Long day?"

"There are four more soon-to-be single people in the world tonight." She put her coat on the stool to her left and her purse on the stool to her right. The bar wasn't too crowded, and Lindsey sipped on her wine and watched the other patrons while she waited for Nat.

One in particular caught her eye at a far booth. He had his

dark hair dropped into his hands, two empty beer glasses before him, and a plate of nachos nearly untouched. Mostly unremarkable on its own, but she recognized him, and she knew what had him hanging his head over his beer.

CJ circled back with a bowl of mixed nuts for her. She slid her credit card and an envelope with a gift card for Bliss's taxi service across the bar. "The guy in the Bliss Bachelors jersey?" She nodded subtly toward the booth. "His drinks are on me."

"Your client?"

"Leave my name out of it, would you?"

CJ grinned and took the credit card and taxi certificate. "Reamed him, huh?"

Her boss had. And in Lindsey's opinion, the guy had gotten the short end of the stick. But she wasn't paid to have feelings. She was paid to get the best settlements for her clients. So she did, and sometimes she watched from the sidelines when her colleagues did the same.

But what was right by law wasn't always what was fair in her gut. And though she was glad for all the people getting second chances at finding happiness—be it with someone else or by themselves—oftentimes the journey was ugly.

She lifted her glass to CJ. "Good wine. Thank you."

He tapped the bar twice. "Nat's running late, but I've got cheese fries in for you." He ambled off to take care of another customer.

Lindsey had taken another two sips when her anti-match-o-meter tingled. First a long, parched heat, then a winter squall, followed by a dewy spring morning and a flipping rainbow. Her fingers tightened around her wineglass and she pursed her lips.

He was supposed to be at Melodies.

But a body slid between her and the stool with her coat on it. "Evenin', Miss Lindsey," Will drawled. "Fancy meeting you here tonight."

"I come here often," she said.

He chuckled softly.

She set her glass down, then twisted her stool to face him. He had his back to the bar, elbows propped behind him, which nicely stretched the white T-shirt over his solid chest beneath his red plaid overshirt. His cowboy boots were crossed at his ankles, and he was close enough for her to catch his subtle scent of bar soap and cotton. Her knees bumped his hip when she turned, and she could count the individual whiskers on his face—they'd be the right mix of soft and scruffy, she was sure —but she channeled her inner baby-eater mask and gathered all her inner willpower to fight the intrigued shiver skittering through her blood.

She generally liked her space. Apparently with Will, she liked a good fight more. "Why are you here?" she said.

"Figured the crowd would be too big at the karaoke bar, what with all the rumors about me being there and all." All his mischief was on display tonight, and that Teflon country boy smile made the smileys on her panties sigh in admiration.

She unclenched her jaw. "Here in Bliss," she clarified.

"Ah. That." He nodded. "My psychic told me to come."

Did he just—he *did*. He was mocking her. "Do you know what I get paid to eat guys like you for breakfast?" she growled before she could stop herself.

He simply grinned bigger. "Not as much as I get paid for writing songs about a girl's… smiles."

Her nostrils flared. Her vision narrowed until she could see one thing—the enemy.

She'd suspected fame had changed him.

Unfortunately, not for the better.

"Hey, CJ," she called, still glaring at Will.

"Yeah?" her brother-in-law answered.

"You know how you're always saying to let you know if someone needs his ass kicked?"

Will's eyes widened. He looked over his shoulder—at CJ, Lindsey presumed, who had Will by a good few inches.

"Letting somebody else fight your battles, lawyer lady?" Will murmured.

"I got time to pop some popcorn and grab a beer first?" CJ said. "Anybody got a video—aw, *shit*, Lindsey. You can't kick Billy's ass."

"Watch me."

"Better tell her you're sorry, Billy, or we'll have Marilyn breathing down our neck," CJ said. "Don't know if you've met the Queen General of Bliss yet, but you will. She's worse than all my sisters put together. And then some."

Will held his hands up. "No offense meant," he said to both of them. Then he turned an overly charming grin on Lindsey again. "Was actually hoping you could tell me about the brunette."

She lifted a brow.

He pointed to his hair poking out under his cap. "The one with the red streaks."

Lindsey froze. His country boy grin was still firmly in place, but she could see something the rest of the bar couldn't.

She could see his eyes beneath his ball cap. They were on the honey brown side tonight, with faint lines at the edges, experience and depth and life making him look far more intelligent—and dangerous—than the simple country boy she'd known for a week in Colorado.

"What brunette with red streaks?" she said evenly.

"The one you thought was a good match for Mikey the other night. Curvy. Had glasses."

Dangerous was exactly what he was. She'd known he was watching her.

She hadn't known how well.

She suppressed a shiver. No man should've been able to read her like that. Especially one she hadn't seen in fifteen years. "I don't believe we know each other nearly well enough for you to make assumptions about me matchmaking. Which I *don't* do."

"Might could have a point." He shifted so he was fully facing her. "Those matches you see—they ever change?"

Lindsey's mouth went dry.

He wasn't—he was *not* here in Bliss for her. He wasn't asking for a second chance. He couldn't be.

Because he wasn't just *Will*. He was Billy Brenton. He was huge, with millions of fans and probably a couple thousand creepy weirdo fans among them who meant it when they offered to have his babies. He didn't have any reason to come back to her.

Especially after how she'd ended things with him.

His country boy smile was gone. So was the mischief. All that was left was an honest, serious question about whether bad matches could turn to not-bad matches, coming from a man who shouldn't have remembered her name, much less her special *talent*.

The man who seemed to have taken particular delight in poking at her in their few minutes together.

A dark presence beside her made her blink. "Jeez, Billy, I step in the john for two minutes, and you go getting yourself in trouble," Mikey said. He gave Lindsey a smile that could've frozen a lava pit.

Lindsey swallowed and dug deep for a steady voice. "No trouble. Billy here was telling me how much he'd love to be a guest judge for the Battle of the Boyfriends next month. He thinks he can find you somebody to play for."

"Don't sound like Billy," Mikey said.

"I heard it too," CJ said. Based on the unusual frown darkening her brother-in-law's face, she guessed he'd overheard most of her conversation. "Said he can't resist that much love in one room, especially if it's yours."

Mikey snagged Will by the collar. "Can't leave him alone for anything. That booth in the corner open?" he asked CJ.

"All yours," CJ said. "Get you started with a beer? Supply of napkins for those numbers?"

"Two Buds," Mikey said. "And you can give the napkins to the ladies." He yanked Will away from the bar with a clear *don't talk to Billy* glare aimed at Lindsey.

Lindsey shivered.

CJ handed back her credit card. He flicked a glance behind her, toward Will and Mikey, then to Lindsey again. "I don't know what's going on here, but if you don't tell Nat, I'm gonna invent my own story."

Lindsey reached for her wine, but her hand shook.

And CJ might've been a big, goofy oaf, but she knew he noticed.

Worse, she suspected Will did too. And she knew he was watching.

She could feel him.

"Hey," Nat said suddenly. She paused and looked between CJ and Lindsey. "What did I miss?"

"Lindsey and Billy, part two," CJ said with a nod at the corner booth.

Nat looked back.

Lindsey refused to.

"Sounded to me like she talked him into being a guest judge for the Battle of the Boyfriends," CJ added. "But you probably shouldn't mention it until tomorrow. Or next time you catch him alone."

Nat lifted her brows, but she didn't ask. Instead, she hooked her arm through Lindsey's, sister intuition apparently kicking in. "We'll be late if we don't go now." She grabbed Lindsey's purse and coat and shoved them at her, then went on her tiptoes to kiss CJ over the bar. "Love you. Work hard. Call you later."

She gave the corner booth a wink and a wave while Lindsey glanced at the lonely, newly divorced guy on the other side of the bar.

He wasn't the reason she didn't date seriously, but she'd seen enough people in his situation to be hesitant to get into a real relationship with a man who was anything less than a bright sunny day for her on her anti-match-o-meter.

She felt the sunshine with Will, but she felt everything else too.

Nat dragged her out into the cold night, where salt crunched beneath her snow boots and her breath hung in a neon-lit cloud. "What in the *world*, Lindsey?" Nat said.

Lindsey had to swallow hard against the lump in her throat before she could find her voice. What she wouldn't have given to be able to talk to Mom now. "We met once," she said while she shrugged into her coat. "A long time ago."

"You and Billy?" Nat whispered.

"Will. His name was Will."

"*Omigod*. I knew you had a secret lost love, but I had no idea—"

"Neither did I." Lindsey shivered and wrapped her coat tight around her.

"Is he here for you?"

"I don't know."

"Are you—"

"I *don't know*."

"Oh, honey." Nat tugged on Lindsey's arm. "Let's go have some cupcakes."

SIX

AFTER TWO FULL days of living on chords, coffee, and pizza, Will had thought getting out would be a good idea. He hadn't expected to run into Lindsey again. Ask around about her, yes. Run into her, no.

Now that he had, he couldn't get her out of his mind.

There was a chance he was pushing her too far. He blamed her stiff lawyer face. It irritated him.

Shouldn't have. She was right—they didn't know each other.

But that fire in her tonight—it inspired another song. The other gals he chatted with at Suckers didn't put a tune in his head. There was something about Lindsey, something hidden — a secret or their history or the way she held her mask in place when he knew there was more going on under the surface—that inspired a world of possibilities and made him want to get home to Vera.

Sacha was right. He'd needed to come here to find his music again. Question was, would he still have it when he left?

The thought made him itch to get back to his favorite girl.

But he was hip-deep in taking pictures and signing autographs, playing the part of Billy when he wouldn't have minded being Will. He wouldn't be Billy without the fans, so he kept his smile on and took his time, but when his phone rang, he checked the readout then excused himself.

Fans or not, when his niece called, he answered.

Will caught Mikey's eye and lifted his phone. "Be right back," he mouthed.

Mikey nodded. Will ducked out the front door and into the darkness, clenching his teeth against the wind. "Hey, peanut."

"Momma saw a picture of you with a girl and she says she's fixin' to yank a knot in your butt," Paisley said.

Will winced and rubbed his shoulder, which had been itching like nobody's business since he saw Lindsey tonight. "Shouldn't you be in bed? What time is it there?"

"Uncle Will," she said, dragging out his name to more syllables than her Southern heritage made necessary, "you're in a heap of trouble here. You need to concentrate."

He needed to hash this out with his niece as much as he needed a hole in his head. "How're Chicken and Biscuits?" Will asked. Paisley's dogs were usually a good distraction. "They settling in good?"

"Yeah, but they miss Bandit. And you're changing the subject again."

Will's heart gave a painful pang at the mention of his dog, but Paisley's tone brought out a grin. Girl would be a handful at eleven and a complete Mari Belle clone by thirteen. A five-year-long tour overseas might be a good idea. "Your momma know you talk to grown-ups like that?"

"Momma says you're just a kid who got old enough to drive, vote and have a job. And a girlfriend. Do I get to meet this one? Momma didn't want me to see the picture. She said I hadn't done anything wrong enough to have to stare at the devil."

Will's grin turned into a grimace. "When was that?"

"This morning at breakfast. Daddy texted her."

Will bit his tongue. Both to keep from asking if Paisley wasn't so sure Mari Belle wasn't planning on yanking a knot in her ex-husband's butt, and to keep from filling his niece's ears with his own worries over Mari Belle giving him the silent treatment all day. Now that he knew that's what it was. "You liking your new school? Making new friends?"

"Uncle Will, you're changing the subject again."

He could almost feel the Mari Belle–inherited I-will-melt-your-skin-with-my-eyeballs glare coming through the phone. "You got a copy of the picture?"

His phone buzzed against his ear.

"That one?" Paisley said.

He pulled the phone away and glanced at the picture message. There he was at Suckers the other night, having a stare-down with Lindsey. But tonight he didn't care about the who and the why behind the picture.

Tonight, he cared about what the picture saw. The camera had put some sad all through Lindsey's slender face. And seeing that sad put a crimp in Will's gut.

He remembered that from fifteen years ago too. The look she'd worn the second day he saw her, when she said she was sure her friends would be there any minute, even though he could see she didn't believe it herself. And he remembered feeling like the king of the mountain when he pulled Vera out, played a tune that made her smile and chased the sad away.

He also remembered feeling like the biggest dummy on the face of the earth when she dumped him onstage at the end of the week, talking into that microphone for the whole tavern to hear. *We're not a good match. I have this gift—this curse. I'm like a psychic matchmaker. And we—we wouldn't make it. Not long term. We're all wrong for each other, like Mari Belle and Ethan. But the point —the point is, we can't do this. I'm going to be president, and the world isn't ready for a First Bubba.*

She'd still inspired songs, even after that. And Will wasn't the brightest guy on the planet, but he still knew he shouldn't get sucked in to caring again. Like she said—they didn't know each other anymore.

"So what's with the girl?" Paisley said.

Will stomped his feet to keep his blood flowing. Dang cold tonight. "She might could look like somebody your momma used to know."

"Is she your snow angel?"

Will swallowed.

Wasn't something his niece was supposed to be old enough to ask.

Ever.

"Where'd you get a question like that?" he said.

"I got ears, Uncle Will. They work real good."

He'd noticed. "You talking to your new friends at school like that?"

"Nah, I'm saving it until they can't live without me," Paisley said.

Will chuckled. "You're your momma's girl, peanut."

"The girl in the picture? She is, isn't she? She's your snow angel. When you get married, I get to be a junior bridesmaid."

Will reached for Vera's strap, but it wasn't there. "Nobody's getting married."

Paisley heaved one of those Mari Belle sighs. "I'll be a *teenager* before I get cousins."

"Old enough to drive and vote, most like," Will agreed. "At least." And that was his biggest regret. He loved playing for a living, loved hearing his songs on the radio, loved being on a stage and the road, but some days, he wouldn't have minded going home every night to a sweet wife and a couple babies and fried chicken on the table.

That was what Lindsey had taken from him. He'd fallen hard. He'd seen what his momma must've felt for his daddy, he'd felt his world crack right down the middle when the girl who had become his everything ripped his heart out of his chest. But unlike his momma, he'd decided he preferred being somebody to being somebody's pet.

Good lesson to learn at nineteen, especially when fame came knocking not that many years later. Even the actresses and other country stars he'd dated over the last decade had agendas.

Will tugged his shirt closer around him.

"At least you and Momma had each other growing up," Paisley said. "I don't have *anybody*."

"You got me, peanut," Will said. "And your momma and daddy, and Chicken and Biscuits, Aunt Jessie and Sacha."

"And Mr. Donnie," Paisley said.

Will grunted.

"He quit smoking, Aunt Jessie says. But Sacha—well. Like Momma says, only thing you get by digging dirt is dirty."

Will pinched his eyes shut. Too dang cold to be standing out here much longer. "Sacha have another one of her visions?" Good Lord help him, if Aunt Jessie was fixin' to have marital problems again, Will would have to clone himself to have enough hours in the day for managing his personal and professional lives.

"No," Paisley said. "But she got creepy quiet every time Mr. Donnie's name came up at dinner Sunday night."

Creepy quiet, Will could appreciate. Being fed a story by his niece, not so much.

And he wasn't sure which one this was. Might could be he'd have to talk to Mari Belle after all.

"Know what else I heard at dinner Sunday night?" Paisley said.

Uh-oh. She had Mari Belle's *you should've told me yourself* voice down too. And he didn't have the first clue what he hadn't told his niece. "What's that?"

"That you're playing at Gellings next month."

"Oh. That." His team had just booked him to fill in for an act that had to cancel a show at Gellings Air Force Base in southwest Georgia. Mari Belle had transferred there over Christmas after working as a civil servant at a base in Vegas for years, much to Aunt Jessie's delight, since Gellings was only an hour from Pickleberry Springs. "You want tickets?"

Paisley squealed. "Does a brick sink in water? Of *course* I want tickets!"

"Your momma okay with that?" Thus far, Mari Belle hadn't let Paisley go to any of his shows. She liked to keep herself and her daughter out of his spotlight.

"Don't you worry about a thing, Uncle Will. I got this under control. And can you get us extra tickets? Momma made friends with Miss Anna next door, now they're in this Officers' Ex-Wives Club thing together even though Miss Anna's engaged again, and I *know* she loves your songs. She had *Hitched* going while we were playing redneck golf last weekend."

Headlights flashed over him. Time to get inside. "I'll see what I can do. Just got spotted, peanut. I gotta run. Give your momma a hug and kiss for me."

"Nuh-uh. Then she'll know we talked."

"Fair enough. You keep on making friends, and I'll get you some tickets."

"Love you, Uncle Will."

"Love you too."

Sirens wailed in the distance. Will gave a silent salute to them. Somebody needed to call 911 on his mess of a personal life.

He trudged inside and gave Mikey the wrap-it-up sign. Will needed to write. Think. Plan.

Mikey wasn't a chatterbox, but he was unusually quiet on the ride to the rental house. Knowing Mikey, he had at least half a dozen phone numbers in his pocket, and he could've stayed out with any one of the ladies, but instead, he was with Will, calling it a night so they could work.

A fire truck wailed up behind them. Will pulled over to let it pass, then continued.

The fire truck turned left.

Will turned left.

Three blocks later, another fire truck came screaming past.

Apprehension strummed in Will's veins.

A glow was visible in the night, pulsing like a layer of doom between streetlamp-lit bare tree branches and the inky black sky.

Will slowed the truck right there at the corner of their street. Fire trucks and police cars and an ambulance blocked the way.

Three houses down, flames from the house—from *his* house—reached out and licked the night while firefighters aimed massive hoses at the fire.

Vera.

Will was out of the truck almost before he had it in park. Mikey was right behind him.

Smoke hung heavy in the air. Will's eyes stung. His throat. His nose. And the crackling. *God*, the crackling fire was like the devil laughing.

Vera was in that house.

Mikey gripped his arm. "Hold on, Will—"

Will lunged forward. "Vera—"

"Whoa, Will." Mikey's grip tightened. "Stop."

"The hell I will. Vera—"

"Billy?" One of the cops approached him. Said a bunch of words. Helped Mikey hold Will back.

Vera was in that house.

Vera, her trusty wooden body, her frets, her new strings. Vera, who'd had his back everywhere from Pickleberry Springs to Nashville to New York to LA, from seedy bars to stadiums.

Vera, who'd helped him write his first song. His last song. Every song in between.

An image of Sacha touching Vera's strap barely a week ago burned in his memory.

She'd known. *She'd known.* And she'd sent him here anyway.

Will fought against Mikey's grip, ignored the cop. "I gotta save her."

The windows of the two-story structure were black holes with red flames shooting out. The roof had already caved in, the fire gorging itself on the wooden structure.

And Vera—Vera was wood.

All alone, burning to death. No more songs in her. No more sitting there, waiting on Will to find her tunes.

"Is there someone in there, sir?" the cop asked.

"Vera—"

"No," Mikey said.

Will rounded on his friend. "She's—"

"A guitar," Mikey said to the cop. "House was empty."

There were three people in Will's life he'd known longer than he'd known Vera.

And one of them was not only letting Vera burn to death, but he was doing it without hesitation.

Mikey suddenly dropped Will's arm. "I left a space heater on," Mikey said. "Oh, shit. Oh, *fuck*. Will—I'm sorry. Man, I'm—"

This time, the stinging in Will's eyes wasn't from the smoke and the ash and the cold.

He spun. He turned his back on his best friend, one of a handful of people who had known him and liked him before he became *Billy Brenton*, and he walked away.

Away from the fire, away from Mikey, away from Vera's grave.

Vera was gone. Bandit was gone.

And Sacha had known.

She'd known.

No way in hell did Will want to know what life wanted to take next.

THE KITCHENETTE at Bliss Bridal wasn't Lindsey's first choice of a place to hunker down with cupcakes and tell Nat about meeting Will over spring break, but Noah wouldn't be asleep for his sitter yet, so they couldn't go to Nat's house, and Lindsey's house was too far away. So they hoisted themselves onto the countertops, and Lindsey told the story to a s'mores cupcake from Heaven's Bakery next door while Nat listened in. Lindsey didn't share all the details, but enough to give Nat an idea of her history with Will.

"I can't believe you never said anything," Nat said.

Lindsey flicked a glance at her sister and shrugged. "He wasn't in the plan. And then there was all the drama with my friends at school and—" She blew out a breath. "I don't like being wrong."

Nat snorted. "No!"

Lindsey brushed off Nat's teasing. "He was a friend when I desperately needed one, and I was a terrible friend in return. And now I don't know why he's here or what he wants. And it's ridiculous to think that he'd be here for me, but—"

"Are you a good match now?"

It was Lindsey's turn to snort. "Seriously? Nat, he's famous, he's surrounded by people all the time, and his love life is probably in *People* magazine every other week. I, on the other hand, am a two-bit divorce lawyer with claustrophobia and a weird psychic gift. How could that be anything other than a bad match?"

"But are you?"

Lindsey picked at a cupcake crumb on her skirt. "I don't do good matches. You know that."

"You pick three-date flings pretty well. *And* you told me to go for it with CJ."

Lindsey slid off the counter. "I have to work tomorrow," she said. "I should—"

Nat's phone dinged. And then dinged again. And a third time. "Jeez," she muttered. She glanced over at it, and her lips parted. "Holy shit."

"One of your new sisters-in-law?" Lindsey guessed.

"Billy's house is on fire."

"*Omigod*." She grabbed her coat. Jerk or not, if he was hurt—

"He's okay." Nat's phone dinged again. "Kimmie thinks. She said—" Another ding interrupted her. "*Damn,* Pepper's hearing rumors he tried to go into the house."

Lindsey's heart went into a panic-dance. "Was someone—"

Nat's phone kept dinging. "House was empty..something valuable inside...he's gone now, took off, nobody knows where...Pepper says he's not answering Mikey's calls...Marilyn's going nuts...."

"Heaven forbid that Bliss gets a bad reputation over this," Lindsey muttered.

"He tried to go into the house. While it was *burning*," Nat said. "Jeez, a guy like Billy can afford anything he wants. I wonder what was in there?"

Lindsey tuned Nat out. She willed her heart to slow. He was fine. He didn't need her. He had Mikey. He wasn't hurt.

But the Will she had known—and Billy Brenton, the Will she *didn't* know—would not have gone into a burning building. He was funny, he might cross a line, and he liked a good joke, but he wasn't stupid and he wasn't reckless. The only thing —oh, *no*.

Nat was thumbing through her phone, managing the incessant dings. "Whatever it was must've been valuable. Rumor is it took three firemen, two cops, and Mikey to stop him. That's crazy."

And probably exaggerated, if Lindsey knew anything at all about small towns. But the part about his trying to go into the house—that wouldn't be idle gossip.

Would it?

She grabbed her own phone and hit the Internet. Three clicks later, she was staring at an article about Billy Brenton and his favorite guitar, Vera.

Vera.

No.

Not Vera.

Despite everything, she hoped it wasn't his guitar. She didn't know enough about guitars to pick one out of a crowd, but she could still see Will's country smile at that roaring fireplace in the ski resort lobby, a guitar at his knee. *My snow angel*, he'd said the second time they ran into each other. This time not literally. *Sit on down. Meet Vera. She's the only other woman in my life, but she ain't too jealous.*

God, the songs he'd played on that guitar that week—and his voice on top of it. None of them were songs she'd heard before or since.

Just playing what I hear, he'd said.

You hear a song in everything? she'd asked.

I do when you're here. She remembered the smile that went with his words. Remembered being unable to stop her own goofy smile in return. Remembered how much smiling they'd done that whole week. How he'd made her feel okay about being *her*, despite her friends ditching her at every opportunity.

She knew he'd noticed, but he hadn't asked for an explanation. So for one week, she got to pretend she was normal. That she hadn't destroyed every single friendship she'd thought she had by telling her sorority sisters they were all dating the wrong men. Instead, he'd listened to her talk about her classes and her family and her big dreams. He'd told her about his family, about his job — he'd been a janitor — and about playing open mic night with his friends and his trusty guitar, Vera.

If he'd lost Vera — a lump settled in Lindsey's throat.

The Will she'd known was gone. And he'd never been meant to be hers.

He could still go screw himself for pushing her buttons the last few days, but if any of her other former boyfriends needed a friend, she'd be there for them.

She grabbed her purse. "I have to go."

"Lindsey?" Nat snagged her by the arm. "Hey, he's okay. Are *you* okay?"

"I need some air. Too many memories in here."

Nat gave her a long, flat stare that was entirely too much like Mom's old *You're not pulling anything over on me* look. "Let me know if you find him. And if you need anything."

"I don't think anyone can give me what I *need*."

"You're not alone, Lindsey."

She blinked against an unexpected sting in her eyes.

She *felt* alone. But she wasn't. She had Nat and Kimmie. CJ and Noah. Dad. She bent and squeezed Nat in an impulsive hug. "I'm a sucky substitute for Mom, but you're pretty damn good," she said to her sister. "Thanks."

Nat hugged her back hard. "You don't need to be Mom. Just be you."

Lindsey almost laughed. Because she was about to be anything but herself.

She was about to be very, very stupid.

SEVEN

WILL WAS HUNCHED over a Hummingbird in a cramped instrument store in a town a ways from Bliss, eyes closed, rocking back and forth, idly picking strings and actively practicing the fine art of denial.

Vera was okay.

Maybe some punk figured out where he was staying, broke in, and stole her, and she'd be on eBay next week. He'd put his people on watch for her. Or maybe she was in his truck, and he hadn't looked hard enough. Or maybe—

He set the Hummingbird aside with a snarl. Vera was a Hummingbird, but this Hummingbird was no Vera. Felt different. Sounded different. Played different. The store's assistant manager—a straggly-haired kid with a goatee that hung almost to his name tag—offered him a Yamaha. Will had played Yamahas before. Fenders. Martins. Brocks. All of them.

But he'd always liked Vera best.

And she was gone.

She was gone, and the music was gone. His dream was gone. His magic—gone.

He snagged the Yamaha with a grunt.

Bells jingled. The kid shuffled away. "Be right back, Mr. Brenton."

The hairs on Will's neck stood up. Then the hair on his arms.

And then a slow, dark, haunting melody slipped into his brain. A bass beat. Then another. Some violin. Lyrics. *Lonely without you, lonelier with you, you make the dawn dark, turn the sunshine to night....*

He focused on the guitar. Tried to shut out the world. But he heard the soft murmur, knew the tone.

She could've whispered in a stadium of screaming fans, and he would've heard her over the crowd. Wasn't his ears listening. His whole body was tuned in.

A shiver washed down his arms and legs, and the half a beer he'd had turned rancid in his stomach.

He looked up.

Yep. There she was.

"Go away," he growled.

Lindsey didn't bat an eyelash. "This place will still be here tomorrow. Take a night off."

A night off. Vera was *gone*, and a night off was supposed to help? He snorted and set the Yamaha aside, then grabbed another sitting behind him. He shifted in the seat. Positioned his hand on the neck of the guitar, wiggled his fingers around the strings. Shifted again in his seat, moved the guitar in his lap, and a subtle scent of smoke wafted out of his clothes.

Will dropped the guitar flat on his lap and pressed his palms into his eyes. "Go. Away."

A hand settled on his knee. "Will."

He jerked at his name in her voice. His hands dropped, pulse leapt, jaw clenched tighter.

She blinked quickly. "*Will* you please listen a minute?" she said quickly, as if she didn't want to use his name any more than he wanted to hear it from her tonight.

"You fixin' to tell me you can match a man to his instrument too?" he said.

"I'm *fixin'* to tell you you're being an ass, and from what I hear, that doesn't suit your image."

He idly picked at the guitar's strings, a usually comforting habit that unfortunately reminded him why he was here.

Because he had to write the songs, and he didn't have Vera to write them with anymore. "Got a lot of fans happy to comfort me," he said.

"For what? Your momma going to prison? Your truck break? Your dog die too?"

Jesus.

His hand curled into a fist. His *momma* was gone. Vera was gone. Bandit was gone. And he was sitting here in the godforsaken frozen North so the girl who inspired his songs could rub it in his face.

"And I runned out of beer," Will said. "You done forgot that one."

Behind them, the kid snickered.

Lindsey skewered him with a look that reinforced the idea that she *did* eat babies for breakfast. But the kid had a smartphone out.

Will uttered a word that would've gotten his mouth washed out in Aunt Jessie's house.

"Put it away," Lindsey said to the kid.

His face went red, his shoulders hunched forward, and he shoved the phone in his pocket. "Sorry, ma'am," he muttered.

She turned to Will, something unreadable but strangely inevitable written in tight lines around her eyes. And then she said the last thing he should've expected, but the only thing that felt right all night. "My house is five minutes away. It's quiet, and I have a guest room and a privacy fence."

He could've gotten a hotel room.

He *should've* gotten a hotel room.

But a hotel room didn't have privacy. Didn't have peace. Didn't have anonymity.

Didn't have his *inspiration*.

Will picked at the guitar strings again. Cast a glance toward the kid. Then to Lindsey. "You gonna be there?"

"I have to work tomorrow."

He kept plucking. Bad idea, staying at her house tonight. Or any night.

But a worse idea was being alone, thinking about Vera.

Finding Mikey. Beating the shit out of him to take it out on somebody.

Will twisted his ball cap around so the bill faced forward. He shoved the Yamaha at the kid. "This one." The kid jumped into action, carrying it past the wall of gleaming guitars and through a mess of drum kits to the checkout counter.

Then Will turned his best *I'm Billy Brenton and I'm the boss* look on Lindsey. "You're driving."

She straightened her shoulders and fired back an *I am a divorce lawyer and I eat babies for breakfast* glare. She pointed to the kid and the guitar. "It stays in the backseat."

Why in the—huh.

Will found an unlikely smile.

It was an ugly smile, but it was a smile.

She didn't want him to play. She remembered how much she'd liked it when he played. Still did, probably. Too much, he'd wager.

"All that twangy, depressing crap will make me crash, and then we'll both be screwed," she said, but her cheeks were pink, and there was enough of a wobble in her voice to confirm what he'd suspected since he saw her Sunday night.

He still got to her too.

"Ain't so opposed to being screwed," he murmured.

Her brows scrunched together. Not a prudish scrunch. More like a *We have too much history* scrunch.

Girl wasn't wrong.

Will ambled to the checkout desk and paid the kid for the guitar, a bag of picks, a tuner and a pack of blank sheet music. Lindsey stayed out of the way, arms crossed over her white coat, lips tight, until the kid showed them out the rear door. In case anybody was looking in, he said.

Out back, Lindsey unlocked one of those hybrid cars. Will could've driven his truck—probably should've, to give himself a quick getaway from her house—but his gut told him to ride with Lindsey.

And when she turned down an alley he hadn't noticed, then circled past the guitar shop that had six people staring in the front window while three others checked out his truck, he blew out a breath he hadn't known he was holding.

Didn't want to talk to people tonight.

He eyed Lindsey's silent profile.

Any people.

"I really do have a psychic," he heard himself say.

She didn't answer, and Will settled in for the ride.

Six eternal minutes later, Lindsey's headlights flashed over a street sign for Joy Street, and four houses down, she pulled into the driveway of a light-colored house. Two stories, newer construction, with empty flower beds lit by fancy lights on either side of her ornate glass-paneled door.

Lindsey led him into the house through a laundry room and into a sunny kitchen with white cabinets, softer white tile floor and shiny stainless appliances like he'd gotten Aunt Jessie last year for her birthday. Lindsey's breakfast nook had a pine-stained table sitting beneath a window trimmed with lacy white curtains.

This fit the girl he remembered. The girl he'd believed in until the end of that week.

Lindsey's slender hips swung through a doorway, outlined all the right ways in that stiff business skirt, and he followed her into an enclosed sunroom off the kitchen.

A comfy looking floral couch and chair set sat around a soft ivory rug over the oak floor. Big picture windows looked out over the dimly lit yard and the privacy fence.

If that was sand instead of a dusting of snow outside, he could pretend he was at the beach house he'd rented in Destin when he first started having trouble writing.

"Make yourself at home," she said. "There's food in the kitchen and clean towels in the closet outside the bathroom upstairs."

A shower was a good idea. But he didn't have clean clothes to change into. They'd all been in the house with—he blinked.

Not yet. Couldn't mourn her yet.

Instead, he set his new Yamaha on the couch, then trailed Lindsey out of the room.

"Television in there," she said with a flick of her wrist

toward the open space at the front of the house near an oak staircase. White blinds closed over the windows, fuzzy white rug in front of two overstuffed white couches, big-screen TV attached to the wall between a smattering of family photos.

Her life. Who she was. What she'd done the last fifteen years.

All that was missing was a dog.

"Feel free to stay as long as you need to," she said.

Couple hours at most, he figured. Long enough to get his bearings, then figure out where to go from here. Somewhere anonymous in Chicago. Or Nashville.

But here in Lindsey's house, he had that slinky feeling making the hairs on his neck and arms stand up. He could hear Sacha's voice. *You need to go back*, she'd said.

He was supposed to be here.

Will watched Lindsey until she looked at him again.

"Mighty nice of you," he said.

"I have my moments." A frown briefly darkened her expression. "Who you do and don't talk to is none of my business, but if your family files a missing persons report because you refuse to answer your phone, I'll make your life hell."

It was enough of a threat to make him pull his phone out of his pocket and hit the power button. He'd shut it off when he left Bliss.

Lindsey showed him the guest room upstairs, a kid's bedroom by the looks of it, complete with a green dinosaur comforter and dinosaurs painted all over the walls. His heart clenched.

Did she—had she—

Not his business, he reminded himself. She'd nailed it at Suckers—they didn't know each other all that well.

But the room was comfortable.

Clean.

Decorated with love for *someone*.

Like his bedroom at Aunt Jessie's. A safe haven for a little boy. Framed pictures of Lindsey and her nephew were scattered around the room, her smiling, the boy laughing.

Happy. With total adoration for the kid. In love, in a manner.

As if she were someone else.

His breathing evened out, but his pulse didn't. *This* fit what he remembered of the girl he thought he'd known too. Big heart hidden under big dreams. "Your nephew stay here often?" he asked.

"Couple times a month."

She turned to the door across the hall—her bedroom, he guessed—but cast one more glance at him. "And I'm sorry about your guitar. For what it's worth."

That thick knot clogged his throat again.

Lindsey ducked her head. An errant strand of honey-blonde hair that had escaped her tight bun caught his eye.

Woman was a mystery. A mystery who'd locked her bedroom door behind her, by the sounds of it.

Wasn't any call for that. Will didn't have any intentions of getting close to her.

He knew better.

Still, Mari Belle was like to have another conniption fit, might even disown him when she found out he'd stayed here unsupervised. Sacha would be pleased, Aunt Jessie scared. But it was only for tonight. For tonight, nobody knew where he was. For tonight, he was simply a guy mourning his guitar in private.

Tomorrow, he'd be Billy Brenton again.

An image popped into his head of Bandit curled around Vera on his tour bus's couch. Will scrubbed a hand over his whiskers.

Maybe he'd be Billy tomorrow. Maybe later.

He dropped Mikey a quick text. *You got a place to stay?*

I'm set. You okay? You safe? came back almost instantly.

Will eyed the pictures of Lindsey and her nephew.

Nope. Not okay. Not safe. *Yep*, he typed. And then he tossed his phone on the nightstand and took himself downstairs to get acquainted with the guitar who would never be Vera.

She was lying. Will didn't have psychic powers, but he knew Sacha. "She need another divorce lawyer?" Will said.

"Don't be silly. Donnie's the best thing to ever happen to her."

And again with the lying. "Sacha—"

"You worry about you, young William. You can't fix anything else until you fix you."

Will bit back a *bullshit*. "Nothing to fix. I'm not broke. Tell Aunt Jessie I'll call her later. Love you." He hung up, then moved to the window and pulled the blinds up to see two cars stop out front. His truck pulled into the driveway, and a girly red number parked on the street.

His phone rang again, but Will didn't have to check the screen to know who was calling. "Mikey."

"Still alive, buckaroo?"

The hesitation and caution in his voice put a rock in Will's gut. They'd been here before, everyone worrying about Will's state of mind over a girl. Will's heart shed a tear and raised a glass to Vera. "Yeah."

"Got your truck and some clean clothes downstairs. Could hit Nashville by nine if we left now."

"Word's out I'm here, huh?"

"Nope. Just used some smarts."

Figured Mikey would use those smarts *now*.

"I'll pop the garage," Will said. "Pull it in."

Wasn't going to Nashville.

The somebody-walked-over-his-grave feeling from last night had faded, but he was getting his own signs that he needed to stay here.

Like writing all night long. Then sleeping like the dead.

"Not so sure that's a bright idea, Billy."

Will wasn't either. Mikey was probably right. Staying in Lindsey's house wasn't smart.

But maybe Sacha was right too.

Maybe he wasn't done here.

He glanced at the notebook next to the bed, filled with scribbles of lyrics, chords, arrangements. Staying wasn't smart for his heart, but it was productive for his art.

Why he was here, after all.

"Not your call," Will said.

He disconnected before Mikey could start cussing like a roadie.

Will stumbled downstairs to open the garage, and Mikey pulled the truck in. Under silent protest, Will was sure. Pepper followed on foot, and Will shut the garage again.

Mikey eyed him cautiously, an apology lurking along with the dumbass accusations. "You look like shit." He stepped into the house and gave Will a man-hug.

Behind him, Pepper offered a small finger wave. "I think you look fabulous," she said.

Will smiled at her. "You sure you're related to Saffron?"

"Unfortunately," she said brightly.

"You get a hotel?" Will asked Mikey. He'd swing by later, show Mikey what he'd been working on and see if the songs would still talk to him outside Lindsey's house.

But Mikey flashed a classic Mikey grin. "Got six numbers last night. Figure I can house-hop for a couple days."

Will swung around to look at his buddy fully.

Because now *Mikey* was lying. If he were house-hopping, he'd smirk and say he had something better. Shove his hands in his pockets and shut up, not inspect the kitchen.

Mikey didn't have to mention his numbers. It was understood. Bragging—something was off.

"Talked to the fire chief," Mikey said.

Will swallowed hard.

Maybe the fire had thrown Mikey off his game. Will could see the truth, the sympathy in his buddy's eyes. Vera was well and truly gone. Not so much as a string left. No tuning knob, no bridge, no frets.

She was dust. Memories. She'd played her final song.

He should've put her in the truck last night. Should've taken her along. "You go and say the sorry word, I'm gonna kick your sorry butt from here to Canada," Will said, his voice too raw. "It's nobody's fault. Happened. It's over. Gotta move on."

He'd dedicate his next Grammy to her, God willing he got

another. Wouldn't ever forget her or replace her in his heart, but it didn't matter if it was Mikey's fault the fire started or Will's fault for leaving Vera in the house in the first place. It mattered that Will still had to be Billy.

Mikey glanced around the kitchen again and did an admirable impression of a Mari Belle sigh. "Shit, Will. Mari Belle's gonna kick your ass," he muttered.

"And your momma's gonna wash your mouth out." Will dialed up his charm for Pepper. "Begging pardon, ma'am. He doesn't get out often."

Pepper humored him with a smile, but she had some curiosity and confusion drawing her brows together. "Related to Saffron, remember? I've heard. Where do you want your clothes?"

"Cassidy called in an order," Mikey said.

Will's assistant was well on her way to a raise. He took the bag from Pepper, and when Mikey got that look—that *I'm gonna talk you blue in the ear* look—Will nodded to the door. "Got a lot of stuff to do. Appreciate the help. Give a holler if you run out of houses to hop to."

Mikey flinched, but still took on that *don't-stay-here-and-be-a-dumbass* look. "Will—"

"I got this one," Will said.

Whether he truly did or not, he still herded his guests to the front door. He did have a lot to do—he always did. Lot more went into being Billy Brenton than writing and singing songs. There were still tour logistics to hammer out, merchandise to approve, marketing and publicity plans, endorsement commitments, his agent and manager and the label brass to appease. He'd used the B word—*burnout*—to get everyone off his back when he ditched Nashville, but it meant they wanted to hear from him more.

To know he was okay. That he'd be ready for tour. That he wouldn't disappoint his fans or any of the dozens of people who counted on the Billy Brenton empire for their paychecks.

So even if he didn't have his personal life under control, he had to convince himself he did.

He thanked Pepper for the help. Listened to Mikey's

orders to call Mari Belle and Aunt Jessie. He'd ask Cassidy to find him a new hotel as soon as he finished messing around with a song that was tickling his brain. He had to work on it now, before he forgot.

Mikey paused on his way out the door. "You're a real mess, Billy-boy."

"Not so much as I could be."

EIGHT

WEDNESDAY WAS a hot mess of a day for Lindsey. Opposing counsel sent ridiculous requests to change already agreed upon terms, a staff meeting went without coffee and her mind kept replaying the soft guitar sounds that had invaded her sleep most of the night. She wasn't sure when Will had finally fallen asleep, but she'd tiptoed out of her house as silently as possible and hadn't spoken to him.

It wasn't that she didn't *want* to talk to him.

It was more that she didn't know what to say.

I'm sorry seemed so long overdue, it would've been meaningless. *Let's be friends* hadn't worked out fifteen years ago and despite being older and wiser, Lindsey didn't trust the swooning the smileys on her panties did every time Will flashed a smile her direction. Which wasn't often, and mostly came with a sarcastic tilt, but still.

She wasn't as immune to her houseguest as a modern single woman should've been. Especially given that he was apparently immune to her.

So she worked late and hoped he would be gone by the time she got home.

She was finishing paperwork when someone knocked at her office door. Her assistant had left an hour ago, and the paralegals had quickly followed. She looked up, expecting to see one of her fellow lawyers in the firm, but instead, her dad stood there.

Much better than seeing Marilyn, even if Dad's appearance brought back memories of the last time he'd come to visit. About a year and a half ago, on a comfortable October afternoon, he'd stumbled in, skin pasty, cheeks wet, brown eyes lost. *It's Mom*, he'd said, his voice cracking. *She's gone*.

Lindsey shut the door on the flashback and blinked quickly. Today, he stood tall, his olive complexion normal, nothing lurking in his expression beyond the normal subtle unease she always thought she saw whenever her occupation came up.

"Am I interrupting?" he asked.

She stood, gesturing him to the client chairs across the desk. "Not at all. Come on in."

He twisted his bowler cap in his hands and took slow steps into the walnut-paneled room. "I was in the neighborhood," he said.

"Your widow support group is tonight?"

He nodded. "Supposed to be a couple new ladies joining us tonight. Always tough, you know?"

Lindsey didn't. She couldn't imagine, and she didn't want to. She crossed around to take the seat next to him. A grin hitched half his mouth under his rapidly salting dark hair. "Your boss know you go barefoot?"

"Yep. I'm writing a cookbook. *The Barefoot Lawyer in the Kitchen.*"

Dad chuckled, and she went back in time twenty years or so, to when she had big dreams and no idea how much she would stand in her own way.

And when none of them knew how to cook. Dad and Nat still didn't, and Lindsey wasn't yet ready to own what she'd been working on in her spare time.

"Your name's come up a few times lately," Dad said. "Thought you might want to know."

Lindsey waited for him to fill in the blanks. She'd let Nat

know Billy's whereabouts, but she didn't know if Nat had told Dad and if Dad, in turn, would've told Marilyn. Not that it would matter for long. She doubted Will was still at her house.

"Did I ever tell you how I asked your mom out on our first date?" Dad said.

Lindsey tilted her head. She'd heard the story several times, and she was positive that Dad's mentioning that story now, in relation to Lindsey's name floating around Bliss, would not be a good thing. "Once or twice," she said.

His chin scrunched beneath a lopsided smile. "I was living over here in Willow Glen, working management at the furniture store."

Lindsey nodded. She missed Mom too. If talking made him feel better, she'd let him talk.

"She walked in looking for a new filing cabinet," he said. "Tell you what, I knew right then I wanted to marry her. So when I found out she worked on The Aisle, I made sure I went for Knot Fest. And there she was, talking to one of those other Aisle people. I walked up to her, and I said, 'Excuse me, the matchmaker said I needed to come talk to you right now.'"

"Had she?" Lindsey asked on cue.

"No, but I dragged your mother to the matchmaker's booth. I figured Gail would either say I was right, that I needed your mother in my life, or she'd out me for lying. At least I'd know either way."

"And?"

"Well, your mother said Gail told her the same thing about the yahoo she was talking to when I interrupted her, but when we got to the booth, Gail clapped her hands and said she knew that seeing your mother talking to another man would make me find my balls. And then she told your mom that accepting my offer of dinner was the best decision she would ever make." Dad chuckled. "Gail was an ornery one. Gave a toast at our wedding that next spring." He slanted an eye at her. "Knot Fest hasn't been the same since she left."

Lindsey's suit itched. "Dad, I'm not a matchmaker." She said it softly, because even though he told people she was on a mission to save the world—she'd used a domestic abuse case she'd assisted with several years ago as her justification to him and Mom for her occupation—she knew he'd always been disappointed that she didn't subscribe to the Bliss mentality.

Not the same way he did, anyway. Bliss believed in getting it right the first time.

Dad swept a quick glance about the room. Her degrees and certifications and awards all hung on the walls, but they felt small and insignificant.

Not enough.

"I know, you do your own thing," he said.

Lindsey bit down on her instinctive desire to defend herself more. She'd long ago learned that a well-delivered eyebrow of *I do not have to explain myself to you*, coupled with the chin tilt of *I am fulfilling a vital role in society, and I do it well* tended to hurry the would-be love crusaders on their merry way. She'd publicly accepted herself, especially when she visited Bliss, and eventually, she'd discovered who among them could accept her, and whom she was better off without.

But with her family—she still couldn't fully explain herself without facing her own feelings of inadequacy.

And Dad was getting entirely too close to one of the tender spots on her not-so-petrified heart.

"Marilyn has been getting ideas," he said into the silence.

Being in her own office made it almost natural to fold her arms and stare down her father.

"I know, I know," he said again. He held a hand up. "I wanted you to know so you can be prepared."

"I've already handled Marilyn."

"Don't think she's done yet," Dad said.

"That's her problem."

Dad grinned. "Glad to know you have a handle on this. I used my only weapon last summer for Nat."

And an effective weapon it had been. Dad had balked almost as hard as Natalie when Lindsey suggested that he get close to Marilyn if he wanted to help Nat in her war against the Queen General, but Dad had been the best person Lindsey could see who *could've* softened Marilyn and her hard-assed *No Divorcées in Bliss* stance.

Not that Lindsey had told Dad the whole truth of what she saw. She *wasn't* a matchmaker, and even if she were, she would never, ever voluntarily say aloud what her internal barometer thought of Dad and Marilyn.

Dad's smile slipped away. "Felt like I was betraying your mother's memory."

"Mom would've been proud of you." Mom and Marilyn had had an interesting relationship too—one of tolerance on Mom's part and a dependence on Marilyn's part, though the Queen General of Bliss didn't like to admit dependence on anyone, and probably didn't even realize she *had* been dependent on Mom. Had Mom been there to guide Nat through saving last summer's Husband Games, things would've been significantly less rocky for all of them.

But the fact that Mom was *not* there was what had made planning the grand finale of Bliss's annual Knot Fest so difficult for all of them, and why it had been necessary for Dad to get creative with helping Nat.

"Still feels like I'm betraying her some days, and Marilyn and I are just friends," Dad added. He gripped the armrests and shifted in his seat. "This Billy Brenton thing—it's something else, having a star here, isn't it? Don't suppose he'll stay long though. Heard on the radio he lost his favorite guitar in that fire last night. Real shame."

"For Bliss, or for Marilyn?"

Dad heaved a dad-sigh. "Isn't that the question. But I meant for Billy. Seems like a good guy."

Lindsey wasn't going there. "Have you considered using your powers to convince Marilyn to quit trying to marry off Kimmie?"

"Bit of a sticky situation there."

"I understand her wanting to see Kimmie happily married and prepared to inherit her part of the bakery," Lindsey said, "but I believe Marilyn could choose more effective tactics."

Dad coughed over a laugh. "You do that lawyer-talk thing pretty good."

"Tact tends to get me further than calling someone batshit crazy."

"Maybe you could find Kimmie a good match," Dad teased.

Lindsey assessed him again. Was he leaning toward Team Marilyn over Team Castellano? A wave of loneliness and nostalgia made her blink. "Where's family dinner tomorrow?"

"Wok'n'Roll." He checked his watch. "Should get going, I suppose. See you tomorrow, hon."

Lindsey stood with him. "Stop by anytime."

Dad didn't grimace like he would've in days gone by, but he did give her a one-armed hug with a gruff, "Go home. You work too hard."

She would've appreciated the sentiment more if she hadn't been afraid of what was—or wasn't—waiting for her at home.

HALF AN HOUR LATER, Lindsey pulled onto her dark street. When she saw the dark blue truck with Tennessee plates in her garage, her raw heart did a girly squealy number the same time her brain went into self-preservation mode. She didn't have much gumption left for the day— fairly normal by this time of night—but she reached deep, deep down to find the stamina to fake it. Shoulders squared, spine erect, eyedrops applied to minimize the evidence of exhaustion, she carried herself from her garage into her kitchen.

And promptly blew out a relieved breath.

It was a disaster—the counters were cluttered with plates, cups, silverware, and Will had even dug out the electric s'mores maker she kept on hand for nights when Noah stayed over. But the man himself was nowhere in sight.

The humming of the heater and the refrigerator were the only sounds in the house. No guitar, no radio, no voices. All normal, except for that truck in her garage.

She let her hair down and kicked off her ivory pumps, then deposited her takeout bag on the table. She should've cooked —it was healthier, and between the hours at her desk and her mid-thirties creeping in, her metabolism wasn't what it used to be—but she'd wanted comfort food tonight.

Lindsey unbuttoned her suit jacket on her way up the stairs, tiptoeing lightly. She turned down the hallway to her bedroom, but paused outside her guest room. The door was open, the dinosaur lamp lit on the nightstand, and her raw heart banged the rest of its rocky casing away at the sight.

Will slept on his stomach on the green dinosaur comforter, his arm dangling over the side of the bed. His fingers twitched, then his hand lifted, reaching for something in his sleep. A guitar? A ball? The dog she suspected he'd lost?

And hadn't *that* been a lovely moment last night? She knew his mother was dead. She remembered that vividly from spring break, because she'd grown up in the land of fairy tales, and there was an adorable orphan boy who wanted someone to love. The boy without a family had chosen the girl without a friend. He'd crept into her thoughts often since her own mother passed away. But last night she'd let out her win-at-all-costs side, and she'd gone straight for his jugular without thinking. She hadn't shoved her foot so far down her throat since the night he pulled her onto the stage in Colorado and told her—and the whole tavern—that he loved her.

But he was here, for reasons God only knew, sleeping soundly.

His breath came out slow and steady. His cap sat crooked on Noah's T. rex pillowcase. If he stayed much longer, he'd need to see a barber. Lindsey had a nearly uncontrollable desire to run her fingers through his hair, to see if it was as soft today as it had been the last time she'd known him. And that thick stubble on his cheeks and chin was long enough to be soft too. The *good* soft. Especially against *her* softer parts.

Intrigue and desire warmed the smileys on her panties.

She turned away.

He could have anyone he wanted.

He could be *good* for anyone he wanted.

And despite everything, or maybe because of everything, she hoped that one day he'd find the woman he deserved.

She tiptoed across the hall to her bedroom, changed into a

fuzzy lavender sweater and jeans, then went downstairs and pulled her chicken Parmesan out of the bag. She opened a Mae Daniels book on her iPad while she ate. Nat had liked the book. Kimmie had raved about it. Lindsey hadn't had a chance to read it yet.

But as soon as she realized the hero was Southern—the charming, drawling, smiling kind of Southern—Lindsey shoved it away.

She had enough of *that* in her life.

"What's wrong, lawyer lady? One of them couples you're splitting up get back together?"

Will peered at her from between the slats of the banister on the top step. Despite his words, his voice was mellow and relaxed. Borderline teasing. How long he'd been sitting there watching her, she couldn't say. Awareness prickled her skin, and the smileys on her panties leapt to attention.

In all the good ways.

In all the *bad* ways.

She wiped a smudge of marinara sauce from her lips. "Yep. Nailed it."

He didn't move, but sat there watching her with his sleepy bedroom eyes.

She pushed away the rest of her pasta. "Did you call someone and tell them you're safe?"

"Called and told 'em I'm not dead. Not so sure about safe yet."

Her pounding heart could appreciate that. "How's Mikey?"

Something flickered in his expression, then shuttered. "Fine. Might could be better if you told me about him and that brunette you didn't want to talk about last night." He stood and stretched. The white t-shirt beneath his red plaid button-down rode up, giving Lindsey a glimpse of chiseled abs and a trail of sandy hair.

Almost the middle of January, twenty degrees outside, and she was suddenly craving an ice cream cone. To distract her. To cool off. To have something else to lick.

He made one of those stretching noises, then dropped his

arms and started down the stairs, bouncing casually, in no hurry, subtly asserting his dominance in her house.

Her blood pressure started an uphill climb. Didn't matter how edible he looked, he didn't get to play man of *her* house.

"You gonna finish that?" Will—no, *Billy*, because he was wide awake now and one hundred percent channeling his inner country rock god—rounded the base of the stairs and eyeballed her pasta with the kind of lust a man usually used on Lindsey herself.

She'd represented a congressman's wife, a popular local news anchor's wife, and the wife of the biggest badass divorce attorney in the county. And she'd gotten her clients excellent settlements in every case. She wasn't easily intimidated, she didn't back down from a fight and she never ran away.

But tonight, she pushed her dinner away and stood. "Help yourself."

Capitulating was apparently the wrong move, because the grin he gave her went past country boy and all the way to redneck. *Here, hold my beer and watch this shit* kind of redneck.

"Saw you got some chocolate chips," he said. "You bake cookies? Got a hankering for something sweet and gooey."

The smileys on Lindsey's panties stood higher and waved at him, but she gave them a silent order to behave.

Even if *sweet and gooey* sounded pretty fabulous to her too. Smeared all over his chest—nope.

Couldn't go there.

Will wasn't fling material. He was lifetime-of-regrets material. And she wouldn't do that to either of them again.

She went to the cabinet over her fridge and pulled out her paternal grandmother's old cookbook, then deposited it on the table.

"That ain't cookies," Will said.

"Closest you'll get from me. I keep everything on hand except motivation."

Those toasted honey eyes connected with hers.

Serious. Curious. Dangerous.

Her stomach launched into a getting-jiggy-with-it two-step,

which should've been anatomically impossible, not to mention *wrong*, but with Will—he inspired her crazy.

His gaze dipped to her mouth.

She swallowed hard. Licked her lips. Lifted her chest. She couldn't help herself. Responding to male interest—it was natural.

She *liked* men. She liked being with men. But usually, she kept that no-longer-petrified organ in her chest out of it. With him—she was already invested.

She always had been.

His eyes lifted again, darker, more intense. "Got a notion I could get you motivated."

He could.

He absolutely could.

His voice was seeping through her cracks again, poking at her softer parts, her feminine parts, her weak parts. "There is one man that I bake cookies for," she said, "and you, Billy Brenton, are not him."

If he was curious about her other "man"—Noah—he didn't show it.

Ego probably told him he didn't need to worry.

"Deep down," he said, still in that hypnotizing voice of his, still holding her captive with that gaze, "I'm just a country boy. Friends and family, they still call me Will. Think he might get some cookies?"

Oh, cookies. The *good* kind of cookies. The kind that was better than butter and sugar and chocolate. She swallowed. Hard. "If he—"

A song split the tension in the kitchen. Something twangy and loud that made Lindsey think about his sister.

Will stepped away from the table, reached into his pocket and answered his phone. "Yes, ma'am?"

Lindsey turned away.

No. The answer was *no*. She couldn't give him any cookies. The baked kind, or the between-the-sheets kind. Not with their history. Not with who they each were today.

Will's conversation was heavy on the *mm-hmm*s and *uh-*

*huh*s, with the occasional *yes* or *no* thrown in. Lindsey took her iPad from the table and walked into her sunroom.

Will's guitar was still there, along with a notebook. Bold handwriting was scrawled over half a dozen papers scattered on her couch.

A pang of yearning hit her in the gut beneath where her dinner sat. How cozy would it be to put on a fire, dim the lights, watch for snowflakes and sit across from him while he strummed his guitar, his fingers working magic, his voice rolling over her and into her and through her? To simply be a girl with romantic dreams and a handsome man and the courage to go for it?

Lindsey backed out of the sunroom.

If he'd been someone else, if they had no history, if they had a true chance at a real future, she might've stayed. But she didn't belong in this room with him. With what made him magic.

She didn't belong with him any more than she belonged with any of the other men she'd dated. She wasn't meant to have a forever. With Will, she couldn't even have a for-now.

WILL WAS HALF-LISTENING to Mari Belle's offers to pray for his better sense to come back since he wouldn't leave Bliss. Watching Lindsey stare at his guitar like she wanted to touch it was too distracting.

Been a long few days. Started okay, went a little nutty, then flushed itself so far down the crapper he couldn't believe he'd ever see sunshine again. But then a smidge of light had come in.

A pinprick, but still light. Here, today, in Lindsey's warm, cheerful home, the pinprick got bigger.

And the music got louder. Wasn't all pretty, wasn't all happy, but it was more music than he'd heard in a long, long time.

Had to be the decorations, he told himself. Couldn't fault her for still having some of that brightness he'd fallen for fifteen years ago. And he could keep the bright separate from the rest of her. Liking her house didn't mean he'd do anything crazy.

Didn't mean he wouldn't be himself around her, but it didn't mean he'd be dumb enough to get ideas either.

"You listening to me?" Mari Belle said.

"Mm-hmm."

One of them Mari Belle sighs told him that was the wrong answer.

Lindsey stepped back, and Will looked at the floor.

"I've got half a mind to come up there myself to drag you home."

Will perked up. Maybe she'd bring Paisley. "I can get you tickets."

Mari Belle huffed.

Girl didn't like it when he tried to take care of her. None of the women in his life did.

Lindsey crossed past Will and went into the living room, knuckles white around her iPad.

Probably not his brightest idea, putting Lindsey and Mari Belle in the same town.

"What say you get *you* a ticket and get on home?" Mari Belle said. "Come stay with me a few days. Paisley would be in heaven."

"Get to meet your friends?" For all the unconditional love Mari Belle claimed to have for him, she put a lot of conditions on him. Like not meeting her friends until she knew if they were worth being friends with.

Apparently he *complicated* her social life by being him. Probably he should tell her about Paisley's plans for his show at Gellings. And that Mari Belle's friends probably already knew about him. But *should* and *would* weren't the same tonight.

"You are the most impossible man God ever put on this whole earth," Mari Belle said.

Considering what she said about her ex-husband, that one dang near stung. "Love you too."

He slid a look at Lindsey.

She didn't bat a lash.

"I'm worried about you," Mari Belle said. "So is Paisley. Will, I got home, and she was crying. She heard about Vera at school."

His throat tightened. "Just a guitar," he said.

"William Brenton Truitt, we *all* know better," Mari Belle said. "Come home. We—"

His phone gave a warning beep, then died, cutting Mari Belle off mid-sentence.

And his work phone—the one he used when he took phone interviews or called in to radio stations—had burned up last night, along with his charger.

He looked into the living room. Lindsey was snuggled into one of her oversize couches with a yellowish knit blanket, looking tired, worn and almost dainty despite being near about as tall as he was.

Pink-tipped toes peeked out from beneath the blanket.

There was a lot of girly hidden beneath her tough lawyer girl walk. And Will was ballsy, but he wasn't one of those perverted types that went digging through a woman's underwear drawer when she wasn't home. If she still wore those smiley face panties—his groin tightened, and for once, it brought back some of his better sense.

Her underwear wasn't his business.

She slid a suspicious eyeball his way like she knew where his brain was going.

He held up his phone. "Battery died."

"There's a charger plugged in next to the fireplace." She dropped her gaze back to her iPad.

He'd been dismissed.

Probably best. Because talking to her, teasing her, being around her felt too natural.

Like if he gave her half a chance, she could suck him into her world again, then crush him again. Exactly as his daddy had done to his momma.

Mari Belle was probably right. He should get out of here.

Instead, he found the cord, plugged in his phone, then settled in to the cozy room.

No cookies or dinner. He wasn't truly hungry. And fun time was over. Lindsey wasn't interested. Will couldn't be. He was here to work on his songs. Nothing more.

Will was feeling too nostalgic about Vera to write, but playing—he could handle playing. He *wanted* to play. He loved music. It soothed his soul. Always had.

He started slow. Something from the last decade or so, some newer country. Nice and mellow. Brad Paisley's "Whiskey Lullaby" was a real good start. Good and heart-breaking. Alcohol and death.

He played for himself, but he wouldn't have minded if the noise bothered Lindsey.

She bothered him just by being there.

He moved on to some David Allan Coe, "You Never Even Call Me by My Name." Lindsey's reflection in the back window jolted, her mouth hanging. Will chuckled to himself, dialing up the twang so thick he could barely understand himself by the time he got to that third verse, the one about momma and prison and that ol' train.

Voices clicked on.

Loud voices, like she turned on the TV to drown him out.

Will grinned to himself and finished the song with a flour-ish, then switched gears again. Something slower. Steve Wariner's "Holes in the Floor of Heaven," one of those senti-mental pieces about a man who lost the love of his life.

Had a feeling Lindsey was working up a good bit of mad.

But she still didn't stand.

Any other woman in the world would've been all up in his business, batting lashes and telling him which one was her favorite song. He knew not to trust Lindsey as far as he could throw her, but he was still curious. Who *was* she? What had she done all these years?

Had she missed him?

Dangerous questions, but Sacha was right.

He wasn't done here.

Truth was, Lindsey had snuck into the front of his mind when he gave in and started working on *Hitched*. He'd seen her and heard her everywhere those few months. And hearing the brass say those songs—those old, sad, lovesick songs of his youth—were his best ever had made him question if he'd truly grown as a musician, or if he was about to wash up. If his best days had been behind him before his career ever started.

Will changed tunes again, this time taking a few liberties with the chords, though not the lyrics, on Jason Michael Carroll's "Alyssa Lies," a good ol' knock-'em-in-the-gut song about a little girl with bad parents.

He was finishing the first chorus when Lindsey stalked into the room.

"Stop," she said.

Warmth crept over Will's ears.

The lady's eyes were hard and hot, her lips set grim as a reaper, and unless Will was way off the mark, he'd gone and pissed her off real good.

He never was the brightest guy on the block—didn't have to be with the other gifts God gave him—but he knew he was wading into quicksand over an unstable sinkhole. He clapped a hand over the guitar's strings, plunging the room into silence.

"Them cookies ready?" he said.

There was a good chance she considered the question grounds for murder. He had a feeling she might've been justified, though he couldn't say why.

"I'm going to bed," she said, the lethal undercurrents in her voice terrifying in a sultry, seductive, sinful kind of way, though Will had the good sense to know she didn't mean to be showing her bedroom side, and he didn't mean to be looking for her bedroom side. "And I swear to God, if you don't stop with the achy-breaky-twangy *crap* that's coming out of this room, I will snap that guitar in half and then light it on fire myself."

She could've probably ignited his guitar strings with one of those looks.

"So... ain't no cookies?" Will drawled.

Wouldn't ever be cookies, unless she was thinking about baking *his* cookies. And he didn't mean the kind with chocolate chips.

Girl was hot.

In every way she could be.

That right there had a song in it. Something strong. Warrior womanish. A minor key, loud and hard, but with some soft, easy moments. He reached for his notebook, scribbled notes. Words. Chords. No full lyrics, just feelings, a theme, an idea.

His heart thumped, a solid bass drum beating beneath the riff in his head.

He didn't notice when Lindsey left. He scribbled more, flipped for a blank page, sketched out an arrangement—guitar, bass, drums, fiddle.

After a while, he noticed voices echoing above him, soft, then louder.

He took a gander at the ceiling and listened.

National Public Radio, he'd bet Vera's strings.

Hell and tarnation.

Didn't have Vera to bet anymore. And he was a doggone fool to have ever said he would've bet any of her for anything.

He set the notebook aside, rubbed his eyes, then went to check the battery on his phone and text Mikey. *Got a minute for a song?*

Ladies Night at Suckers came back two minutes later. *Can be there in 30 if you need me.*

Will shook his head at the screen. Something wasn't right. Mikey should've invited Will out. Said they could talk tomorrow.

Offering to leave ladies night?

Will had a sudden thought, a suspicion so crazy, it made his staying with Lindsey seem sane.

He glanced at the clock. Barely twenty-four hours since they were last at Suckers. Time for Mikey to be moving on to his second phone number, if Mikey was being Mikey.

You sick? Will texted.

Eat shit, buckaroo.

Will scratched his whiskers, sent another look at the ceiling where Lindsey's NPR was still playing.

He texted Mikey again. *Where you staying tonight?*

Dude. Ladies Night. Quit breaking my groove.

That was more like Mikey. Will slouched on the couch, glanced at the reflection of the empty couch in the front room. Then he shoved to his feet and went to the kitchen.

He'd get to the music soon enough. But for now, he had something else to do.

NINE

LINDSEY WASN'T an early riser by choice, but given her case load and her houseguest—who had been awake God knew how long last night—she was showered and dressed before the sun. She had enough drama at work with divorce season dawning. She didn't need it at home too.

Yep, that was why she was tiptoeing in her dark house, slingbacks dangling from her fingers, barely breathing for fear the noise would alert Will to her presence outside the bedrooms.

But halfway down the stairs, she paused.

A light shone in the sunroom. Either *Billy*—the ass—hadn't been to bed, or he didn't care about wasting energy.

But then she noticed something else.

She sniffed. Then sniffed again.

Her house smelled sweet. Like sugar and chocolate and melted butter.

Like cookies.

She hit the bottom of the stairs and flipped on the light switch over the breakfast nook.

The glow was bright enough to filter into the kitchen, where her counters were spotless, the sink empty except for two cookie sheets in the drying rack. A plate of chocolate chip cookies sat on the table.

Lindsey's mouth watered.

Her family had never been big on cooking or nutrition, but despite the sugar and TV dinners she fed Noah when he came to visit, she couldn't eat anything she wanted anymore without feeling it in the fit of her clothes. So she'd been teaching herself to eat healthier, which meant branching out into learning to boil water and watching the occasional Food Network show. She'd mastered the art of oatmeal, and had she not worked late last night, she probably would've baked a chicken breast and put it over some leafy greens.

Cookies for breakfast—she shouldn't.

"They don't bite," Will said from the doorway to the sunroom.

For everything else he did loudly, the man could move quiet as a ghost. He padded into the breakfast nook, white socks on his bootless feet, and took a cookie. His sandy hair was mussed, and he'd ditched the overshirt in favor of only a white T-shirt that highlighted the slant of his shoulders and gave her a glimpse of solid biceps and forearms. His eyes sported the evidence of an all-nighter, and he smelled like cotton and fresh-baked sugary goodness.

On his way to the fridge, he took a big bite, as natural as if he'd been in her kitchen every day of his life, showing off jeans stretched across a squeezable ass. "Not poisoned either."

He grabbed the milk, then pulled two glasses out of the dishwasher and poured them full. "Eat up, lawyer lady. Don't want you getting hungry for any babies today."

He was the only man Lindsey had ever been susceptible to, and he was making it worse this morning.

She sat. Slowly, because now her kitchen smelled like both cookies and *breakfast date*.

There was sunshine in her kitchen even though the stars were still out.

There had been sunshine in her whole house since he'd stepped into it, even with all the god-awful sounds coming out of his guitar last night, even with the history swirling between them, and she couldn't deny it.

He put the milk before her, then offered her a cookie.

"Thank you," she said.

His eyes crinkled when he smiled. "Not a morning person?"

"I'm not a people person."

"Bet that cookie might could change your mind."

His grammar had both irritated her and endeared him to her fifteen years ago. Because the corners of his lips always tilted up whenever he said something that would've made Lindsey's grade school English teachers twitch. They still did, as if he knew he was abusing the English language, but he also knew where he came from, he liked talking that way and he didn't give a good gosh darn what prim and proper people thought.

She'd envied that. For all her talk of what she intended to do with her life, the big things she'd accomplish, how she'd go into politics and save the world, how she'd be so much bigger than a housewife in some Podunk town—he had something she didn't.

He had personality and talent and inherent charm. He'd been everything he needed to be so he could reach his dream and shoot past it, all the way to the edges of the galaxy.

She'd severely underestimated him then. Consciously.

Subconsciously, though, she had to have known. She'd wanted what he had—his easy grace, his comfort in his own skin, his simplicity.

He *was* simple. In the best way. He wanted something, and he went for it.

And despite the digs he'd aimed at her, after watching him everywhere else, after hearing her coworkers and friends and family talk about him, she suspected he hadn't sacrificed *who* he was to be *what* he was.

Whatever he wanted from Lindsey this morning, though, it could be neither simple nor easy.

She bit into the cookie.

The world may have gone a bit unfocused, and a moany whimper may have slipped through her lips. Butter and sugar and still-melted chocolate. Goodness and happiness and perfection to start her day.

Lindsey was in love.

With the cookie. Not with the man who made them.

The man who was watching her with amused interest, his gaze lazily focused on her while his lips tipped up in the corners beneath his whiskers.

She swallowed, resisted going Cookie Monster on the rest of the cookie and took a sip of milk instead.

"Like 'em?" Will said.

"They're okay."

He laughed softly. "You're a hard nut to crack."

"I know very few people who enjoy being cracked." But if he didn't quit using those sleepy eyes on her over his chocolate chip cookies, she'd be one of them.

"Notice you're not getting all objectionable over being a nut though."

She chose to let *that* comment pass. Because being *objectionable* would've required using her mouth for something other than eating his cookies.

Will slouched in the chair across from her, still watching her eat. His strong fingers wrapped around his milk glass, veins visible beside the bones of his hand, fingernails short and clean.

His hands had learned her body when they were younger. Learned her body and played her body. Like his eyes, they bore evidence of more experience. A scar on his index finger. Tanned skin. The lines in his knuckles more pronounced.

And he could use those hands for everything from playing his guitar to baking cookies to stroking a woman's most sensitive parts.

He'd undoubtedly be better now than he'd been then. And she'd had no complaints then.

His lids slid lower, as though he could hear her thoughts. See where her mind was going. That her body was fully onboard.

But they weren't *there*. They couldn't ever be *there*.

But perhaps—perhaps they could honestly be friends. This time. "I helped with a domestic violence divorce case a few years ago," she said. "Our client's daughter almost died. Your song—I don't like it."

He inclined his head. "My apologies. Won't play that one again."

"Thank you."

"You nail his ass?"

"The DA did. I helped her get out." She'd had nightmares off and on for months, but she'd kept that to herself. Because she hadn't lived the horror. She'd only seen pictures. She didn't have the right to complain about her cozy life.

She'd made regular donations to local women's shelters and to legal assistance funds ever since too.

Will took a long drink, never breaking eye contact, then put his glass down with a *plunk*. "You ever make any good matches?" he said abruptly.

All her senses went on alert.

There went that country boy grin again, making her panties' smiley faces swoon and making Lindsey wish she had the sense to burn them and go for a more sensible underwear choice. Something lacy. Maybe satin. Or commando.

"Don't try that *I only do bad matches* stuff," he said. "Or that *I don't know what you're talking about* stuff. I know you set your sister up."

Damn man's cookies still tasted like heaven, even when he was provoking her. "I know my sister, and I trust CJ. Not being a bad match isn't a guarantee for lifelong happiness, but I knew enough about each of them to believe they had a good shot if they committed to a relationship." She crossed her arms. If she could lay it out there, then he could too. "How long have you had a psychic?"

"Since my Aunt Jessie took us in when I was six. Sacha lives next door. She helped raise us."

Lindsey opened her mouth.

Then shut it. He *had* mentioned that fifteen years ago. She should've remembered, because she'd almost found the courage to tell him about her *gift* early that week. Something had stopped her—her own fears, or a suspicion that Will didn't believe in psychics despite having one in his life, or perhaps simple embarrassment. It was so long ago, Lindsey couldn't remember why.

"Sacha can't get lottery numbers right for anything," Will said with a shrug and a dangerously disarming grin, "but when she says something that makes my hairs stand on end, I listen."

"She told you to come here."

"Yep. Told me yesterday to stay." His grin receded, and he looked past Lindsey. "Think she knew Vera's days were numbered."

Lindsey shivered, but she covered it by taking one more cookie and standing. She wasn't running away because they were sharing life secrets. But she did need to make a tactical retreat. This was enough of being friendly for one morning. "Thank you for breakfast. I need to get to work."

"Your friends," Will said. "They know why you do what you do? Do any of them really know?"

She stopped. "What do I do?" If he was referring to her profession, she'd already told him the same as she told everyone else. That good people shouldn't be punished all their lives for mistakes.

He didn't break his concentration on her. "You could be setting folks up instead of helping 'em get divorced. You honestly believe in second chances, or are you doing the next best thing to what you were born to do?"

Lindsey swallowed. They didn't know each other well enough for this conversation.

Or for him to have made that supposition. Or for him to have cared. "That's quite romantic of you, but I don't do good matches."

He shrugged over a cookie. "You pegged Mikey with one the other night."

"Not being a bad match doesn't guarantee a good match, and if half of what I've heard about Mikey is true, I wouldn't set him up with anyone. Even Marilyn Elias."

Will choked on his cookie. Lindsey was positive he hadn't met Marilyn, but apparently he'd heard of her.

"All the stories about Mikey are true," Will said, "but they leave out the part where he's loyal as they come to his friends. Day he settles down, it'll be for good."

"Perhaps you should write a song about *him* then."

"Like writing about pretty ladies better."

And their underwear, she silently added for him while she rinsed her cup and put it in the dishwasher.

"Was why Sacha told me to come here," he added quietly. "To find the music again."

Lindsey's heart fluttered, and her hands wobbled. She snagged a towel without looking at him.

And have you?

She wanted to ask, but she wasn't sure she could handle the answer. Instead, she grabbed her purse and coat and shuffled toward the garage. "Well. Good luck with that. Excuse me, but I have marriages to correct and babies to eat."

"Wait a minute there, lawyer lady," he said, entirely too close.

Sneaky man and his sock feet.

He touched her shoulder, lightly, barely a squeeze of his fingers, but there was a possessiveness in his proximity, in his voice.

"You're forgetting your lunch."

He reached into the fridge and pulled out a Styrofoam container that looked suspiciously like last night's leftovers. It was in a plastic bag, and he dangled it by one finger. "Thought you could use it more."

She avoided any physical contact when she took the bag. "Thank you."

He turned toward the sunroom, running a hand through his hair. "And your shoes."

She looked at her feet.

"Dammit," she muttered.

He chuckled.

And the scary truth was, listening to Will chuckle was almost as good a start to the day as eating his cookies.

LAST NIGHT, sometime after he did his dishes and before he baked cookies, Will had gotten his eyes crossed looking Lindsey up on the Internet. She volunteered for the occasional community event. She played in a summer softball league, and there were rumors she'd anonymously made a notable contribution to the local high school's show choir group for new costumes. She was mentioned in her sister's wedding announcement. And that was about it. Other than a lawyer review page equally full of praise from satisfied clients and scathing reviews from their exes, Lindsey's life wasn't the open Web page his was.

He needed to quit thinking about her and keep his head straight.

The lady still had secrets. And she didn't want to share them with him. Her eyes said otherwise, but Will had listened to her eyes before, and look where that got him.

So he'd be nice, treat her the same he would any other woman in his life—fun for now, but not meant to last—and this time, he'd be the one doing the leaving. He wouldn't let his heart get involved. He was here for the songs and nothing else.

Way early this morning, he'd done a dang good job with the writing again.

Hurt that he'd had to do it with the Yamaha. He'd played plenty of guitars other than Vera over the years, and had at least a dozen or so he used on tour, but he always wrote with Vera. He had since Sacha gave her to him.

Writing with another guitar felt like he was being disloyal to Vera's memory. So he told himself she'd made her sacrifice to put him in the place he needed to be to write again.

But between the emotional roller coaster, the mental taxation of writing again, and the rest of the business his team kept throwing at him, he was exhausted. So Will hit the sack as soon as Lindsey left and awoke again around noon. Didn't take more than fifteen minutes of being alone before Will wanted company. Even his music wasn't enough of a distraction.

He wasn't born to be lonely. He liked being on the road, traveling with his band and crew, always having someone to talk to. Liked people. Usually.

But he didn't want to go hang with Mikey. Didn't want to go check out a restaurant or a bar, didn't honestly have time to kick back and go to the movies. Much as he wanted to not be all by his lonesome, he didn't want to invite anyone to his hiding spot either. Good hiding spot it was, too—he hadn't seen a hint that anyone was watching Lindsey's house, and rumor was that he was in Chicago proper instead of out in the burbs of the burbs. After losing Vera so soon after losing Bandit, there was one place Will wanted to go.

He sent Cassidy a couple notes about work stuff—he needed a new business phone and computer, someone to get in touch with the insurance company and the owners of the house that had burned down, and studio space at a local radio station for some rough cuts—then sent Mikey a text to keep his buddy off his back. After a quick search on his phone, he snagged his coat, pulled on his boots, and took himself on out of the house.

Twenty minutes later, he parked at a plain double-wide on this side of Bliss. A simple wood sign said he was in the right place. He locked his truck and crossed the gravel walk to the concrete step, then went in.

He stopped in the small, empty entryway and propped his forearms on the counter. The barking from the door behind the counter had announced him. No need to ring the desk bell.

Sure enough, the door swung open a minute later. "Hush, Killer," a familiar voice said. "That's no way to make a first impression."

And there was Pepper Blue swinging around to face him while the door shut behind her. "Oh, hey, Billy." She treated him to a whole-face smile while she smoothed her dark hair. "What brings you here?"

"Looking for a friend."

A subtle blush colored her cheeks. "Human or canine?"

"I'll take both. You working two jobs?"

"Nah, I volunteer. Triple bridezilla morning at the boutique, so I'm taking a long lunch. Want to come on back?"

Somebody *woof*ed behind the door. *Friends.* "Yeah."

The dogs were in a wide, bright room that smelled like friendly mutt and old concrete. Other volunteers and workers were visible through the glass window of the door into the next room. A litter of friendly yappers in a pen next to him jumped all over each other like fans in the pit at one of his shows. A spaniel mix in the pen across the way jumped and sniffed at him. A few of the dogs barked, but most followed the spaniel's lead, watching and sniffing and wagging their tails. Will reached over the pen and rubbed the spaniel's head, which earned him a doggie kiss.

"That's Ginger," Pepper said.

"Isn't one of your sisters named Ginger?"

"Yep, and this one looks just like her." She flashed him an unapologetic smile, then leaned over a pen to give a gangly redhaired setter a double-handed ear-scratch. "And this is Barbie. I've been lobbying to have her renamed *Saffron*, but nobody's going for it. They look alike too, don't you think?"

Barbie flopped to the ground and showed them her belly, tongue lolling to the side.

"That they do," Will agreed.

In the pen past Barbie, a tan dog with a black snout and black-tipped ears lay on his belly, nose between his paws. Looked like a lab-boxer mix. His brows twitched, and his sad, dark eyes followed the action in the room, but otherwise, he didn't twitch a muscle.

Just laid there, watching. Waiting.

Pup looked like his dog just died.

"That's Wrigley," Pepper said. "His owner was a state trooper."

Her tone filled in the rest. Wrigley's owner wouldn't be coming home.

Will bent to rub Wrigley's rough fur. "Feel for you, pup," he said softly.

Wrigley nosed at Will's arm, but that was all he did.

"He's four," Pepper said. "We thought we'd found a family for him, but they returned him. They assumed he'd be more energetic at home. No dice."

Wouldn't take much for the dog to perk up, from what Will could see. "He healthy?"

"As healthy as they come."

Wrigley crept forward, still on his belly, and watched Will. His doggie lips were making a doggie frown, all kinds of pitiful written in his eyes.

"Seriously, that's about as excited as he gets."

"You need a rawhide bone, a Frisbee and some warm weather, and you'll find some happy again, won't you, boy?" Will said.

Wrigley crept another inch forward. Will rubbed the pup's head, but he still didn't get up.

"We've tried toys and treats, changing his food, everything," Pepper said. "He's just a quiet dog."

Will hadn't come looking for a new pet. More to hang for a while and recharge his batteries. Dogs were great—they loved you without question. Didn't care if you went out and played for a crowd of twenty thousand, so long as you came home at night. Forgave you for taking them to the vet. Didn't ask anything but to be fed and exercised, kept warm and clean and loved.

And this one here—this one needed an unconditional friend as bad as Will did. "Wanna go for a drive, pup?"

Wrigley's tail wagged. His whiskers twitched, and he raised his head, those soulful eyes asking if Will meant it.

Wasn't any doubt.

Will meant it.

"Get a move on, then," Will said. "Can't get in a truck if you don't get up off the floor."

Wrigley stretched his neck. Gave a sniff. Seeing what Will was made of, Will figured.

He waited.

With a heavy dog-sigh, Wrigley scooted into sitting position, showing off the white stripe that started on his neck and covered his belly.

Pepper inhaled a soft breath.

Wrigley, though, got a hint of stubborn in his expression. *I'll sit for you*, he seemed to say, *but I ain't making any more effort till you prove you mean it*.

Will pulled his keys out and dangled them. "You coming?"

Wrigley sniffed at the keys, but he didn't move any farther.

"Oh, don't tease him," Pepper said. "You can't—there's an application and a waiting period and—"

"And there's some perks to being a superstar," Will said.

"But you—what will you do with him while you're on the road?"

Will slanted a look at her. "He goes with me."

"You can do that?"

"Course. Took Bandit out with me for years. Saffron didn't mention it?"

"Actually, she didn't talk much about you," Pepper said.

Will put a hand to his heart. "Aw, now, that's cruel. Blow to a man's ego."

Pepper's grin was as familiar as her sister's. "You weren't Dylan." She gestured to Wrigley. "What will you do with him until you go out on the road?"

Take him home. What Lindsey would do when Will brought a dog into her house until he went on the road—Will felt a smile creeping on.

Kick him out of her house, that's what she'd probably do.

Might could be some goodness in that too. Comfortable as he was getting, as much writing as he was getting done, he wasn't likely to leave on his own. And this morning had reinforced the idea that he needed to get out before he got too attached again.

"Won't be a problem," Will said. "He trained?"

"Of course he is."

Wrigley echoed the answer with a disgusted snort. He watched Will. Waited.

"Fixed?" Will asked.

"Yep."

"You go on and get whoever you need to so I can take my new friend here for a ride."

"Saffron did mention your ego," Pepper said, but she couched it with a friendly grin, and she went to the door into the next room and waved through the window to one of the ladies.

"Hear that, Wrigley?" Will said. "We're breaking you out of this joint."

Wrigley stood, gave a full body shake, and then nosed Will's hand. And an hour later, Will's wallet was relieved of a hefty donation, and he had a new best friend sitting in his passenger seat.

Life was looking up.

TEN

PEPPER HAD BEEN RIGHT—WRIGLEY wasn't much into balls or Frisbees, or maybe he had enough common sense to want to stay inside where it was warm. The pup was curled at Will's feet in Lindsey's sunroom Thursday evening, listening to him noodle out a melody on the Yamaha. Paisley had called to say hi to the family's newest canine, and then Aunt Jessie had called and squealed like a grandmama after Will texted her Wrigley's picture. But when Will asked what Aunt Jessie and Sacha were doing, Aunt Jessie had clammed up and said she needed to go, because Donnie was taking her out to the Pork'n'Fork for dinner and she still needed to get herself gussied up.

Left Will with a sinking in his stomach. He had few memories of being six years old, but the ones he had were vivid. Second biggest was Sacha bringing him Vera. The biggest was of him lying in that twin bed on the squeaky springs, listening to Sacha telling Aunt Jessie that she *could* do this, she *could* raise two babies. That Will and Mari Belle were her destiny. That a place like Pickleberry Springs helped their own, and that Sacha would be there too. That Aunt Jessie wasn't alone.

Will had little enough left in his life that made him feel like the regular ol' country boy he was at heart. His family might not have been conventional, even by Southern standards, but something being off with Aunt Jessie and Sacha—that didn't help.

But tonight, he had his dog and his music. He told himself Aunt Jessie and Sacha were probably fine, just being girls who sometimes needed their space. And this time next week, he would forget anything felt off, that the best thing he could do for all of them was to get back to normal himself. The Yamaha wasn't worn in the right spots like Vera had been—no scratches or scars or evidence of life yet—but she'd do.

The back door knob clicked. Without hardly giving it a thought, Will switched from his noodling to strumming a song his buddy Tyler Blue had written, "Rain Dance," about a guy who fell in love with a girl while watching her dance in the rain. Will had seen Lindsey dance in the snow, but not in the rain.

He wanted to though. See the carefree side of her she'd had when they met. See her face light up, her smile glow. That all-wet part wouldn't be half bad either. The lady would be sexy as hell all wet.

He clapped a hand over the strings and plunged the room into silence.

Didn't need to be thinking about Lindsey in the rain. Or Lindsey being happy, or Lindsey being sexy. He was packed and ready to go. He'd been planning on clearing out before she got home, leaving a thank you note, but he'd wanted one more afternoon in a comfortable house before he and Wrigley set out to find a new place to crash.

Working on that new song, he'd lost track of time.

Been a long time since that happened. It wasn't a love song, wasn't a hate song. Simply a song about hanging out, drinking beer, loving life. Good old-fashioned country music. Inspired here.

His fingers itched to strum again, but he set the guitar aside instead.

He made to stand, turned to the door, and there she was, shuffling through the kitchen, barefoot. Her light hair was tied back so tight it looked painted on, her skin paler than it should've been, exhaustion etched in the slope of her back and shoulders.

Will started toward her. The chair next to her clattered, and she yelped. "Ow!"

That would hurt. Stubbed toes sucked. "You okay, lawyer lady?" He leaned in the doorway, watching her turn those tired brown eyes toward him, sizing him up as though she was deciding if he was asking about her toe or her day.

"I'll live. Thank you." She set another plastic bag on the table. "Leftover Chinese if you're hungry."

He'd planned to grab something on his way to a hotel, but Chinese sounded decent. So did company, even though he knew better. She turned toward the stairs with a barely noticeable limp in her gait.

"Eat any babies today?" he said.

She pinned him with a suspicious side-glance. He shouldn't have asked. Didn't need to get more attached. But she'd let him stay here for two nights and days now. She'd offered him dinner last night, let him raid her fridge, bake cookies, brought him dinner tonight. She hadn't offered anything else. He hadn't asked.

But she'd been friendly, if guardedly so. Not starry-eyed. No agenda. And he'd been on the lookout for an agenda. Best he could tell, the biggest difference between the woman standing here and the girl he'd known fifteen years ago was life experience.

"No babies," she said finally. "And despite the Queen General's best attempts, I didn't play matchmaker for her daughter either. I did, however, help save a village of dinosaurs from sweet and sour meteor-droids. For purely selfish reasons, I promise. Dinosaurs taste almost as good as babies."

The Queen General. She was that Marilyn lady that the folks in Bliss had mentioned a time or two. Supposed to be scary. His team told him they'd fielded three phone calls from her already inviting him to welcome receptions and offering him a key to The Aisle, which he figured was what a town like Bliss did instead of offering keys to the city. He wanted to ask about the matchmaking part, but it wasn't his business what she did or didn't do with her gift.

Even if Mikey was hanging his hat at the home of one Miss Dahlia Mallard.

"Don't seem likely, you and that Queen General lady running in the same circles," Will said.

"My father is *special friends* with her. We have family dinners on occasion."

"You want, I can have my psychic talk to him about that."

The corners of her mouth wobbled until she gave in and put her pearly whites on display. With her lips spread in a full-on smile, he got that funny feeling in his belly, right under where his heart started drumming one of those painful-but-good beats.

"That's very kind of you," she said. "But I've got this one covered."

He didn't doubt it. "What I hear about that Queen General lady, even a baby-eater like you might could need some backup with that one."

"Don't tell me the great Billy Brenton is afraid of a crazy old lady from a little town in the middle of nowhere."

"I grew up in a little town in the middle of nowhere. I know what those crazy old ladies can do. Darn right I'm scared."

Lindsey blinked at him.

He winked, and then something even more terrifying than meeting her Queen General happened.

She tipped her head back, put a hand to that delicate neck, and she laughed.

It was a little peal of laughter, but the music in it filtered into his soul and made his heart beat out a stronger rhythm, sending electric shocks through his veins.

He wanted to bottle that laugh, that happy twinkle, that bright smile, and put it in a song.

This was the girl he'd fallen for in Colorado. Part insecure, part confident, but bright and happy and shining beneath it all. He had a notion she didn't laugh like that for just anybody.

Darned if that wasn't a better feeling than the first time one of his albums went double platinum.

"At least she's not Southern too," Lindsey said.

Will inclined his head in agreement. Couldn't find his voice to say anything.

Not when that honest smile of hers was making him wonder again why she'd pegged him for a bad match for her all those years ago. What he could see, they got along fine.

And when she went to work untying her coat and slid it off her shoulders, his gut tightened.

So did his groin.

Now *that*—that, a man could get behind.

Bad, bad idea, his brain said.

But everything else about him was jumping onboard.

This was the girl he missed.

She was still in there. Tucked under layers and layers of stiff, uptight lawyer lady, that girl he'd met—the one he'd laughed with, the one he'd gotten drunk with, the one he'd gotten matching tattoos with—that girl was still in there.

But she was more too. More than he'd known. Fifteen years ago, she hadn't mentioned the psychic matchmaker thing until the minute she broke up with him. What wasn't she telling him now?

More important, why did he care?

She set her coat over the chair, then reached for the buttons on her stiff suit jacket. "The better news for you," she said, "is that she doesn't enter the lair of evil divorce attorneys like me. So you're safe for now."

"Not so sure I'd agree, so long as you keep taking your clothes off."

Her hands froze, and the happy slid right off her face. Wary curiosity took its place, her soft brown eyes watchful, lips tugging down, upper body subtly leaning back.

Will liked the happy better. He wanted the happy. He *needed* the happy.

Her gaze dipped to his lips.

She wanted to kiss him. Whatever she thought about being a good or bad match for Will—and it hadn't escaped his attention that she hadn't come right out and said one way or another lately—he *knew* she wanted to kiss him.

He knew she wanted to be that carefree girl who danced while the snow fell down. Who would dance in the rain too.

"My apologies," she said softly. She took a step back. Then another.

It wasn't a retreat—her stubborn side was coming out, all those barriers slamming up to block out the girl she was hiding underneath that frigid lawyer lady exterior.

"You seeing somebody?" It was the dumbest question he could ask her, but he had to know.

"That's none of your business."

He hitched a corner of his mouth. "So that's a no."

"It's a *none of your business.*"

He didn't move, didn't follow her while she made her way to the steps, but he knew how to keep a woman's attention even when he knew she was right about that *very bad idea* thing. "I ain't pretty enough for you?"

I'm still a bad match for you?

"Your ego doesn't need my stroking."

He tilted an eyebrow.

Let her think about what else she could stroke if she had half a mind.

The way her brows slammed down over her pinkening cheeks—she was thinking it. Getting agitated by it too.

Good agitated, he guessed. Unless he was losing his touch.

"Anybody ever tell you you're pretty when you smile?" he murmured.

"Once. But he doesn't exist anymore."

That one hit him in the heart.

She was wrong about that. Probably should've done the *I remember you* thing different. Maybe she'd open up if he said the words.

Maybe they could do some forgiving, some healing. Looked to him like they could both use it. Or maybe once they stopped doing the not-talking-about-it thing, she'd tell him he still wasn't a good match for her.

That she was good for inspiring music, but she wasn't his to keep.

She looked at him once more, like they might've been sharing some thoughts, but then her gaze slid past him, went wide, and all the shrieking floodgates opened.

"What the *hell* is that?"

Ah.

That.

What with her distracting him, *that* had slipped his mind.

Wrigley scooted himself into the doorway right next to Will.

"What's what?" he said to Lindsey.

"That *dog*."

Will scratched the whiskers on his chin, made a show of looking right, left, up, and down. Winked at Wrigley. "I don't see no dog."

He slid a glance at Lindsey. Yep, looks could kill, and he was dying about fifty deaths here.

She marched up to him, bringing a whiff of flowery shampoo, fried egg rolls, and something innately *Lindsey*, and went straight to where Wrigley was sighing a sad, lonely dog-sigh on her kitchen floor. His brown eyes tracked her movement, all full of *I need somebody to love me*.

"*This* dog," Lindsey said, pointing between them at Wrigley.

She was close enough for him to touch her cheek. To kiss those pink lips. To taste. "Him? He ain't a dog. He's my friend."

Her jaw stretched open, as though she were winding up to give him a good ol' what-for.

Will couldn't hide his grin. This one looked to be even better than last night's what-for. She was fixin' to toss him out on his rump. And he was fixin' to enjoy it.

Before Lindsey could utter a word, Wrigley scrambled to his feet and nudged her hand. She jumped, looked at the pup's big, brown, silent *love me, lady* plea, and then the funniest thing happened.

That stiff, uptight, gonna-give-you-a-talkin'-to melted away, and danged if it didn't look like the girl fell in love.

Her shoulders softened. So did those brown cowboy-killers. Her jaws of doom closed, leaving lips slightly parted, and she touched hesitant fingers to Wrigley's fur. Wrigley arched into her touch, some *love me more*? going on there. She stroked his head, and his tail wagged.

"He doesn't bite," Will said. "Likes a good scratch behind his ears."

"How do you know?"

"Most dogs do. Not so complicated. Not like people."

"Nat's allergic," she said softly, more to Wrigley than to Will. "We never had dogs."

Her fingers skimmed his fur like she couldn't figure out where his ears were, but the simple gesture sent blood surging to Will's groin.

He wouldn't have minded having her fingers on him like that.

He tucked his hands in his pockets and stepped into the sunroom, watching. A girl without a dog, and a dog without a home.

He blinked quickly. Swallowed.

Right special sight there.

"If it makes any messes on my rug, you're cleaning it," she said.

"He's a he, and he ain't so fond of baths."

She sent him a laser death eye. "If *he* makes any messes *anywhere*, you're cleaning *everything*," she said.

Wrigley nosed her hand, looking for more love. She squatted, met him at eye level. "We can be friends," she said, "because it's not *your* fault you're here."

Wrigley licked her cheek.

Dang dog hadn't licked *Will's* cheek yet.

"And stay off my furniture," she said to Wrigley.

He thumped his tail.

Lindsey gave him one last long look, then stood. She turned, and her words were soft, but he heard her all the same. "Gonna have to try harder than that, country boy."

"To piss you off, or to win you over?" He was right smart like that.

"Depends on how bad you want to hurt."

The girl always had been the smarter of the two of them. Would've been nice if she hadn't had to prove it.

Mikey had nailed it. Will was looking to join the Dumbass Hall of Fame.

Because he was staying here in Lindsey's house. Dog and all.

He didn't trust her all the way yet, but she still held a piece of him no one else had ever come close to touching.

WHEN LINDSEY GOT her job after law school and moved to Willow Glen, she'd bought a cute bungalow in a modest neighborhood where everyone knew everyone else. She hadn't had much time to socialize outside work, but she'd still met most of her neighbors. She'd learned their kids' names, and she recognized their pets.

But four years ago, a flood had completely wiped out her street, among other places here in Willow Glen and over in Bliss.

Some of her old neighbors had stayed, salvaging what they could. Some had torn down their homes and rebuilt on the same land. And some, like Lindsey, had moved to higher ground. She liked her house well enough—it was functional and modern, and since it was new construction, she didn't have to worry about maintenance on her appliances for a few years. There were enough bedrooms for Noah to have his own and for Lindsey to keep a home office.

As a house, it was everything she needed.

She called it *home* because that was what people called the house they claimed as their own. But having Will in it made it feel homier.

Having Will in it was also giving her ideas she had no business having.

And having Wrigley—that was scary on a whole new level.

Friday morning, when she realized she was sharing her oatmeal with a dog, she bolted out of the house so fast her shoes left skid marks.

She should've had a fit about Will bringing a dog into her house. She should've kicked them both out. A person staying a few nights was one thing, but a pet—what if it had fleas, or peed on the furniture, or got into the cabinets or chewed her towels or ate her secret stash of Hershey bars?

But Wrigley's sad, soulful eyes—his *I don't have anybody else to love me* look—she'd melted. Lindsey was such a sucker.

She hadn't lied. Nat's allergies had kept her family from having pets. But Lindsey had wanted a dog.

She'd wanted a dog more than she'd wanted to breathe most of her childhood.

After her spring break with Will, she'd wanted anyone or any*thing* that would love her. She'd found it in her neighbor's black lab during her summer internship.

No judgment, just love.

It had reminded her of Will.

And now, she had Will, and she had a dog. Sort of. Once he found a new house to rent—or decided to bail on Bliss— they would both be gone. She knew he had a concert in Georgia in a couple of weeks. She'd heard him talking to his management on the phone about it. And then a tour, recording more albums, more touring.

He was temporary.

Even if she and Will could make peace with their past, she'd never be the partner a public figure like Billy Brenton needed. He was surrounded by people all the time. People wanted to talk to him, wanted to talk about him, wanted to talk about who he was with, pass judgments. She couldn't tolerate that scrutiny aimed at her and her gift. She couldn't tolerate the scrutiny *he* would endure for her gift. Good for him that he was comfortable having a psychic, but being half-raised by one was different than dating one. And with her discomfort in crowds on top of it?

She couldn't date him, because he made her match-o-meter malfunction. He wasn't a good match. Or maybe he was, and she was overthinking it. Or maybe he wasn't, but she wanted him to be anyway.

So Friday night, when the cleaning crew arrived at the law firm, she went home and tucked herself into her home office to do a little extra work, earplugs firmly in her ears. Will had been plugged in to a laptop computer, his guitar next to him and earbuds in his ears, murmuring something to himself, and she was fairly certain he hadn't even realized she was home.

She was perusing online menus, contemplating the deep philosophical question of chicken or steak on a salad—but what she wanted was cheese fries from Suckers—when the unmistakable scent of yummy food wafted into the room.

Lindsey's stomach growled. Once again, he'd made her mouth water.

The man was *so* good with the torture.

Fleeing the house for food was tempting. But it would've been rude.

Unless he hadn't made enough for her too.

That would've been rude.

She logged off the remote connection to her files in her downtown office, and was about to close her Internet browser when the smell got stronger.

"You hungry, lawyer lady?" a voice drawled behind her.

It was a muffled voice, but it came through the earplugs. She pulled them out, then twisted away from her desk to face him.

Today, he wore a blue plaid button-down open over his white T-shirt, and his stubbled cheeks looked freshly trimmed. But what caught her attention most was the plate he carried, heaped with stir fry, and the glass of white wine in his other hand.

If the man had flaws, she couldn't remember what they were. "I am," she said. "Thank you."

"Promise to behave myself if you want to come on downstairs and eat with us."

With any other man, she would've asked what the fun was in behaving herself. Instead, she nodded, then followed him downstairs.

While Wrigley lay at her feet, Will told funny stories about life on the road and alternated it with asking loaded questions with an innocent delivery. What did a lawyer lady do for fun? How did she sleep at night with all those dinosaurs across the hall? Was it true she'd also played matchmaker for CJ's co-owner at Suckers? He didn't mention Mikey.

Funny, because Lindsey had heard Mikey was staying with Dahlia instead of at a hotel. The same Dahlia that Lindsey had pegged as a not-bad match for Mikey and that Will had asked her about more than once.

Lindsey's plate was empty, her wine nearly so, when Will pushed back his empty beer glass and leaned his elbows on the table. "You're not so bad when you relax a little."

"And you're not so bad when you're not playing god-awful music."

There went the killer country boy grin, with a full eye-twinkle to go with it. Good thing the man didn't have dimples, or he probably *would* cause heart attacks every time he used them. He was giving the smileys on her panties heart palpitations as it was. They practically leapt off the cotton. *Smile at me! Look at me!*

"What kind of music do you like?" he asked.

She swirled her wine and told herself to get a grip. "I don't listen to much music."

"Ever?"

"Lady Naga could walk past me on the street and I wouldn't have a clue."

He sucked in his cheeks as though he was trying not to laugh. "What about Justin Beaver?"

"Him either. What's so funny?"

Will shook his head and held up a finger. After a minute, his eyes were still dancing, green flecks peeking out amidst the brown, but he'd stopped snickering. "You're one in a million, lawyer lady. You ever listen to anything but NPR?"

"Nope."

"Gotta branch out some. Try some heavy metal. Grunge rock."

"Grunge rock?"

He nodded, all fake seriousness. "You look the type."

And there she went, laughing at him.

She never laughed in January. It was a refreshing change. Also dangerous.

Wrigley sniffed the air. She tossed him a piece of chicken. He lunged for it as though he hadn't been fed in months, then scrambled to a sitting position at her side.

"People at the shelter said he wasn't ever this active," Will said. "He likes you."

So Wrigley was a shelter dog. She fed him another piece of chicken. "Do you have to return him?"

"I don't take my dogs back." The offense was heavy enough to make her feel guilty, even though she hadn't meant it that way.

"I didn't know if you were borrowing him"—she lifted an eyebrow—"to annoy me."

Wrigley grunted in Will's direction, and Lindsey smiled. "He didn't either." She stood to take her plate to the sink. "Thank you, again, for dinner."

"Worth eating?" he asked.

"It was surprisingly good."

He stood with his own plate and padded after her. She could've told him to leave it, that he cooked, she'd clean. But that felt too domestic. Too much like what her parents would've done.

At the thought of her parents, an unexpected lump settled in her throat.

Mom would've liked Will.

Rather, he would've charmed her out of her heels. She wouldn't have just liked him. She would've adored him.

Will bumped her shoulder at the sink, and awareness flared deep inside her, deeper than just the smileys on her panties. She fluttered a hand. "I've got this. You can go—do whatever."

"No trouble." His voice was right there, right in her ear. "Like to clean up my messes."

Was she one of his messes?

She turned on the faucet to rinse the plates. "Still. I can handle this."

He was between her and the dishwasher. And he'd apparently decided he was done behaving himself, because he was watching her with a singular concentration, as though he were putting all his effort into sending subliminal messages that she needed to drop everything—including her clothes—and kiss him.

"Excuse me," she said, but he'd broken so soundly through her barriers at dinner that her voice wobbled.

He took the plate from her hand. Set it in the sink. Killed the faucet. Stepped closer, his intentions clear.

Her breath came in short, shallow bursts. When she kissed a man, she kissed him on *her* terms. Always with an escape route clear.

Will anchored his arms on either side of her, trapping her against the countertop.

She didn't like being crowded.

But she didn't want to escape.

Didn't want to be in control.

She wanted him to kiss her. She wanted him to lead. She wanted to feel his lips, his tongue, his teeth. The scrape of his stubble. The solid wall of his chest.

The scents of cotton and beer tickled her nose.

He was going to kiss her.

"Dessert?" he said, that voice rumbling over and through her, fracturing those cracks in her resolve.

She needed to say no. She needed to push him away. "Y—yes."

He leaned closer, his lips a breath away, and then—

And then he pulled away. Let go of the countertop. And shoved a plate of cookies between them. "Me too."

When she didn't immediately move, he shrugged, took a cookie, then put the plate down. "My Aunt Jessie's recipe," he said. "Lady can cook." He gave a nod, took a man-size bite, then sauntered to the sunroom.

Will twenty billion, Lindsey zero.

Again.

ELEVEN

LINDSEY WAS scarcer than snowflakes in a Georgia summer on Saturday. Will didn't hear her get up, didn't hear her leave, didn't know when she was fixin' to come back.

So he called Mikey and got scarce too, settling in for working on some songs at Dahlia's house.

Dahlia.

Mikey's not-bad match, according to all that stuff Lindsey wouldn't say. Will wondered if Mikey had figured that out. Probably not. Probably wouldn't want to know either. Still, Mikey had spent more than a normal amount of time with Dahlia this week.

Her house was across the street from Vera's final resting place, so Will stopped and said a few words. Wanted to cross the yellow tape, go digging, see for himself if he could find any of her strings, but Mikey pulled him over to Dahlia's sparsely furnished ranch before Will got into places he wasn't supposed to go.

"Dahlia's a little tight on money right now," Mikey said. "She runs this funky ice cream shop in downtown Bliss. Has a dirty flavor tasting next Saturday. We should go."

Huh. Mikey was acting nervous. Like a girl.

"Holy shee-ite," Will breathed. "Girl's got you smitten."

"Shove it, *Billy*," Mikey grunted. "You comin' for ice cream or not?"

Lindsey had *nailed* this one.

Will's heart triple-timed it on a two-beat rhythm. "Miss seeing your ass mooning over a girl? Never. Be like hiding from the show at the end of the world."

Lindsey was better than she would admit. Maybe she *could* see the good matches too.

Or maybe Dahlia had heard Lindsey pegged her as a not-bad match for Mikey and was taking advantage of the situation. "She using you?" Will asked.

"Don't talk shit about shit you don't know anything about," Mikey growled. "Dahlia's good people. I'm getting tickets. Telling everyone you're going. She needs a boost. Shut up and be there."

Will grinned and pulled out his Yamaha. "Sure thing, Mikey boy."

They worked until Mikey had to disappear and meet someone at The Milked Duck—named by Dahlia's great-aunt, Agnes Mallard, Mikey said—and then Will went to check on Wrigley.

Saturday night, Lindsey was still hiding out somewhere. Mikey was hanging with Dahlia, so Will took himself over to Bliss and went to Suckers. Pepper was there, along with the odd but strangely adorable Kimmie Elias. When Will assured Kimmie that his management had sent him to anti–mind-control training, and that he wouldn't let her mother brainwash him into marrying Kimmie so her mother could get her hands on his money, she talked about freaky fortune cookies instead of her dreams about Will creating a turtle-rito, whatever that was.

All in all, not a bad night. And the food was pretty decent.

When he got to Lindsey's house, he found a note on his guitar saying that Wrigley went out for potty shortly before 10, but nothing else.

After dinner last night, and that near-kiss, and watching Lindsey love on Wrigley, living in the bedroom she'd decorated special for her nephew, and now hearing stories from

Pepper and Kimmie about what Lindsey had done for Natalie and CJ and various other people around town, it was clear the lady was more than a divorce lawyer with a secret gift for matchmaking.

To hear her friends and family talk, she was sounding more and more like the girl he'd fallen in love with.

But she didn't show *him* that part of her. Not today.

Then, he'd known she had secrets. But she'd still let him in.

I love you, she'd whispered in the dark, skin to skin, body to body, heartbeat to heartbeat.

He'd heard her.

Not just once.

He'd felt it too, in the stroke of her hand, the brush of her lips, the burn of her gaze when she'd led him across that final bridge from boyhood to manhood.

She'd loved him.

Of course, her dumping his ass cold the next night, talking into that microphone for all the tavern to hear, on a stage where he'd sang her a song from his heart and proclaimed his undying love for her, that hadn't been love. That had been hell to recover from. Took him months to be able to look at a microphone again.

But she'd had something that had been missing from all the girls he'd known growing up: big dreams, confidence in her smarts, her acceptance that he wasn't the bookish type she was, and a desire to spend time with him anyway.

An unwavering belief in his dreams for him, right until that moment onstage.

You can do it, Will. You're amazing. You need a plan and a little courage, but one day, you'll be a superstar.

He'd thought fifteen years was enough to let go of how they'd ended, but the memory of loving her so hard, so deep, of believing she loved him too and then doing a complete one-eighty, kept nipping at him. It bugged him all of Saturday night on into Sunday morning. She'd slipped out of the house early again. Mikey had texted a do-not-disturb-except-in-case-of-dire-emergency message, which Will took to mean he was planning to score with Dahlia—poor girl—

and which meant today would be another day of just him and his dog.

But by late morning, Wrigley had used up all his energy and was snoring by the fireplace, and Will wanted a human to talk to. He knew Suckers was open, and they had good food.

Plus, going there again fed the rumors that he was camped in Bliss rather than one town over.

And it wouldn't ruin his day if Lindsey was there.

This early on a Sunday, the place was brighter and near empty. Lindsey wasn't there, but Natalie and her little boy were. The lights were high and the music was low while she swung her foot and flipped through a dress catalog. She looked his way when he approached.

"Well, hey, Billy," Natalie said. "Pull up a seat. You hungry?"

Will nodded.

Noah sat on the ground near her, singing to himself and playing with dinosaurs dressed in pink and holding baseball bats. Lindsey had mentioned the little boy's dress fascination and his dinosaur obsession over dinner Friday night, and it wasn't hard to see why she'd talked about her nephew with a big smile. Kid was cute.

CJ popped out of the kitchen. "How you doin', man?" he said to Will.

"Getting by. Y'all enjoying married life?"

CJ and Natalie grinned at each other, and Will's heart gave a hollow thump. He'd always thought he'd get the wife and kids while making it big would fade into a dream. Instead, he'd made it big and now wondered if he'd ever get a family of his own.

"It's okay," Natalie said.

"I was gonna say fair," CJ said, but they were grinning bigger at each other.

"Y'all make a good burger?" Will said. "Could go for some of them cheese fries too."

Natalie and CJ shared another one of them looks happy couples could pull off.

"Lucky you, the cook's here," Natalie said. "CJ's idea of

gourmet is putting Spam on a plate, and the burning water gene runs deep in my side of the family. Which you've probably already figured out."

Huh. Now that she mentioned it, he hadn't seen Lindsey cook much more than breakfast.

"Burger and fries, coming right up," CJ said.

He went to the kitchen. Natalie tossed her short, dark hair and gave Will a speculative look. "Did you really take a dog into Lindsey's house?"

Now there was an interesting topic to discuss with her sister. "Those two are soul mates."

"You're a handful, aren't you?"

"Goes with being this irresistible." Will grinned at Noah. "Bet he is too."

Natalie gave the little boy behind her an indulgent smile. "Most days." She peered closer at him. "Noah, did you have an accident?"

Will glanced back again too. The kid had a wet streak all down the front of his shirt.

"Mo-om," Noah said. "I don't have accidents. I use the toilet." He grinned big. "I even wipe myself."

Will nodded. "Me too, man. Me too."

"I meant with your *drink*," Natalie said. She grabbed a handful of napkins and pressed them to Noah's chest and belly.

"Are you married?" Noah asked Will while the boy was getting wiped down.

"Nope," Will told him.

"Are you *going* to get married? My mommy makes pretty dresses. If you ask, she'll —"

"Oh, no!" Natalie lunged for a glass next to a coloring book and crayons, scooped out some ice, and tossed it on the floor. "Meteors are attacking your dinosaurs! Run, dinosaurs, run!"

Noah scrambled to his feet. His laughter echoed off the walls, "Oh, no!" he wailed in a falsetto voice. "Meteor-droids!" He took off skipping around the tables, making his dinosaurs fly.

Natalie brushed her hair off her forehead and slid onto her

stool. "Kids," she said with a wry smile. "We're working on teaching him not *everything* in real life revolves around weddings, but it's tough, living here."

"Imagine so," Will said.

CJ reappeared with a glass of water for Will. "He ask if you want Nat to make you a dress?" he asked.

"No, honey," Natalie said in that sing-song, you're-in-trouble voice. "Meteors attacked his dinosaurs first."

"Guess you lucked out," CJ said with an unrepentant grin. "Get you anything else to drink?"

"Not unless you've got some real sweet tea."

"Got iced tea and sugar packets."

Will shuddered. "No, thanks."

What they lacked in sweet tea, they made up for in company. Other than Mikey and his family, Will wasn't often around people who treated him like a regular person. With Natalie and CJ, it might've been the Lindsey factor, might've been that CJ's sister had played in Will's band, but there was nothing starry-eyed about either of them. No angles, nothing they seemed to want from him.

So today, he enjoyed himself, being himself. He was debating asking if the bakery delivered cupcakes when he realized Noah was singing something awful familiar.

Off-key and off-beat, but he was singing a Billy Brenton original to his dinosaurs.

Will choked on a laugh.

Words weren't quite right either.

"*Lookin' for those bow spangle smiles,*" Noah crooned.

"Oh, lordy." Natalie hid her face behind her hands, but her shoulders shook with silent laughter.

Will spun on his stool.

Noah held the pink-dressed tyrannosaurus in his right hand, making it sing to the blue-dressed triceratops in his left. "*Ain't never been a mime, too like, too old, Air I was, moan on the gold…*"

"Back up, back up," Will said over another laugh. "*Ain't never been the kind,* Noah, bud. *Ain't never been the kind.*"

He walked Noah through the first verse. They hit the

chorus, and Noah burst into song all on his own again. *"And she's glowing me her gritty miles, bunny miles, dime word miles…"*

"Whoa, whoa," Will interrupted. "Dime word?"

"He, ah, thinks you're saying A-S-S-Y instead of *sassy*," Natalie said, "which would cost me a dime to his college fund."

"Got it," Will said. *"And now she's showing me her pretty smiles, funny smiles, sexy smiles, her sassy smiles,"* he sang for Noah.

Noah chimed in on the rest of it.

She wears her biggest smiles, her brightest smiles, her secret smiles, her underneath-it smiles.
And she's wearing them just for me.
My snow angel's smiles are just for me.

Will grinned at the kid, but Natalie stared at Will with a half-confused, half-thinking-hard-enough-to-make-her-brain-smoke look.

Uh-oh.

She blinked, then shook her head. But her eyebrows were still scrunched like she had a notion about something.

His heart kicked out a *you stepped in it now, pal* rhythm, coupled with the hair standing up on his neck.

"Did you—" She stopped herself.

Will felt an unusual warmth in his face. CJ walked out of the kitchen with a burger and fries. He looked at Natalie, did one of those silent-questions-to-the-wife looks.

"What exactly are your intentions?" Natalie said, and while Will had heard Bliss's Queen General lady had some scary to her, Natalie was plain terrifying.

He gulped. "Ma'am?"

"Your intentions," she repeated, making every syllable sharp and distinct.

"Regarding?"

"Regarding the subject of that song."

Will sometimes had to wear his Business Billy face, and he was good at putting on a show, but he wasn't good at lying. And Natalie didn't appear to be good at tolerating being lied to.

The lady's eyes had gone dark as night.

"Billy, you're in trouble," Noah whispered.

"Looks like," Will agreed.

Natalie folded her arms over her chest. "My sister can take care of herself, but that doesn't mean I won't end you if you're playing with her, and I don't care who you are. In fact, *because* of who you are, if you hurt her, I'll end you, and then I'll bring you back to life so I can end you again."

Will glanced at CJ, who had the half-afraid, half-admiring look of a guy who got off on watching a woman on a power trip. "Might could need that to go," Will said to CJ.

"Oh, no," Natalie said. "Stay. Enjoy the music."

"*Face* the music?" Will said.

"That too." She smiled sweetly, which was even more terrifying than her intentionally scary face. "It's the least you can do for teaching my son a song about my sister's underwear."

Will bit his tongue.

Because otherwise, he'd ask if Lindsey still wore those smiley face panties. And even he knew that was a bad idea.

But if Natalie was putting it all out there, Will probably needed to clear the air with Lindsey about it too. No more talking behind it. No more pretending it didn't exist.

It was time to put the past to rest.

LINDSEY WASN'T unfamiliar with working on the weekends, but she usually stuck to one day or the other, generally no more than six or eight hours total.

By early Sunday afternoon, she'd racked up ten, and that was after spending yesterday morning at Bliss Bridal being fitted for a wedding gown she'd never wear for anything other than Nat's promotional pictures for her new line of dresses. Lindsey spent Saturday afternoon with Dad and Noah at a crazy, jam-packed bouncy house place close to her office. So it had been natural—and a blessed, quiet, uncrowded relief—to swing in and do a few hours of paperwork instead of going straight home last night.

Today, she'd risen early so she could finish what she started at the office yesterday. But now, Lindsey was hungry, and she wanted to be home. Whether or not Will was there.

And she refused to think about which option she preferred.

She could've kicked him out—between the dog, the music and the memories, he shouldn't have been her favorite house-guest. But between the dog, the music and the memories, he was inspiring ideas and feelings she shouldn't have.

Her heart—and the smileys on her panties—squealed when her garage door lifted to reveal his big dark blue truck inside.

He wouldn't be here forever. And she knew she shouldn't let him be anything more than a friend.

But Will was her weakness.

He had been from the minute they met.

And neither her internal match-o-meter nor his big, public life—compared to her need for a simple, private life—could change that.

She softly opened the door into the house. Twangy music came from the living room.

She tossed her purse onto the counter, kicked off her mules, put them next to his cowboy boots and shrugged out of her coat, listening.

"*...Soon I was tumbling into the snow, with my face all about to hit the ground...*"

She couldn't hear the song without thinking of nineteen-year-old Will, flashing that country boy grin, using that line —"*Baby, that ain't no way to break a man's fall.*"

There were other instruments, and his voice sounded different. Still Will, but not the same. He wasn't playing the song on his guitar. It must've been on the radio.

In the living room, she found Wrigley on the floor at Will's feet while he lounged on the couch, watching himself on the television.

Not the radio. His music video.

Shot at a ski resort.

Will flicked a glance at her, and she felt warm sunshine. "Five weeks at number one last fall," he said conversationally.

The song played on. Lindsey's heart tripped over itself. She hadn't seen the video, and she couldn't reconcile the man lounging on her couch with the man on the television, flashing a *wink-wink* every time he sang the word *smile*.

"Congratulations," she murmured.

Will lifted a brow at her, and the sunshine she'd felt when she walked into the room morphed into a typhoon.

Congratulations? the brow said. *That's all you have to say? I wrote a song about your underwear and made millions off it, and all you want to say is* Congratulations?

Tell him he's an asshole, her brain said. *What kind of creep writes a song about a woman's underwear?*

"I'm sorry," she whispered, straight from her heart.

Not because he didn't deserve an ass-kicking for writing a song about her underwear.

But because she needed to say it. She needed to know if he could honestly forgive her.

If she could forgive herself.

Not because they had a future. But because she needed to let go of the guilt from the past.

"That's a right good start," he said, his voice on the husky side.

Wrigley whimpered. He stood, shook and trotted to Lindsey's side.

She didn't know what else to say. Or how. Apologizing was a skill she'd voluntarily unlearned when she came home to Bliss as a divorce lawyer.

She'd had to, or she wouldn't have survived.

"You know what's always bothered me?" Will's voice was raw, his eyes steady but seeping with old injury. "You knew. That whole week, you knew you'd leave. All that *friend* stuff was bullshit, and we both know it. Why'd you do it? Why'd you let me in when you knew you were fixin' to just kick me out again?"

Why, indeed? Of all her regrets in life, hurting Will had always been the biggest. "I didn't mean to. I didn't *want* to. And I thought I had it under control. But I was a know-it-all nineteen-year-old who had alienated all her friends by telling them that my psychic powers said none of them were in good relationships. I was a freak who didn't know how to be a friend. But you—you were funny and sweet and goodness personified. You made me feel like a person instead of a weirdo. And I hoped we could leave the week as friends, and that you'd never know how terrible I could be."

He blinked twice, three times, before his mouth settled into a grim line. "Yeah, that didn't work out."

"No. It didn't."

"You could've told me. You could've *trusted* me."

"We were a spring shower, Will. Warm and sweet and *short*. I'm sorry—I'm *so* sorry for how I ended things. I was then, and I am now. But it doesn't change that we wouldn't have made it."

"And now? What are we now?"

He was warm breezes and roses and beach sunrises with Kimmie and Pepper and Nat and all those women he'd taken pictures with last Sunday night. And he was *everything* with Lindsey. The good and the bad. The sweet and the ugly. The hope and the doom.

Because she wanted him badly enough that she couldn't judge?

Or because they would be the biggest train wreck of the century?

"Why are you here?" She hated the cracked punctuation of her voice. "What do you want from me? What are you looking for?"

"You make me hear the music." His voice was as steady as her pulse. He hunched forward and thrust his fingers through his hair. "You do. Just you. Like nobody else ever has. I want —I *need* to know if there's anything of the girl I fell for left under there."

Her hands shook. The TV flashed images of the fireplace— the same fireplace in the same ski lodge with the same buffalo head over the fireplace.

He'd gone back. He'd walked where they'd met. And he'd let his people tape it and show it to the world, set to the tune of a song about her *underwear*.

He wanted to know if there was anything of the girl he'd known under there?

She gripped the bottom of her ivory cashmere sweater, and she lifted it over her head and tossed it aside. "Is *that* what you wanted to know?" she said, vulnerability—damn *vulnerability*—making her voice squeaky.

His gaze was so intense, so focused, so determined, she couldn't have looked away if she'd wanted to.

"Could we make it now?" he said. "Are you supposed to inspire my songs forever?"

Lindsey's heart ached so hard it almost stopped. Could they? Or couldn't they? "I have a rule. Three weeks or three dates, whichever comes first. That's it. I don't do commitment. I don't do long-term. I don't do love. Those are my terms. You can take them, or you can leave."

He stretched on the couch, his eyes making a slow perusal of her body. Her skin quivered. He may as well have been licking her body for all the *yes, please*s coming from her smiley face panties.

And she couldn't deny her own *yes, please*.

This was a bad, bad idea. It wouldn't be a normal three dates or three weeks. He'd changed her world once before.

If he stayed, he would change her life again. Even knowing what she was offering, even knowing what she'd sacrifice when it was over, she offered it anyway.

Because she wanted him. Plain and simple, even though she knew it couldn't last. She wanted Will Truitt. Again.

"Kissing part of this deal?" His voice—raw, throaty, unsteady—inspired a pull of longing between her thighs as much as the words themselves did.

"Yes."

His eyes went dark. "Touching?"

"Yes."

"Lights on or off?"

"Yes."

His scorching gaze slid down her body once again. "Clothes on or off?"

She popped the button on her jeans and hooked her thumbs under the waistband.

He leaned forward, his breathing audibly quickening. Her core pulsed in time, hot and needy and ready.

This was a bad, bad idea. Even with boundaries.

Because he was the one man who could make her break her own rules. And she would still have to let him go.

She took her time, sliding her jeans off first one hip, then shifting to push them down the other, enough to show him that the smileys on her bra matched the smileys on her panties.

And that permanent smiley on her hip.

"Yes," she said, her voice as unsteady as his. "Clothes on *or* off."

He swiped a hand over his mouth, but she heard his murmured *Christ almighty*. He lifted his hooded eyes to hers. "Three weeks," he said.

"Or three dates. Whichever—"

He stood. "Three weeks." He stepped into her space, brushed his thumbs over her ribs, his hands on her back, his mouth moments from hers. "Three weeks. Say it."

Three weeks.

Three weeks with Will. Her raw heart was working up a sweat. She licked her lips. She should outline option clauses, early termination terms, fidelity boundaries.

But this was Will. *Her* Will.

"Three weeks," she whispered.

"Starting now." He wasn't looking at her eyes anymore. Nope, he was staring at her lips.

His head dipped close.

His jaw brushed hers.

A jolt of pleasure danced across her skin.

She remembered this. *God*, she remembered this.

She closed her eyes, inhaled his scent—cotton and soap and guitar—and took a leap of faith that she could put herself together again when they were over.

She touched the soft hair on his face. His hands drifted lower until they settled at her waist, his fingers squeezing into her rear, his body molding against hers as though he'd been born to fit her, and his lips touched hers.

Her breath caught, and she leaned into his kiss. Lips, tongue, teeth, everything. She kissed him, and he kissed her back, his mouth playing hers with the same skill as his fingers played his guitar.

Kissing Will made something inside her burst free, something innately *her*—a dance, a smile, a laugh. His touch, his lips, his very essence settled an irritation she'd felt so long she hadn't realized it could be soothed, like a small part of her soul coming home.

A kiss this right shouldn't have been so terrifying.

She had one hand at his neck, holding him right where she wanted him, the other exploring the hot skin beneath his T-shirt. Her breath came in short pleasured whimpers, and she desperately wanted to wrap her legs around his hips to soothe the ache growing between them. Will's hands were decidedly less steady, his breathing more ragged, but his body still solid against hers.

A shiver raced through her body, and she felt it pass through him too. He eased out of the kiss, pulled his hands back. He pressed his lips to her forehead. "It's a deal then," he said, and he turned away, walking out of the living room while she stood there with her shirt off, her jeans half-down, and an aching pulse beneath her smileys.

"Whaa…?" she stuttered.

He'd been turned on too. She knew it. She'd *felt* it.

He was already halfway through the kitchen. "Gotta write a song," he said.

"A *song*?"

Her only answer was the sound of guitar strings.

TWELVE

WILL WASN'T sure how long he was buried in the music, but when he looked up, his neck was stiff and his fingers sore, darkness had fallen, and a plate of food had magically appeared on the end table beside him.

Smooth?

Probably not.

But *holy* sweet Jesus. He'd liked Lindsey's kisses when he was nineteen. Three weeks of them now might near kill him. He grinned to himself, a masochistic, *you idiot* kind of grin, but still a grin.

Three weeks.

He had a notion to mess with her on that idea. But he had a promise of three more weeks of inspiration, and he didn't plan on wasting it or jacking it up by getting attached again.

Still, he probably needed to make nice with his muse.

He stood and stretched, felt blood coming back to his hind end. The food smelled good. Not down-home cookin' good, but still good. There were definitely mashed potatoes and green beans on that plate beside him. The meat, he wasn't sure about. Pork chops, maybe, or chicken. A light was on in the living room, so he grabbed the plate and the silverware Lindsey had left him, and he went in search of her.

Never much did like eating alone.

She was curled in the corner of the couch under her blanket again, reading something on her iPad. Wrigley was snoozing away on the floor. Will took a seat in the center of the couch, close enough that his leg sat against her toes, and settled the food on his lap. "Heard a rumor you can't cook," he said.

She didn't look away from her reading. "You know rumors. They're always true."

She had him there. According to some of the tabloids, he had fourteen love children, two with aliens and one with the sister of Bigfoot.

He eyed his plate, half-suspecting he was about to get a mouthful of some super-hot-sauced dinner meat, maybe with a side of habanero peppers inside, but when he took a bite, all he tasted was gravy-slathered pork chop. Not bad. "You a secret chef, lawyer lady?" he said after he swallowed.

"I'm a woman of many secrets," she said, still not looking up.

That, he believed.

He ate another three bites, watching her read. There were subtle dark smudges under her eyes, and she occasionally tucked her hair behind her ear as if she didn't realize she was doing it. He caught himself reaching for Vera's strap.

Funny. Lindsey had been his world for less than a week fifteen years ago. Barely any time at all. And he still didn't know her. Not well, anyway. But sitting here with her was still cozy and homey and comfortable.

If he ignored her *three weeks* edict. He was good with having three weeks of inspiration.

Wasn't sure how he felt about the expiration date. Or with her idea that she didn't do love.

Was that his fault? Did some other jackass need a whoopin'?

Or was it because of what she could see?

"Good book?" he said into the silence between bites.

"Wikipedia."

He grunted and went back to his plate, still watching her. Must've been interesting. She was so absorbed, he might as well have not been there. Not fair. Having his leg against her toes was making him remember her kiss. Hot and deep, right and wrong. That article must've been spectacular. Probably not something for a case. But what—

He choked on his mashed potatoes.

She lifted a brow and slid those deceptively innocent brown eyes in his direction. "Are you okay?"

He remembered the dry sense of humor. She controlled the spark of ornery better now than she had then. But he caught it. It was a glimmer, a shift in her gaze, a twitch at the corner of her mouth, but he saw it. He clapped himself on the chest, right where those potatoes were stuck behind his breastbone. "Great," he managed.

She passed him a cup of water from behind her, and after watching him successfully swallow a gulp, she returned her attention to her tablet.

Turnabout for walking away from that kiss, if he knew anything about women.

The bigger problem, though, was in what he suspected she was reading. "My Web site's more reliable," he told her.

"And slanted to make you look like a saint," she said. No shame there. Not a blush, not a bit of hesitation. "But I assume that's intentional."

Will set his dinner aside and put his arm over the back of the sofa, leaning closer to her, trapping her toes under his leg. She kept her focus on her iPad, but he saw the flutter of her pulse in her neck.

Girl wasn't unaffected.

He wasn't either. She inspired more than his songs.

She was pretty. Intriguing. And as far as he could tell, completely indifferent to his being Billy Brenton now. "Not quite fair, my life being an open book on the Internet, and yours being all private. Couldn't even find a Facebook page for you."

She flipped a cover over her tablet and set it aside, then looked at him, big pools of milk chocolate that could've either been inviting him in or warning him to stay out.

He shifted closer to her. "Still planning on being president one day?"

"As it turns out, public speaking is a talent I neither currently possess nor have any hopes of mastering." Her toes burrowed under his leg, tickling and teasing his hamstrings, but her gaze dropped and the softest blush washed over her cheeks. "The signs were there from my first Miss Flower Girl pageant, but after the incident in Colorado—well. Denial is hard to continue with that many witnesses. I still hate microphones. I almost hyperventilated during my toast at Nat's wedding."

Wrigley pushed his whole body to standing so he could put his head in Lindsey's lap. She smiled at him and scratched behind his ears, and dang if that dog didn't smile back at her.

And dang if Will wasn't jealous of the dog. Should've been Will telling her it was okay.

He remembered the *incident* in Colorado well. He remembered the lights of the stage, remembered the crowd *aaw*ing when he pulled *his girl* up there with him, remembered her panicked smile while he told the whole tavern he loved her. He remembered her blurting into the microphone that she didn't love him. That she *couldn't* love him. That her mystical powers said he was all wrong for her. He remembered his heart breaking. He'd heard it. Heard it crack, felt it break into chunks. But it didn't feel like it had happened to *him* anymore.

He'd made a good life since those days. Wasn't right to hold a grudge against her. She'd been nothing but hospitable and nice, hadn't made him any promises, hadn't hinted that she would.

If he liked her, it was his problem.

Not hers.

She tilted her head at him, still stroking Wrigley between the ears, thoughts of her fingers stroking Will instead popping into his mind and stirring his blood.

"Why Billy Brenton?" she asked.

Good question, that. Took him back more than a decade, and he almost smiled. "Hadn't been on a stage in a while when Mikey and me got our first gig in Nashville." It was half the truth, anyway. No sense telling her how many months it took him to not hear the snickers and gasps of the crowd in that tavern, to not hear her saying *"We're not supposed to be together. We won't make it. I know these things,"* every time he and Vera stood in front of an audience. "Felt easier, performing behind another name, being somebody else for a while. The guy who did the booking at the club kept calling me Billy, so I went with it. Gave him my middle name instead of my last name. How it's been ever since."

A faint line appeared between her brows, like maybe she knew there was more to the story.

"How'd your parents take you becoming a divorce lawyer?" he asked before she could press it further.

The line smoothed out, and a humorless smile teased her lips. "Not well."

"That good or bad?"

"I didn't do it to rebel. I did it to be normal." She picked at a loose thread in her afghan. "I know I'm *not* normal," she added quietly. "But this is as close as I can come."

Will could appreciate that. Probably not the way she meant it—most days, he was amazed in a good way over how not-normal his life was—but he had his moments of wanting normal.

Of wanting what she'd given him since he moved into her house five days ago.

"I repaid them for their contributions to my education." Her fingers stilled in Wrigley's fur. "I don't apologize for what I do. I don't judge The Aisle people for making money off doomed couples. I buy a bachelor in the Christmas auction every year. I help my family's boutique sponsor contestants in the Miss Junior Bridesmaid and the Miss Flower Girl pageants. The people who can accept me do so, and the rest of them—well, that's their problem."

Will swallowed. That part about her buying a bachelor didn't sit so good.

She burrowed her feet deeper under his leg. Her squirmy toes tickled, but in all the right ways.

"We didn't know each other well then, either, did we?" She

said it softly, but those pretty eyes of hers were serious and steadfast.

He'd been an open book. He'd told her about his job, his friends and his passion for music. He'd told her about Aunt Jessie and Sacha, about his momma dying, about Mari Belle being the best and the worst sister in the world. He hadn't mentioned his daddy being in prison, but then, Lindsey had been a lady. No need to sully her ears with that.

Lindsey, though—she was right. He hadn't known her. He'd known she had secrets, and he hadn't pushed. Probably should have. But she'd done things for him that week. She'd believed in him. She'd encouraged him. She'd made him believe in himself despite Mari Belle and Aunt Jessie and near about everyone else in his life not taking his music seriously.

Even knowing Lindsey had secrets, though, he didn't care. Because most of that week, he'd seen a girl with a big heart, big smarts and a big dream. A girl with courage and determination on a level he'd never knew existed.

A girl who'd inspired his own courage and determination. *If you want something, go for it. No one else cares if you reach your dream. Believe in yourself and don't let anyone tell you that you can't do it.*

He caught himself reaching for Vera's strap. "I knew enough." He tapped his chest, right where his heart had started hammering. "This here? It's pretty reliable. Don't matter why people are who they are. Matters that they *are*. And you—" He had to swallow, because stripping naked and taking himself out in the snowy front yard would've left him less exposed than what he was about to say. "You were what I needed."

Her toes had quit tickling his leg, but the raw, wary, warning tilt to her mouth and lips hit him somewhere she couldn't physically touch.

Don't get close, it said.

I made the rules, you need to stick to them, it said.

She's right, you're an idiot, his brain agreed.

He leaned closer to her, brushed a lock of hair off her

cheek, then let his fingers explore the silky strands, the curve of her ear, the soft skin on her neck.

"Will—"

"Be a long three weeks if I can't say thanks for the inspiration."

She stayed stiff as a statue, but he held her gaze, let his fingers drift into her hair to massage her scalp. Finally, her breath came out on a soft sigh, and her lashes lowered. In that hollow spot in her neck her pulse was still fluttering faster than hummingbird wings, but the stiff, frosty, unflappable, baby-eating divorce lawyer wasn't there on the couch with him anymore.

She wasn't the girl she'd been—there was something not bright enough, not determined enough, not free enough—nor was she the coldhearted lady he'd wanted to believe she was a week ago.

But she was the lady who made him feel like his life was shifting into place.

He knew it was elusive. Knew it couldn't last. But he clung to the feeling anyway.

Why don't you do love? was on the tip of his tongue.

It was the smart question to ask. *Any* question that kept him from moving his fingers from her hair to her lips was a good question. But he didn't want to be smart.

He wanted to just *be*.

With Lindsey.

"If you kiss me and then leave me again to go write another twangy song," she said, eyes closed, lips barely moving, "I swear to God, I will snap that guitar in half and feed it to you for breakfast."

"You use the prettiest words."

One lid lifted.

Will grinned at her.

Her lips twitched in the corners then parted. She was smiling at him, a full, open, honest grin that set his ticker beating harder.

"It is utterly unfair," she said, shooing Wrigley away and tossing aside her blanket, "that your country boy smile isn't illegal." She pulled her feet from beneath him, but then she swung a leg over him and straddled his lap, still smiling at him while she took his cheeks in her hands and pressed a soft, open-lipped kiss to his mouth.

Will's pulse kicked up the tempo. He gripped her hips and pushed against her, parted his lips to make way for her tongue. Music exploded inside him. Electric guitars, keyboard, fiddle, bongos. No words, just the white-hot melody of their bodies.

The intoxicating scent of her shampoo tickled his nose, but the intrigued woman scent was stronger—heady and spicy and *everything*.

He wanted her.

He wanted her fast and hard, then slow and leisurely, all night long. In his bed. Against the wall. In the shower. Everywhere.

Not to keep the music talking. But because he wanted her.

Right here.

Now.

He slid his hands under her sweater. She moaned into his mouth and arched into his touch, and what little blood Will had in his brain surged to his groin.

All thought disappeared, save one word—*mine*.

He stroked the curve of her spine, pushed her shirt up, feasting on her lips, tasting sunshine and peaches and heaven in her hot mouth. Her hands were on his ears and in his hair, and god, there was too much fabric between their bodies.

She wriggled against him, and he damn near exploded.

The hallelujah chorus had nothing on the tunes she was sparking all over his body.

She broke the kiss, arched back and tossed her sweater aside.

Will's mouth went dry, just as it had earlier.

One cup of her black bra was adorned with a winking, red devil-horned smiley face.

He traced the edge of the satin with fingers that weren't as steady as he would've liked, then dipped his fingers under her jeans. "Like that you match under here."

She ran her hands under his shirt, over his chest, her cool

touch igniting shivers over his skin. "Is this a ploy to get another song out of me?" she asked.

"It's a ploy to get you out of your pants."

"And what, exactly, are you planning on doing once you get me out of my pants?"

Will felt his lips curving up again. "Darlin', you leave the details to me."

"I assume those details involve my satisfaction?" Her smoky voice drifted over his skin and seeped into his bones.

"Twice over," he said.

Her eyes were dark as night, her shoulders trembled, but she leaned in and pressed her lips to the corner of his mouth while her fingers traced his nipples. "Now?" she murmured.

"Now," he agreed.

She slid off his lap, quirked a *take your clothes off* eyebrow, then shimmied out of her jeans.

And Will had thought his mouth was dry a minute ago.

"Get moving, cowboy," she said, fisting her hands on the red ties at the sides of her hips. His gaze snagged on the smiley face tattoo on her left hip, then on the winking smiley at the triangle of black fabric between her legs.

He had to swallow twice to find words.

Fifteen years. He'd been all over the world, had his pick of women, played to bikini-clad crowds on beaches, and *this* woman—softer and curvier than she'd been at nineteen, less perfect, more perfect—this woman stole his breath, stole his words, stole his soul.

Every time.

She snapped a finger. "C'mon. Strip." But her lips were tilted up, and there was warmth, if not outright affection, glowing in her expression. "You need a hand?"

Lord almighty, she was fixin' to kill him.

He nodded.

She laughed. A beautiful, amused, sexy, *I'd love to rid you of your pants* laugh. "Been a while?" she murmured while her hands went to his belt and those glorious breasts hung right at eye level.

He nodded again.

"That won't get you a pass on good performance," she whispered. She nipped at his ear and unbuttoned his jeans, and she could've said near about anything she wanted, and he still would've caught her face in his hands and kissed those lips.

She wasn't shy about kissing. Not hesitant, not coy. He fumbled for the condom in his pocket, then lifted his hips so she could shove his pants down—all the while kissing her, with her kissing him right back. Cool air touched his legs, then, with his pants stuck around his ankles, she climbed on, kissing and stroking and rubbing him.

They'd been fast and hard and uncoordinated at nineteen.

Now, he wanted to thrust into her, but he wanted to kiss her forever. See where else her hands would go, feel the weight of her breasts in his palms, enjoy the heavy throb of anticipation in his groin. He pulled her closer, their tongues tangling, and he unhooked her bra with one hand. She moaned into his mouth and kissed him deeper.

He would've let her do anything right then.

Because he'd never kissed another woman who put so much enthusiasm into being with *him*.

Not Billy. Will.

She rocked against his erection, and a flood of sensations crashed over his skin. "Lindsey," he gasped.

She untied the strings on her panties.

"Sweet Christ Almighty," Will whispered.

She took the condom from him, and with nimble fingers, opened it and rolled it down him.

Her hands, her fingers, her touch, her kiss, her body—she was everything.

He near about lost himself when she slid over him, taking him inside her, tight and hot and perfect around him.

She felt so *right*. Natural. Like she was born to ride him. Like it hadn't been fifteen years. Like she'd never left him.

"Lindsey…"

"Will," she whispered, bucking over him, eyes dark and intense on him. Her breathing was ragged, cheeks flushed and bright, lips swollen.

Beautiful.

His. His like no one else would ever be. Like no one else ever could be.

She flung her head back, riding him harder. "Lindsey," he said again.

She closed her eyes.

Closed them against him, closed him out. A moment later, she arched her back and cried out, and his body reacted instinctively, joining her physically even though his heart was having performance anxiety.

She was *his*, but she wasn't.

I don't do love, she'd said.

But with her, he didn't know any other way. Even when he wanted to protect himself, he knew.

She was the only one who made him hear music. The only one who made him feel home. The only one who wanted nothing more than for him to be plain, simple Will Truitt.

He'd had four hours of his three weeks, and already, he knew three weeks wouldn't be enough.

Not by a long shot.

Her limbs seemed to melt, and he used his last ounce of energy to roll them so she was beneath him on the couch.

Because she was *his*.

Question was, this time, how long could he keep her?

LINDSEY DIDN'T RETREAT to her bedroom. No, a retreat would've been cowardly. Instead, she lay with Will, enjoying his weight and their soft smart-ass getting-to-know-you-again volleys until she lost feeling in her legs. When she shifted, he gave her his best adorable, irresistible country boy grin, then shoved off her. "*Now* can I go write a song?"

"Another one? Your stamina is amazing."

He snagged her hand and dropped a kiss to her knuckles while his gaze took a slow meander over her naked body. "Ain't seen nothin' yet, lawyer lady." He nodded toward the sunroom, a subtle invitation to join him.

He'd played for her fifteen years ago too, when he was a simple janitor who liked to goof off with a guitar. And she'd liked listening to him.

Too much, in fact. She could claim she hated country music all she wanted, but Will—his guitar, his voice, his songs—he *was* the music in her life.

"Try to keep it down," she said. "I have to be in top baby-eating form this week."

The warm specks flickered out of his eyes. He tugged his pants on, then snagged his shirt off the ground. "Extra twang, coming up." Despite the subtle shift in his expression, he sounded cheerful and unaffected by her rejection, perfectly happy to have been sexed up then turned down for anything more intimate.

Exactly how she liked her relationships.

But a relationship with Will was more complicated.

He turned away, giving her a beautiful view of the curve of his back, the muscles in his arms and the smiley face tattoo on his left shoulder blade.

He'd kept it.

All these years, he'd kept his matching mark.

He pulled his white T-shirt on, and her heart gave a pained thump.

She smelled a thunderstorm brewing and felt light as a happy spring morning.

In fifteen years, no man had made her feel like Will did. Appreciated. Accepted. Adored.

And in three weeks, she would say good-bye to him again. For good.

THIRTEEN

MONDAY MORNING, Lindsey awoke alone. Will was passed out on Noah's bed across the hall, and while she was disappointed he hadn't snuck into her room for a late night romp in the sheets, she was also relieved.

Boundaries were good.

She worked past dark Monday night and got home to a note that Will had gone out to Suckers, and to call if she wanted him to bring anything home for her.

She didn't. She had a craving for cheese fries, but she shared some chicken with Wrigley instead and had a salad on the side, then texted Will a short message: *Long day. Another tomorrow. Drive safe.*

He was asleep in Noah's bed again, breathing heavy but not snoring, when she crept out of the house Tuesday morning. When she got home, he was in the kitchen, cheerfully whistling to himself and making pan-fried steak. They had a cozy dinner as he told more stories about life in country music, which she countered with stories about Noah and Kimmie, who were honestly the two most fascinating people in her life. After dinner, when they bumped into each other while cleaning the kitchen, she pressed a kiss to his scratchy cheek and thanked him for dinner. He gave her a one-armed hug, told her she was welcome, and that she looked exhausted and should get some sleep.

He'd spent too much time talking to his management team about endorsements and tour schedule changes today, he said, and he had to work on a song.

No kiss back. No lingering touches. No *let's get naked* vibes.

It was as though he were nothing more than a friend.

Which should've been a good thing. She liked friends-with-benefits relationships. No emotional entanglements. No expectations. No drama when his three weeks were over.

She had two weeks and four days left with him. So Wednesday night, even though she had three more cases to catch up on and Will had said he had tons of work to do too — it seemed country music superstars worked as hard as divorce lawyers — she shut her computer down and went home.

Will and Wrigley were in the sunroom, the man snoozing in the middle of the couch, his phone sliding out of his hand and his feet propped on the coffee table. Wrigley lifted his nose and sniffed at her. She scratched his ears, and he soaked in the love, panting happily.

Will hadn't moved. His breathing was deep and rhythmic, slow and steady. Not a snore, but not silent either.

Lindsey stepped out of her shoes. Still, he didn't move.

But he was *here*. Comfortable in her house. Unguarded. Peaceful.

Happy?

If he'd been any of her other short-term boyfriends over the years, she wouldn't have given his happiness more than a passing thought. But she hoped Will was.

Because despite how little she'd been here since Sunday, having him in her home made her happy. Warm summer, bright blue skies, sprinklers-in-the-sun happy. Heart full, not just smiling-panties happy.

It was the most dangerous happy she'd ever had. And here, just the two of them, with Will being *Will*, she almost trusted her sixth sense.

She almost believed they could be butterflies-and-rainbows happy forever.

She should've logged in upstairs and caught up on email.

Instead, she stepped into the kitchen and eyed Noah's favorite cabinet.

She *could* stand to work off some steam. She'd had to wear her growly face entirely too much in the office this week.

Five minutes later, she returned to the sunroom, plate in hand.

Will's breathing stayed slow and deep.

The blinds were open, the room bright from the overhead light, and dusk was settling outside. But with the privacy fence, no one could see in. She set the plate on the arm of the couch, then flicked open the buttons on her suit jacket and slid it off. Cool air touched her shoulders and arms.

When she unzipped her skirt, Will's left eye slid open. His right eye followed, and his breathing stopped. "Am I dreaming, or is this a really good day?" His voice was husky with sleep, and it made Lindsey ache to hear more.

"Depends. Is that a phone on your pants, or are you happy to see me?"

He tossed the phone aside, and the tent in his sweatpants left no question that he was happy to see her. "C'mere, pretty lady," he said.

She did.

But not before she shimmied out of her skirt and shell too.

"Lord have mercy," Will breathed.

Lindsey straddled him on the couch, rubbed herself against his bulge and watched his gaze wander over today's smiley faces. "No mercy for you tonight." She pressed a quick kiss to his lips, angling back when he tilted his mouth closer to hers.

He tangled his fingers in her hair and tried to pull her close. "Gonna tease me?"

"I'm fixin' to treat you."

His smile went wide, and he added a chuckle that made her smileys swoon. She reached for the plate and plucked the treat off it. The chocolate had melted and swirled with the marshmallow oozing out between the two graham crackers. She swiped a finger full of sugary goodness. "How do you feel about s'mores, country boy?"

His erection pulsed between her legs. "Real good." His voice was huskier, his eyes hot.

She slid her finger into his mouth, and when he sucked on it, she felt the pull all the way to the deepest parts of her womanhood. She rocked against him.

He caught her wrist and held the s'more steady while he swiped at the marshmallow goo. "Your turn, pretty lady."

Her lips parted. She swirled her tongue around his finger, tasting sweet chocolate and marshmallow, and then she gave his finger one long, hard suck.

"Sweet hallelujah," Will breathed. He bucked against her.

She brushed his lips with the treat. "You want a bite?"

"I want *you*."

She tossed the s'more on the plate and slid her hands under his T-shirt to the light hair on his solid chest. He cupped a hand behind her neck and pulled her close. His lips suckled and teased hers while he expertly unhooked her bra with one hand.

She rocked against him and parted her lips, her tongue darting out to tangle with his.

All his sounds were new, but they felt familiar—the low groan deep in his throat when she tweaked his nipples, the gasp that escaped when she rocked her hips harder against his erection, the rumble of *more* when he fisted his hands in her hair and held her tighter against him.

Lindsey thrust harder against him, yanked at his T-shirt. "Make me feel good."

He shifted and helped her tear the shirt off, then hooked his thumbs in the elastic of her panties. She lifted, helped him scoot them down, then reached for his pants.

Someone knocked on the door.

"They'll go away." She tugged at his pants, and he thrust his hands into her hair and claimed her lips.

The knocking came at the door again, but it was followed by another sound.

A key.

"Oh, *shit*." Lindsey leapt off Will's lap. "Nat?" she called.

"It's Dad."

Will's eyes went wide. "Oh, *shit*," he echoed.

"Hold on, I'm coming," Lindsey yelled.

"Or *not*," Will muttered. He yanked his pants on and grabbed his shirt while Lindsey dove into her clothes.

Wrigley looked toward the kitchen.

"Hold on a minute, Dad," Lindsey called.

"Lindsey?" Dad called. "You have visitors?"

"I—it's—kind of." She flipped her hair out from beneath her jacket as he walked into the sunroom.

With Marilyn trailing behind him.

Dad's eyes went round as they swiveled between Lindsey and Will. Marilyn—generally unflappable—did a guppy impersonation.

"This is a nice surprise." Lindsey's heart shouldn't have been hammering. She was an adult, this was her house and she had nothing to be ashamed of. But her breastbone was taking a beating anyway. "What brings you two by?"

Dad cleared his throat, then took two awkward steps back. "Thought you might want to go out for dinner before our widows group. Guess you're busy."

"No, we're—" She glanced at Will. He lifted a brow. What *were* they? "We're hanging out," she finished. Lamely.

"You got a dog," Dad said.

Wrigley lifted his head, pointing a wary eye at Marilyn.

Smart boy.

"He's mine." Will stepped beside her. Not close enough to touch, not far enough away to be simply friendly. His easy, people-like-me country boy grin was out in full force, emphasizing the Billy in his personality.

She could still recognize Will in there too. A mature, confident, make-no-excuses Will.

But the thunderclouds and tornadoes moved in, hovering at the edge of her anti-match-o-meter.

"Lindsey's been real nice, giving us a place to stay," Will said.

Dad's mouth hung open for a second, glancing again between Will and Lindsey. "Looks like," he said.

The half-eaten s'more on the couch arm didn't say

anything, but it sat there like a chocolate marshmallow elephant, everyone obviously aware of it, no one wanting to mention it.

Lindsey was almost positive she had a streak of marshmallow over the whisker burn around her lips and on her neck. But she refused to squirm.

Marilyn squared her shoulders and set her chin. The Queen General had entered the building. "Billy, it is so lovely to finally meet you. I'm Marilyn Elias, president of Bliss's Bridal Retailers Association and chairperson of Knot Festival. And by the power vested in me as a direct descendant of the founders of Bliss, I hereby welcome you to our quaint little corner of the world. It's our most esteemed pleasure to have you nearby. I trust your accommodations have been adequate?"

"Couldn't have asked for better, Miss Marilyn, ma'am."

"I would be more than happy—"

Dad slid her a side-eye, and she stopped.

Will's country boy grin stayed in place, but there was a keen awareness in the flicker of his gaze. Fifteen years ago, he'd said he wasn't much of a scholar.

He didn't have to be. He was smart about people, about music, about life. "Dinner sounds like a right good plan." Will put his hand at the small of Lindsey's back. Those warm honey eyes connected with hers, laugh lines crinkling, his country boy grin turning to a rueful, private smile. And she couldn't help but smile back.

He'd always made it impossible not to smile back.

Dad cleared his throat.

"Real good timing, actually," Will said. "I was fixin' to call Pepper Blue tomorrow to talk about that judging gig with your Battle of the Boyfriends, but seeing as you're here now—"

Lindsey choked on her tongue.

Marilyn tittered, that obnoxious, fake giggle that Nat called her devil laugh. "Oh, Billy, how lovely! By the power vested in me as chairperson of Knot Festival, I hereby accept. We would be delighted to have you, playing *or* judging."

"Aw, now, can't play for you." He put an apology into the

tilt of his lips, then topped it with a wink. "Take too much attention from the real talent of the night."

The man was annoyingly charming. "The Battle of the Boyfriends is almost four weeks away, *Billy*," Lindsey said.

Pointedly.

Will lifted a brow at her. *So?* it said.

"Tour rehearsals don't start until after that," he said. "Told my management team this afternoon. Be an honor to do it. Love giving back to little towns. Came from one, you know."

This has nothing to do with you, his words said.

But there was a dare lingering behind his words.

Go on. See if you can let go after three weeks. I'll still be here.

Lindsey swallowed hard. "That's very kind of you."

Marilyn tittered again. "Such generosity," she said.

"Aw, shucks, ma'am. Ain't nothin'."

"And how delightful that your dear friend Mikey has found true love in Bliss too. I've always said it's the town of fairy tales."

Will nodded. "Yep. Never seen Mikey smittened before."

Marilyn's eye twitched. "Smitten."

"Suppose it depends on where you come from, Miss Marilyn."

"Where I come from," Lindsey said, "it's dinnertime. Pizza, anyone? I'll call it in."

"Dinnertime," Dad agreed.

"I might could be up for that," Will said.

Marilyn's eye twitched again, which would've been funny if Will wasn't playing games with *all* of them. Teasing Marilyn with her grammar, playing the Billy card to win Dad's approval, pushing Lindsey's buttons because he could.

Lindsey grabbed the s'more plate and stepped out of the room to call in a pizza order. And even though it was on par with leaving Will to swim with the sharks, she left him with her guests and went upstairs to change out of her work clothes. When she returned to the sunroom, everyone had taken seats. Marilyn was perched primly in a chair, Dad at one end of the couch, Will lounging at the other end. Not a problem in general.

But the conversation was not good.

"We used to have a matchmaker," Marilyn was saying, "but our hopes for our next matchmaker have thus far not materialized."

"Looks like you're making do," Will said.

"It would be easier to bear, were there not a uniquely qualified person living so close by. Who has also been asked to judge the Battle of the Boyfriends."

Three sets of eyes swivelled to Lindsey. Wrigley stared at Marilyn with a doggie frown that bordered on *I'm fixin' to growl at you.*

From Wrigley, that was positively dangerous.

"Enough, Marilyn," Dad said softly.

"Simply making an observation," she said. "Lindsey, I don't believe I've ever had the privilege of being in your home. It's quite lovely. Rather unexpected."

"Fits her well, what I've seen," Will said.

As though he belonged here too.

As though he were staking his claim.

As though he had a right to an opinion.

He shouldn't have. But he did.

No small part of her that wanted to know what he thought of not just her house, but also her life. Her choices. Who she was.

She needed to let him go now.

Because she wouldn't be able to keep her own terms when his three weeks were over.

BY THE TIME Lindsey's dad and the crazy Bliss lady left, Lindsey looked like she would've rather been plucking her nose hairs with rusty tweezers. She collapsed onto the couch in the sunroom, head in her hands, her whole body sagging like she wanted to dissolve into a puddle.

"Didn't have to invite 'em to stay," Will offered.

If that was supposed to be a glare she aimed at him, she was missing the mean in it. Her eyes were red-rimmed and puffy. Not as though she had been crying, but more like she was exhausted. "You could make friends with a possessed unicorn, couldn't you?"

"Probably so. We both fart rainbows."

She gaped at him for half a second before a sad laugh slipped out. "I should show *you* to the door too."

Probably so on that too. He was getting attached when he knew better. Aside from the havoc she might play on his heart, he didn't have time to go chasing a girl. His next album was delayed, management was talking about adding stops to his tour and last time he talked to Aunt Jessie, she'd clammed up completely and said she had to go when he asked how Sacha's monthly moonlight aura-cleansing went.

Aunt Jessie and Sacha disagreed sometimes, but Will had never seen them out-and-out fight. Whatever was going on, he figured they'd make up soon enough.

So he did what he did best lately—he stuck his head in the sand, pretended his life and his family and his career were all in order, and he retreated into his music.

He grabbed his Yamaha and sat next to Lindsey, crowding her while Wrigley took his spot at her feet. "Wouldn't kick me out, would you?" Will pressed a kiss to her hair. "Who's gonna do your dishes if I go?"

"I'll hire a pool boy."

"Pool boy can't do this." He strummed the Yamaha, looking for the notes in "Three Little Birds." Didn't take long to find them, and before he started singing, she shifted.

"I know this song," she said.

He grinned. Didn't surprise him. He'd pushed her mostly out of his brain the last fifteen years, but some songs—like this old one—always made him think of her. "Sing it with me," he said.

"Not a chance."

"Aw, c'mon, lawyer lady. Can't be that bad."

"Yes, it can."

He skipped the first verse, went straight to singing about everything bein' all right. And she leaned into him, her head nodding on his shoulder while he sang.

She fit there, snuggled up to him while he played. He treated her to another Bob Marley song, then switched into some Colbie Caillat. His crew would make him turn in his man card if they heard, but all that "Brighter than the Sun"—it fit Lindsey.

It fit what he felt when he saw her. When he touched her. When she ran her fingers over his arm, his leg, his guitar. When she pressed a kiss to his shoulder, giggled at the lyrics he improvised to be about her so he could listen to her sweet laugh.

Didn't make any sense she couldn't feel it too, but she'd still put that three-week limit on him. And the girl wouldn't have her mind changed.

Not easily.

Good thing Will had some experience in fighting his way to the top. Couldn't help wondering what he'd lose to get there this time though.

"Never did finish that s'more," he said eventually.

Lindsey pushed his guitar away, then climbed into his lap. "You play dirty, Will Truitt."

He didn't have to concede or argue the point, because she touched her lips to his, opened her mouth to him, and treated him to something better than all the s'mores in the world.

LINDSEY HAD A VERY strong suspicion why Will didn't breach the threshold of her bedroom, and by Saturday morning, she was equal parts relieved and frustrated by it.

No, that wasn't true.

She was way far gone on the frustrated end of the spectrum.

She shouldn't have been—her couches had gotten plenty of action—but he was wearing her down. Making her want to invite him *all* the way in.

He'd made her house more into a home every day. Some nights by making dinner, others just by being there with

Wrigley while she cooked, a good bit by putting music back into her life, but mostly by being her friend.

It was what had worn her down fifteen years ago too.

Why do you let them treat you like that? he'd asked after seeing her friends give her a subtle snub for the umpteenth time.

There's more to it than I can explain. But it's my fault. I stuck my nose where it didn't belong and said things about things I don't really understand. It was all she'd told him, because she hadn't wanted to confess to her *gift*. She'd wanted to be normal.

Still deserve better, no matter what you did, he'd said. *So long as you meant good*.

He'd treated her as though she were normal. Kindhearted. Human—she made mistakes—but forgivable.

Better, he'd treated her as though he *liked* her.

She hadn't realized how much she needed him and his friendship until she'd crossed the line she couldn't uncross. There had been no mixed signals from her match-o-meter fifteen years ago. He'd been her spring rain shower. Warm and refreshing, but still wet and cloudy. Fleeting. Not meant to last.

Now, though, every time she walked into her house she felt sunny days and rainbows. Yet every time he had to play Billy Brenton—whether it was on the phone, or to tease her, or even when she was at work and someone mentioned him—she felt ice storms and droughts coming.

She shouldn't have given him three weeks. She should've walked away.

And now, she had only two weeks left.

This wasn't his normal life, he'd admitted. He was surrounded by people—by the cameras that taped his weekly BillyVision videos that he put on YouTube for his fans, by his crew, by his management team, by his band. And then there were the interviews, the parties, the small gigs in crowded bars and lounges, the benefit shows for charities. He usually wrote songs for his next album on his bus, he said.

His tour bus. A box on wheels. A nice box, by the sound of it, but still a box that was skinnier than a lane in the road.

The thought had nearly given her a panic attack, and he

wouldn't even be on said bus during their fifteen days left together.

Even if her match-o-meter hadn't been out of whack, their lifestyles were. So Saturday morning, while he was sleeping—sprawled on his stomach cross-wise on her guest bed, his mouth slightly ajar, his hair still mussed from what her fingers had done to it last night—she gathered a few necessities, and then tiptoed downstairs. She let Wrigley out for a potty break and filled his food bowl, and she'd started a note telling Will that she would be out doing family things all day—a final dress fitting with Nat, then time with Noah to keep her Most Favored Aunt status—when someone knocked on the door.

Lindsey gave herself a quick mental pep talk, then peeked through the decorative window beside her door. She'd wondered how long it would take Mikey to make his way over here. Will hadn't said as much, but Lindsey knew Mikey wasn't a fan of hers.

But it wasn't Mikey standing on her doorstep.

And it wasn't a nosy reporter who had sniffed out Billy Brenton's location.

Nope.

It was a vaguely familiar light brown-haired woman with perfect makeup and perfect clothes, including a perfect red peacoat, and a perfect scowl marring the lips and cheekbones she shared with her brother.

Lovely.

Lindsey squared her shoulders and opened the door. The face, she recognized from fifteen years ago. The new last name she'd learned by reading Will's Wikipedia page.

Mari Belle Truitt-York swept cool, assessing hazel eyes over Lindsey. Her lips pursed, and her grip tightened on her Coach bag. "Once wasn't enough?" she said in her own Southern drawl, more refined and softer than Will's, but still quite effective when it came to speaking volumes without raising her voice.

Lindsey stepped aside and swept an arm in invitation. "He's upstairs, sleeping. Make yourself at home."

Mari Belle's chin tilted. Slightly, but it was enough.

She wanted a fight.

She stepped across the threshold. "Quite adorable," she said.

"Thank you." Forget the note. Lindsey would text Will her plans. "Long flight?"

"Honey, I'm not here to discuss my air travel."

Lindsey almost smiled. "So are you here to see Will or me?"

She didn't answer immediately, instead stopping to study Lindsey's family pictures on the wall around the television. "Whichever one of you can be talked into any sense," Mari Belle finally said.

She'd have the most luck with Wrigley. Except Wrigley had wandered into the room and was eyeing Mari Belle the same way he'd eyed Marilyn Elias the other night.

"Do you know how many families the Billy Brenton empire feeds?" Mari Belle said.

"You'd best tread carefully if you intend to impugn my character," Lindsey replied, her lethal lawyer voice going head-to-head with Mari Belle's verbal sword.

"I don't need to be crass." Mari Belle turned to face Lindsey. "Your little stunt fifteen years ago? It didn't end on that stage. Not for my brother. He was a kid then, no responsibilities, no one to let down. But now? He has people who count on him. He has people who need him. And you mess with his head. Let. Him. Go."

Lindsey's heart hammered in her throat. But she held Mari Belle's glare without flinching. "None of us are kids anymore." She lifted a finger and twirled it about the room. "And he's not a captive here. This is his choice."

"Not entirely."

Lindsey folded her arms and lifted the lawyer brow.

Mari Belle gave the eyebrow back, with a little Southern spunk thrown in. But then she heaved a sigh big enough to rattle the windows. "You don't know, do you?"

A shiver prickled Lindsey's skin from her toes to her tailbone and all the way to her scalp.

Something was wrong. Something was very, very wrong. "Did he have my secret baby?" Lindsey deadpanned.

"If you care about him at all, you'll make him leave, and you'll make him think it's his idea."

"And why am I going to do that?"

"Because I don't want to lose him again."

It wasn't Mari Belle's *I* that got to Lindsey. Nor was it her *lose him*.

It was the *again*.

"We're not kids anymore," Lindsey repeated.

Mari Belle gestured to her own face, to the subtle lines of age. "Here, yes. But here?" She fisted a hand over her heart. "Nurture can't fix the nature he got from our momma. And he has too many people counting on him for you to do him like our waste of a father did her."

There hadn't been details on Will's father in the Wikipedia article. Nor did Lindsey know the details on how his mother died.

She dropped her arms. "I think you're overestimating—"

"No. I'm not."

There went Lindsey's shivers again.

Fifteen years was a long time to hold a grudge. But if Mari Belle's theatrics were based in even a fraction of truth, perhaps Lindsey didn't have the full story.

A furry, warm body nudged her leg. She absently settled her fingers into Wrigley's rough fur. "This is a temporary arrangement, and he knows it," she said to Mari Belle. "There's not much more I can do."

"Do your little psychic matches change?"

There was a hitch in her voice—a small thing, but enough to be noticeable. Enough to make Lindsey wonder if she wasn't asking purely for Will's sake.

Lindsey had, after all, included Mari Belle in her public declarations that night in Colorado about who didn't belong together.

"On rare occasions," Lindsey said.

"And has it changed with my brother?"

It had changed.

It had most definitely changed.

"I've been very clear with Will about what I can and can't offer him. And he's been very clear with me about what he wants too. Perhaps it's time you trusted him." She turned and reached for her coat. "Enjoy your day, and stay as long as you need. There's coffee in the kitchen. I'm sure Will will be glad to see you."

Honestly, she had no idea as to the truth of that. But she did love killing people with kindness. They never expected it out of a cutthroat divorce attorney, and they looked like fools if they got snotty back.

Mari Belle obviously appreciated the tactic, because her lip curled and her eyes went flat, but she replied with a sugary sweet, "That's too kind of you," that made Wrigley growl.

Lindsey rubbed his fur again. "Be nice, boy." She nodded to Mari Belle. "Excuse me. I'm late for my bridal gown fitting." And she would've left her house with a smile, except she was too worried Mari Belle was right.

FOURTEEN

WILL WAS VAGUELY aware of being on his tour bus, the motion rocking and lulling him, making him want to sink deeper into sleep. But there was a giraffe in ninja clothes staring at him from atop his childhood dresser in the corner, and the back end of the bus was open, with Vera flying on a string behind.

He reached for her, but his hand found soft denim over firm flesh instead.

The rocking stopped, but then a feminine voice spoke. "Remove your hand from my rear end. Where do you think we're from, Arkansas?"

Will bolted awake, and bright green assaulted his senses. Bright green, dinosaurs and an unmistakable Mari Belle glare. He squeezed his eyes shut again. Everything but Mari Belle made sense.

"I have to say," she said, "for the way the rest of the house looks, I wouldn't have expected this of Lindsey's bedroom."

And Mari Belle was still here. Wasn't a dream after all. Will grunted. He rolled off the bed and smothered her in a hug, pushing her face into his T-shirt to muffle the oncoming talkin'-to. "Good to see you too, MB."

She pulled back with a near-smile. "You find your brains, I

might return the sentiment. Wanna tell me why *she* has a wedding dress fitting today?"

Will wasn't the quickest banjo player in the band, but he knew that sentence was meant to terrify him.

Not being terrified probably should've terrified him too.

Wrigley padded into the room, giving Mari Belle the same look that he gave the crazy Bliss lady the other night. "That coffee I smell?" Will said.

"Yep."

"Good." He went downstairs, Mari Belle and Wrigley both on his heels, but both of them silent. Not so unusual for the dog. For MB, though—that had Will worried. He checked his phone and found a message from Lindsey—*Hanging with Nat and Noah today. Have fun.* It took him another minute before he laughed out loud.

"Yes?" Mari Belle said.

Probably would've been nice of him to tell Mari Belle that Lindsey's dress was for her sister's new gown collection, but he liked keeping her on her toes. Instead, he poured a cup of coffee for his sister and let her assume what she wanted. "You here about Aunt Jessie and Sacha?"

Mari Belle heaved one of her trademark sighs and accompanied it with pinching the bridge of her nose. "There's not enough coffee in the world to tackle *that* one."

Will shivered. Hard to pretend everything was fine and he wouldn't have to pick whose house to go to first for Christmas, with Mari Belle confirming a problem. "They fighting over Donnie?"

"Of all her husbands, he's not the one I would've picked for them to break up over."

Will reached for Vera's strap, then almost cussed out loud when he caught Mari Belle watching.

Aunt Jessie and Sacha's friendship had outlasted three of Aunt Jessie's marriages, a couple of overnight stints in the Pickleberry Springs slammer—*We weren't trespassing, we were traversing a different ethereal plane*, Sacha had said both times Will bailed them out—and a breast cancer scare for Sacha two years back. Them fighting—over *Donnie*—wasn't right. Guy was fairly useless, far as Will could see. "Ain't that bad, is it?" Will said.

"It wouldn't be if Sacha would quit having her damn visions." Mari Belle latched on to the coffee and inhaled as though she were looking for life itself. "And if y'all would quit listening to her."

"She's family."

"She's a nut job."

"Still family."

"Aunt Jessie's family. And Aunt Jessie's picked Donnie over Sacha."

Will's stomach flipped as if he were on a roller coaster and dueling banjos rang out between his ears. His momma drank herself to death, his daddy went to prison, he'd had his share of trucks that broke down, his dog died and now the two women who had done the most to raise him—the two women who showed him what true friendship looked like, what supporting each other through thick and thin meant—were letting a man come between them.

His relationship with Lindsey probably fit in a country song too, but he didn't want to think on that too long.

"Lesson in there, Will," Mari Belle said. "Time to pick your smarts over all the psychic woo-woo."

He reached for a coffee cup of his own. They wouldn't agree on this one. Mari Belle never had warmed up to Sacha like Will had.

But then, Mari Belle hadn't been the one in the family telling him to go for his dreams when he came home from Colorado broken. She hadn't been the one telling him he was strong enough to heal his broken heart and find real love one day.

And Mari Belle wasn't the one who believed he should be here, where the music was talking to him again, and where he'd found Lindsey living out a life that was nothing like *her* dream.

He'd once sworn he'd love that girl with all his heart, forever. The longer he was here, the more he wondered if his purpose here wasn't to find his music but to help Lindsey find her joy.

If maybe the two were related.

Wouldn't be sharing that with Mari Belle though. Not when he already knew what she'd think of the idea.

"Go on then," he said. "Get it all out."

Mari Belle leaned her jean-clad hips onto the opposite counter and gave another big ol' Mari Belle sigh. "You already know everything I'm fixin' to say. So why do I need to say it?"

Alarm bells went off in Will's brain. Loud *abandon ship* alarm bells. Wasn't like Mari Belle to skip a chance to give him a good what-for. Especially after coming all this way.

"To make yourself feel better?" he said.

"It won't make me feel better, because you'll do whatever it is you plan on doing anyway, and I'll be the bad guy. Again."

Will tugged at his collar. He went for Vera's guitar strap —*dammit*. Would've been easier to deal with the hootin' and hollerin' than it was to deal with the fact that Mari Belle came up here to tell him she gave up.

She'd just taken guilt trips to a whole new level. "You've never been the bad guy," he said.

"No?"

"You've been the one we could count on to keep us straight. Even when we don't listen."

"You *don't* listen. None of you do."

He spread his hands. "Listening now."

"You didn't talk for a month after spring break," Mari Belle said softly. "To *anybody*."

Heat crept along his ears.

"And when you *did* start talking again," Mari Belle said, "you weren't you. Will, I'm happy as anybody that you made it, but you weren't you when you left for Nashville. I kept waiting for Mikey to call and say you'd drunk yourself into a ditch, that you got run over, that they needed me to come identify your body. Do you know how that feels? And now you're going right back to the girl who started it. No telling how it'll end this time."

Will wrapped an arm around his sister. "I'm being smart this time."

He was. He was getting good and attached, but he was being smart. Reminding himself Lindsey hadn't answered a few questions, that she'd given him a deadline, that he was here for the songs.

And if in the process he happened to put that smile on her face instead of the one just on her panties, then good for both of them.

"*This time.* This time, Will," Mari Belle said. "You hear yourself?"

He did. And he knew what she was thinking. "This ain't like what Momma did." The words left a trail of acid all the way from the bottom of his lungs on out his lips.

Probably because he wasn't so sure it was true. Lindsey wasn't the cheating type, but she was the heartbreaker type.

"You've got a lot of Momma in you," Mari Belle said, soft-like and gentle, which wasn't like Mari Belle at all. "I don't give a good glory what this does to your career. I don't want to lose my brother. She broke your heart. She broke *you.*"

"She didn't—"

"She *did*, and you talking about *this time* won't convince me," Mari Belle said. "You want a girl who only wants you once you make something of yourself?"

"Now hold on—"

"*Everybody* cares. Whether they want to or not, everybody cares."

"So you two had a good talk before she left this morning?"

Mari Belle crossed her arms. "She was quite gracious and polite and said all the right things."

"Bet that put a bee in your bonnet."

"You and I both know it's not what's on the outside that counts."

"Damn right. And she sees *me*. Not *Billy*. Not the guy onstage. Not the guy with the fans and the record deals and the big fat bank account. *Me.*"

Mari Belle heaved her *he's done gone and fallen off the turnip truck again, bless his heart* sigh. "Will—"

"She won't hurt me. Not like that again. I came here for the songs. Ask Mikey. Haven't written this good in years. I've got two more weeks before she's kicking me out, and I'm fixin' to use 'em. Got a good life to go back to this time. Got people who'll keep me going. Being here—I ain't Momma, Mari Belle. I won't give up on life if a girl doesn't want me. I've got people to live for. Got you. And Paisley. Aunt Jessie. Sacha. And a whole lot more."

"You're a damn fool driving yourself to a second heart-break, you know that?"

Will let himself indulge in a Mari Belle sigh. "You hanging out a while? Mikey's got a girl you should meet. We're going to her place for some ice cream thing tonight."

"You're fixin' to keep on being a moron, aren't you?"

"I'm fixin' to keep being me."

THE DRESS NAT had wrapped around Lindsey made her itch.

Not because there was anything wrong with the fabric, but because Lindsey couldn't help wondering what Will and Mari Belle were doing. If he'd still be there when she got home tonight. If she should've skipped the fitting and date with Noah and stayed home instead. Or perhaps if she should simply toss Will's belongings out the window and change the locks before either of them got more attached.

"You're not going to give us any details at all, are you?" Nat said around a mouthful of pins. They were over the show-room of Bliss Bridal, and Nat was working her magic with the dresses.

"Do I ever?"

"My mom didn't look near as disappointed as I would've expected about Billy being at your house," Kimmie piped up from her block across the room, where Nat's assistant was attacking her with pins too. "It's like somebody slipped a Xanax into her morning frosting."

"So you're saying she's hatching another plan?" Nat said.

"My last fortune cookie *did* say that the unexpected would

be both a blessing and a curse, but to beware of those who claim to have all the answers."

"That's a remarkably normal fortune," Lindsey said.

"Yes, well, I also dreamed she and Billy had a secret love child named Zanziboo who had the power to sneeze Tater Tots."

Nat chuckled. "No need to have magic psychic match-making skills to know *that* one would never work."

"Logic would dictate," Lindsey agreed.

The door banged open and the Queen General herself stepped in.

Kimmie's face went jaggedly scarlet. "Mom," she stammered. "This isn't—I'm not—we're—"

Nat was on her feet before Lindsey registered that she'd taken the pins out of her mouth. "Kimmie. Quiet."

Kimmie went mute. Lindsey pursed her lips to hide a smile. Nat and Marilyn weren't the enemies they'd once been, but they were hardly bosom buddies.

"Lindsey," Marilyn said. "By the power vested in me as president of the BRA, I require a word."

"And I require appointments." Natalie made a shooing motion. "You'll have to wait your turn."

"I'm afraid if we're going to have the Battle of the Boyfriends showcased in *Rural Reality*, we need a commitment *now* from Bliss's resident matchmaker to judge."

"And that relates to your needing me… how?" Lindsey said.

Marilyn smiled.

An honest, open, about-to-be-a-pain-in-the-ass smile. "My dear Lindsey, we've already discussed this. It's time you came home."

"Now wait a minute," Nat bristled.

Lindsey snagged her shoulder. "Down girl."

"She can't—"

"Watch and learn, young one." She assumed her best *I don't care what's in your frosting because I eat babies for breakfast* smile and narrowed her sights on Marilyn. "No."

Marilyn's happy faltered. "Bliss needs—"

"No." Lindsey did plenty for Bliss.

"And you've demonstrated excellent judgment—"

"No." Nudging Nat toward CJ was one thing. She'd had her reasons. Noticing that Mikey and Dahlia weren't bad together didn't mean she was a matchmaker. She hadn't even told anyone.

Except Will, and he wouldn't have told Marilyn.

Would he?

"Your father thinks—"

"For the final time," Lindsey said, "*no*." She mimicked Nat's shooing motion. "We're done here."

"We are *not* done, Miss Castellano."

"You are *so* done," Nat said.

"Kimberly—" Marilyn started.

Nat cleared her throat.

"You look lovely, dear," Marilyn said to her daughter. Her gaze turned to Lindsey and lingered a moment longer. She didn't say anything, but even after she left, she was still in the room.

"She's going to cream your spinach," Kimmie whispered.

"She has *Billy* judging the Battle of the Boyfriends. That wasn't about getting Bliss featured on *Rural Reality*. It was about her getting all of what she wants."

"She wants you to move home to Bliss and become a matchmaker?" Nat said.

"She wants Lindsey to find *me* a man," Kimmie said glumly.

"She wants to still be relevant in a time when Bliss is changing." Lindsey shifted on her block. There was nothing Marilyn could take from her. Not her job, not her home, not her self-respect. And even though Marilyn had brought three eligible Bliss bachelors to the last family dinner as prospective dates for Kimmie—under the guise of wanting to discuss some kind of official Bliss business while Nat was available too—Lindsey hadn't played along. "In her own misguided way, she probably also thinks this is her way of showing Dad that she accepts me. And it won't work. On any count."

But Lindsey's stomach still wobbled as though she'd been

boxed into a crowded elevator, and her muscles spasmed from the effort of holding still.

"Did she really ask you to help find me a husband?" Kimmie whispered. Her big baby blues were full of the open, vulnerable innocence that made Lindsey's heart ache. Kimmie had spent most of her life placating her mother, which was no small job. And while Lindsey suspected Marilyn wanted what was best for Kimmie, she didn't believe Marilyn could truly know what was *best* for Bliss's favorite quirky baker.

"She knows better," Lindsey said. "*You* are the only person who gets that choice, Kimmie. Don't let her take it from you." She twisted on the dressing block. "Did you put a puff on my butt?" she said to Nat, because she was about done with this psychic matchmaker thing. "I've never known a bride who wants her ass to look bigger."

"It's flattering. Trust me, you need the extra curve." She squatted and grabbed her tape measure. "Enough about the dresses. I want to hear about *Billy*. Why is it such a big secret what he likes on his pizza? Dad won't tell."

"The better question is what he likes in his cupcakes," Kimmie said. "And does he need a baker on the road? Mikey comes in from time to time, but he never talks about Billy at all. Just Dahlia."

"Those two are crazy adorable, aren't they?" Nat said. "I *never* would've seen that coming. Are you guys going to the tasting at The Milked Duck tonight?"

Lindsey had heard Dahlia sold out of tickets for the Risqué Flavor Tasting within two hours of the announcement on social media that Will would be there. Standing shoulder-to-shoulder with half of Bliss crammed into a tiny ice cream shop? Lindsey shuddered. "Too crowded."

"The Billy factor," Nat murmured.

And there went the thunderclouds in Lindsey's match-o-meter. Thinking about Will as Billy was enough to set it off.

Nat squinted at Lindsey. "Not an easy problem to solve, is it?"

"It's not a problem either of us intends to solve." Her reflection taunted her. A spinster posing in a white fluffy wedding gown. "Are you going, Kimmie? You and Dahlia could cater bridal showers together if you created some risqué-named cupcakes."

Kimmie's cheeks went their signature blotchy red. "My mom would string my beans. Heaven's Bakery doesn't do *that* kind of business."

"So do it on the side," Nat said. "What can Marilyn do to stop you? *And* then you could have assets that we-all-know-who can't touch."

Kimmie's baby blues were as wide as her cheeks were red. She darted a glance between Lindsey and Nat. "I could do that?" she half-whispered. "I mean, is it legal?"

"Did you sign any kind of contract or agreement with your mother when you started working at the bakery?" Lindsey asked.

Kimmie shook her head.

"Mom didn't have me sign one either when I started working here," Nat said. "Tradition holds enough weight on its own around here."

But traditions were changing. This time last year, having a divorced woman running a shop on The Aisle had been near scandalous. Bliss had embraced the Internet, reality television, and lavish weddings that cost as much as the gross domestic product of some third world nations, but otherwise, the little town hadn't yet caught up to even the second half of the twentieth century, never mind the twenty first.

"Did you sign anything when your mom sold half the bakery to pay for Knot Fest?" Lindsey asked. "Is your name on any of the business documents anywhere?"

"No."

"Then you're probably free and clear to have some fun with Dahlia." Lindsey still had a few friends from law school — it helped that she'd quit acknowledging her *gift* by then — and for her own piece of mind, she planned to give one of them a call on Monday. See if he could do some digging to make sure Kimmie wouldn't get in trouble with anyone other than her mother for using her talents to benefit herself for once.

They spent the next hour gossiping, making up sexy-sounding cupcake flavors, and pretending Marilyn didn't exist and that Lindsey was normal. When Lindsey left to get Noah from CJ, she hugged both Nat and Kimmie tight.

Because *they* were home, and they were her best friends, and one day soon—too soon—she would need them more than she could tell them.

WILL WASN'T surprised Lindsey declined his offer to take her to Dahlia's ice cream tasting Saturday night. He had a nice time with Mikey and Mari Belle, but he was mighty glad to get home to Lindsey's house all by himself, loaded down with dirty-named ice cream flavors to boot.

He found Lindsey reading in her living room—a book this time, instead of his Web page—and he got an honest smile when he handed her a carton of S'mores ice cream. "Wasn't on the menu, but I special ordered it for you," he told her.

"Thank you." She scooted down the couch and patted the warm seat. And since Will wasn't one to pass up the opportunity to touch the pretty girl who liked the country boy under all the Billy Brenton sparkle, he settled next to her with his own carton of ice cream, a chocolate number Dahlia called Chocolate Orgasm.

Rightly so.

"Never would've thought Mikey and me were coming here for him to find a girl," Will said. "Like her, though. She's good people. Good eye, lawyer lady."

Lindsey stiffened. "I'm not a matchmaker."

She had one of those woman-tones, the kind that meant he was supposed to understand what she wasn't saying, but he didn't have the whole Lindsey handbook.

Not yet.

"You got reason to think they're not good together?"

She shook her head, but she stayed stiff.

Will put his ice cream down and fingered the silky strands of her light hair. "Not making fun, you know."

"I know."

She probably would've yanked him a new one if she thought he was, so he figured she believed him. But it still took a while of his thumbs massaging her shoulder blades before she relaxed.

"I was invited to be one of the judges for the Battle of the Boyfriends again today," she said eventually.

"By the crazy cake lady?"

"She wants me to move to Bliss."

She hadn't said much about why she lived a town over instead of closer to her family. Will figured it was because her office was nearby. And there weren't any divorce lawyers in Bliss.

He'd checked. Simple curiosity. Because the lady did seem to like her hometown.

He had a notion she wasn't being invited to judge as a divorce lawyer. "That what you want?" he said.

"I want to be *me*."

"Who are you?"

She twisted to give him a *don't be a dumbass* look that was as loud as one of Mari Belle's sighs.

"Not talking about what you *do*," Will said. "Or what you don't do. Talking about who you *are*."

The glare faded, but the wariness that followed wasn't any better. "What I do defines me."

"What you do traps you." Wasn't his business, but he couldn't stop himself. "We're all more than a job or a gift. Me, I play the part of Billy. But deep down? I'm a kid from the sticks with a mishmashed little family and a guitar. I own that. *That's* who I am. Who are you?"

He felt her shiver. "I'm about two seconds from leaving this conversation," she said.

"If you knew who you were, you wouldn't be talking to me about the crazy cake lady wanting you to move to Bliss." Good thing she wasn't leaning on him anymore, or she'd feel how fast his heart was running. The girl was a mess. All put together on the outside, still fighting who she was on the inside. And he had a notion he was the only person in the world who could see her struggle. "If you knew who you were, you'd be fixin' to stay, or you'd be fixin' to go, but you wouldn't be sitting here thinking on it. Not with me. I'm gone in two weeks. You gotta live with you forever."

Her eyes went wide, body stiff, lips tight. There was that flash of panic, of pain, of fear.

He wasn't wrong. She liked him. Not for the exercise, but for the talking. For the listening. For the friendship.

"Your rules, remember?" he said.

She blinked quickly, then pulled herself off the couch. "My rules." She fumbled with the lid on her ice cream. "Let Wrigley out once more before you go to bed. And warn me the next time you have visitors coming."

Told him a lot, watching her retreat.

Didn't tell him if she still thought he was a bad match for her, or if she was scared to commit to his being a good match. Either way, he knew one thing for sure.

The lady was all mixed up on the inside.

Didn't take a psychic to see what she needed.

It took a man who could be bigger than himself, whether she loved him or left him, to show her that every last bit of her was perfect just as she was.

FIFTEEN

MARI BELLE LEFT for home around noon on Sunday. She got in a few more good sighs, along with a semi's worth of hints that Will needed to get his rear end to Nashville or Georgia, but he was still glad she'd come. Would've liked if Paisley had come too, but she'd spent the weekend with Aunt Jessie and Donnie.

Will also wished Lindsey hadn't been gone before the sun came up—catching up at the office, her note said—but he figured life was probably easier that way. Especially since Mikey was hanging out, moping.

His budding romance with Dahlia had gone for a hike through the pig slop, and now, while they were supposed to be working, Mikey was plucking out the same tune on his guitar. It was something new that should've been fast and fun, but instead sounded like a hound yowling over being plugged up.

The guy needed a drum kit to beat on instead of an old six-string.

Mikey being torn up over a girl—this was new.

Mikey being torn up over the girl Lindsey pegged as a good match—even if she wouldn't say so—was interesting, but probably only to Will.

Neither of them were making much progress on the songs for the next album. So when Will's phone rang, he breathed a sigh of relief at the distraction. Then grinned at the face on his screen. "Hey, peanut," he said into the phone.

"Uncle Will, I've given this a lot of thought, and I think you should take me on tour this summer."

Will choked on air. He stood and stretched, then went to the kitchen. "You talk to your momma about that?"

"Uncle Will. I go for the easy sell first. What do you think I am, eight? Besides, once you get married, you'll need a babysitter on the road, and won't it be better if I'm already used to the lifestyle?"

Crazy girl. Almost irritating too, because now he was wondering what Lindsey looked like in that wedding dress yesterday. "You having fun with Aunt Jessie and Donnie?" he asked Paisley.

"Yeah. I wanted to go looking for the Pickleberry Springs treasure with Sacha yesterday, but Aunt Jessie said Sacha was gone. Uncle Will, she told Aunt Jessie that Uncle Donnie wasn't in her future. But Aunt Jessie *really* likes Uncle Donnie. And he's nice. He bought me an ice cream cone and let me listen to Taylor Swift all day. But if Sacha says he's gone, he should be gone. Right?"

Even Will knew this was dangerous territory. Paisley wasn't supposed to be old enough for dangerous territory yet. Or ever. "All you need to know, peanut, is that boys are trouble," Will said. He needed to give Sacha a call, see what was going on there.

See if he could get his family patched back together.

Paisley did an admirable impression of a Mari Belle sigh. "Uncle Will. If I wanted that kind of advice, I would've called one of Momma's Officers' Ex-Wives Club friends. She must've yanked that knot hard in your butt if you won't tell me what you think. You know you're the only one with any sense when it comes to Sacha, right?"

"Nice seeing your momma," Will said. "Wish you could've been here too."

"Uncle Will," Paisley said, dragging his name out to about fourteen syllables. "Did you miss the part where I'm not eight anymore? You're changing the subject."

"How about I promise to call Aunt Jessie and Sacha right now?"

"That's the best I'm gonna get today, isn't it?"

"Yep."

"Well, you better call her quick, because there's a for sale sign in her front yard."

Will's heart went on a bender.

Sacha—moving? No.

No.

She'd baked him brownies when he got skinned knees. She'd taught him to read a map, taken him out hunting fairies when he was six and told him not to hurry into flirting with girls when he got older.

"Womenfolk overreact sometimes, peanut. It'll blow over," Will said.

He talked to Paisley a few more minutes about school, her new friends, the dog next door, anything and everything, all the while telling himself she was wrong about that for sale sign.

Before she let him go, she made him repeat his promise of extra tickets for her neighbors to go with them to his show at Gellings Air Force Base weekend after next, then made him promise to think about letting her come out on the road with him.

He'd think about it.

Other guys took their whole families out on the road. But the odds that Mari Belle would trust Paisley to him were pretty much zero. Even if he could talk Mari Belle into it, Paisley's dad would probably nix the idea.

Will put in a quick call to Sacha, who said she needed to get ready for a psychic convention over near Savannah, and told him to write good songs today. When he asked if she was selling her house, she told him he needed to worry over taking care of *him*, not her, and all but hung up on him. So he called Aunt Jessie, who gushed about how polite and sweet Paisley was and how much Donnie loved her too, and how nice it was to have Paisley and Mari Belle and *real family* close again, and then said she had to go prep a big ol' fried chicken dinner.

Both conversations left him with that sick feeling in his gut as if his life wouldn't ever right itself again. Wasn't like he was a kid anymore, but it still sat wrong that his family was breaking.

He grabbed himself one of the cartons of ice cream he'd bought at Dahlia's flavor tasting last night—girl made good ice cream, and the names were right funny too—and took himself to the sunroom.

Mikey was frowning over the computer, listening to a recording Will had made. "What is this crap?" Mikey said.

"The good kind of crap. You do me a favor?"

"Does it involve us leaving?"

"Involves you asking your momma to check and see what's going on with Aunt Jessie and Sacha. Paisley says Sacha's house is for sale."

Mikey finally looked up. "Sacha's moving?"

"Sounds like it." And the thing with Sacha was, there was no telling if she'd move the three blocks it would take to be across town in Pickleberry Springs, or if she'd up and move to Mexico. All depended on what her visions and the spirits told her to do. "You still friends with that private investigator lady?"

Mikey's face went an unusual ruddy color. "Yeah."

"Might want her number myself if things go bad." He hoped it wouldn't come to that, but he couldn't let Sacha walk away.

She was still *Will's* family, even if she wasn't Aunt Jessie's anymore.

"Sure." Mikey's gaze dropped to the ice cream, and he grimaced. "Put that shit away."

"You wanna talk about it?"

"We girls now? Eat ice cream and talk about our feelings?"

Better than talking about Sacha and Aunt Jessie. "Goes good with the pouting you got going on."

"Ain't one to talk, buckaroo."

Will shrugged and dug into the ice cream. Hazel's Nuts, it was labeled. "You name this one?"

Mikey growled.

Will took that as a *yes*. He took another bite. Swallowed.

Damn good ice cream. "Girl who can make ice cream like this doesn't come around every day."

"Shove it."

"You want, I can put in a good word for you."

Mikey leveled a flat stare at Will. The kind that usually meant nothing good was about to come out of his mouth. Might could've meant one of them would end the day sporting a black eye too.

Will should've asked Lindsey if she had any valuables in here she didn't want getting broke.

"You playing matchmaker like your girl now?" Mikey said.

"She's staying out of this one. Told me she liked Dahlia too much to make the girl suffer."

Mikey shoved to his feet and paced in front of the fireplace. "She said something about us?"

"You believe it if I tell you?"

"No."

Will shrugged again.

Mikey scraped a hand over his bald head and made a quick turn. "You know what? Who needs this shit? Lots of girls out there. I'll just — I'll just go find another one."

First time Will had *ever* heard Mikey hurting over a girl.

He shivered one of those shivers he got when Sacha took it in her mind to tell him something.

Lindsey saw more than she believed.

"Could go get her back, man," Will said to Mikey.

"No point." Mikey pushed a fist into his other hand. "Even if I was a one-woman kind of guy, she doesn't want me. And I — I don't deserve her."

Where was Mari Belle when a guy needed a good sigh? "Then get over it. We gonna write songs today, or you gonna be a girl?"

Mikey eyed the guitar he'd brought over. Then Will's ice cream. "Suppose we're writing."

And for a few hours, they were almost who they used to be. No girls, no pressure, no family problems. Just two buddies working on making something big while a dog snoozed at their feet.

Same as they'd done almost half their lives.

LATE MONDAY AFTERNOON, Lindsey was debating how many ibuprofen it would take to get rid of her headache when her assistant buzzed in. "You have a visitor, Miss Castellano."

She grimaced. She'd successfully avoided Will since Saturday night, but there had been something in his expression that had told her their conversation about who she was wasn't over. And that it wouldn't be over until he said it was over, not even if she managed to avoid him the entirety of the next two weeks.

Who she was wasn't his business.

But she had to wonder if she could interpret her match-o-meter readings about him better if she *did* know who she was. No one else made her doubt her career and her choices. Not the way Will did.

The people in Bliss thought she'd turned her back on their core beliefs. But Will didn't care about Bliss. He simply believed in her gift. He accepted it. He didn't think it made her weird, and he didn't question it. He quite possibly understood it and accepted it better than she did.

The problem was, she didn't *want* the gift. And she didn't know how to explain it to him.

"Send him in," she said to her assistant.

The door opened, except it wasn't Will who strolled through her door.

Lindsey straightened her lips and her backbone.

Four. She should've popped four ibuprofen, at least an hour ago.

She nodded once. "Mikey."

He was in his usual Billy Brenton ball cap, a red pullover, tight jeans, cowboy boots, and his growly face was firmly in place. He shut her door with an ominous click.

But the bloodshot eyes and sadness radiating from him

suggested he wasn't here to reinforce Mari Belle's message from Saturday.

Lindsey leaned back and gestured to the two chairs across from her desk. "Make yourself comfortable. Coffee? Water?"

"Are Dahlia and me a good match?"

He had a droop in his posture, stubble on his cheeks and the desperate look of a heartbroken man.

"Are we a good match?" he repeated into the silence.

She gave herself a mental shake. "Do *you* think you're a good match?"

"See, I know the answer to *that* question, and it doesn't answer the one I asked you."

Were he anyone other than Will's best friend, she would've suggested he take his hostility and shove it somewhere the sun didn't shine, then had the firm's security help him with that. "We've met once? Twice?"

He paced behind the two brown leather chairs opposite Lindsey's desk, a flurry of color against the dark paneled walls. "Don't go talking in circles around me," he growled. "I got other bones to pick with you too."

"In case you missed the sign on the door, I specialize in bad matches. Specifically, in terminating marriages at the request of the people who make their decisions about the validity of their relationships for themselves."

He stopped and turned to fully face her, pulling himself to his full height. "Are we a bad match?"

Every instinct Lindsey possessed instructed her to evade the question. This was Will's best friend. If she gave him bad love advice, if she gave him false hope, or if he decided she was lying because he wasn't inclined to believe her, she'd be screwing things up for one of the few people in Will's life who had always loved him simply because he was Will.

No pressure. No pressure at all.

But was Will right?

Did she truly *own* who she was? Or had she been hiding from herself, messing with her own cosmic balance by ignoring what made her unique?

"I don't know Dahlia well," Lindsey said, "but she strikes

me as the sweet, kindhearted type of woman it would be all too easy to walk all over."

Mikey paced more, adding a knuckle crack to it. "Are we a bad match?" he repeated.

"And I don't know you well," Lindsey said, "but I have been subjected to dozens of BillyVision episodes, and you don't strike me as the type to settle down, never mind with a small-town, plain girl like Dahlia."

He rounded on her. "Don't you *ever* call her plain."

Lindsey lifted a practiced brow. "Is she your usual type?"

"My usual type sucks." One corner of his mouth started to hitch, but a scowl took over. "*Jesus*. I can't even make a blow job joke." He pointed at Lindsey. "Last time. Are we a bad match?"

"I don't know what she's putting in her ice cream, but it appears to be working."

Mikey growled.

Lindsey swallowed a smile. Wasn't so hard with the way her heart was suddenly tripping as though she'd had too much coffee. "I barely saw you together," she said, fully aware that she was tiptoeing a line that a divorce lawyer probably shouldn't toe, "but I did not notice any overt signs that you were a bad match. For whatever that's worth." She didn't particularly want to tell him, but she *did* want to know how it felt to say the words aloud. And it felt easy. Not right, not wrong. Not simple, not complicated. Just easy.

"So we're not a bad match," Mikey asked.

"How much do you like her?"

He dropped into a chair and thrust his head into his hands, then mumbled something.

"I'm sorry?"

Mikey eyed her from beneath his ball cap, gray eyes swimming with sadness. The guy looked more pathetic than Wrigley. "She dumped me."

"You want her back."

There went the suspicious eye again.

"Why are you here, Mikey?"

He slouched. "To tell you to leave Will the hell alone." And even with the pain and the heartbreak and the desperation still haunting his expression, there was a steely rigidness behind his words.

There went her shivers again. First Mari Belle, now Mikey.

She'd hurt Will fifteen years ago. She knew that.

But such strong warnings from his sister and best friend all these years later made her wonder what she didn't know.

Lindsey grabbed one of her business cards and scribbled Bliss Bridal's number on the back. "The Battle of the Boyfriends is coming up. I believe you're acquainted with Pepper Blue. She's on the planning committee. She'll get you registered. And then you go grovel. Go grovel and beg and promise Dahlia everything you can give her, but don't you dare lie to her. I don't do good matches—that part's up to you. If you want her, go get her. If you don't, leave her alone. But don't blame me for your choices."

He took the card. "If you hurt Will—"

"There is nothing you can threaten me with that could possibly be any worse than what I've already threatened myself with," she said.

Not because she wanted to admit it, but because Mikey mattered to Will.

"I hate it here." Mikey fanned the card against his fingers. "Cold. No sweet tea or fried okra. You're here. But I got a notion I might be staying."

"How lovely for all of us."

Mikey stood. "I wasn't here," he said.

"I can agree to that on one condition."

He crossed his arms.

"When you marry her, don't even think of asking me to give a toast."

"Ain't gonna be a problem." He stepped toward the door. "And don't hurt Will."

"He's a big boy. He can take care of himself."

Mikey's growly face popped out again.

"But I'm glad he has friends like you watching out for him," Lindsey said with a sweet smile.

"I really don't like you," Mikey grumbled.

"And I'm okay with that."

She was such a liar.

She didn't mind being disliked. But she did mind being hated by Will's closest friends and family for reasons she didn't fully comprehend.

Mikey left her office, and she turned to log off her computer. Five minutes later, she was on her way home.

SIXTEEN

AS SOON AS Lindsey walked into the house, she heard Will. He was talking to someone, but when no one answered, she realized he was on the phone. She pulled her shoes off, then made her way through the kitchen.

"Been getting a lot of work done," he was saying. "Yeah. Good songs. Wrote one for you too, Aunt Jessie. I call it 'Shut That Door and Take Off Them Muddy Shoes Before You Ask Me for Sweet Tea.'"

Even as her heart still tripped after Mikey's visit, Lindsey smiled. That was Will. *Her* Will, the Will she remembered.

He was right. He knew who he was.

"Wanted to write one for Sacha too, but she's not answering today," he said. "You know anything about that? Where she might be?"

Lindsey started toward his voice.

"Now, hold on," he said. "You're changing the subject on me, and Mari Belle's overreacting. All y'all keep acting like I don't have the sense God gave a rock, but I—"

Lindsey paused in the doorway to the sunroom. Will stood at the window, facing away from her, phone to his ear, ball cap backward and curls peeking out. He was in a green plaid over-shirt and the jeans Lindsey loved—the things that denim did to his rear did things to the smileys on her panties. But even with the broad shoulders and ass to admire, her gaze lingered on his white socks.

She wasn't a sock person. Honestly, who was? But she was a *home* person. And Will, in socks in her home, was *home*. Snow fluttered outside, barely visible in the rapidly darkening evening. And a blizzard warred with a beach sunrise on her match-o-meter.

She breathed slowly, deeply, savoring the subtle scent of him that had lingered in her house since he arrived.

Home.

She'd called this structure *home* since she bought it. But it had never been this warm kind of home before.

"Not fair to judge her on who we were fifteen years ago," he said.

Lindsey froze.

"Sacha ain't wrong on this, Aunt Jessie. I need to be here. And you need to listen to her. You need to give Lindsey a chance. People change. For the better as often as for the worse. You the same person you were before you met Donnie?" Will's voice was getting thicker, his drawl stronger. "Lot of life lessons happen in a decade. And I ain't Momma. Don't you start too. Not when you're throwing out your lifelong best friend for a guy you haven't known more than two years."

A rough tongue licked Lindsey's hand. She blinked against an unwelcome sting, and went to her knees to scratch Wrigley's fur. "Who's a good boy?" she murmured.

She saw Will turn in her peripheral vision. Wrigley flopped to the ground and showed Lindsey his belly, so she gave him a good, double-handed belly rub.

Thirteen more days, and she'd have to say good-bye to Wrigley too.

"Looks like my dinner just got here," Will said into the phone. "Gotta go. You go talk to Sacha and make up, then tell her I said hi and call if y'all need bail money again. I mean it, Aunt Jessie. Get on back to causing trouble. Love you."

Will pocketed his phone and turned all the way to face Lindsey. "Hey."

Wrigley's tongue lolled out the side of his mouth. Lindsey kept rubbing until she found the spot that made his leg twitch. "Bail money?" she said as evenly as she could manage while Wrigley's leg fired away.

"Sacha does moon worship sessions in ol' Farmer Beauregard's cotton fields every full moon, and she and Aunt Jessie are always out looking for the legendary Pickleberry Springs treasure where they ain't always welcome. Don't mean any harm, but some of the sheriff's deputies got sticks up their butts."

The man had an interesting family, she'd give him that. But it didn't change the fact that they didn't like Lindsey. "So dinner's on you tonight?"

He stepped toward her, hands in pockets, taking his sweet Southern time. "Your turn to cook. Got everything you need in there. Fresh okra for frying, turnips for soup, pig snout for kabobs..."

"Great. I'll call Mari Belle for the recipe. She might could tell me how to make sweet tea too."

"Getting the hang of it, lawyer lady. I'm impressed." He held out a hand, but she didn't know if it was an offer of a truce, that they forget what she'd heard and how many members of his family hated her, or if it was a simple gentlemanly offer to help her to her feet.

Either way, she took his hand.

Though everyone who mattered to him told him to walk away, though Lindsey herself told him to walk away, he was still here.

And she was still glad.

He didn't stop with pulling her to her feet though. He also pulled her against his warm, solid body. He pressed his cheek to hers, threaded his fingers through her hair, cradled her head. "Missed you."

I missed you too. "Songs dry up?"

"No. I missed you."

She leaned into him, forcing air into her lungs, then out again. His breath on her neck should've inspired those good tingles and his fingers in her hair should've made the smileys on her panties sit up and beg for attention too.

Instead, her skin itched and her chest couldn't expand big enough. She didn't need to feel trapped with Will. He wouldn't hurt her. He didn't mean to crowd her.

Still, she yanked away. "Back in a minute." And she darted out the back door.

The winter air enveloped her, the darkening sky hazy with snowflakes that spread into infinity. Her nostrils stuck together, and the rush of cold air was like ice in her throat. But her lungs opened, and the tension in her shoulders faded to a shudder.

"Lindsey?"

Will was tucked into the doorway, a shadow against the bright lights from inside the house.

"Tell me about your parents," she said.

He scuffed a socked foot against the doorframe. She wanted him to hug her again, but she also wanted him to stay where he was. She wanted him to answer, and she wanted him to tell her it was none of her business.

She wanted him to enforce her three-week rule, with all the requisite precautions of *not* getting attached, because she was failing at staying within her own boundaries.

"Don't remember my daddy," Will said. "Everybody says my momma was crazy in love with him, but he wasn't dependable. In and out of her life, couldn't keep a job, spent some time in prison. Mari Belle remembers him coming by from time to time. He'd say the right things, my momma would take him in, and then he'd be gone. One day, nearabouts Christmas, she saw him kissing another woman. Went crazy mad, started drinking, and didn't stop till she was dead."

"Were you living with your aunt then?"

"She took us in after."

Lindsey rubbed her hands over her arms, loneliness and pain and fear crashing through her on behalf of the little boy he'd been, of the loss he'd suffered. "That's awful."

"Don't remember much of it. Mari Belle does, but she doesn't talk about it." He stepped outside, stocking feet and all.

"We got lucky. Probably better off with Aunt Jessie and Sacha anyway."

He stopped an arm's length away from her.

"After spring break"—she sucked in another icy breath, blinked back the sting behind her eyes—"what happened?"

She didn't want to know. The don't-fall-harder rule demanded that she let it go. But she *had* to know.

Because he mattered. He mattered, and she'd hurt him, and she didn't want to hurt him again.

"Truth?" he said.

She didn't answer. And her baby-eater glare at the implication she didn't want to know the truth was half-strength.

He shifted toward her, but then rocked on his heels and blew into his fist. They could've had this conversation inside, where it was warm. They *should've*. But she had already waited too long to ask him.

"Wasn't pretty," he said.

"How not pretty?"

"I loved you." His voice came soft, lyrical, sad. Neither of them had ventured into the L-word territory, and hearing it from his lips put a pang in Lindsey's chest. "I loved the way you smiled at me, the way you threw yourself into life, the way you knew what you wanted. The way you kept going and trying and smiling even when your friends were snubbing you. I didn't have much direction then, but you made me want it. Made me want to be somebody, so the next time we met, you couldn't tell me I was just some bubba."

"I was so wrong, Will."

"I hid away for a few weeks, writing songs." His words were getting softer, sadder. "Aunt Jessie made me eat. Mari Belle called from school four times a day, even if I didn't talk to her. Sacha kept telling me she was having visions that I'd have a good life, that I'd get what I needed, that I was perfect the way I was. Mikey tried to help me write some songs, but I was crazy. Knew what I wanted to say, didn't want anybody else to help."

"I'm sorry," she whispered. It was woefully inadequate, but it was what she had.

He ducked his head. "That first week after, I knew what my momma was feeling, being so crazy wrapped up in someone. Won't lie—I had some moments of feeling like my life was over. But the more I wrote, the better I felt. Still couldn't stop writing though. Needed to write. Needed to play. Needed to believe in myself the way I thought you did for those few days."

She didn't know if her shivers were coming from hurting him or from the cold, but she couldn't stop. And she didn't want to go inside. She didn't want to be warm.

She wanted to be right again. Whole. Not sorry anymore.

"Wasn't all you," he said. "I let 'em think it was, some days because I missed you, some days because I hated you, but some of it was me looking for where I fit. Killing the doubts. Aunt Jessie, Mari Belle, they didn't want me to go after my dreams. They didn't want me disappointed when I didn't make it."

"You were all alone."

"I wasn't, but I was. They loved me. But they didn't know how to make me feel invincible. Not like you did. Sacha told me to go for it, but even when she had her visions, I didn't believe her the way I believed you. She didn't say anything about my dreams until after you did."

"Will, we had less than a week—"

"Lightning strikes in a millisecond, changes the world forever."

No. People didn't change other people like that. They couldn't. "How long did you write?"

He rubbed a hand through his hair, then down his whiskers. "A month. Maybe longer. One day, I ran out of songs to write. Guess I used up everything I had bottled up all my life. So I went back out in the world, found songs in more places, about more things. Kept building that catalog like you told me to. Told Mikey I was going to Nashville. They all thought I'd lost my mind. They didn't see me like you saw me. Back home, in school, I was always Mari Belle's dumb kid brother, not a guy who could be somebody. I kinda thought I'd lost my mind too, but you—you saw me different. You showed me that I could see me different. I held on to that. Somewhere in the back of my mind, I always hoped you still believed in me too."

"I used to wonder if you were selling tires or still sweeping floors."

"My two backup plans," he said.

It should've been funny, but it wasn't. "I didn't know you made it until you walked into Nat's wedding. I felt like such a fool. And now, Mari Belle, Mikey, your aunt—they're right, Will. You should walk away."

His steady gaze didn't waver. "Why?"

"Because you built this. This big life, the dreams, the superstardom. *You* did. This is yours, and you need to keep it. I always thought you'd still be in Pickleberry Springs, raising a bunch of kids with a sweet woman who liked to listen to you play with your band at the local hole-in-the-wall."

"Wouldn't have been a bad life."

"But you *are* Billy Brenton. You can say you're a simple country boy with a guitar, but that's what makes you a superstar. *You.* All of you. You're a gift to the world, and I can't be a part of that world."

He tugged at his shirt, a familiar gesture she'd come to understand meant he was reaching for his guitar. "Why?"

"Because I'm a mess. Because *you* make me a mess. And you have too many people who need you for me to make you a mess again." She pointed between them. "We're toxic, Will. We screw with each other's heads, we—"

"I wrote *Hitched* about you. Not just 'Snow Angel Smiles.' The whole album. It went platinum in a month. Set all kinds of records. Won some big awards. It's been out a year, and I still get over a hundred emails a week from people who say one song or another on it touched their life. That ain't toxic, Lindsey. That's goodness out in the world."

That wasn't her. It wasn't them. "It's been *years*—"

"And you stuck." He tapped his heart. "You stuck here. For *years*."

"That was you. Your songs. Not my influence. It's all you."

"It was *you*." He pulled out his wallet and shuffled through it, then held out a folded paper. "You know why I went to Nashville?"

She eyed his offering then took and gingerly opened it. The creases were so worn, the paper so soft, the ink so faded, the words inside were barely legible.

"Step one," he said. "Write a bunch of great songs."

Her breath caught.

"Step two," he continued. "Take them to Nashville. Clean toilets until someone recognizes your genius."

"You kept this?" she whispered.

"Step three." His hands settled at her waist. "Show them you can play and sing too."

"Step four, take over the world." She dropped her head to his shoulder, still clutching the paper.

"*You* drove me to Nashville," he said into her hair. "Without you, Billy Brenton wouldn't exist. *You* did that. You were my inspiration. Still are. After *Hitched*, I couldn't write. Here, I can't stop."

"It's not me."

"It's you. It's always been you." His scruffy cheek brushed hers. "Come inside," he murmured, his breath hot on her ear. "Let me show you."

She clutched him and buried her nose in his neck. *I love you.* She always had. *Stay*. Forever.

Here.

With her.

"Will, I can *not* give you more than another thirteen days. I shouldn't even give you thirteen more minutes."

"Deal's a deal, lawyer lady. And since you're dumping me again, I have to get a lifetime's worth of songs out of the next thirteen days."

"Will—"

"Aunt Jessie, Mari Belle, Mikey, they're all wrong. You didn't break me. You showed me who I am. Who I could be." He brushed a thumb over her cheek. Snowflakes settled in his lashes and his whiskers. "About time I return that favor."

And like that, she surrendered. "Okay," she whispered.

He pulled her inside, then shut and locked the door. He

lowered the lights, then lowered her to the sunroom couch, then lowered his mouth to hers, and he loved her.

He loved her like he couldn't live without her. He loved her like he knew her better than she knew herself. He loved her like they truly could have their forever.

And for one night, she let herself indulge in the fantasy too.

WILL HAD twelve days to break through Lindsey's barriers, and he didn't plan to waste a single minute.

He knew he'd most likely fail—she had given Wrigley an extra-long hug on her way out the door to work this morning —but he also knew the lady saw something when she looked at him. The same kind of something she saw when she'd looked at Mikey and Dahlia.

He even had a good grip on her objections to him. To *them*. She didn't like crowded spaces, and his life as Billy was one crowd after another. She liked her privacy, and he lived life in public. She knew his family didn't like her, and she'd had enough of not being liked for one lifetime.

He could solve all of her problems one way or another. Tonight, he was starting on that last one. Suckers wasn't too crowded on a Tuesday night. Sure, there were a few fans asking for autographs and pictures, but not like there had been at first. The town had gotten used to him, and they were pretty darn good at giving him space.

Mikey and Dahlia were with them. His buddy had made up right good with his girl this morning, right there in Lindsey's house while Will had to listen. And he'd heard things he didn't want to in the process, so Will made Mikey promise to come out and give Lindsey a real shot.

And because Dahlia was as good for Mikey as her ice cream was sweet and perfect, when she agreed with Will, big ol' tough Mikey had agreed with a goofy grin on his face.

He was even behaving himself tonight, making a real effort and everything, including Lindsey when he told stories. "Hey, Billy, you remember that time Saffron switched all the toothpaste in the band bus with diaper cream?"

"Oh, gross," Dahlia said.

Lindsey grimaced over her wine.

"Remember all y'all hollering about it." Will remembered discovering the prank the hard way on his own bus too.

"I don't understand that," Dahlia said. "Don't you *look* at the toothpaste tube before you put it on your toothbrush?"

"You do when you're at my house," CJ said from behind the bar.

"Your wife know that?" Mikey asked.

He grinned. "Nah, I'll let her figure that out on her own when the time's right."

Lindsey's gaze was stuck on something across the room. Will followed it, and discovered she was watching a preppy guy and a bookish-looking girl. The dude was trying hard to get the lady's attention. And by the soft smile on Lindsey's face, and by the shivers on Will's neck, he was betting the dude had a good chance. "Playing matchmaker?" he murmured to her.

She started. "Just watching."

"Good match?"

She frowned briefly, then turned to him with mixed messages shooting out her pores. "They're not bad." She shrugged, but it wasn't a casual shrug. It was a stepping-out-of-the-comfort-zone shrug.

Will watched the lady shake her head at the guy, then slide off her stool and gather her coat.

Lindsey didn't move.

Will nudged her. "You should say something."

She slid a glance at him. "I don't know them."

"But they're a good match."

"No, they're not bad. There's a difference."

Mikey and Dahlia were sitting there, happy as lovebugs in spring. And Lindsey was the only one who saw that coming. Will nodded toward them. "Pretty sure you're better at this *good match* stuff than you give yourself credit for."

"Nice try. I don't know them, but I'm well-known around here. They'll think I'm trolling for clients."

"Or she might think twice about leaving."

"If it's meant to be, they'll find each other again." She turned her attention to her wine.

"Hey, Billy, tell Dahlia she needs to come see the show at Gellings," Mikey said.

Will absently nodded at Dahlia, even though he was tracking the other girl's path toward the door. "You should come. Be a good time."

"We still got VIP tickets?" Mikey asked.

"Think so. Call Cassidy."

Will could stop the girl. But she hadn't made any sign she recognized him, which put him in a worse spot than it put Lindsey. Because a guy setting up another guy—especially one he didn't know—was about the same as a divorce lawyer playing matchmaker. Awkward, unexpected, and more than a little uncomfortable.

He could see Lindsey's problem here.

"I can't take time away from The Milked Duck," Dahlia said.

"Sweet pea, time off's necessary for your creativity," Mikey declared. "Can't keep making perfect ice cream without new inspirations. Ain't that right, Billy?"

Will spun on his stool. He was fixin' to stop the girl walking out, because somebody had to.

His reputation could take the hit. If it helped show Lindsey that she needed confidence in the good as well as the bad of what she saw, then it was what he'd do.

But the door swung open, and a mess of chaos walked in the door.

Kimmie balanced two boxes in her mittened hands. Her gait was clipped and dread dragged her lips into a frown that set Will's shoulders to hunching.

"Sorry we're late," she said. "Mom had to mash someone's potatoes, and then the cupcakes fell over in the car."

The girl Lindsey had been watching slipped out the door. Kimmie slid the boxes between Will and Mikey, and she popped the lid open on the top one. "Sorry about your face," she said to Mikey.

Dahlia squealed and clapped her hands. Mikey's jaw came unhinged. And Lindsey laughed the sweetest peal of laughter Will had ever heard.

A dozen cupcakes were in the box, all decorated with a remarkable likeness of Mikey and his bald head. Except for the smushed-up part on some of them.

"Darlin', those are perfect." Will pulled out his phone to snap a picture. He let go of his own plans of matchmaking, saying a prayer Lindsey was right and her good match would make it work for themselves. "Mikey's momma's gonna be right proud."

"I had a dream you had a psychic mongoose who could control the weather, but then it started raining turtle shells, and the ninjas knew if they could get the mongoose to eat bacon, it would snow fairy dust instead."

"Kimmie." Lindsey smiled. "Will's a friend."

She emphasized the *Will* and the *friend* part, and he had a moment of thinking she was still doing him the bigger favors in their relationship. Wasn't often he got to be *him* out in public.

Kimmie swiped at a curly blonde flyaway and shoved it behind her ear. "He's still smokin' hot, and I'm not convinced my mother hasn't made a voodoo Lindsey cake to destroy your chances so she can set me up instead."

Lindsey squeezed Will's thigh with her free hand, which he took to mean *don't treat her like a weirdo*. "He is hot," Lindsey agreed, "and he's also a *friend*, and we'll take care of your mother."

Kimmie glanced around the room, her gaze lingering on a table of men who played baseball for the Bliss Bachelors, the local minor league team. "Actually," she started.

"Aw, shit," CJ said.

Kimmie winced so hard Will thought even her hot pink shirt got in on the wincing.

Marilyn marched through the door, Lindsey's dad on her heels.

"Yeah," Kimmie said quickly. "Sorry. I tried to text you, but she had her cell-signal blocker on."

"She has one of those?" CJ said.

"She channels it naturally when she's displeased."

Kimmie shot another look at the table of men.

"They're all terrible matches for you," Lindsey said.

Kimmie blew out a breath and flashed a pained smile. "Thanks."

Marilyn descended on them. "Billy. So lovely to see you again." She did a fancy-lady air-kiss to his cheeks, then grimaced at Mikey. "And...you too. Lindsey, Dahlia. You're entertaining our guests?"

"Best hospitality I ever had," Mikey said.

"That's because you're getting laid again," Dahlia said. "But I'm warning you, it better not get all same-old, same-old, now that you're serious about me."

Marilyn made a strangled noise. Will choked on his own spit. Lindsey's shoulders shook with soft laughter. "I like her." She raised her glass to Mikey. "Well done."

Mikey stood and grabbed Dahlia by the hand. "I'll show you *same old*, woman."

"Not in my bathroom," CJ said. "Take it out back."

"Screw out back. I'm renting us an airplane. You're about to join the Mile High Club, sweet pea."

"I don't know if you should aim so high to start," Dahlia said. "You can only go down from there." But she still finger-waved to the group. "Kimmie, I'll call you later. Lindsey, I'll make him say five nice things about you before I put out." She grabbed the top box. "Can we take these cupcakes? Thanks so much!" And the two of them danced out the door.

"*This* is why I never enter this establishment," Marilyn said.

"Oh, I don't think that's the only reason," Lindsey replied.

Her dad slid a *behave* look in her direction, but Will grinned.

That was his girl. Cheeky and spunky and bright.

"Whiskey, Arthur?" CJ said.

The older man shuddered like he'd never met a whiskey he

liked. "A coke. And I'm getting Noah a drum set for his birthday."

"Go great with the three sets my sisters already sent him."

"Pretty sure we're trumped for life, Dad." Lindsey patted the stool on her other side. "Might want to rethink that whiskey."

"No whiskey," Arthur reiterated.

"You sure?" CJ said. "Marilyn's buying."

"She's not allowed inside unless she buys a round," Lindsey murmured to Will. "I made her sign a contract."

Will got the feeling there was more to that story, but he didn't ask. Instead, he smooched her cheek, right in front of her father and the crazy cake lady and everyone in the bar. "A woman of many talents. I like it."

"Cupcakes, Billy?" Marilyn said. "Lindsey tells us you like peach cobbler, so Kimberly created these for you."

"I had a dream that coconut dinosaurs could play harmonicas made of fire icicles," Kimmie said.

Will looked between mother and daughter.

"No, she's not adopted," Lindsey said.

"You get used to it, man," CJ said to Will. "Life in Bliss." He turned and rang a bell. "Round on the QG," he called.

A halfhearted cheer went up in the joint, most of it from a guy deep in his cups at the far end of the bar. Three tables cleared out, their occupants dropping cash on their tables and darting for the door. CJ muttered something and left to take care of the baseball players and the few others who stayed.

If Marilyn noticed, she didn't give any indication. She simply smiled brighter—and scarier—at Will. "Did Lindsey mention she'll be judging the Battle of the Boyfriends alongside you?"

"Marilyn…" Arthur said.

"Think she mentioned she's washing her hair that night," Will said.

Lindsey squeezed Will's leg again. And he was near about certain that one was a *thank you.* "How's the cabin this week?" she asked her dad.

"Peaceful. Quiet." Arthur eyed Will. "Should come on out

this spring if you're still around. Have a man weekend. CJ, you'll bring Noah?"

"Anytime," CJ called.

"Right on a pond," Arthur said. "See a lot of deer."

"Fishing good?" Will asked.

"Best, unless the girls come. They get to talking, and the fish go into hiding."

"I don't think Billy's relocating to Bliss, Dad," Lindsey said.

"It's lovely here in the summer," Marilyn interjected. "Have you seen the official brochures for Knot Festival?" She made a noise that would've been a giggle from any other woman, but which sounded more like a monkey sneezing off-key to Will's ear. "Our dear CJ and Arthur are both former husbands of the year. And you missed *quite* the show watching them compete at the Golden Husband Games."

And they thought his Southern-talk was bad? Will made a note to ask somebody to translate all that later. "Sounds like some good entertainment."

"It was something," Lindsey said. She passed him a cupcake sprinkled with cobbler crumbles over peach pie filling, then took one for herself. Kimmie, Will noticed, was diving into a slice of coconut cream pie.

"It's her chocolate," Lindsey said to Will. "The cupcakes aren't poisoned."

"Lindsey," Arthur said.

"Oh, isn't she funny." Marilyn tittered.

Lindsey looked at her father and Marilyn. "Not something I'm generally accused of," she said lightly. Will watched her in the mirror over the bar, and when shivers raced down his neck again and he realized what he was seeing, he choked on his cupcake.

Lindsey turned to him, brows raised. "You okay?"

He looked past her to her dad, then back and raised his own brows.

Lindsey's cheeks went pink and her eyes wide. "Don't—"

"Wouldn't dream of it," he forced out. "You driving home?" He reached for his beer. Would take at least four of those to get rid of the images forming in his head. Lindsey didn't think her dad and the crazy Bliss lady were a bad match.

"And now you see why I don't want the *gift*," she muttered.

He did.

He definitely did. He wouldn't want to live with that sort of knowledge either.

"You two are simply adorable," Marilyn declared. "Such a shame we weren't able to get the *Rural Reality* people to come to the Battle of the Boyfriends. The cameras would love you, and it would've been such a boost for Bliss to be featured."

Lindsey shifted, and Will could tell she was working up a good what-for. So this time, he squeezed *her* leg. "Talked to my people," he said. "We're fixin' to bring cameras. Do a two-part BillyVision episode on Bliss."

Marilyn blinked. And then blinked again. "Billy Brenton, you are *too* kind. By the power vested in me as a direct descendant of the founders of Bliss, I hereby pronounce you an honorary Justice of the Peace of Bliss."

And again he needed a translation. He nodded to her with a full-on Billy smile, because that seemed the most appropriate reaction. "Thank you kindly, ma'am."

Lindsey studied him, eyes flickering with something he couldn't read.

"I got a fortune cookie that said shame would be brought to my home through the interference of nefarious forces," Kimmie whispered.

Lindsey held Will's gaze a moment longer before shifting her attention to Kimmie. "That's an eventual inevitability."

And even though Marilyn did that devil giggle thing again —and Arthur grunted, and CJ snickered—Will had a feeling Lindsey was right.

SEVENTEEN

THEY DIDN'T STAY LONG at Suckers. Lindsey had to work tomorrow, and despite Will's insistence that he could party all night, he'd been tugging at his middle shirt button and getting that lost-in-thought, need-to-write-down-a-lyric look. In the car, he popped a CD into the player—his album *Hitched*, he said—and they both lapsed into a comfortable silence.

She got the feeling he wasn't listening to the music, but she was. And she decided he was evil for playing it while she was driving.

It was a lifelong love story, starting with a song about a simple guy who liked to hang and drink beer with his buddies, going into "Snow Angel Smiles," and on to songs about heart-break, then redemption—"Turned," that song was called, dark and twangy and bright and hopeful at the same time—then marriage and babies, with a couple hanging-with-the-boys, doing-country-things songs thrown in too. Hard work and fun and life. She suspected it ended with grandbabies, but the album wasn't done playing when she pulled her car into the garage. *This* was the album he said he'd written about her.

And she wanted to keep it. She slid the CD from the player and tucked it into her purse.

If Will noticed, he didn't comment. "Nice of you to give

Bliss some extra publicity while you're here," she said while they walked into the house.

He blinked at her, clearly returning from whatever world he lived in when he was thinking about his songs. "Fun town. I like it." He grinned then, completely unashamed, and added, "Besides, that whole Most Married-est thing they have going fits the theme for *Hitched*. Good publicity angle. My people want me to head to Cherish next."

"The love capitol of Louisiana?"

"You've heard of it?"

"We're practically sister cities." She frowned at him. "The Battle of the Boyfriends is a week after our deadline."

"Yep."

"How many microphones does your crew bring?"

"Enough to keep you away that night. Don't even think of coming. My security guys will have orders to restrain you if you get anywhere near the stage or judging table."

Pressure built in her sinuses as though a storm was brewing. He was taking care of her yet pretending like he didn't know it. "Wouldn't be the first time I've been restrained by security," she said, "but it probably wouldn't be as enjoyable as the last time."

His eyes went smoky. "Handcuffs?" he said, his voice on the husky side.

"That's between me and the officer."

He visibly swallowed, and his gaze drifted down her body. "You still got 'em?"

She let her minx side out with the smile she gave him. Then she turned and swung her hips on her way to the stairs. And when they reached her bedroom door, she grabbed him by his plaid shirt, and she pulled him inside her private haven.

WILL WOKE up the next morning to bright sunshine streaming on pale yellow walls. He was buried in a fluffy mound of a white down comforter, and his guitar was in the wicker rocking chair beside the bed.

Write me a happy song today, Lindsey had written on a sticky note stuck to the guitar.

He leaned into the pillow, inhaled the sweet scent of Lindsey surrounding him.

He was officially a goner.

Wrigley nosed Will's arm. He rolled over to scratch the pup's ears. "We got eleven days, boy," he said. "Think we can convince her to keep us?"

Wrigley wagged his tail and panted a smile.

"Yeah, you're a given. It's me we gotta work on."

Will knew how to woo a girl, and he had the money to do it with the best of them. Didn't have any problems seducing Lindsey's body.

But it was her heart he wanted, and that couldn't be bought with chocolates and flowers. Probably couldn't even be won over with a song, not if the whole *Hitched* album hadn't done it. She still had her ticker locked tight.

She'd always had his. Always, right from the first day he met her. *I don't like country music*, she'd said with that adorable nose wrinkle she didn't use so much anymore. *It's too depressing.* He'd played her a song, and he'd watched her discover a world she hadn't known existed, and he'd wanted to spend his life showing her new worlds.

He'd changed her mind about his music, and in return, she'd changed his entire life.

"You think she's happy?" he said to Wrigley.

Wrigley's nose twitched.

"Right. One person can answer that, and no telling if she'd deem us worthy of knowing." Lindsey hadn't been happy on spring break. She'd been lonely. She'd been lonely and lost and faking her way through it, but she'd still found smiles for him. Real smiles. Right up to the end.

But she was still keeping him at arm's length. Even finally inviting him into her bedroom, she'd kept her distance. She didn't look at him when she came. She didn't shut off her brain, didn't let go. Physically, yes. Emotionally—she was still holding back.

He thought on it all day while he worked, some with

Mikey, some alone, and by the time she got home long after sunset, looking for all the world as if she'd used the last of the fight in her, he had a plan.

He met her in the kitchen and helped her out of her wool coat. "Looks like all those babies gave you indigestion today," he murmured after pressing a kiss to her cheek.

She leaned into him. Briefly, but enough for him to squeeze in a hug too.

"I had to read three opposing attorneys the riot act today."

"They come around to your way of thinking?"

"Of course." She pulled back and flicked the buttons open on her suit coat, and Will had to fight hard to keep enough blood in his brain to concentrate.

"I don't like microphones, but I can argue a phone to death," she said. Some color was coming back to her cheeks, some life into her eyes.

"Good to know."

She slid off her suit coat, then reached for the zipper on her skirt. She fiddled with it while she gave him a coy smile. "Did you write me a happy song today?"

He had to swallow twice. "Yep."

She pulled the zipper down half an inch. "Can I hear it?"

"Yep."

Took everything he had to resist reaching for her again.

She tilted her head to the sunroom.

Dang woman. Seducing him with her body, sealing those walls around her heart again.

"In Georgia," he said.

She stopped with the zipper, and the coy look on her face shifted into suspicion. "In Georgia? Your happy song is called 'In Georgia'?"

He had a notion he was getting a glimpse at what she did on that phone all day long. "No. Week from Friday. Come to Georgia. Got a pre-tour show at a military base not far from where I grew up. You come, I'll play you your song."

"Will—"

"Three weeks aren't over until next Sunday," he said.

"Don't even have to miss much work. 'Sides, when's the last time you had a vacation?"

She was fixin' to demonstrate some of those arguing skills. He could see it.

But Will hadn't lived here for two weeks without picking up on a thing or two. He stepped into her space, grasped her hips, two fingers sliding between her skirt and her smiley panties. "Think on it." He brushed his whiskers over her cheek and sucked on that patch of skin under her ear.

Dang if the girl didn't melt right into him.

"You're cheating," she whispered.

"Ain't seen anything yet, pretty lady."

He just hoped he could follow all the way through.

LINDSEY HAD LOST HER MIND.

Perhaps it had been Will's well-reasoned argument that she'd agreed to three weeks. Or his irritating point that she had no clients Friday—mostly because he'd called and booked himself all day. Or that she would have plenty of time in the office on Sunday afternoon, since he didn't intend to begrudge her those last few hours of their negotiated three weeks. Or his charmingly overbearing insistence that he had more than adequate means to provide her lodging and transportation.

Or perhaps it was the growing panic she felt at how quickly the days were skipping by.

But most likely, it had been his offer to let Wrigley stay in Bliss when he left on tour. She could write joint custody paperwork, he'd said, and he'd sign whatever she put in front of him.

She'd been torn between hugging him, crying and flipping him off, so she'd settled for agreeing to go to his concert.

She wouldn't keep Wrigley—much as she loved the dog, he was Will's, through and through—but he'd broken her with the offer.

And then there was the situation with his aunt and his aunt's best friend.

The two most important women in his life, fighting because of a man.

Will hadn't asked Lindsey if she'd weigh in on the situation, but this was his family. The family that had come together for an orphaned little boy. The family that been there for him the last time she left him. The family who would be there for him again this time.

She didn't even know if his aunt or the psychic would be at the concert, but if she could use her gift to help heal their rift, then she'd be here, in Georgia, to do what she could for Will before their time was over.

So here she was, nine days later, on a beautiful sixty-five-degree day in sunny, bright, southern Georgia, giving her name and identification to an efficiently intimidating official at the entrance to Gellings Air Force Base. The security made her uncharacteristically nervous—probably because CJ, whose first wife had died in combat while stationed at Gellings, had told her horror stories about base security from his short time of living here. Lindsey had been distracted enough by everything else to not realize he was being his normal doofus self. But once she was through the gate, the security to get to Will himself was almost worse. He and Mikey had hit the road early yesterday to get here for meetings with his team, sound checks and photos with the troops, and interviews with local reporters. Now Will was more guarded than Fort Knox.

But finally, she was allowed inside the small office building where Will and his band and crew were gathered before a pre-show meet-and-greet.

His *people*.

And he had a ton of people. People with clipboards, people with earpieces, people with cameras, people with instruments.

It was a good thing they were officially over on Sunday, Lindsey told herself, ignoring the hiccup in her chest. Because she was not built to be anyone's long-term anything, especially a man whose life involved this many people around him all day, every day.

Here, he wasn't her Will. Here, he was Billy Brenton. She spotted him almost instantly. His back was to her, and he was deep in conversation with four people around him. More than the backward ball cap and the plaid shirt over the finest butt in country music—and no, she didn't need to see the rest to know she was right—it was the way he held his arms, the curve of his shoulder, the mole on the back of his ear.

She knew him.

She knew him, and she loved him. But she couldn't have him, because standing in the doorway of the crowded room was making her chest tight and her skin itch and her mouth dry. In match-o-meter land, she was hovering above the earth, between a sandstorm and a brilliant blue sky.

She hadn't been meant to be with the nineteen-year-old Will. They'd both been too young, too inexperienced. They hadn't found their lives yet.

And now, she'd come to realize, she wasn't a bad match for the grown Will.

But Billy Brenton was a terrible match for her. And she couldn't have one without the other.

Will stopped, and when his head turned toward her, his face lit beneath his ball cap with the biggest, sweetest, most genuine Will smile.

Her heart—and her smiley faces—gave a soft, happy, sappy sigh.

"Glad you made it, lawyer lady," he said with a wink.

And then, in case she hadn't been sure he meant it, he handed the paper to one of his people, crossed the room and kissed her silly.

She was crazy to kiss him back—next week she'd be nothing more to these people than one of Billy's old girlfriends. But kiss him back she did. She kissed him with a desperation she didn't want and couldn't shake. She dislodged his hat and had her fingers in his hair, breathing in the scent of him, tasting his mouth, trying to squeeze more out of every next moment than she'd captured in the entire time he'd lived in her home.

He pulled back and dropped a kiss to her forehead, then straightened his cap and turned her into the room. "C'mon. Meet my crew."

He didn't introduce her to everyone, but she met his manager, his assistant, his crew lead, all the guys in his band and his publicist. She met his lights guy, his wardrobe manager and his caterer.

Will, her sweet, simple country boy, had a *wardrobe manager*. And a *caterer*.

Every person in the room showed him an innate respect. Some called him *boss*. All were overly polite to Lindsey, with the exception of Mikey, who was simply Mikey.

He and Dahlia had come over for dinner four times this last week, and while Lindsey wouldn't call him a friend, he'd at least become less hostile. And today, he gave her an honest smile.

Probably because he knew she'd be skedaddling out of Will's life soon.

Mikey topped his smile with a kiss to the cheek and a "Glad you could make it" that was heavy on believability and light on sarcasm.

Had to be the in-love-with-Dahlia effect. Dahlia had had to stay in Bliss—a last-minute emergency at the ice cream shop had derailed her plans, which was probably as disappointing to Lindsey as it was to Mikey. She could've used a friend.

"Good call on that girl, lawyer lady," Will murmured to her as they moved on to the buffet. "But don't go looking too close at the rest of my crew, okay? Won't be easy to replace Mikey out on the road."

"Replace him?"

"He's moving to Bliss. Knew it was coming, but he gave me formal notice this morning. Soon as I find a new drummer, he's gone."

"She doesn't want him on the road?"

"All his choice. I've been telling you that boy's smittened. Can't deny I'm looking forward to giving him bad marks when he plays in the Battle of the Boyfriends next weekend though." Will squeezed her hand and smiled at her. "You need some air, or are you okay?"

"I'm okay."

She wasn't, and he could probably tell, but other than a sideways glance, he didn't push.

Too soon, he had to leave for his fan meet-and-greet. Most of his entourage went with him. Lindsey opted to stay behind. Will insisted she fix herself a plate of food and said he'd see her again before the show. No one seemed to mind her sitting in the corner reading a book. But when Will and his people returned, there was a different energy about the room.

After greeting her with a peck to the cheek, Will leaned against a table next to her, but he was distracted, his head bopping to music Lindsey couldn't hear. Several others did the same. Earpieces were handed out, guitars appeared, and random songs and notes started floating about the room.

"Warm-up time," a guy carrying a case of water bottles said to her. "Opening act's on now. Good show if you want to go watch it."

Mari Belle popped into the room, accompanied by a young girl. Will looked up, and after a minute, he blinked, like he finally realized what he was seeing. "Hey, peanut."

"Hey, Uncle Will!"

Mari Belle released her grip on the girl's collar, and she darted past Will's crew to hug him. "Are you fixin' to sing my favorites tonight?"

"They're all your favorites."

Lindsey smiled at their banter.

"How's Wrigley doing?" Will asked.

"Uncle Will, that is the laziest dog God ever put on this green earth. He didn't even move when Biscuits mistook him for a girlfriend. You sure he's got a pulse?"

Lindsey laughed. That sounded like the Wrigley she knew and loved. The girl turned to her. "Are you Uncle Will's snow angel?"

Mari Belle sighed. "Paisley—"

"Yep," Will said. "Paisley, meet Miss Lindsey. Lindsey, my nearly perfect niece. She's watching Wrigley for me this weekend."

Paisley grinned. "He means all-perfect niece. Uncle Will promised I can be a junior bridesmaid when you get married."

Lindsey's heart launched into a painfully fast sprint. She wrapped her cardigan tighter around her, even though the room was more than adequately warm. "How old are you, Paisley?"

"Ten going on thirty-five."

It was impossible not to laugh. "You're your momma's girl, aren't you?"

"Much to my daddy's chagrin."

Will gave her light brown hair an affectionate tug. "Hush, you. Talk more'n your momma does, and that's impressive."

"I *am* standing right here," Mari Belle said with a sigh.

"Makes it more fun," Will said. "Y'all excited for the show?"

"Oh, yeah." Paisley flashed another grin at Lindsey. "It's my first Billy Brenton concert."

"Is it?" Lindsey said.

Paisley nodded. "For real. Momma said I was too young before."

"I was too," Lindsey said.

Paisley grinned bigger.

"Hope it'll be worth the wait." Will winked at Lindsey. "I'm singing songs for both of y'all tonight."

"Thirty minutes," a guy boomed out in the middle of the room.

"That's our sign," Mari Belle said to Paisley. She gave Will a quick hug. "Don't fall off the stage this time, okay?"

He flashed her a smile, but his eyes were going distant again.

"Sing good, Uncle Will," Paisley said.

Mari Belle didn't talk to Lindsey aside from aiming an eyeball of *leave my brother the hell alone* in Lindsey's direction.

They paused to give Mikey hugs, then left the room. Will reached for the middle button on his plaid overshirt, and a frown drew his brows together.

Vera.

He was still reaching for Vera.

Lindsey slid closer and pressed a kiss to his newly trimmed

whiskers. "I'm wearing a new set of smileys today," she whispered.

He wrapped his arms around her and pulled her close. "Hell, woman. Gonna be thinking about *that* all through the set now."

"You're welcome."

"Leave Billy alone," Mikey said. "Can't go messing with the pre-show routine, or he'll miss all the good notes."

"Says the guy who gets to sit behind his drum set the whole show," Will grumbled. He squeezed Lindsey's hand. "Band time. See you after the show?"

She nodded. "That song better be worth coming all the way here."

"All of 'em are."

"Even the twangy crap?"

"Especially the twangy crap." He hadn't said as much, but she knew he knew how much she loved listening to his music.

And that her car radio now had a country music station programmed into it.

With an unfiltered Will grin, he kissed her. "Be looking for you. Get a set of earplugs. Gets loud out there."

A stagehand led Lindsey out of the building and loaded her in a golf cart for a short drive in the dark across a stretch of asphalt to a hangar that housed Will's stage. Crew members were moving microphones and God knew what else, transitioning the stage from the opening act and getting it ready for Will.

With the pass Will's people had given her, Lindsey entered the VIP section off to one side of the stage, roped off from the masses in the folding chairs that lined the rest of the hangar. Fifteen or twenty other people were in the VIP section, but more were trickling in. Mari Belle and Paisley were there, chatting with a couple who put into Lindsey's mind a pretty sunrise over a lake. Paisley pulled Lindsey into their group and introduced her to Miss Anna and Mr. Jackson. Neighbors, apparently.

They reminded Lindsey of the couple in that Mae Daniels book she'd finally finished. He was Southern military, she was northern put-together, both of them completely into each other. And with them as witnesses, Mari Belle was even pleasant.

"Will tells me you're breaking up with him on Sunday," she said to Lindsey while Paisley was in the midst of telling their friends a story about her dance class this week.

"We have an understanding."

Mari Belle slanted her an odd, unreadable look. "You told him you weren't a good match then."

Lindsey's stomach cramped. "We weren't."

Mari Belle kept staring.

"Do you believe in psychic matchmakers?" Lindsey said softly.

Mari Belle didn't answer. But something flickered over her features. Uncertainty, perhaps. Something mulish, as though she didn't want to believe, and was frustrated with herself for even considering the possibility.

"Your aunt isn't coming?" Lindsey tried again.

"She can't get on base," Paisley said. "Too many run-ins with the sheriff while she was out looking for the treasure."

Mari Belle heaved a sigh. But her friend Anna clapped her hands with glee. "I love the South," she said, sounding every bit as northern as Lindsey. "It's so colorful here."

"Momma! Momma, look," Paisley said. "It's Uncle Mikey!"

Will's band appeared onstage. Rumblings started in the crowd, and the lights inside the building flickered, then lowered. A steady drum beat kicked in, then the rest of the instruments, and then the stage lights came on, and there was Will, completely himself, completely Billy Brenton.

Opening his show with "Snow Angel Smiles."

Lindsey's heart cracked so hard it could have bled.

They were almost over.

He looked over at her and smiled that open, wide, killer country boy smile. And even with her very soul weeping—*this* was the man and the life she wasn't meant to have—she smiled back at him with everything she had.

Because neither of them could afford for him to see how badly she wanted all of him.

———

WILL FORGOT how much he missed being onstage until the moment he stepped on one again. And then it was magic — the lights above him, the stage beneath his boots, microphone in hand, his band behind him, the muffled sounds of the crowd sweeping through him. He wasn't Will Truitt anymore. He wasn't the guy in a questionable relationship with a girl who was fixin' to leave him in two days. He wasn't Aunt Jessie's nephew, Mari Belle's brother, Paisley's uncle. He wasn't the guy worried that Sacha was mostly unreachable since she put her house up for sale. Right now, in this moment, every fiber of his being hummed in tune to the thrill of being Billy.

He loved playing military bases. They weren't the biggest crowds, but they screamed and cheered as if they were. And they were good folk, all of them. Made the world right so he could keep being Billy Brenton.

And to the side of the stage, Lindsey smiled at him — that special, secret, *I know you're singing about my underwear* smile.

He winked at her.

She blew him a kiss.

And danged if that didn't make him feel like he was putting on the best show of his life.

He worked the stage and the crowd in the hangar, getting his groove on, his body moving to the rhythm of the song, the audience singing along, and soon they were moving into "Tap Dancing," a hit off the album before *Hitched* about a guy drinking until he thought he had rhythm. Lindsey was trying to clap along, but the girl's sense of time was near about as bad as she claimed her singing was.

But she was trying. She was here. Close enough to touch.

He wanted to stop the show and kiss her. Gave it a good long thought too, but Mari Belle would've kicked his rear end from here to Thursday for exposing Paisley to that. And Lindsey didn't like the spotlight.

About halfway through the show, he finished "Weekend Cowboy," his first smash hit to go double-platinum, and he grabbed the Gibson that was waiting for him center stage. His crew had his mic stand waiting, and he took a seat on the stool they'd put out while he was dancing out front. His band shifted effortlessly into the opening chords of "Better Me," Will's most popular ballad. Lindsey's song would be next. He glanced over at his snow angel.

She was gone.

Mari Belle was there. Paisley too. A blonde he'd been introduced to at the meet-and-greet. But no Lindsey.

Must've run to the ladies' room, he guessed. Or went in search of food.

Or the crowd had gotten to her.

He gave the Gibson a strum while the audience cheered and hollered. "Y'all know this one, huh?"

He scanned the audience again, a dark mass of standing-room-only crowd spilling out of the hangar. No sign of Lindsey's blonde hair, her light purple sweater, her smiles just for him in the VIP section though.

She had about three minutes before he'd pull her song from tonight's set list.

Wouldn't be an all-bad thing, though. Meant he'd have to sing it for her later.

Just the two of them.

They were over on Sunday? She could think it all she wanted to. But Will, he'd get his girl. He might not get to keep his mishmashed little family, but even if it took all his life to convince her, he'd get his girl.

EIGHTEEN

"YOU'RE sure it's okay to be out here?" Lindsey said to Jackson. Mari Belle's neighbor had noticed her struggling to breathe in the growing crush of the crowd in the VIP section, and he'd walked her out for air.

"Better than you passin' out in there." He smiled at her in the dark—a warm, adorable kind of grin that his fiancée seemed to fully appreciate. "Don't get on military bases much?"

Lindsey shook her head.

"All good out here tonight. If you get somewhere you shouldn't be, somebody'll steer you back."

"Good to know." The night air was cool and refreshing, and the tingling in her fingers and toes slowly receded. Will's voice drifted out into the night. A month ago, she never would've considered it possible that she'd be standing on a military base, listening to Will sing. But here she was. "Your wedding's coming up?"

"Next month." His grin went even more adorable. She was such a sucker for the Southern boys.

"Congratulations."

"Thank you kindly, ma'am."

She studied the dark-haired man. "Can I ask you something?"

"Yes, ma'am."

"Do you deploy often?"

He chuckled. "Me? Nah. Air Force paid for my engineering degree. Like to keep me behind a desk and use my brain instead. I get sent downrange maybe every few years or so, at most."

"Oh."

The music changed inside, slowed down. Lindsey was missing Will's show.

But she couldn't breathe inside the hangar.

Too many people, too many bad matches, too much subtle hostility still rolling off Mari Belle.

Too much of her self-imposed deadline breathing down her neck. She had to walk away from Will in less than forty-eight hours.

"I go TDY a fair amount, but I reckon ol' Billy travels more than I do," Jackson said.

"TDY?"

"Temporary duty. What civilian folks call business trips."

"Ah."

"My Anna Grace, she's one of them takes-care-of-herself types." He tucked his hands in his pockets and rocked on his heels. "Still hate to leave her, though. Miss her when I'm gone."

Lindsey couldn't help smiling. "You two are ridiculously cute."

"She gets all the credit for that part."

Will's voice washed over her, echoing over the crowd's roar inside the hangar.

They loved him.

Thousands of people, and they loved him. He could've had anyone, and he kept coming back to Lindsey.

"You gonna go with him out on tour?" Jackson asked.

She shook her head. "We're not—" She blew out a breath. "Will is one of the best men I have ever known," she said. "But Billy Brenton—that's not the kind of life I fit into. He was born to be a superstar, and I—I'm not the best he can do."

"Usually the kind of thing a man likes to decide for himself."

"I've been a divorce lawyer for ten years. Trust me, I know how it ends when one party asks the other to sacrifice their dream to make a relationship work."

"Still his choice to make." Jackson looked at the hangar. "A year ago, I thought I liked being all by my lonesome. Thought serving Uncle Sam was good enough for me. Would've said the same as you, that it's not fair to give up a career for love. But my Anna Grace—she's worth everything. I was born to wear the uniform—and my Mamie says I make it look good—but I'd quit my job in a heartbeat if that's what it took to keep her."

"But then what would you do?"

"Life ain't about what you do. It's about what you do for the people you love. And I don't know Billy—don't know Will —but I reckon he'd be as happy in a little country bar as he is on a big stage." He grinned. "But don't go telling my Anna Grace or Mari Belle I told you so. They'd chew me up one side and down the other for taking the wrong side."

"You don't miss much."

"No ma'am."

"Lindsey! Hey, Lindsey!"

She glanced over at the unfamiliar voice, and suddenly a spotlight was on her, a microphone was shoved in her face and two guys crowded her. She could make out crew IDs and nothing more as she blinked into the light.

Her pulse crashed in her ears, panic bubbles erupted in her chest, and she tasted the acidic bite of terror. She tripped back one step, two, before a solid grip steadied her.

The other two bodies, the spotlight and a camera jostled into her. "Billy said this is your first concert," the same voice said. "That true?"

"Wanna tell his BillyVision viewers what you think of it so far?" another voice said.

No. *No.* She didn't. She couldn't.

She opened her mouth, then snapped it shut. The microphone leered at her, taunting her. *Say it*, it said. *Tell us every-*

thing, Lindsey. Tell the world you're a psychic anti-matchmaking divorce lawyer and that you're dumping Billy tomorrow.

She swallowed against the words rising from her chest. Bile nipped at her throat and she fought the words she wanted to spill into the microphone. "I—he's—"

Thousands of people watched BillyVision. Being Billy was Will's life. She'd been wrong fifteen years ago. They hadn't been bad for each other because she'd be president and the world couldn't handle a First Bubba. They'd been wrong because she was never meant to be president, and she couldn't handle Billy Brenton's life.

"Oh, hey, we need to get you a Billy T-shirt."

Lindsey's knees turned to rubber. "I don't—You can't—Will—" she choked out.

"How about you fellas give the lady some room?" Jackson said quietly beside her.

The light went out, the microphone disappeared and suddenly there were two men standing between the dots marring Lindsey's vision while she gasped for air.

"You okay, Miss Lindsey?"

"Just wanted to give the boss a surprise. He digs you. Thought he'd like seeing you on camera."

"You need some water or something?"

She declined, lungs heaving, fingers tingling. Will's crew hadn't meant any harm.

But her pulse was zinging. Her legs quaked with aftershocks and her stomach was wound tight. She swallowed hard. "You startled me," she forced out.

It was the only thing she could think to say to keep her dignity intact without causing problems for Will's crew.

"Sorry again, Miss Lindsey."

"Didn't mean any harm, ma'am."

"Here, have a bottle of BillyWater."

This time, instead of a microphone, they thrust a water bottle with Will's picture on the label at her.

"Can we get you a chair?"

"Or walk you inside?"

"I got a peppermint too, if you want that."

They were sweet, all doing their best to make her feel better, but these were the *good* guys. What if they'd been the local press, or *People* magazine, or Katie Couric, or the *National Enquirer*? What happened when someone shoved a mic in her face and asked the hard questions? *Are you dating Billy for his money? Is it true you dumped him onstage fifteen years ago? What makes you think you're good enough for a superstar to love? Hey, can you tell me if those two people over there are a good match? What's it like to be a weirdo?*

She and Will weren't in Willow Glen anymore. Her Will wasn't her Will anymore.

She swallowed hard again, this time against the grief welling up.

She had to let him go. She wasn't built for a public life. Sooner or later, she'd repeat her mistake from Colorado, or her mistakes from college with her *gift*, and his family, his friends —they were all right.

This time, it would be worse. This time, instead of building him up for his destiny, she'd tear it down, piece by piece, by being the freak show in Billy Brenton's life. The girl who couldn't handle crowds. Who panicked over the sight of a microphone. Who wanted him to stay home, with her, every day, and never go on tour again.

She couldn't ask that of him. He'd been hers for a month, but in his regularly scheduled life, he was Billy. The BillyVision videos, the way he lost himself in writing songs, that broad, unfiltered country boy smile that lit the whole stage when he was on it—Will loved being Billy. He was *born* to be Billy.

And she would only be in his way.

Will's voice echoed out of the hangar, half-drowned by the crowd singing along with him.

She was missing part of his show.

The only show she'd ever see, but not the last show he would ever perform. He had thousands of crowds to entertain still, and she wasn't the woman he needed by his side.

"You want to go back, or you need more air?" Jackson said.

Lindsey gulped in one more big breath.

She wanted to go home. She wanted to run away, pack her bags, and move to Siberia with Kimmie.

But she couldn't run out on Will.

He deserved an honest good-bye this time. "I'm ready," she said.

They returned to the hangar with the BillyVision crew flanking them, the camera off. Will was alone onstage, all the lights down except a single spotlight on him. He was settled on a stool, adjusting his mic. He scanned the crowd, then gave his guitar a strum. Something sweet but hard came out. He looked at Lindsey. "Y'all want to hear something new?" he said.

The crowd went wild. Even through her earplugs, Lindsey heard the roar.

"This one here's going out to a special lady tonight," Will said. "She asked me to write a happy song."

Lindsey's heart stuttered. She'd almost missed her song.

She shouldn't have asked him to write it. She didn't belong in his life. She wasn't strong enough to live in his life.

He smiled, and then music poured from his fingers.

It filled the hangar, the sounds of strength and softness, and wrapped around her. The sounds weren't comforting, weren't comfortable, but they were *right*.

She didn't want to let the sound in. But she couldn't walk away. Because this could be the last thing he ever gave her.

"A black heart don't know how to love, that's what they all said," he sang.

Lindsey's breath caught on a lump in her throat.

That smile, it lies, those eyes, they hypnotize, but ain't nothing can hide the dark inside.

Wait. This—*this*—was his song to her?

Maybe he *did* understand the end was coming.

He closed his eyes, and he went all into the song.

But that heart, it wasn't born coal,
Took a lifetime to freeze it cold,

She's what they let her believe, can't dance, can't sing, can only hide.

Hiding.
He thought she was hiding.
And he wasn't wrong.
"But she's more," Will sang.

> *She's more than she knows,*
> *She's more than she shows,*
> *The world can't see it,*
> *She's hiding it deep,*
> *But my girl, my angel,*
> *Your black heart glows.*
> *Oh, baby, that rainbow in your heart glows.*

Lindsey hugged herself tighter.
He was—his song—he could *see* her. He saw how she thought the world saw her, and he saw so much more.
You believed in me, he'd said.
He opened his eyes, slid a look at her.

> *She listened to the judging, watched them shut her out,*
> *Misunderstood, called wrong,*
> *She hurts, but she's strong,*
> *So she took a pen and wrote it on her heart.*

He was telling her story.
More, he was telling her he believed in her.
He believed she could be everything he needed her to be.
She blinked quickly.
This was *not* a happy song.
Will closed his eyes again.

> *A whole world of being alone,*
> *Of being told she don't belong,*
> *And now her heart's colored over, black ink, sharp stings, a girl apart.*

"But she's more," Will sang.

She's more than she knows,
She's more than she shows,
The world can't see it,
She's hiding it deep,
But my girl, my angel, your black heart glows.
Oh, baby, that rainbow in your heart glows.

The music changed. It went deeper and softer, the combination of sounds and rhythm and speed making her heart beat in time with the music.

He took an audible breath in the microphone.

Now it's my turn to paint your heart, put the color back on your soul,
Red and blue, yellow, green, let me show the world the you that I know,
Trust me one more time,
Love me one more time,
I want to write our best story on your heart.

"Because you're more," he sang.

You're more than you know,
And you're only starting to show,
The world's gonna see it,
Don't hide it deep.
My girl, my angel, your rainbow heart glows.
Baby, let that rainbow in your heart glow.

Lindsey was short of breath and her cheeks were wet.
He loved her.
Will loved her.
He knew her, he *saw* her, and he still loved her.
But love wasn't always enough.
Not when she could never be the girl *Billy Brenton* needed.

SATURDAY MORNING, Lindsey and Will slept in. Considering how late his show went, and then the extra hour he stayed afterward to sign autographs from the stage, she was surprised either of them moved before noon.

She hadn't mentioned her encounter with his BillyVision crew. She didn't want to get them in trouble, but more, she selfishly wanted one last day with Will, with no thoughts of Billy.

But then he asked if he could take her an hour down the road to Pickleberry Springs. To his home.

To a place where Lindsey was quite possibly the only person qualified to help his family.

She knew Sacha most likely wouldn't be there. That Will hadn't heard from her in a week, that Mikey's momma was reporting there wasn't a person in Pickleberry Springs who had seen her and that Will had hired a friend of Mikey's to track her down.

But his Aunt Jessie would be there. Aunt Jessie's husband would be there.

And even though Will didn't ask Lindsey to use her *gift*, she knew he'd be watching to see what she saw.

"Will," she said, "this won't change *us*."

She wanted to go with him. But she needed to be strong. She had to say good-bye to him tomorrow. Today was the last day she had to help him. She *had* to walk away tomorrow. She had to stick to her rule.

For both their sakes.

"You ever been in the land of moonshine and armadillos?" Will asked.

She shook her head. He told her to hustle her cute little butt on up into his truck and let him be in charge for one day out of twenty-one. So mid-afternoon, they pulled into Will's hometown. It was on the run-down side, with shops needing new paint and roads needing patches. But every person on Main Street waved at Lindsey and Will as they drove through, most of them before they realized who was driving.

A tattered sign across the road advertised a 5k for wounded warriors over Presidents' Day weekend, and a group of Girl Scouts sold cookies outside the small-town grocery store. There was an honest-to-God Curl Up and Dye hair salon sharing space with a taxidermist. An antique store housed in a bright red single-wide trailer. A shed with a home-made Deer Processing sign next to a wooden stand with Boiled Peanuts painted across the top.

"Boiled peanuts?" Lindsey said.

Will smiled at her, glowing with pride and affection for his hometown. "Culinary delight," he said. "Not in season, though. See? You hadn't come, you'd never know they existed. You're welcome, for exposing you to some culture."

He waved at another passerby stepping out of Elsie's Diner. "Good fried catfish there," he said. Then he flipped on his blinker and hung a right away from downtown. Two minutes later, he took a left on Billy Brenton Lane—"Was Mildred Street growing up," he told her with a ruddy hue coming to his cheeks. Then he stopped the truck at the curb of a dinky ranch with holly bushes under the front windows. Pansies lined the short walk to the little white house.

The house next door, equally dinky but painted a sunny yellow, had a real estate SOLD sign stuck amidst the rainbow pinwheels spinning over the brown grass. A sign in the front window advertised psychic readings, and a Winnebago was parked out front.

Will's gaze caught on the Winnebago, and he visibly relaxed, a short, relieved breath slipping between his lips.

But Lindsey shivered.

She was wrong. She shouldn't be here. She didn't deserve to meet his family, didn't deserve to interfere and weigh in on a situation that was none of her business. "Will—"

"They all know you're gone after tomorrow."

"Do you?"

She'd needed to say it for a long time, but she hadn't had the courage.

He turned in his seat to face her, his eyes the most serious she'd ever seen. "You like being a divorce lawyer? It make you happy?"

Her fists clenched instinctively. So did her jaw. "So now *you* want to judge my choices too."

It was an easy fight to pick.

But Will didn't blink or flinch. He just kept that steady gaze on her. "Ain't judging. Asking. I know why you do it — got some appreciation for that — but I've been watching you, Lindsey. I don't care what you do, so long as you're doing what makes you happy. Eating babies, swimming with the sharks, spinning on a stripper pole in Vegas, whatever. But that shine I saw when we were kids, that light you had when you talked about changing the world — it's not there anymore."

Even with his steadfast focus, there was a desperation in his voice, as though the cracks in her life were his failing. If he could've been this guy — this sweet, honest, determined man — without the Billy factor, she would've crawled into his lap and asked him to marry her and promised him she'd spend the rest of her life doing nothing more than making him as happy as he'd made her the last three weeks. She'd always thought she was even-tempered, but he'd weathered mood swings and a constant ticking clock and her gift — her *curse* — with unwavering grace and humor and dedication.

"I heard you," she said. "I heard the song. I know. But Will, not every gift is a blessing. Not every talent should be in the spotlight."

He opened his mouth, that stubborn look telling her she was about to get a Will Truitt–style talkin' to. But then a creepy-crawly sensation slunk down her arms and spine, and a single rap at her window made her jump.

She turned and found a tall, dark-haired, dark-eyed woman gazing down a long nose at her.

"You came."

Even with the windows closed, Lindsey heard her. And suddenly she understood what Will meant when he talked about the hairs on his hairs standing up. Lindsey wasn't one to ruminate on mystic essences — having an internal anti-matchmaking barometer was quite enough — but she shivered all the way from her hair follicles out to the edges of her aura.

Will hit a button to roll Lindsey's window down, then swung his own door open and climbed out. "Christ Almighty, Sacha, don't sneak up on people." He walked around the truck and gathered the wispy woman in a tight hug, the bottom of her long flowery dress ruffling in the breeze.

Sacha wrapped her arms around him and visibly squeezed him back. "Look at you. I haven't seen you this content in years."

"Good to be home. Good to see *you* home."

"And you brought her. Good. We *all* need her."

Will frowned. He let Sacha go, then opened Lindsey's door. Before he could make introductions, Sacha wrapped her arms around Lindsey and grasped her tightly. "You'll do what needs doing," Sacha whispered. "Be brave. Be bold. Trust yourself. And you'll find the balance you seek."

The atmosphere shrank, the houses and trees and cars and Sacha all closing in around Lindsey. The ground went wobbly, and the pungent odor of old burnt oil assaulted Lindsey's nose. She forced air into her lungs and willed her heart to slow.

"Sacha. Let her go."

Will's quiet order was effective. The woman released her hold, and when she turned her dark gaze on Lindsey this time, the intensity was gone. She continued to study Lindsey while Lindsey studied her. Sacha's face was devoid of makeup, she wore no jewelry, no embellishments anywhere, save a toe ring. Her dark hair hung straight. Her shoulders and elbows were bony and pointed, and the muumuu hid her figure, but her grip was stronger than her figure would've indicated.

Sacha's lips wobbled and her brows knit together. "Having a gift makes for a lonely life," she said. "True friends make all the difference."

It was, and they did. And Lindsey suspected that even Will, having all the complications of being Billy Brenton, couldn't fully understand what the freak factor did to finding those true friends.

Lindsey honestly couldn't fully understand either. She didn't live her *talent* like Sacha did.

"Aunt Jessie will come around." Will leaned against his truck. He looped one arm around Sacha, grabbed Lindsey's hand with the other. "Donnie doesn't have anything on you, and she'll figure that out soon enough."

"I've fulfilled my destiny here," Sacha said. "It's time I move on."

"Time you stay put," Will said.

"You may have bought my house, but you can't make me stay."

"You might leave, but you'll still be *my* family," Will shot back. "Appreciate it if you quit ignoring my calls."

Sacha didn't answer. Instead, she eyed Lindsey.

A tremor started deep in Lindsey's bones.

"I should've waited until you came," Sacha said. "Jessie loves him too much to believe me, and now I've broken my own family."

And Aunt Jessie most likely hated Lindsey enough that Lindsey's opinion would carry negative weight.

Sacha was screwed.

"In my experience," Lindsey said, "there's never a good time to tell your friends anything they don't want to hear about their love lives."

"Never?" Sacha said.

Five little letters, carried by a tone that said there were as many reasons as there were stars.

"Will's right," Lindsey said. "You should take his calls. Having a *gift* can make for a lonely life, especially if you shut your family out."

Sacha pursed her lips, then patted Will's chest. "Come see me before you leave."

"You staying that long?"

"William. Such a question." She pulled away from him with a reluctance that bespoke finality. Lindsey hadn't yet been able to quell her shivers, and they got worse when Sacha's gaze lingered on her. "Fearlessness would suit you. You're hiding your light as sure as you hide your smiles."

She didn't say good-bye but instead turned and floated to the clapboard bungalow next door, her flowered muumuu trailing behind her.

Lindsey turned a baby-eater glare on Will, because it was easier than wondering if Sacha would leave as soon as they were out of sight. "Did you tell *everyone* what 'Snow Angel Smiles' is about?"

He rubbed a weary hand over his face. "Didn't have to. You know how hard it is being a teenager with a psychic pseudo-mom?"

Despite everything, there she went, smiling at him all over again, falling harder for this adorable country man.

His answering grin was half-strength. "You wanna go see my old bedroom?"

"Is that a pickup line?"

"Come on inside and you'll find out."

How was a girl supposed to resist an offer like that?

NINETEEN

MUCH AS WILL wanted to show Lindsey his bedroom, Aunt Jessie took priority.

When they pushed into the house, she spun toward them. She was wearing one of his older Billy Brenton T-shirts over pink polyester pants. Her curly hair fanned out in back, her clear blue eyes wide, a flash of disappointment drawing them down before she found her smile. "My Will. You're home."

She'd been staring at her wedding photo on the floral-papered wall. Over the years, Aunt Jessie had had various wedding pictures hanging in that spot. Only thing that changed was the groom. When Will and Mari Belle moved in, it had been one of four pictures on the wall. Aunt Jessie had added more pictures of the three of them as they grew — Aunt Jessie, Will, and Mari Belle. At the beach in Panama City. Catching fish in the Flint River. Standing around Mari Belle with all her awards when she graduated high school.

Last time he'd been here, there had been more.

Because last time he'd been here, half the pictures had had Sacha in them too. Now, instead, there were blank spots on the wall, nonfaded squares that felt like bruises on his heart.

Sacha would leave again while he was here. He knew she would.

But he'd track her down. He wouldn't let her be alone. Wouldn't let her believe she'd lost them all.

He pulled Aunt Jessie into a hug, even though he wanted to shake her. "Missed you at the show."

"You're much better among smaller audiences." She squeezed him hard—harder than Sacha had, and Sacha had near about squeezed the stuffing out of him.

He kissed the top of her head, then let her go and turned to Lindsey, who was wearing a mix of her serious lawyer lady mask and undisguised sympathy. Those sharp eyes of hers had made a quick sweep of the room, and he had a notion she knew it was all wrong.

"Aunt Jessie, meet Lindsey. She's been helping me write songs."

"Lovely to meet you," Lindsey said.

The two of them watched each other for a minute. Lindsey's calm and relaxed act was almost convincing, but Aunt Jessie eyed her like she would an alligator.

"Got any sweet tea?" Will said to Aunt Jessie. Because any Southern woman worth her salt offered the alligators sweet tea too.

Aunt Jessie huffed. "What kind of a question is that, young man?"

He grinned at her. "Lindsey here ain't ever been south of the Mason-Dixon line before. Dadgum shame, don't you think?"

"Actually, I've been to Disney World," Lindsey said.

"Oh, honey, bless your heart," Aunt Jessie said. "Disney World ain't *south*. Y'all didn't happen to see Donnie's car in town when you came in, did you?"

"Can't say we did," Will said. "You want a glass, Aunt Jessie?"

"No, thank you, honey."

"Mikey's in town too today. Thought we could have him over. Fry up some chicken and okra. Make some cornbread."

Aunt Jessie moved to the window, pushed the gauzy curtain out of the way and peered at the road. "Sure, sure. Y'all go on in and see what I got in the fridge."

"Thinking about catching an armadillo too," Will said. "Add some fried butterflies on the side."

Lindsey choked on air, but Aunt Jessie nodded again. "Sounds good, hon."

"Aunt Jessie."

She turned. Her mouth wobbled and she blinked quickly, but Southern steel shone through.

She'd never had as much steel as Mari Belle, but she didn't let that stop her.

"Don't you go judging me." Her voice cracked. "You bring *her* into my house, and you want to tell me I'm wrong to pick love?"

Will held his hands up. "Not judging. I'm worried."

"I'm sixty-two years old. It's high time I took charge of my own life, and I don't take kindly to people telling me who is and isn't good for me."

"People make mistakes, even when their hearts are in the right place."

"What heart's in the right place when it's trying to break mine?"

"The kind that's loved you longer."

"*That* kind told you to go chasing a girl who's fixin' to dump you tomorrow."

Lindsey pursed her lips together. Will clamped down on the instinctive need to defend her.

Difference between his situation and Aunt Jessie's was that Lindsey was meant to be his.

He knew she'd miss him. He knew she cared. He knew she was scared.

And he knew he was man enough to be steady, to be her *friend*, even from afar, as long as it took for him to give her the courage that she'd once given him.

"I'll go take care of the sweet tea," Lindsey said quietly.

He let her go—not because he wanted her to, but because he understood she needed to.

"She still is, isn't she?" Aunt Jessie said. "She's still fixin' to dump you."

He wasn't here to fix him and Lindsey. He was here to fix

Aunt Jessie and Sacha. "Why do you love Donnie so much, Aunt Jessie?"

She sucked a big breath through her nose, her brows shooting halfway up her forehead. Her eyes went misty, and she touched a hand to her heart. "He knows me. Right here. Like he's known me all my life. I know you don't trust anybody new, and I know Mari Belle don't trust anybody male, but Donnie doesn't want anything from any of you. He wants me to be happy being *me*. Lord knows he's not perfect, but he's perfect for me. I've never wanted more to keep my vows to any man like I want to keep my vows to him. And if you're taking sides, you—you can—"

"Not taking sides." He wasn't one who could argue with listening to his heart. Even when he knew he was heading for stormy weather, even when he knew it would hurt, he couldn't help but follow his heart now that he'd found it again.

Looked like he and Aunt Jessie both had some of what his Momma had had. "Just want you to be happy, Aunt Jessie. And you don't look real happy today." None of the women in his life looked real happy lately.

She turned to the window. "Life ain't always beautiful."

That was the honest truth.

"How about I go get you a glass of sweet tea too."

"You're a good boy, Will. Always have been. I just don't want to see you get hurt."

"Want the same for you, Aunt Jessie."

In the kitchen, Lindsey had found the old flowered Corelle glasses and the jug of sweet tea. Will settled his hands at her waist and pressed a kiss to her forehead. "You try any yet?"

"I thought you'd like to see the show."

Will forced a grin. "You eat Kimmie's cupcakes, you can drink sweet tea. I got faith in you."

She wrinkled that cute nose, but when he let her go, she held the cup to her nose, gave a big sniff, and then took a gulp.

The shudder wasn't as big as he expected, but it was still cute and funny as all get-out.

"That is *sweet*," she said.

He clinked his own glass to hers. "Welcome to the South,

pretty lady. You notice if there's any okra in the fridge? Not letting you leave without trying some of that too."

"I wouldn't even know what it looks like."

"Looks like a big ol' bag of dee-licious."

While she humored him with a halfhearted laugh, he grabbed another glass from the cabinet. Didn't like standing there pretending everything was fine, because it wasn't.

Lindsey didn't want to be there. Aunt Jessie didn't seem to want either of them there. And Sacha would be gone before Will was done delivering Aunt Jessie's tea.

Here it was, his last day of being plain ol' Will Truitt before he spent the next nine months being Billy Brenton, and everything was all wrong.

He wanted Sacha to come over and make her secret cornbread recipe. To *stay*. He wanted Aunt Jessie to fuss that Will was making a mess helping bread the okra. He wanted Paisley to jump around, interfere with everybody and chatter away. He wanted Wrigley underfoot, and Mari Belle's dogs too. He even wanted Mari Belle sighing over some such thing or another.

And he wanted Lindsey to fit into it all.

The front screen door banged against the doorframe before he could carry Aunt Jessie's glass in to her.

"Nat's first husband was a real prick," Lindsey said softly. She had a clear view of the living room. Will didn't hear anyone talking, so he guessed Aunt Jessie had stepped out front.

Hopefully not to give Sacha a what-for. Will angled closer to Lindsey.

Donnie's truck was in the driveway.

Will's heart kicked up like it was fixin' to win a NASCAR race.

Lindsey could solve this. She could tell them all who was right—Sacha or Aunt Jessie.

And then Will could put his family back together.

Lindsey put a hand on his arm. "I broke my own rule and told Nat she shouldn't marry him. I tried the *you're not happy* tactic instead of the *because I can see it* route, but it didn't matter.

People believe they love whomever they believe they love. And it sucks for the people who get hurt in the name of love."

"He's not a bad guy," Will said. "He's just kinda useless. Got some kind of inheritance, and he's been chasing bad business ventures for as long as Aunt Jessie's known him."

"You think she's his backup plan when the cash dries up?"

He shrugged, watching Jessie hustle up behind Donnie on his way into the house.

"When they got married, Sacha said they'd make it," Will said. "Never said that about Aunt Jessie's other husbands. Just said getting married was the right thing for Aunt Jessie to do at the time. Thought maybe somebody in our family could find that true love this time."

"Has Sacha ever been married?"

"Nope. Says knowing too much gets in the way of following her heart."

"Hmm."

"Hmm, interesting, or hmm, you can relate?"

The screen door opened. "Donnie, please, not now," Jessie said. Her voice was hushed, cracked, as though she didn't want it carrying through the house.

As though she didn't want to be saying it at all.

Will stepped into the living room and sized up his uncle-in-law.

The older man was plump, with a receding hairline and a bulbous nose. His usual outfit was a three-piece suit, but today, he was in baggy jeans, sneakers and a loose brown polo sporting dust streaks.

Looked like the streaks Will's crew got moving boxes of merchandise around.

Will's gut tightened. "Afternoon, Donnie."

The older man wouldn't meet his eyes. "Afternoon. Didn't realize you were in town."

Aunt Jessie was hugging herself, shifting from foot to foot.

"Y'all have plans this afternoon?" Will said. Bright. Happy. As if he were standing on a stage, playing for a crowd instead of watching something he didn't understand going down in his aunt's living room.

As if his heart wasn't pounding like he'd run ten miles.

Lindsey put a hand to his back, a subtle *I'm here*.

"Don't want to make a big fuss," Donnie said, "but I finally figured out I ain't what Jessie needs. I'm clearing out my stuff. Won't take long."

"He's staying," Aunt Jessie said. "Will, tell him he needs to stay." She looked past him, pointed to Lindsey. "*You*. You're supposed to know these things. *You* tell him he needs to stay."

"Jessie." Donnie started to look at her, but his eyes pinched shut, his mouth twisted, and he turned away from her. "Don't need to be making this harder."

"Then don't leave." Aunt Jessie sent a desperate look at Will. "He's the love of my life, and *that woman* said he needs to go, so he's going. Tell him not to leave. *Tell him to stay.*"

Beside him, Lindsey's gaze flitted between Aunt Jessie and Donnie. There was a wrinkle in her nose. Her brows shifted down. And she studied Donnie's retreating backside with a singular concentration that gave Will's heart the shivers.

"Why are you doing this?" Lindsey said quietly.

Donnie froze.

Will did too. He'd heard her lawyer voice, her telling-a-fun-story voice, her bedroom voice, but he hadn't heard *this* voice.

The *you're wrong on a cosmic level* voice.

"What's really going on, Donnie?" Lindsey said.

Donnie's face had gone pale, and he seemed to be struggling with what to do with his hands. "It's what's best for everybody. I ain't in her future. Suppose all y'all heard that by now."

"Why aren't you in her future?" Lindsey said.

"Quit asking him questions and tell him he needs to stay right here." Aunt Jessie had always been prone to tears, but these tears were different. These were heart-cracking, life-shattering, world-ending tears.

"I don't know what the truth is," Lindsey said, "but you owe it to your wife to tell her all of it."

She had Donnie's full attention now. He mopped a hand over his pale forehead. "Ain't your place—"

"Did you cheat on her?"

"Of course not."

"Did you want to?"

"Now that's just plain insultin'."

Will wasn't Donnie's biggest fan by any stretch of the imagination, but there was an honest ring to the man's answer.

"Are you still married to someone else?" Lindsey said.

"Now you listen here, missy—"

Lindsey didn't stop. "Problems in the bedroom?"

"Never," Aunt Jessie said. "Not ever."

Will grimaced. He'd have to thank Lindsey for *that* visual later.

"Money problems?" Lindsey suggested. "Religious differences? You want children and she doesn't? I've been a divorce lawyer for ten years. I can keep going all day."

"I'm dying," Donnie blurted. "You happy now? I'm dying."

He sagged against the wall that used to hold pictures of the whole family. "I'm dying," he repeated, softer.

Silence descended like a thick smoke. Will tried to pick his jaw up off the floor. Lindsey gripped his shirt where her hand had been resting on his back.

And Jessie stood there, gaping, her heart—her *life*—breaking before his eyes.

Will moved first. In three steps, he was at Aunt Jessie's side. He knew something about heartbreak. Knew something about being left behind. Hell if he'd let her think she was alone.

"Got cancer." Donnie swiped at his eyes. "End's coming. My momma had cancer. My daddy had cancer. Now I got cancer. I took care of 'em both for nearabouts ten years, all said and done. Ain't pretty. Jessie, darlin', you deserve a better life. You deserve a man who's whole, who can keep taking you out to the Pork'n'Fork, who can keep up with you goin' out and havin' fun. You got the whole rest of your life ahead of you. Don't need to be turning you into a nursemaid. You've given up enough for me. I don't want you doing any more."

Jessie shrugged out of Will's reach. "Donnie Boyd, you are

the dumbest man God ever put on this planet, but you're *my* man, and I'll be danged if I'm letting you get away with this."

"Jessie. Been a good two years, but I can't ask you to spend the next forever taking care of me till I die. Sacha was right. I—"

Jessie mauled him with a hug. "You hush. You ain't going through this alone, Donnie. Not so long as I got breath in me and a heart in my chest." She had a clenched fist buried in Donnie's shirt while she tilted a look at Will, then at Lindsey. "We're right, us two. He's *mine*. In sickness or health. He's supposed to be mine. And I'm his."

Lindsey nodded. Once, but it was an honest nod, the truth echoing in the sadness and longing and sympathy in her eyes. "You're a beautiful match."

Will's heart swelled to twice the size of Texas.

He wouldn't have picked Jessie and Donnie to be forever, but if Lindsey would put stock in them, then Will could work harder on accepting Donnie. She *did* see. He had the same shivers on his shivers that he got when Sacha was dead-on.

And turned out, Sacha might not have been wrong. And that put a crimp in Will's heart for his aunt.

While she fussed over Donnie, Will took Lindsey by the elbow and steered her to the backyard. And when they stood outside in the warm Georgia sunshine, he wrapped his arms around his girl and rested his forehead on her shoulder. "You see that coming?" he asked.

"No," she whispered. "I thought maybe he was doing it for Sacha, not for… that."

"They really good together?"

She hesitated, went stiff against him. But then she put her arms around his waist and softened with a whole body sigh. "Yes."

For how long was anybody's guess, but Sacha hadn't been wrong.

Will had to get over and tell her. Jessie would need her now—would need *all* of them—more than ever.

"Bet it feels good to say that," he said into Lindsey's hair.

And there she went, getting all stiff again. "Will."

He let her go and hoisted himself onto the top of Aunt Jessie's picnic table, his feet on the bench. "After seeing all the people who get married for the wrong reasons, wouldn't it be nice to nudge couples together who have the chance to get married for the right reasons?"

He was pushing her buttons, but she wasn't biting. No stubborn lawyer face coming out, no stubborn just-plain-being-Lindsey face either. Instead, she nodded. Once. Again. "It would."

That bass drum kicked up in Will's chest. He reached for her hand. Soft, smooth, with pink-tipped nails. She squeezed his hand back. She was all woman, all beauty, all strength.

And she was finally figuring out how much *more* she was too.

"You feel like making any other matches today?" He couldn't keep the raw, husky hope out of his voice. He wasn't on a stage, wasn't talking to reporters or deejays or fans.

He was talking to the woman who had always been his world.

Her gaze dropped. "Will," she said again.

"Don't tell me you're leaving tomorrow because we ain't good for each other. I know you don't like crowds. I know you don't like being in the spotlight. You don't have to be, Lindsey. I can fix that."

"Stop," she whispered.

He slid off the table, cradled her face in his hands, her soft hair cascading around his fingers, and tilted her head so he could see those pretty, teary brown eyes. Wasn't anything in the world that could've stopped him. "I didn't ask for three weeks for me. I asked for three weeks for you. A long time ago, you believed I had what it takes to be a star. You believed in me. Now it's my turn. I believe in you. I believe in who you are, who you are under the suits, under the baby-eater lawyer lady, under the smileys. And I'm gonna keep believing in you as long as it takes, until you're ready to believe in *us*."

A tear dripped on her cheek. Her chin wobbled. But instead of tipping up like they were supposed to, her lips drew down. Instead of crinkling in happiness, her eyes had hopeless misery written in them. "I can't," she whispered.

His heart let out an *oomph* like it had been socked in the gut.

"Will, you are an amazing man—"

"Stop," he growled.

"—and you could be happy with any woman in the world."

"I'm looking at the woman I want to be happy with."

"No, *listen*. Listen to me. I've seen you with Pepper, with Kimmie, with Dahlia and Nat and Marilyn, with all those women who wanted your signature at Suckers. And you're a good match for all of them. *All* of them. You can do so much better than—"

"*Stop.*" She was wrong. He couldn't do better. He didn't *want* to do better.

He ignored the quaking in his gut, in his bones, in his soul, and stared *into* her, willing her to know what he knew. To understand that in this case, *he* knew better. "And what do you see when you look at me with you?"

"Everything." The word was barely audible but it boomed through his ears anyway. "Typhoons and rainbows. Earthquakes and sunshine. Thunderstorms and spring flowers. Everything."

"That good or bad?"

"*I don't know.*" She inhaled a shuddery breath. "But I do know you can be happy with someone else. *Anyone* else. You should be happy, Will. You deserve to be happy. I want you to be happy. But I can't be the one who makes you happy. I can't."

His chest hurt from all the pounding behind his ribs and his arms trembled from the effort of holding her without squeezing so hard she couldn't leave. "I can fix the Billy stuff. I can make it go away."

"Will, let go." More tears streaked down her cheeks. "You have to let me go."

She didn't mean taking his hands off her.

She meant taking his heart off her.

"You're wrong," he said.

She pulled out of his grasp. "So go get a second opinion." She wasn't mean, wasn't angry. Simply matter-of-fact. She brushed a tear off her cheek. A pained look creased her forehead. "I'm sorry, Will. I'm so sorry." She took two backward steps, then turned and fled the backyard.

He followed after her. "Lindsey. Lindsey, wait." She wasn't leaving. She couldn't leave. They weren't done.

Even tomorrow, they wouldn't be done. They had a future. They had things to work out, but they were meant to be together. He was hers. He'd always been hers.

She kept fleeing. Head down, power-walking away. Sacha stepped between the houses and dangled something that flashed in the light. Her dark hair lifted in the wind, and her dark eyes flashed a *storm's coming* warning.

Lindsey stumbled to a stop. Will saw her hand reach out to touch Sacha's.

"No—" he started.

But it was too late. Sacha had already handed over the keys to her car. "Leave it at the airport."

"Stop!" Will said.

"Let her go, William." The vision voice. She was using the vision voice on him. "She's meant to go, honey. She did what she needed here. She's meant to go."

Lindsey skittered into Sacha's Winnebago, fired the engine, and then his life, his love—she sped away down Billy Brenton Lane.

And Will stopped.

All of him. He just stopped.

Stopped moving, stopped breathing, stopped feeling his heart beating. He hunched over, broken.

He knew where Lindsey lived. Knew where she worked. He had her phone number, her email address and he knew how to get in touch with her family.

But knowing where she was didn't change that she didn't want him.

And not because he was Billy Brenton.

But because even Will Truitt had never been good enough for her.

A steady hand settled on his shoulder, right where his smiley face tattoo burned his skin. "Come inside. Sit with me awhile."

"You—you let her go. You *helped* her go."

"You have to let her go too. It's her journey now, and you can't help with what she must do."

His hairs stood on end. The hairs on his neck, on his arms, on his legs. He shook Sacha's hand off. "Tell Aunt Jessie I'll call her later," he choked out.

And Will left too.

Lindsey didn't believe in him anymore. This time, he had to be the one who believed in himself.

TWENTY

WILL SPENT Saturday night holed up in a seedy motel halfway between Pickleberry Springs and Gellings Air Force Base. He sent Aunt Jessie a text message to call him anytime, sent Sacha a text message that he still loved her even if he didn't want to talk to her for the next forever, but she owed him not moving away, and then he sent Mikey a message that he'd hit the Dumbass Hall of Fame and discovered it wasn't all it was cracked up to be, but he'd be in Nashville on Sunday night.

But first, Will had to get his dog.

After lunch on Sunday, he pulled over at a modest house not far from Gellings Air Force Base. He had a nameless guitar instead of Vera and no dog on the seat beside him yet.

He also had a lifetime's worth of achy breaky songs bleeding out his heart, but none of them sounded like music.

After an obligatory knock, he used his key to let himself into his sister's house. Voices echoed somewhere in the house —more than just Mari Belle's and Paisley's voices. He turned around—he'd call Mari Belle and have her bring Wrigley out —then a squeaky bark greeted him and Biscuits, Mari Belle's terrier, lunged for his leg.

Chicken, her boxer, ambled into the foyer for some sniffing-and-greeting business. Wrigley poked his head out of the dining room. So did Mari Belle.

"Aw, Will," she sighed.

Paisley barreled around the corner too. "Uncle Will! Where's—"

Mari Belle snagged her daughter and clapped a hand over her mouth. "Go get Uncle Will a piece of pie and a glass of milk."

"Yes, ma'am."

She danced off, and Mari Belle eyed him. His shoulders crept to his ears.

Been a long time since she looked at him like that.

Wasn't undeserved. Some, but not all.

Wrigley stood, gave a lazy shake, then ambled to him, sniffing, peering around behind Will. *Where's my girl?* his dog seemed to ask.

Will bent and gave Wrigley a good rubdown and nudged Biscuits off his leg.

Wasn't anything else he could do.

"C'mon, sit down." Mari Belle led him to her dining room, all three dogs following along at their own pace. "My apologies for my brother," she said to her guests. "His brain took a vacation a month ago and his heart's paying for it today."

He wasn't feeling like being Billy Brenton today, so if they were expecting another song-and-dance, they were in for disappointment.

Mari Belle yanked on his shirt and dragged him into a seat. "Anna, Jackson, this is Will. I don't know if you were properly introduced the other night. Will, my neighbors."

He remembered the lady from the meet-and-greet. She smiled at him. "Hi," she said in a Minnesota accent, and on the starstruck scale, she was doing a right good job of almost keeping to the bottom.

He nodded.

Mari Belle shoved him into a chair, then tweaked his ear.

He yelped.

"I swear to sweet baby Jesus," she said, "if you don't say

something, I'm gonna whoop your hind end until you can't sit for a week."

He leaned back and folded his arms.

Like to see her try.

'Sides, wouldn't be any worse than what he was doing to himself.

Mari Belle sat next to him, still giving him the mother of all *don't be a dumbass* looks.

"Here's your pie, Uncle Will." God bless Paisley. Sweet girl hadn't picked up on the ugly flowing around this morning. "Miss Anna made it."

"Thank you, peanut."

He slid Mari Belle a *happy now?* glare.

He could talk.

Didn't want to, but he could do it.

"Hope you like s'mores pie," Anna said. "It would've been sweet potato, but Jackson doesn't share."

Will eyed the chocolate and marshmallows, arranged all pretty and neat on a graham cracker crust. His stomach rolled over. "Looks right good." Looked like it would make him sick.

Made him think of Lindsey's ice cream. Her s'mores maker. Her licking melted chocolate and marshmallow off his fingers.

"Momma's trying to teach Miss Anna to bake biscuits," Paisley said, "So Miss Anna's teaching Momma and me to bake pie. What's your favorite pie, Uncle Will? And what about Miss—"

"Paisley, the dogs need to go out," Mari Belle said.

"They just came in," Paisley said.

"Have you finished the dishes?"

Paisley slid from the table again. "If y'all are talking *grown-up* stuff, I can still hear you in the kitchen."

"Go."

"Leave her be," Will said.

Mari Belle's *don't be a dumbass* eyeball turned into the dual eyeballs of *don't disagree with me in front of my daughter.*

Will stared right back.

She picked up a coffee cup with a classic Mari Belle sigh. "What did she do this time?"

Wasn't talking about Paisley, and he knew it.

But the stink of it all was that Lindsey hadn't done anything. Nothing but been honest with him, and he couldn't handle it.

They'd all warned him. He hadn't listened.

"You talk to Aunt Jessie today?" he said.

Mari Belle's lashes fluttered in one of her annoyed eye flickers, but she nodded over a sigh.

Didn't much matter what Will's love life looked like. Aunt Jessie's would be hard enough on all of them.

Probably he should've offered to stay behind in Pickleberry Springs and help, but they were better off without him right now. He'd hire extra caretakers if Aunt Jessie needed help, he'd make sure Donnie saw the best doctors, he'd damn well make sure Sacha stayed in town and that Aunt Jessie patched things up with her best friend, if she hadn't already. But emotionally, he couldn't be what they needed. So he'd go to Nashville. Tour rehearsals started soon, and there was a mountain's worth of publicity and other business stuff he had to attend to. And he'd gone and committed himself like a dummy to being in Bliss on Saturday night.

He'd been certain Lindsey was scared of what she knew.

He'd had no idea she'd just been being honest.

Friends can kiss, right? she'd said fifteen years ago. And he'd missed the clue.

I don't do love, I don't do commitment and I can only give you three weeks. It's my rule, she'd said this time.

And again, he'd been the dummy who ignored it.

We're a much better match now than fifteen years ago, but you're still better off with anyone but me.

He eyed the pie again. Didn't hurt so bad this time, Lindsey running away from him.

Might could've been because he was numb. Might could've been because he still had Mari Belle and Paisley and Aunt Jessie and Wrigley and Mikey and Sacha.

Or might could've been, he was lying to himself.

"You quit talking again, I'm gonna yank that knot till your kidneys bleed."

Paisley leaned in the doorway to the kitchen, watching and being uncharacteristically quiet. Across the table, Anna and Jackson shared a look. Anna had been watching Will curiously. "Did you break up with your girlfriend?"

Will's grip tightened around his fork. He needed to eat a bite. Prove to Mari Belle he was fine. Ease those worry lines creasing Paisley's forehead. Get out from the spotlight of a stranger asking after his personal affairs.

"She wasn't his girlfriend," Mari Belle said.

"I was going to be a junior bridesmaid and babysit," Paisley stage-whispered. She sent Will a dirty look that should've made her momma proud.

"Oh, for God's sake," Mari Belle said with one of her sighs. "Paisley, honey, Uncle Will will buy you a new tea set instead, okay?"

Paisley heaved her junior version of a Mari Belle sigh. "Uncle Will, would you like some Pepto to go with your pie?"

"Oh, honey, you've got it bad," Anna murmured.

Will gave her the *Don't talk to Billy Brenton like you know him* look.

She sipped something out of her teacup. "Is this because she's a Yankee?" Anna said.

"Yankees aren't all bad," Jackson drawled into his pie. "Once you give 'em a chance."

Will's jaw went unhinged and dangled. "Did y'all call her a *Yankee*?"

"Unlike *some* families," Mari Belle said to Jackson, "we judge people on who they are, not where they're from. And *this* girl—"

"Watch your mouth," Will growled.

"—has a history of wreaking havoc on my brother's emotions," Mari Belle finished.

"My experience, the only ones that get to you are the only ones that can make you truly happy," Jackson said.

"And exactly how many have *gotten* to you?" Anna said.

"Oh, three, maybe four." But his grin and wink aimed at Anna said otherwise.

One girl in a lifetime could do a man like that.

And Will's one girl didn't want him. Again.

He shoved his pie away.

"Does he look happy to you?" Mari Belle deadpanned.

"Darkest days of a man's life are the ones where he's found his girl but doesn't think he can have her." Jackson forked another bite of pie. "Don't reckon she's got it much easier. Anna Grace gave me a right good fight about needing to do that independent woman thing, not wanting to follow me around all the time when the military moves me, but your life makes ours look simple."

Independent woman thing. Yeah, Lindsey had that. Always had.

"Lady doesn't like the spotlight, does she?" Jackson continued. "Your crew scared her right good."

Will's head jerked up. His BillyVision crew. They'd been behind her during her song Friday night. They'd scared her away. He'd have to talk to them about—no. He clenched his jaw.

Lindsey would've left anyway. It was what she did. Difference was, this time, she'd told him she would.

"It's so easy to lose your own identity in a regular relationship, and you don't even realize you're doing it until it's over," Anna said. "But being a superstar's girlfriend? Getting all that attention? That's even harder."

Will grunted. *He* was the problem. *His* job was the problem. What about hers? She wasn't even doing what she was supposed to be doing.

And what would her life look like if she walked away from a successful career to be a full-time psychic matchmaker on the road with him?

His stomach clenched.

Lindsey wasn't built like Sacha. She liked having a traditional job. She liked stability. She liked taking care of herself.

And being with Will—being with *Billy Brenton*—would've made her give all that up eventually. He could've found her another job—lots of guys' wives ran charitable foundations, worked part-time from the road, found worthy causes to champion—but she hadn't even given him the chance.

Because her psychic woo-woo matchmaker senses went haywire where he was concerned.

Mari Belle let loose another of her sighs. "I don't think she was after your fame and fortune, I'll give her that. But I still think you're better off without her. Is Mikey going to Nashville with you?"

Nashville was another problem.

Lindsey didn't like crowds. She'd been rejected by friends in college because of her gift and by the townspeople of Bliss because of her job. Being Billy Brenton's girlfriend would put her in a spotlight no matter what Will did.

Another place to be judged.

Another place to be rejected.

He got it.

He did.

But she still didn't want to give him a chance to make it all right.

He shoved to his feet. Mari Belle was right. *Lindsey* was right. He and Lindsey were better off apart. "I gotta hit the road." He patted his leg, and Wrigley pushed to his feet once again. "Call me if any of y'all need anything."

Paisley darted into the room. "Don't go, Uncle Will. You barely got here."

He squeezed her hard, a big ol' lump threatening to choke him. "Miss you already, peanut. I'll talk to your momma about that plan you had for the summer."

She let him go with a whoop. He nodded to Jackson and Anna. "Appreciate y'all watching out for these two." Even if he didn't appreciate them butting into his own personal private life.

Mari Belle walked him to the door and wrapped him in a tight hug. "Take care of yourself, okay? Call me. Every day. Every hour, actually. That would be better."

He nodded.

She worried. He knew.

He worried too. But he couldn't afford to go to that dark place that was creeping at him from all angles again.

He had to go be Billy Brenton.

LINDSEY'S SKIN ITCHED EVERYWHERE.

She'd taken off the wedding dress over two hours ago, but she still felt the satin and lace, still smelled the flowers, still felt the ache in her cheeks from forcing a smile throughout Nat's photo shoot this afternoon.

And she wasn't done yet. Because Nat wanted to celebrate the launch of her new line of Bliss Originals bridal gowns. So here Lindsey was, on a crowded Friday night, hunched into an impossibly small personal space bubble in Suckers, watching the out-of-town wedding crowd.

The guests came in for weekend weddings in Bliss. They came to Suckers to hook up with other wedding guests, then disappeared as if they'd never been here. The ones who smelled like one-night stands, she didn't mind. She'd done enough itch-scratching in her life to get it. But the ones who smelled like desperation?

Those made her head and her heart hurt.

She could spare them long-term pain if she interfered. But she didn't know how to be tactful about it.

Or why any of them would listen to a random crazy woman in a bar who was doing a horrible job of hiding her own personal heartbreak.

The itch in Lindsey's skin flared.

Will would be back tomorrow for the Battle of the Boyfriends, and he was bringing a camera crew. Doing what he promised for Bliss.

She missed him.

She didn't have the right, but she missed him.

"That was fun, wasn't it?" Pepper said beside her.

Lindsey forced a smile. "Yep. A blast. And none of the dresses burst into flames for being worn by a divorce attorney."

"Or pre-brides." Pepper's shoulders slumped.

"Pre-brides?"

Pepper grimaced. "Is there really no legend of the pre-bride in Bliss? That seems so unlikely."

"If there were, I would've heard of it," Kimmie said over her coconut cream pie on Lindsey's other side. It was practically the first thing she'd said all day. "We have the widow-maker, the groomsman curse, and the golden bouquet hex. But the pre-bride legend? That's a new one."

"Pepper's got it bad," Cinna said. She was slinging bottles behind the bar beside CJ tonight. "Her last fourteen boyfriends have married the girl they met after they broke up with her."

"Seven. *Seven.* Not fourteen. And sometimes *I* did the breaking up." Pepper tossed a piece of ice at her sister. "No one invited you to this conversation."

"Just because you dated half of them before you signed up for Facebook doesn't mean it didn't happen with them too. It just means you didn't hear about it." Cinna grinned. "Too bad hanging with Billy didn't count as dating or maybe Lindsey would have a ring on her finger instead of some tears in her beer."

"Too bad drinks don't mix themselves." CJ popped up behind her and swatted her with a towel. "Get back to work and quit being obnoxious."

"I'm the baby. Being obnoxious *is* my job."

Cinna slid down the bar, sassing three groomsmen and winking at a fourth on her way.

"I totally get why some animals eat their young," Pepper said.

"Yeah, but if Mom and Dad had eaten her, Sage would've had baby syndrome," CJ said.

"I could've lived with that."

Kimmie slid her coconut cream pie past Lindsey and over to Pepper. "Here. You might need this more than I do."

"Really?"

"Well, no, but I almost didn't fit in my dress today, and that'll interfere with my mom's efforts to marry me off." She shuddered, then eyed the pie.

CJ pushed another piece onto the bar. "Got enough to go around, and your mom's gonna have to go through me before we let you get married off. To a man of your choosing. Who loves you with or without the dress. Eat up." He added a second glass of white zin for Lindsey, then went to check on Nat, who was hunched over a camera with her photographer.

Kimmie and Pepper both poked at their pie.

"Does Bliss have any ways of breaking curses?" Pepper said.

"Supposedly there's an old troll lady who lives under the country club, but you have to be able to sing the alphabet in her native language, which is a cross between Minion and Mandarin."

Lindsey peered at Kimmie. "Seriously?"

"Yeah, she—oh, wait. No, that was a dream. Sorry. No curse-breakers."

"Evening, ladies," Dad said. "Mind if I join you?"

Lindsey turned. She hadn't realized he was coming tonight. He was alone—no Marilyn—and he was wearing a melancholy expression she recognized all too well.

She tucked her hair behind her ears. "Have a seat," she said.

Dad eyed Kimmie's coconut cream pie, then winced. "Go light, Kimmie. Don't want you having bad dreams."

Lindsey glanced about for an empty stool, and a woman at a table caught her eye. She had plain brown hair with bangs that needed a trim, little makeup, and she wore a chunky sweater that hid her figure. When she realized Lindsey was looking at her, she pulled her purse tighter into her body and shifted her gaze away.

Lindsey's heart swelled, beating fast. Her nose started running, and pressure built in her sinuses.

She smelled tulips.

She looked around and spotted someone else she recognized.

Her throat clogged.

"Here, Dad. Take my stool."

"You sure?"

"Yeah. Way crowded tonight. I'll celebrate with Nat another time."

She needed to leave. Take her coat and her purse and go.

Instead, her wobbly knees moved away from her stool without grabbing her personal belongings.

One step. Then two. Three. All the way to the table halfway between the steel semicircle bar and the door, to the girl hugging her purse. "That guy over there—" Lindsey pointed to the man she and Will had seen talking with the girl a couple weeks ago. The couple Will had urged her to say something to. "Let him buy you dinner."

"I'm sorry?"

"He likes you. Let him buy you dinner."

The girl cast a covert look at her Romeo-in-waiting, who was casting a covert look at her instead of chatting with his buddies and the four women around them.

"I don't know him," the girl said.

Lindsey didn't either. And her heart was fixin' to pound right on out of her chest—*damn* those Southernisms still sneaking into her brain—but she knew. She *knew*. These two needed to meet. "The bar's open until two. Lots of people around. Say hi. Tell him your name. Ask him where he's from. Tell him about your job. Or just go say hi. If nothing else, you'll make his night."

Before she could say anything else, Lindsey walked away. She rolled her shoulders and rubbed at her hip, then swiped at her nose. She itched again. Not from the dress, from the fabric, or from anything she could touch.

But it was almost a *good* itch.

Like she'd taken the first step in shedding skin that didn't fit her anymore.

"Whoops," she said when she returned to the stool where Dad was sitting. "Forgot my purse."

"You're leaving?" Nat appeared at her side and gripped her hand. "CJ's bringing us cheese fries. And you *have* to see this shot of you by the wedding cake monument. It's gorgeous."

"The dresses were gorgeous. That was all you."

"No, *you* were gorgeous. Please, Lindsey? Five more minutes? We all have to call it quits early because of the Battle of the Boyfriends tomorrow night."

"We haven't toasted the dresses yet," Pepper said. "You have to stay."

"And I could use a whiskey," Dad said.

Lindsey blinked at him.

"Dad?" Nat tilted her head. "What's wrong?"

"I had a dream fluffernutter sandwiches were marching on the capitol," Kimmie said over her pie. "And then they reached for their swords, except the swords were really bombs, and the bombs were fortune cookies, and then they popped like popcorn, and it was like, *Poof*! A bajillion fortune cookies, all with freaky fortunes. They were everywhere. And now—and now—"

"I've had to terminate my friendship with Marilyn," Dad said.

Nat's lips parted. Kimmie's cheeks were bright and splotchy, her chin wobbling so hard her nostrils were twitching too.

Kimmie had always borne the brunt of her mother's personality, and Dad's friendship had made the Queen General significantly more human.

Lindsey's itching got worse. It went under her skin, beneath her muscles, but she couldn't scratch her bones. Couldn't make it go away.

Because—because—

"Why?" she said to Dad.

"You know, I thought I could change her," he said slowly. He nodded to Nat. "When she was giving you such a hard time, I thought I could be a buffer. Remind her we were in the business of making magic for *people*, and that we were all on the same team. I thought she was getting better. Especially after the Games last summer. But then..." He shook his head. "She crossed a line." He lifted a finger to CJ. "Whiskey. The good stuff."

CJ nodded.

"What line?" Lindsey said. Her stomach fluttered, her heart begged for a break and that thick knot of icky emotions grew bigger behind her nose and eyes.

"You know what I missed most when your mom died?" he

said. "I missed those minutes at the end of the day. She'd ask me how my day was, and I'd ask how hers was. We'd talk about you girls, about the shop, about committee meetings. Simple, but it's what I missed. Last summer, it occurred to me —Marilyn hadn't had any of that. Not for years. She didn't have anyone to unwind with at the end of the day. She was who she was because she was alone, and she didn't know how to be any other way. So when she was so rotten to you, Nat, I thought I could change her. I thought I could make her better for all of us. For all of *Bliss*."

Nat rubbed his back. "You did, Dad. She's still crazy and annoying, but she's better. And Bliss is better too."

"What line did she cross?" Lindsey repeated.

Dad wouldn't look at her.

"Dad?"

He took a shot glass from CJ and tossed it back, then sputtered out a cough. Dad's eyes watered, and a trickle of bubbly moisture dribbled out the corner of his mouth. "What in the—" he gasped.

"Ginger ale," CJ said. "I've seen you drunk. Can't be responsible for that again. Don't you worry, though. I'll charge you like it's top shelf."

"Finger paints and science kits for Noah's birthday," Dad rasped out.

"Pretty sure Margie and Saffron already have those covered," Pepper said. "Try a set of jacks. It's the only thing none of us are brave enough to buy. We *know* that comes with retribution."

"And payback's a bitch," CJ growled at his sister.

She snorted. "So? It's not like *I'm* ever getting married and having kids."

Lindsey watched Dad until he looked at her. "What did Marilyn do?" she said.

He scrubbed a hand down his face. "She said somebody needed to talk to your boss, so we could get you to doing what you should've always been doing. And I told her—I told her she could accept *both* my girls for who you choose to be, or she could get out of my life."

Nat shrank, quick injury flitting across her features.

Dad hadn't told Marilyn to shove it when Nat was taking the brunt of her shenanigans.

Kimmie wiped a smudge of cream off her nose, then took another bite from her pie.

"Six months, I've been patient," Dad said. "Six months, I've believed she could be better. I thought she *was* better. Your mother had a lot of respect for her, you know. Said she was a good friend in her own unique way, but it meant putting up with all the eccentricities, and knowing that she wouldn't even realize you were being her friend. But what she did to you, Nat—I was wrong. I can't change her. I shouldn't have tried. I'm sorry, hon. I'm sorry, and I'm done. You girls—you deserve better. Lindsey, I don't understand why you do what you do, but I'm proud of you. And you don't have to change for me—or for some boy—or for *anybody*. I'm done accepting people into my family who want you to. Either one of you."

"Dad—"

"You know what stings?" He fiddled with his shot glass. "She's a real pain in the ass some days, but she *understood*. She knew how hard it was to be lonely. She made me less lonely, but I—there are plenty of people to be friends with."

"Dad," Lindsey said again.

"I know. I'm sorry. Kimmie, I'm sorry to you too. Not fair to talk about your mother like this."

"Mmph," Kimmie said around a mouthful of pie. Her big blue eyes were shiny and tilted down with a morose acceptance. She'd probably known all day. No wonder she'd been quiet.

Lindsey bit her lip.

Compared to being unable to honestly tell Will they were a good match, this should've been easy.

Did bones have layers? Because hers were itching inside now. Itching and burning and protesting.

She never wanted to do this.

Never wanted to know.

She'd sworn a blood oath with herself to never tell *anyone* what she knew, because no good could come of it.

But Kimmie was miserable. Kimmie was bound to be miserable for the rest of her life if Lindsey didn't say something.

And Dad was sad. Sadder than he'd been since last spring, before he became friends with Marilyn.

And Marilyn—without Dad, she'd return to being the Queen General robot.

Or worse.

Payback wasn't a bitch. Grief was. And fresh grief—Lindsey knew a thing or two about that.

So she turned her back on every promise she'd made herself, every oath she'd sworn to herself, every bit of determination to ignore what she'd known for almost a year.

"Dad," she whispered, "Marilyn's a good match for you."

Nat choked on her drink. Pepper dropped her wine, the glass shattering on the floor. And CJ lost control of the soda hose.

Lindsey ducked but still got hit with the sticky stream of liquid. Dad, Kimmie and Nat all dove for cover while Pepper flew across the bar and grabbed the soda sprayer. "Smooth, Princess," she said to CJ.

"Like to see you keep it together if *you're* faced with having Marilyn as your mother-in-law."

Lindsey's eye twitched.

Nat straightened with a giggle. "Oh, *God*, Lindsey. That was mean. Don't do that to Dad."

Lindsey pulled out one of her favorite lawyer expressions.

"You're serious?" Nat said.

"You're serious?" Kimmie echoed, significantly more hope in her baby blues. She reached for her pie, now doused with wine and soda, and went in for another bite.

Dad eyed Lindsey. "You're serious."

"I'm not saying not to let her stew for a few days to come to the realization of what she's lost"—oh, the irony and the pain —"but don't write her off because of us. Nat can handle Marilyn. I can handle Marilyn."

She *could*. She could handle Marilyn.

It was the rest of her life she was still sorting out.

But the truth was, much as she cringed at the thought of more family dinners with Marilyn, of the Queen General of Bliss hosting them for Thanksgiving, of having to put up with Kimmie's mother more—telling Dad the truth felt good.

She grabbed Nat's hand. "And you. You and CJ are a fantastically good match too."

"Duh." Nat pulled her in for a hug. "You already said it, even if you didn't."

Across the bar, the girl with the bangs and baggy sweater approached the preppy guy who'd been eyeing her. They shared a tentative smile, and Lindsey smelled a whole field of spring flowers.

Like she'd put her own brand of happiness into the world.

Will would've been proud of her. She clenched her fist to keep from reaching for her phone.

She didn't have the right to call him or text him. She'd walked away. This was *her* fault. And now she needed to leave him alone to find his own happiness.

It was the hardest thing she'd ever done, and it had involved dodging his phone calls the first half of the week, but it was *right*.

He had a bigger life, and he deserved to move on to someone who could love him without question. Someone who was an honestly good match for him. Someone who could be his forever without question, who could be as good with Billy as she was with Will, who could fit into all of his worlds, the superstar world and the simple country boy world.

She hoped she hadn't broken him too badly for that.

Because the world would be a better place with a mini-Will or five running around in it.

Lindsey blinked against the stinging and snatched her coat. "I need to go," she said.

"Aw, Lindsey," Nat sighed.

Pepper reached over and squeezed her arm. "I'm sorry. You two looked happy together. Cinna's right. I should've dated him first for you."

Lindsey waved them both off. "I'm beat. You guys have fun." She eyed the mess on the bar and the floor. "After you get cleaned up." She gave Dad a half-hug. "Don't wait so long that Kimmie starts talking about Marilyn channeling her displeasure to swallow The Aisle whole again, but give her a chance to admit she's been wrong. I'll drop by and see you tomorrow." Then she gave Nat a quick hug and a peck on the cheek. "I'm proud of your dresses, Nat. Mom would be too."

"She'd be proud of you too, you know."

"She wouldn't, but that's sweet of you to say."

And knowing she had family and friends who would tell her comforting lies like that was all that would be keeping Lindsey warm tonight.

TWENTY-ONE

AFTER ONE TOO MANY glasses of wine after she got home Friday night, Lindsey was up with the sun, headache in full force, and nowhere she had to be.

But staying home—yeah.

Not happening.

Nat and Kimmie were both helping Pepper with the Battle of the Boyfriends all day. So was CJ. So since her favorite nephew needed a grown-up, and Lindsey needed a distraction, she went for a double dose of coffee, her happiest smiley face panties, and packed her s'mores maker into her car.

A while later, she and Noah clomped into Dad's weekend cabin. When Lindsey and Nat had lived at home, the cabin was Dad's weekend retreat away from all the girls. Now that he was retired and widowed, he was out here as often as possible. Lindsey hadn't been in a while, but it was obvious Marilyn had.

There were touches of her everywhere. A KitchenAid mixer on the counter, matching white throw pillows on the couch, wilted daisies in a vase on the mantel. And like last night, Dad was wearing a shade of melancholy that complemented Lindsey's very, very well.

Noah didn't seem to notice, and between Candy Land, s'mores and a snowball fight, they were all almost in a good mood by late afternoon. Noah nodded off between Lindsey and Dad on the couch by the fire. And Lindsey wanted to.

But she couldn't.

"I met Will on spring break my sophomore year," she said quietly.

Dad nodded for her to go on.

And she did.

She told him the whole story, about losing all her friends in college because she told them who should break up with their boyfriends, about the awkwardness of going on spring break with them anyway, about Will slamming into her on the ski slope, about her wanting a friend and finding so much more.

She left out the part about sleeping with him. Let Dad assume whatever he wanted.

She told him about their final night over spring break, how Will had pulled her onstage at the tavern, sung her a song, told her he loved her.

And then about how she broke his heart.

Publicly.

Loudly.

Humiliatingly.

Dad didn't comment, so Lindsey pressed on.

She told him why she switched law specialties—she'd barely gotten through law school with every presentation getting harder to bear instead of easier, every moment of speaking in front of a crowd terrifying her more and more, about choosing to go into family law to correct the wrongs she wasn't brave enough or strong enough to prevent.

Dad sat there, his arm draped across the back of the couch, circling both her and Noah, and he listened. And when she was spent, he nodded once more. "Always knew you didn't want the family business," he said. "Never knew you were working it in your own way anyway. Giving people second chances—that's honorable, hon. Don't even want to think of where Nat would be now if she hadn't gotten out of her first marriage. Haven't always understood how you do it every day, haven't always liked it, but you've got a bigger heart than you know. You take care of Nat and Noah and Kimmie. You came over to Bliss and supported us all in your own way, even before most people accepted what you do. Lot of ways, you're bigger than Bliss. I've *always* been proud of that. Hope you know it."

"Not always," she whispered. "But thank you."

She dabbed at the corners of her eyes and glanced at the clock. She had to go to get to the Battle of the Boyfriends on time.

And she needed to be there.

Not as a judge. Not to see Will. But to see how it felt to go as herself.

As the woman she'd been born to be, with the gifts she'd been given, Lindsey *had* to go.

Some of those couples might need encouragement. And that was a skill Lindsey needed to work on, no matter what it ultimately meant for her career as a divorce lawyer.

"You going tonight?" Dad asked.

She nodded. "It's time to see if I can find where I truly fit."

"That what you want?" Dad said.

It wasn't what she'd wanted most of her life. But it was part of who she was, and she'd be happier embracing it than denying it. "I want to put more happy in the world."

"Always have, hon." Dad heaved a Dad-sigh. "And there wouldn't be a song about your underwear floating around the radio if you hadn't."

Lindsey swiped her eyes again, this time over a laugh. She fixed a tray of fruit, cheese, carrots, and crackers for them, then she left Dad with official Noah duties and went to see about her own life duties.

WILL HADN'T EVER FOUND his team suffocating before, but all the meetings about the tour and the next album and this problem and that problem and this other problem were enough to make him want to gouge out his eyeballs this past week.

And now he was in Bliss when he wanted to be anywhere but here, lingering backstage with the other judges for the

Battle of the Boyfriends. His crew was out in the Bliss Civic Center's theater, capturing footage of the crowd as he'd promised the crazy Bliss lady they would. He had left Wrigley at the hotel with Cassidy, who was wrangling a few business details for him, and then put on his biggest, brightest Billy face to get through tonight. He'd done his own shots with the BillyVision crew, schmoozed with his fellow judges, answered questions for a couple of local reporters.

And now he wanted to get this over with and get gone.

Someone slapped him on the shoulder. "Doing okay, man?" Mikey said quietly.

"Yep."

"How's Jessie?"

"Real good." Will should've been spending his last weekend off in Pickleberry Springs with his family. Truth, though, was that he didn't want to be there any more than he wanted to be here. "Donnie saw a doctor this week who said they caught it early enough. And Mari Belle said Sacha had a vision that Donnie's fixin' to kick cancer's ass, and it won't come back."

"Good sign," Mikey said.

Will shoved his fists into his pockets so he wouldn't be tempted to deck his buddy. Mikey never took Sacha's side, but he hadn't said a bad thing about her since Sacha gave Lindsey a getaway car.

Mikey hitched a shoulder, his casual act almost the right shade of innocent to be convincing. "Sacha's nuts, but she's still good people. Not like it would help right now if she said he was gonna kick the bucket."

Will grunted.

Mikey tilted a look at him, then heaved an admirable impression of a Mari Belle sigh. "Gotta hand it to you, bucka-roo. Doin' better this time than you did the last time she did you in. Still here. Still walking, talking, and getting shit done."

Will clenched his jaw so hard his teeth should've cracked. He didn't give a damn about getting shit done. He wanted —

He wanted his girl.

No. He wanted the woman he thought was his girl to want to be his girl.

"But funny thing." Mikey said. "Last time, you couldn't quit writing. This time you just quit."

Will reached for Vera's strap.

Mikey was right. Will had quit. He was showing up for meetings, doing what needed doing as Billy, but the music —

The music was gone.

Vanished. *Poof.*

Dead.

He'd written four good songs in Bliss, plus three more he and Mikey had done together, and he had the bones for at least fourteen more. But those fourteen?

He'd handed them to one of his favorite songwriters in Nashville before he left town yesterday. Told him to make them into something decent, because Will couldn't do it.

He didn't want to.

"Never thought I'd say this," Mikey said, "but the girl made you happy. Being Billy ain't everything. The band and crew — they're good at what they do. They'd find other work if you wanted to hang it up."

"Dahlia putting happy heart sprinkles in your Cheerios too?"

Mikey grinned. "Nah, it's all the ice cream." He tucked his hands in his pockets. "Seriously, Will, don't let being Billy be your whole life if there's something else you want."

Not the advice Will ever would've expected out of Mikey. Being in love had addled the boy's brain.

"Oh, hey, Billy." A slender dude in his mid-thirties hitched his brown dress pants, then stuck his hand out. "Lou Lovely. WEDD radio. Great to see you again. Didn't get to talk much at karaoke after Nat's wedding, but I've been playing your songs since 'Weekend Cowboy' landed. Love your music."

Will dug deep for his Billy mask and shook the deejay's hand. "Thanks, man."

Mikey shifted away. "Now, Billy-boy, don't go giving me the good scores because we're friends," he said louder.

"Don't think you have anything to worry about, Mikey."

Annoying as Mikey could be, Will would miss him when he finally found the right new drummer. Mikey knew when Will was Will, and when Will needed to be Billy. A new drummer wouldn't even know *Will* existed.

Seemed to be fewer and fewer people in the world who did. Will wasn't even sure he wanted to exist anymore.

Why not just be Billy? When he was Billy, people talked to him. When he was Billy, people loved him.

When he was Billy, people didn't send his phone calls straight to voicemail or tell their assistants that they were unavailable to talk to him.

Not like Lindsey had.

But when he was Billy, he had to write songs. And those songs had dried up.

"You staying with Lindsey again this weekend?" Lou Lovely said.

Will's head jerked up.

The deejay chuckled. "Would've liked to have been a fly on the wall when you brought a dog into her house. Bet that was a sight."

"Who—" Will started.

"Oh, hey, there, Billy." Pepper Blue slid between them, all gussied up in dress pants, heels, a silky-looking blouse and chunky green jewelry. "Lou, Marilyn needs a word. Mikey, *get out*. No socializing with the judges or you're disqualified and I won't let you onstage, and we don't want to disappoint Dahlia, now do we?" Pepper latched on to Will's arm and steered him away from the two other men. "CJ's been interviewing for a new cook at Suckers, and this crazy thing happened. He found a former army cook who supposedly knows how to fry okra. Who knew? Anyway, we had him whip up a batch for tonight for the judges to try. Have you seen the food table yet?"

"Not hungry, but thanks," Will bit off.

She squeezed his arm tighter. "It means the world to Bliss that you're here. I'm new to all this, but everyone keeps saying there hasn't been a crowd so big for the Battle of the Boyfriends since they almost got Adam Sandler to come judge the year after *The Wedding Singer* was in theaters." Her phone dinged. She whipped it out, and Will's gut went tight at the name on the readout.

Lindsey.

Pepper angled the phone away from his view. "But you're way better than Adam Sandler," she said.

Will nodded at the phone. "She here?"

Pepper got one of those pained looks that Mari Belle usually paired with a sigh. "Do you want her to be?"

His pulse kicked it into high tempo, making his temples ache. "What I've learned, doesn't much matter what I want there." He turned to the table. "Fried okra, you said?"

"And sweet tea," Pepper said. "Mikey stole some earlier and said it was almost as good as his momma's."

"Huh."

Pepper took two slow steps backward and tapped the name tag on her lapel. "I need to go get the contestants in order. If you need anything at all, holler at any of us wearing one of these. And thank you again for being here. It's really, *really* nice of you."

She didn't say why, but Will knew. There was half a chance he'd run into Lindsey tonight. And in that half a chance, there was all of a chance she'd pretend she didn't know him.

Like she had a month ago.

If he could've been regular ol' Will Truitt, he would've turned around, walked out that door into the frigid February weather, and kept on walking until he lost himself.

But he had a dog, he had his family, and he had a crew counting on him. So Billy Brenton was staying in the building.

And he'd be every bit of the superstar they expected to see tonight.

Because *that* was who he had to be.

LINDSEY ARRIVED at the large theater in the Bliss Civic Center for the Battle of the Boyfriends shortly before curtain time. There were sixteen boyfriends, fiancée-wannabes, or boyfriends-to-be performing in this year's talent show.

Usually the performers were in their late teens or early twenties, all men who wanted to publicly declare for their women.

Only in Bliss.

Profits from entry fees and ticket sales went to local charities, and inevitably someone Dad's age would enter, or someone would completely embarrass himself, or someone would totally surprise the girl he had his sights on by going up there alone, not in a relationship, and dedicate his performance to the woman he wanted to date.

Small-town drama at its best, and it was romantic and sweet and perfect, even during the train-wreck moments.

Lindsey didn't want the distraction of the crowd, so she texted Pepper and asked for a key to one of the box seats. Unfortunately, the box gave Lindsey a clear view of the judges' table. But fortunately, she could hide among the curtains and watch.

The theater was rapidly filling. The battle was due to start in five minutes. Lou Lovely, a local deejay that Lindsey had dated a lifetime ago, was already at the judging table. So was a favorite local TV anchor lady. Mr. and Mrs. Hart, Bliss's gourmet chocolatiers, were the official judges from The Aisle this year. One seat was still empty at the table.

Will's—no, *Billy*'s seat.

Lindsey couldn't afford to think of him as Will. Nor did she have the right.

The door opened, and Kimmie slid into the box with Lindsey. "I *do* do not want to be here."

"Fortune cookie?"

"I ate an entire coconut cream pie last night."

Lindsey turned to stare at her friend. "An *entire* pie? Before or after the slices at Suckers?"

"After. With a full-strength Kimmie colada chaser."

"Oh, Kimmie. Were the dreams bad?"

"Let's just say I didn't know owls had testicles, and they should never sing."

Lindsey didn't want to ask. She didn't want to know. Still —"Owls?"

Kimmie grimaced. "Some things, you can't un-dream or un-remember."

"Or un-hear," Lindsey agreed. "How's your mother?"

"Did you know there's a level past Queen General? It's Her Majesty, the Supreme Grumpy Eminence, and she passed *that* about six hours ago. I'd ask you to tell her I tried to talk you into using your woo-woo powers tonight, but she'd know we were lying, and I'm not sure Bliss is ready to deal with that level of her displeasure."

"Perhaps the sheer force of her personality will finally chase off her silent partner at the bakery."

Kimmie gave a wide-eyed head-shake *no*. "He came by this morning," she whispered. "I thought she was going to castrate him with a frosting spreader."

"Instead of using her psychic powers?" Lindsey deadpanned.

Because this was *normal*. And normal was good.

"Well, with her telekinesis. The spreaders were all the way across the kitchen." Kimmie visibly shivered. "And you know what's weird? I think he *liked* making her mad. I think every time she gets mad, he gets more determined to not give her what she wants. *Any* of what she wants."

"You truly should consider moving."

"But where will I find another you?"

Unexpected tears stung Lindsey's eyes. She squeezed Kimmie in a hug. "We could move together."

Go. Somewhere. Anywhere. A beach, maybe.

Will liked the beach. He'd said he used to find one when he needed to write songs.

"Possibly to Alaska," Lindsey said.

"Siberia, I was thinking."

A rumble went up in the crowd, and Lindsey's raw heart went on an off-key, off-tempo drum solo.

Will was here. *There*. Walking across the stage to the judges' table, waving to the crowd, smiling his killer Billy Brenton smile for the crowd.

"I'm fine," Lindsey said before Kimmie could ask.

She wasn't fine. She was missing something, but she didn't know if it was something she'd ever been meant to have.

She simply knew that after Will, she would never be the same.

She hated herself for walking away—for *running* away from him, but she'd had to. Even while embracing who she was, she was still a mess. And he—he deserved a good match.

Not chaos. Not uncertainty. Not fear.

A *good* match.

Fearlessness would suit you, Sacha had said.

Lindsey shivered.

Will took a seat next to the news lady. The flashy blonde was a terrible match for him. A thunderstorm after a tsunami.

The lights dimmed, and Lindsey turned her attention to the stage, where a spotlight lit Marilyn stalking to the microphone. She introduced the emcees, who introduced the first performer, and the battle began.

Lindsey hadn't been to a Battle of the Boyfriends in years. Some of the performers were pretty great. And some of the matches were great too. Lindsey saw awkward where others wouldn't have—when the third performer brushed past the second performer's girlfriend, Lindsey realized who the better match would've been, but she'd take care of that later.

But then a guy brought a guitar onstage instead of using the karaoke music, and she braced herself.

She looked at the judges' table. Will leaned his cheek on his palm, his attention focused on the stage. His free hand picked at the middle button on his omnipresent plaid overshirt, and her heart panged again.

He was still reaching for Vera.

Mrs. Hart leaned into him, and he turned to her with a smile and replied. Lindsey suppressed an eye roll. He was a drought with the older lady. Not that she'd go after Billy Brenton—she and Mr. Hart were well-matched and old enough to be his parents—but Lindsey still looked.

An hour into the show, there had been one surprised girl— she'd gone running up the aisle to hug her new boyfriend, a twenty-something bank teller, and Lindsey had felt a spring rain shower.

Her heart had let out a sob.

So had the smileys on her panties.

She and Will had been a spring rain shower, once upon a time.

Four performances later, Mikey walked onto the stage.

And he was carrying a guitar.

Lindsey suppressed a shiver and swallowed the rock in her throat. Her eyes stung.

This wasn't getting easier.

She missed Will. She missed him sitting in her sunroom. She missed his smile over the dining room table. She missed his teasing, she missed his pushing her, she missed his loving her.

And now his best friend was here, a guy no one expected to ever settle down, to sing a love song to a girl who was a good match for him.

Why couldn't Will have been Lindsey's match?

Had she felt everything because she wasn't supposed to use her sixth sense when it came to her own relationships? Had she felt everything because she was so afraid she would mess up, even if they were a good match, that she'd mixed the bad signs in with the good? Or had she felt everything because she wanted him so badly, she willed the good into being there along with the bad?

Mikey settled onto a stool onstage and adjusted the microphone. "Evenin', y'all," he said. "I'm new here to Bliss, and it's been a crazy month, but coming here is the best decision I ever made in my life. Dahlia, sweet pea, I love you."

"You did good with that one," Kimmie whispered.

"I didn't do anything with that one."

"You do more than you know, Lindsey."

Lindsey didn't answer, but she did reach over and squeeze Kimmie's hand.

Mikey's fingers hit the guitar strings, and the sound took Lindsey back to her sunroom, to a day not all that long ago when she'd come home to find Mikey visiting Will, the two of them working on a song together. Joking, playing, starting and stopping.

Tears blurred her vision.

He'd been happy that day. Will had been happy. She had too. Then Dahlia had arrived with ice cream, and they'd all been happy together.

Mikey leaned into the top microphone and sang. His voice was shaky, not as deep as Will's, not as *right* as Will's. But that cocky smile he flashed to the audience said he knew he wasn't a singing sensation, and he didn't care, because he had his own talents, and he had his girl.

Lindsey didn't hear the words. She didn't *want* to hear the words. She wanted to bolt.

To leave the theater, to leave the Civic Center, to leave Bliss.

To go somewhere and cry like she hadn't let herself cry since Mom died.

But she'd survived losing Mom. She would survive losing Will.

"He's really pretty bad," Kimmie whispered.

Lindsey choked on a laugh-sob. He was. But he was out there, unafraid of being bad, unafraid of being mocked, unafraid of failing.

And what did he have to fear?

Dahlia adored him. Lindsey doubted there was a single person in the theater who *couldn't* see it.

Mid-song, Mikey slapped his hand over the guitar strings, plunging the room into silence.

"Enough of that," he said. He stood, put the guitar on the stool, and then reached into his pocket and went to one knee.

The crowd gasped. And that was before the room erupted in rainbows from the light filtering through the massive rock he held out for all to see. "Dahlia Mallard," Mikey said, loud and clear and booming without the assistance of the microphone, "will you marry me?"

Cheers erupted. Clapping, laughter, and joy echoed throughout the theater. Whistles rang out. Dahlia jumped onto the stage, leapt into Mikey's arms, and shrieked, "*Yes!*" loud enough for her voice to carry all the way to Willow Glen.

Will was on his feet, clapping and smiling with the rest of the judges, but it wasn't his Will smile. It was his Billy smile.

He should've had his Will smile for his best friend. He should've been able to be himself here in Bliss.

Was that Lindsey's fault? If she'd been brave—if she'd been fearless, like Mikey, unafraid of what everyone would think of her, unafraid of being judged—would Will be happier?

"And we're gonna disqualify ourselves from winning so ol' Billy here doesn't have a conflict of conscience in his judging," Mikey said into the microphone. "I got my girl. Don't need a trophy."

The crowd laughed and cheered more. On their way off the stage, Mikey and Dahlia stopped at the judges' table. Will reached over, gave Mikey a man-hug, then kissed Dahlia on the cheek.

A sandstorm. Dahlia would've been a terrible match for—

Lindsey straightened.

Will had bad matches.

Will had bad matches.

Her heart shot into her throat. She fisted her hands to stop the shaking in her fingers, but the quaking spread up her arms.

She could see Will's bad matches. If she could see his bad matches, then she could honestly see his good matches too.

Because she'd let herself use her gift for good?

Or because she'd let him go? Because she had nothing left to lose by reading his matches anymore?

As if he'd heard her thoughts, he twisted and looked up.

Right at her.

Their gazes locked. And held.

Lindsey didn't move. She didn't blink, didn't breathe, didn't twitch a single muscle. Will sat there, those soulful, injured brown eyes boring into hers for the eternity of half a second.

And Lindsey smelled roses. Roses and daisies and sunflowers. She felt sunshine, a warm spring breeze, dewy morning grass under a brilliant blue sky.

No thunderstorms. No hail. No locust plagues.

Just goodness.

We're right for each other, and you know it, he seemed to say.

Will's eyes dropped. He faced the stage again where the final contestant approached the microphone.

In ten minutes, Will Truitt would walk out of Bliss forever.

Brave.

Could Lindsey be brave? Was she supposed to be brave?

Fearless.

She wouldn't get another chance. Billy Brenton was untouchable. And Will had taken the hint and quit calling after Tuesday.

Unafraid.

She could very well make a fool of herself if she tried to stop him tonight.

Or maybe she could fully step into the shoes of the woman she was always meant to be.

Lindsey stood so fast she tipped her chair over. "I have to go," she said to Kimmie.

"But —"

"If I don't come back, follow your heart. Don't let your mother boss you around, and don't settle for any man who doesn't worship you like the fabulous, unique, *perfect* woman that you are. Do you understand me?"

Kimmie gawked at her.

Lindsey didn't wait for an answer. Instead, she bolted out of the box.

She had something she had to do.

TWENTY-TWO

WILL COULDN'T SIT STILL. His knee wobbled, his toes tapped, his fingers drummed. He didn't even hear this last performer.

That look on Lindsey's face after Mikey's performance—she saw something.

She saw something, and he didn't know what. But the way those chocolate brown eyes had widened, the way those kissable lips of hers had parted, the way her gaze had bored into him—*through* him—had stood all his hairs on end.

She said he deserved better. But what about *her*? Who would stand beside her and believe in *her*?

She'd disappeared from her seat, and he'd made up his mind.

Will Truitt wasn't leaving Bliss until Lindsey Castellano knew exactly how important it was to him that she was happy. He had let her leave Pickleberry Springs, he'd quit calling her office, but what kind of a man would he be if he walked away from the one woman in the world who needed him for *him*?

The kid onstage finished his song, said something to a Tamara, then squinted into the theater. A rustle of uncomfortable laughter rippled behind him.

"Oh, dear," the sweet older lady on the other side of him

murmured. "This happens once or twice every year. I'd hoped we'd escaped it."

The kid squinted out into the audience. His face was getting red. "Tamara?"

Will felt for the kid. But Will didn't know where Lindsey was, and he needed to *go*.

To find her.

A sudden commotion broke out offstage. Most of the theater couldn't see it, but the judges had a decent view.

"Oh, dear, again. Marilyn's been not entirely happy this week," his fellow judge whispered.

"That woman is crazy when she's not happy," the news-woman on his other side whispered.

The kid onstage slowly backed up.

A murmur grew in the crowd.

Then a bigger commotion happened offstage, spilling out onto the stage itself. Marilyn, Pepper, and a dude Will didn't recognize, all pushing back against something.

No, some*one*.

The crowd's murmur grew to a rumble.

And then another person stepped out onto the stage, pushing right past the crowd trying to keep her out.

Her jeans hugged her hips, one of Will's favorite sweaters clung to her breasts, and there was a war going on with her facial expressions. Hardheaded stubbornness and terror and — and something Will's ol' ticker was afraid to believe in.

"Oh, no," the sweet lady murmured. "She doesn't sing."

Will scrambled to his feet, then just stood there. His heart was fixin' to bounce right on out of his chest.

"Billy?" the news lady said.

He didn't answer.

Because Lindsey had grabbed the microphone.

And Mikey was right behind her with a guitar.

Lindsey made a *get on with it* gesture at Mikey, who swallowed hard, glanced at Dahlia in the wings, and then at the ground.

The rumble in the crowd was getting all-out riot loud.

Marilyn Elias charged center stage, but Lindsey flung an

arm out and pointed at her. "Stop," she said, her voice coming through the mic, "or I'll spill every secret I know about you."

Marilyn froze.

The crowd's rumble was somewhere between discomfort and *yeah, this'll be a good show*.

Lindsey stepped fully to the mic, but she didn't look at it.

She looked at Will. Long and slow, those milk chocolate eyes searching his face, his eyes, his soul.

He pressed a hand to the throbbing in his chest.

"I love you," she said.

Behind her, Mikey said, "Sorry for this," then plucked out the first few notes of a song.

Will's mouth went dry.

He knew that song.

He *wrote* that song.

He made to move, but Lindsey pointed to him, and she kept pointing. "Stay."

She missed the cue by a good three beats. Mikey went back to the lead-in chord, but she squeezed her eyes shut, took a breath that echoed around the whole theater and took half of Will's oxygen away, and then she started singing.

Or her best impression of it, anyway.

It's a lonely life we live, running and chasing and looking for that next gig,
None of us are ever going to be better than we're gonna be,
Not when all we want is just to be what we want to be.

"Is she hiding a wet cat in her throat?" the news lady said.

"Shove it," Lou Lovely said to her.

Lindsey had a death grip on the microphone. She swayed onto her toes, then rocked back to her heels, over and over while she warbled the song.

She knew the words.

Every word.

Lindsey hit the chorus—what was supposed to be the chorus, anyway—and she looked right at him.

But when we let the love in, we're a better we than we are a better me,
Better you, better me, better free, better we,
We're all the better that can ever be. You and me, forever, into eternity.

Will's skin was too tight, his lungs too small, his bones too rubbery.

She wasn't looking *at* him. She was looking *into* him. Not demanding to see, but asking that he look at her.

That he *see*. That he understand. That he accept her.

That he believe in her.

That he trust her.

That he love her.

He needed to stop her. She didn't have to do this. Didn't have to finish.

He got it. He heard her loud and clear.

Some heckling started from somewhere behind him and echoed through the theater.

But if Lindsey heard it, she didn't show it.

He pushed his chair out of his way.

She put a hand out.

Stop, it said. *I have to do this*.

No, she didn't. The only thing she had to do was to love him.

He stepped around the couple beside him and ignored the laughter and shrieks growing in the crowd. Lindsey had started the second verse, but she faltered. "*Stay*," she said to Will. "Let me finish."

Her cheeks were wet, her eyes wide, her hips swaying offbeat under the soft pink sweater that framed her figure all the right ways.

And he wanted to hold her and kiss her and love her.

Away from the crowd, away from the cameras, away from everything.

He surged toward her, but she was still too far away. He remembered her and microphones. The things she said into them.

We're not right. We don't match. I see these things. We won't make it. I can't love you.

Now, her cheeks were fire truck red, her knuckles whiter than snow, and the spotlight made her hair glow. "I was wrong. You have bad matches."

He froze.

No.

No, not again.

"But they're not me," she whispered, the microphone picking up her every word.

Will's breath left him in a rush. He stepped toward her again. And she stood there, talking faster and faster the closer he got. "I love you, Will Truitt. And I'm sorry. I'm so, so sorry for what I did last week. I was wrong. When I look at you, I see sunshine. And flowers. And rainbows and puppy dogs and chocolate chip cookies. I love you," she said. "I love you, and—"

Will reached her. He hit the kill switch on the microphone.

"—and I love you as Will, and I love you as Billy, and I'm scared to death, but I'm *here*, and I'm staying. With you. If you still want me."

She was one hell of a woman.

She'd sung for him.

She'd braved a microphone and a crowd and him and herself to be here.

He pulled her into his body, stuck his nose in her hair. "I love you, Lindsey. I've *always* loved you."

Will Truitt needed to get his pretty lady off this stage. To stop her quaking, to get her out of the spotlight, to show her how badly he'd missed her, how desperately he loved her, everything he would do for her.

Billy Brenton, though—Billy needed to kiss her. Right here. In front of all these people. He needed to show the world that this woman who couldn't carry a tune was *his* woman. He wrapped his arms around her, felt the soft cotton of her sweater, the press of her breasts against his chest, then the silk of her hair between his fingers, the scent of her shampoo teasing his nose, and finally, the taste of her on his tongue.

A drum beat in his soul. A guitar riff. A fiddle and tambourines. *Music.*

Will Truitt was a simple country boy who fully intended to marry above his station in life. The first time he'd met Lindsey, she'd given him music. The second time, she'd given him hope.

And this time, she'd given him everything.

He would never again let this woman go.

MAYBE MICROPHONES WEREN'T the devil after all. Lindsey wasn't planning on repeating her performance anytime soon, but she'd lived through it. The sun wasn't up yet, so there was no telling if her house had been egged or toilet papered overnight in retribution for what she'd done to everyone's ears, but she didn't care.

Because she had a perfect moonlit night at the beach right here in her bedroom, and that wasn't something anyone could take from her.

Will's hand slid along her bare belly and he pressed a kiss into her shoulder. His low morning voice rumbled over her skin. "You been lying awake all night staring at that trophy?"

The trophy. Those crazy people in Bliss had declared her the Battle of the Boyfriends winner. First woman in history, worst singer *ever*, and yet, she'd taken home first prize. "Yep. You caught me." She rolled into him, skin to skin, as close as she could get, and let her fingers roam his body, smiling so hard she felt it in her cheeks. "I only sang for the trophy."

"That one goes right next to my Grammy."

Her hands drifted lower, and his mouth found that sweet spot on her neck. "Don't want to leave," he said.

She squeezed his rear end. "I can be in Nashville Friday night. Unfortunately, I have some cases I need to see out, so I can only stay the weekend, but I'll let my boss know I'm not taking on anything new."

"Don't go quitting your job on account of me. Already got my people working on getting me a lighter schedule so I can be home more. We'll work this out."

"Home?" The word put a warmth in her chest.

"Here. With you." His lips moved to her ear, sending electric sparks all over her body. "Anywhere with you. Doing whatever you need to be doing."

She snuggled into the crook of his shoulder, letting his hands and mouth and body wake her in the best of all possible ways. "I wanted to be president to change the world," she murmured. "I chose to be a divorce lawyer to help good people fix unfortunate situations. But there's so much more I can do if I quit hiding. I have a gift that could guide ordinary people toward extraordinary love. And I have you. So I think it's my duty to see how I can use *all* of my talents to be my own kind of superstar." She didn't want to be a kept woman, but she also wasn't too stubborn to overlook the possibilities that came with the kind of life Will had as Billy Brenton. She'd made a difference on a small scale in the last decade. With him beside her, she could make a difference on a bigger scale.

"Also gotta quit hiding those smiles under here." Will's thumb brushed her hip over her smiley face tattoo.

"Good call. I should get rid of those. Just toss them all out."

He flipped her onto her back, pinning her to the bed. "Don't you dare, pretty lady." The hard length of him settled between her thighs, and she wrapped her legs around his hips.

He tilted his mouth to hers. "You do that, I'm gonna have to rethink this plan I have where I marry you and strip you out of those smileys every night."

Her breath caught, and her eyes went misty.

She hadn't thought she would ever get married. A husband, kids, a dog—she'd thought she'd be happy without them.

But now, she couldn't imagine anything, *ever*, being better than making a life with the one man who understood her inside and out. "I love you, Will Truitt," she whispered.

His lips found hers, and he kissed her—long, slow and deeply—and then brushed her hair away from her cheek. "I love you too, my beautiful snow angel. What say we make some new memories?"

She said yes. Just as she always would from now on to her sweet, perfect country man.

EPILOGUE

Later that year…

"YOU EVER HEAR of anybody else crashing a baby shower?"
Mikey said to Will while they peered into a ballroom over-
flowing with women from Bliss. Christmas lights twinkled
from the walls, and pink-and-blue wrapped presents spilled
out in a massive pile that made the twelve-foot tree in the
corner look too small.

"Ah, Mikey, I remember a time when this many women
would've been your heaven," Will said. "Or you nervous
because you haven't performed in public in too long?"

Mikey snorted. "I don't get nervous. And there wasn't _ever_
a time I would've walked into a baby shower to get phone
numbers."

"Got an old BillyVision episode that says otherwise."

CJ strolled over, glanced in the room, and then slapped
Mikey on the back. "Go easy on him, Billy. Fatherhood is
scary as shit the first time."

"You got a four-year-old the first time," Mikey shot back.

He pointed into the room. "You tellin' me you ain't gonna pass out the first time you watch Nat try to push a—a—"

"Watermelon," Will supplied.

"—Watermelon out her—out her—"

"Vagina," CJ said.

"*Jesus*. I need some ice cream."

A distinct laugh drew Will's attention to the ballroom. Lindsey had taken a seat between a very pregnant Natalie and an equally pregnant Dahlia, her own belly still at the cute stage, not yet ready to pop. On Nat's other side, Kimmie was talking and gesturing over her own baby bump.

Ah, Kimmie. That'd been fun, watching her fall in love. Came with one of Lindsey's finest moments, in Will's opinion.

He smiled while Lindsey's laughter grew stronger, Nat and Dahlia joining in, and Kimmie added her own unique giggle-snort.

"Hush," Nat said to Kimmie. "You're gonna make me have to pee."

"Get in line," Dahlia said.

"There's enough stalls for all of us," Kimmie said, "but first we'd have to stand up again."

More laughter rolled through the room. Lindsey caught sight of him, and her smile went wider, her eyes softer, all of her prettier. He blew her a kiss, and dang if the pretty lady didn't go pink in the cheeks.

Got him right in the heart. She always had. Always would.

"We've gotta go now," Will said to the guys, "or they'll be taking turns going to the bathroom from now until this shindig's over. Ready, Mikey?"

Mikey swiped a hand over the sweat on his bald head. "Yeah. I'm ready."

"CJ?" Will said.

CJ lifted his instrument. "Got my cowbell. Would have my kazoo too, but Noah hid it."

Will grabbed Yvette. The old Yamaha would never be Vera, but Lindsey had insisted the guitar needed a name. And she'd been right.

Just like she'd been right that all of Bliss would turn out

for a quadruple baby shower, with all the gifts being donated to local women's shelters. That lady was something else. Hadn't taken her but two months to figure out the best way to organize a nonprofit legal assistance fund for families in crisis, and barely another two weeks to put her plans in motion.

Will had offered the capital to get it going, but Lindsey insisted all she wanted was a little of his time and connections. He'd played a benefit concert for her in Chicago with some of his best and biggest buddies in the country music industry, and she'd even gotten onstage to thank everyone for coming out without tossing her cookies.

Already, her organization had funded legal fees to help two women secure divorces from abusive husbands, and helped a paycheck-to-paycheck family adopt an orphaned nephew who'd been on the verge of going into foster care.

That one had hit home. Could've been Will when he was a kid.

Lindsey had always been special, and now the world was getting a glimpse of everything that she was capable of. Without the fear, *she* was learning what she was capable of. She'd nudged four couples together in the last month without their hardly realizing what was going on too. But the best part, in Will's opinion, was that she was happy.

And he'd never been happier himself.

"Gentlemen," Will said, "let's go crash a baby shower."

And that's exactly what they did.

THE COMPLETE JAMIE FARRELL BOOK LIST

The Misfit Brides Series:

Blissed (CJ and Natalie)
Matched (Will and Lindsey)
Smittened (Mikey and Dahlia)
Sugared (Josh and Kimmie)
Merried (Max and Merry)
Spiced (Tony and Pepper)
Unhitched (Ben and Tarra)

The Officers' Ex-Wives Club Series:

Her Rebel Heart (Lance and Kaci)
Southern Fried Blues (Jackson and Anna Grace)

Jamie Farrell's Pippa Grant Titles:

The Mister McHottie World:
Mister McHottie
Stud in the Stacks
The Pilot and the Puck-Up
Royally Pucked
Beauty and the Beefcake

Rockaway Bride
Hot Heir
The Hero and the Hacktivist
Charming as Puck

The Bro Code Series:
Flirting with the Frenemy
America's Geekheart

Standalones
Master Baker (Bro Code Spin-Off)
Exes and Ho Ho Hos

Co-Written with Lili Valente
Hosed
Hammered
Hitched
Humbugged

The Bluewater Billionaires Series
The Price of Scandal by Lucy Score
The Mogul and the Muscle by Claire Kingsley
Wild Open Hearts by Kathryn Nolan
Crazy for Loving You by Pippa Grant

ABOUT THE AUTHOR

Jamie Farrell is the alter ego for USA Today Bestselling romantic comedy author Pippa Grant. She believes love, laughter, and bacon are the most powerful forces in the universe. When she's not writing, she's raising her three hilariously unpredictable children with her real-life hero.

Visit Jamie's website at:
www.JamieFarrellBooks.com
Follow Jamie on Facebook at:
http://www.facebook.com/JamieFarrellBooks
Follow Jamie on Twitter at:
http://www.twitter.com/TheJamieFarrell
Sign up for Jamie's newsletter at:
http://www.subscribepage.com/JamieFarrellNews